She tripped, and fell . . .

Luke, reacting instinctively, turned and grasped her in his arms. Melissa, startled by her near fall, found herself held gently but firmly in his arms, her body tight against his, her face only a fraction of an inch from his face, her lips only . . .

Such a warm riot of feeling boiled through her that she felt as if she were temporarily bereft of her senses. She had never swooned in her life and thought it an affectation, but now she felt that she might do so at any moment. Her knees felt weak, her heart was palpitating, she was at once removed from and aware of everything about the situation and conscious of every place their bodies touched.

Part of the feeling was fear, but it was fear of herself rather than him. *My God!* she thought, *was this what falling in love meant? If it was, how could people stand it? It was so deliciously, excitingly terrible!*

And then she heard Luke groan—a sound of anguish, not of pleasure, and as she registered this, their lips were no longer a fraction of an inch apart, but were touching; and the warmth and the sweetness and the thrill that coursed through her body were beyond her experience.

Dimly, Melissa perceived that she should tear herself away. She knew that she was allowing him and unprecedented intimacy, yet she could not move.

Melissa, awash in the tumult of her feelings, suddenly released from long repression, was lost. . . .

* * *

P9-ARL-220

Now Melissa felt very tired, very relaxed, and very satisfied, as if she had been scoured clean of all other emotions. She felt a great swell of tenderness for this man who had brought her so much pleasure.

So this was making love! So this was the thing that happened between men and women. No wonder they kept it shrouded in secrecy! No wonder society frowned on it without the sanctions of marriage. Otherwise, why, everyone would be doing it all the time. No work would be done. No houses would be cleaned. It was the most glorious pleasure she had ever known.

He sighed. "It *was* wonderful. I loved every minute of it. I've wanted to make love to you from the instant I saw you standing there so proud and independent on the veranda of your daddy's plantation. The thing you don't understand, Melissa, is that with men . . . well, to put it bluntly, to a man, making love to a woman does not always mean that he wants to marry her. Do you understand at all what I'm trying to say?"

* * *

Understanding was not enough. All that Melissa was sure of was that she felt a sense of terrible loss and betrayal. It was too cruel to find love, and then lose it, all in one brief night.

But it was love, wasn't it . . . and that was something. Both an ending and a beginning . . .

Love's Raging Tide

Patricia Matthews

PINNACLE BOOKS   LOS ANGELES

LOVE'S RAGING TIDE

Copyright © 1980 by Pyewacket Corporation

An original Pinnacle Books edition, published for the first time anywhere.

First printing, January 1980

ISBN: 0-523-40659-2

Cover illustration by Gary Rudell

Printed in the United States of America

PINNACLE BOOKS, INC.
2029 Century Park East
Los Angeles, California 90067

This book is dedicated to
Dr. Frederick Shroyer,
scholar, gentleman, author, critic, teacher and friend,
with many thanks and much affection.

LOVE'S RAGING TIDE

I am the land and you are the water,
Rushing, urgent,
You sweep me away.
Child of my age, a sheltered daughter,
You, a man who
Makes his own way.
Coming together in the darkness,
Soft summer earth and river wide,
Part of the earth is gone forever,
Forever part of love's raging tide.

Love's Raging Tide

Chapter One

It was one of those late spring days that only Mississippi can produce, a day so soft and balmy that the air felt like flower petals against the skin, a day full of awakening and promise; and the sight of it made Melissa Huntoon want to weep.

She stood on the spacious, pillared veranda of her ancestral home, looking out over the broad acres that had belonged to her family for two generations, and her eyes burned with the effort to remain dry. She swallowed past the hard lump in her throat, and gripped the handle of the pink parasol that her granddaddy had brought her from Paris, the year before he died.

The day should be gray, she thought; the clouds full of rain like unshed tears. Today, Great Oaks would ring to the auctioneer's hammer. The plantation itself—two thousand acres of Mississippi bottomland, some of the finest cotton land in the South—had already been taken over by the bank. Today, everything in the house would go to the highest bidder.

Melissa smoothed the full skirt of her dress with her hand. From a distance, she knew, she would appear well dressed. Only close inspection would show the neat patches and darns that held the now-fragile cloth together. The dress, she thought, was like Great Oaks itself—impressive enough on casual inspection, but badly flawed. In the case of Great Oaks, it was debts, endless debts, incurred against the property before and after her father's death. When the day was over, Melissa would be left with little more than the clothing she wore and a few personal trinkets. It was not much to show for twenty-one years of life, not much with which to start a new life.

Bitterly she watched the stream of horses, buggies and carriages coming up the driveway. Like vultures, she thought; except they couldn't even wait until their prey was dead!

Melissa knew very well that all of them weren't here to bid. Many of them were here simply to gloat on the downfall of the high and mighty Huntoons. Jean-Paul, her father, would have greeted them with a round of buckshot; and she sorely wished that she might do the same.

However, she had no choice. Amalie, her personal maid, and the only one of the servants left, had advised her to stay inside, out of sight until it was over; but Melissa could not bear the thought of hiding inside, as if she were afraid of these usurpers. She was the mistress of Great Oaks until the day was over, and until then she would appear before them as she and her family always had, proud, with her head held high. Let them stare, these *nouveaux riches*, these Johnny-come-latelies. Let them see what a Huntoon

2

looked like. It might be their last chance to see real quality!

She heard soft footsteps behind her, and did not need to turn around to know that Amalie had come out on the veranda to join her. The knowledge lifted her spirits. Amalie had been with her as long as Melissa could remember. The older woman had been her nurse, her mother, her friend, and her confidante. And at least Melissa would be able to take Amalie with her when she left.

A shabby carriage drove past the veranda, and a woman's pinched, tight-mouthed face turned in her direction. The woman's eyes were bright with avid curiosity, and Melissa stared haughtily back as the carriage passed on to the stable area where the horses of the prospective buyers were being tended.

Another of the sightseers, Melissa thought. In these Reconstruction times, there were not many in the South with the wherewithal to buy property and furnishings, even at auction prices, and obviously this woman was not one of the fortunate ones.

The traffic was increasing now, as more and more people arrived, and Melissa felt Amalie draw close to her side. "Are you all right, little one?"

Melissa nodded and reached for the older woman's hand. Not trusting herself to speak, she squeezed it fiercely.

Melissa's mother had died some years back, of a fever, and her father, wounded in the war, had come home to cough his life away. The war years had been difficult for Melissa, but not nearly so difficult as watching her beloved father, the man who had been so proud and strong, grow weaker every day, and seeing his face as he was slowly forced to relinquish

3

his dream of once again seeing Great Oaks as it had been—a busy, thriving plantation.

Melissa, with Amalie's help, had struggled to run the plantation on her own; but it was not to be. With the slaves freed, and the family fortune given freely to the Confederate cause, there was only the house and land left when the war was over. There had been no choice but to mortgage the property to the bank in town.

If the bank had remained in Southern hands, she probably would have been granted loan extensions, but the bank itself failed, and it was taken over, along with a stack of overdue mortgages, by a man named Simon Crouse—better known to the local populace as the Carpetbagger.

The Carpetbagger was a smallish man, who appeared taller because of the proportions of his body. He was, as some of the women were fond of remarking, "well set up," with small, neat hands and feet, and a large head, with a thick growth of brown hair which, if you didn't look too closely, gave him a noble air.

However, Melissa was one of those who *did* look closely. The war years had made her expert at judging human nature, and despite Crouse's good manners and elegance, she had seen and taken note of the greedy flicker behind his dark eyes, and the unrestrained sensuality of his mouth, when he thought he wasn't under observation.

Always, from the first time they had met, Simon Crouse had made her uncomfortable. His dark eyes, moving cautiously over her body, made her feel violated, and she always felt a sort of dreadful *eagerness* in the man, a secretive greediness, that she was hard put to set into words, but which made her feel some-how threatened.

Melissa knew that many of the ladies around thought him attractive, even though he was a Yankee moneylender, a carpetbagger of the worst sort. If he kept on his way undeterred, he would soon have his greedy hands on most of the state of Mississippi. She had to admit, in all fairness, that the fact that he now owned Great Oaks had some bearing on the way she felt about him.

And speak of the Devil! Coming toward her was a handsome carriage, drawn by a fine pair of matched horses, throwing up dust, and jouncing importantly up the great drive. She recognized the carriage as belonging to Simon Crouse.

But what drew Melissa's attention was the man on the large black horse, riding alongside the carriage. The horse was magnificent, the trappings luxurious for these impoverished times, and the man himself was certainly imposing—young, well built, handsome, and expensively dressed. It was obvious that he was accompanying the carriage. What connection could he possibly have with Simon Crouse?

The carriage moved around the curve in the drive-way, and stopped at the bottom of the steps, in front of Melissa.

Melissa felt her heart begin to pound, and she tried to compose herself. She must handle this confronta-tion with dignity. That was all she had left.

"Miss Huntoon!" Crouse had climbed down from the carriage, and stood awaiting her on the bottom step. He doffed his tall hat and inclined his head.

He's like an actor, Melissa thought with distaste.

Crouse turned to the man on the black horse. "I

would like to present my dear friend, Mr. Luke Devereaux. Mr. Devereaux, Miss Melissa Huntoon."

Luke Devereaux swept off his broad-brimmed hat. "It is my pleasure, ma'am," he said in a deep voice. His hair was a rich brown color, and his brown eyes had a slightly golden tint. His full mouth wore a musing smile.

Melissa returned his gaze coldly. "I am sorry that I cannot say the same, sir!" she said tartly. "The circumstances being what they are."

His smile remained in place. "I am in no way responsible for your circumstances, Miss Huntoon."

"Perhaps not," she directed a scathing glance at Crouse, "but you may be held responsible for the company you keep, and certainly Mr. Crouse is responsible for my plight!"

"My dear Miss Huntoon, that is simply not true," Crouse said with a superior smile. "I have always deplored a lady involving herself in business matters. Not only is it demeaning, but the female mind simply has no grasp of the problems involved. Your plight is a prime example of that fact. The bank held the mortgage on this plantation, and the payments were sadly in arrears. My foreclosure is nothing more than sound business procedure."

"You may call it what you like, Mr. Crouse, but that does not excuse this humiliating auction today."

"That, Miss Huntoon, is not my doing either. You *do* have other creditors, my dear, and I suppose they believe they are entitled to due consideration."

"Daddy collected many fine art objects over the years, paintings and the like. Many of them are priceless. Now, today, they will be sold off to people who have no idea of their true value!"

"Now there you are mistaken. I fully appreciate them," Crouse said with infuriating smugness. "And that is precisely why I am here today. There are several paintings that I fully intend to have for my very own."

"You?" Her voice was scornful. "What do you know of art, Mr. Crouse?"

His smile grew strained, and Melissa knew that she had stung him. The thought gave her pleasure, but she was also a little intimidated by the suppressed fury in his eyes.

"I don't suppose that a young lady like yourself, isolated, as it were, in this charming backwater, has had a chance to learn much about the sophistications of the larger world," he said. "If you had, you would have learned not to judge people so quickly. The fact that I am a banker does not mean that I do not appreciate the artistic things of life. In truth, I already have an excellent and extensive collection of art, and I intend to add to it this day."

Melissa felt herself flush, and suddenly her bravado failed her and depression took its place. "I don't suppose it really matters," she said dully. "After today, none of it will belong to the Huntoon family."

Crouse moved closer to her, turning his back on Luke Devereaux. Melissa stole a glance at the man on the horse, but he was apparently watching the parade of visitors as they came up the large, circular driveway.

As she looked back, Melissa saw that Crouse was now quite close to her. Too close! She could see the high color on his prominent cheekbones, and the hungry glitter of his dark eyes. She wanted nothing so much as to draw back from him, but she did not wish him to think that she feared him.

"There *is* a way your lovely things can remain in your possession, Miss Huntoon."

She stared at him, as her heart leaped in sudden hope, then plummeted. She did not trust him. It had to be a trick of some kind. She whispered, "How?"

His voice was low. "Become my wife. Become Mrs. Simon Crouse."

Melissa felt as if her body had lost all heat. She could only stare at him in consternation, as he looked at her intently, his mouth slightly open and his eyes bright with something that she could not put a name to.

Her mind was chaos. "Why?" she finally managed to whisper, although this was only one of the questions that tumbled pell-mell through her mind.

He smiled slightly. "I need a wife. I have spent years building up my fortune, and now I wish to enjoy it. I have chosen Great Oaks to be my permanent residence, and I would like you to share it with me."

He leaned even nearer, and his eyes burned into Melissa's with frightening force. "Be my wife, Melissa. I can make you happy. Then you will not need to leave Great Oaks, nor lose the family possessions you hold so dear."

The stasis that had paralyzed Melissa broke, and she almost staggered backward, until she felt the bottom step against her foot. The contact seemed to give her strength.

Again Crouse moved toward her, and she swung her parasol around so that it formed a shield in front of her, its sharp point directed at Crouse's chest. His smile faded and his mouth tightened.

8

"Mr. Crouse," Melissa said softly but distinctly, "you presume too much! Whatever made you think . . ." She shook her head. Simon Crouse, I would not marry you if I were starving and you had the last loaf of bread in the world! I look upon you as my enemy. I thought you knew that!"

Crouse's high color slowly faded, and his expression was blank with shock. Despite her own confusion, Melissa sensed that he really had had no inkling of how she felt about him, impossible as it seemed.

"Take care, girl," he said, and his voice was as taut and sharp as the flick of a whip. "I am a dangerous man to cross. Perhaps you had better reconsider your words!"

Melissa, looking into those blank eyes, felt sudden fear. She shivered, as she thought of the water moccasin she had once stumbled upon, coiled by the side of a stream. Crouse's eyes now held the same deadly, mindless stare.

She conquered her fear. "I don't need to reconsider," she said, her voice as soft as his. "I spoke my mind. I hate you, Simon Crouse. You are everything that I find despicable in a man, and I would never, never become your wife. I would certainly much rather starve first!"

The corner of Crouse's mouth twitched, and he raised his hand as if to strike her, but paused as Luke Devereaux stepped between them.

"I think the auction is about to start." Devereaux's voice, speaking in a normal tone, seemed to break some kind of terrible spell, and Melissa found that she had been holding her breath.

Crouse turned away, and then in a swift, lethal movement wheeled back to face her.

"So be it," he said in an icy voice. "And what you said, about starving to death. That could very well come to pass, you know. In fact, I shall do everything in my power to see to it, and I have a great deal of power in Mississippi, far more than you can imagine. Good day to you, Miss Huntoon."

"Going, going, going! Gone!"

The auctioneer's rusty voice rasped out over the crowd like the cry of a crow. He struck the top of the table with his gavel, and Melissa raised her chin a trifle higher, and struggled to keep her expression noncommittal. Amalie had gone back into the house, and Melissa now stood alone on the broad veranda, not far from the table behind which the auctioneer presided.

As the auctioneer's cry died away, a portly, red-faced townsman, flanked by his two beefy, equally red-faced sons, thrust his way impatiently through the crowd, and stomped up the veranda steps to claim his prize: a beautiful, hand-carved wine cooler that had originally come from France.

Ever since Melissa could remember, it had rested in a place of honor in the huge dining room of Great Oaks. The wine cooler had always been a particular favorite of hers because of the carved faun's head that adorned the lid, and the plump bunches of carved grapes that ornamented the cherrywood sides and corners, gleaming roundly against the smooth, polished background.

Now this lout of a townsman would cool his common wine in the chest that had once held the fine French wines favored by her father and grandfather. Melissa's expression was disdainful as she watched the sweating men lug the heavy chest down the steps. She would not give them the satisfaction of knowing that she cared.

As they struggled down the steps and across the yard, Melissa's thoughts went back to the last family dinner at Great Oaks, the last time they had all been together in the great dining room, before the war, a million years ago, it seemed . . .

The long dining room had been alight with candles, the light flickering warmly over the Sèvres porcelain and the heavy silver flatware. In the center of the long table, banked by bright summer flowers, sat the magic fountain—or so the children always called it—an elegant, hourglass-like construction of silver and crystal that spouted a clear stream of water toward the ceiling. When the force of the water grew low, the hourglass section reversed, top to bottom, and the water rose anew, like magic, into the air.

The day had been hot and still, with the full power of summer, but there was a slight breeze now, and all of the tall windows were open to the night air and the odor of nightblooming jasmine, which filled the room with its seductive scent. Because of the heat, the ladies and girls all wore their thinnest gowns, and Melissa thought that her mother and the other ladies looked like princesses in the soft, pale dresses, fragile with lace and embroidery. The men, encouraged by her father, had removed their coats, and sat exposed in their elegant white shirts, laughing and flushed with the freedom her father had granted them.

Above the laden table, the shoo-fly, a large carved wooden fan that hung from the ceiling, moved slowly back and forth, operated by a house slave. The movement of the shoo-fly created a cooling breeze as the air was conducted over the blocks of ice that sat on the corners of the table, melting in their silver salvers.

At the head of the table was Melissa's grandfather. He had refused to insult tradition by removing his coat, and his full white beard shone silvery against the white of his coat front.

Joseph, the black serving man, took a bottle of pale red wine from the wine cooler; the wine bottle gleamed with droplets of moisture. Joseph held it for the old man to inspect. Melissa, sitting next to her grandfather, smiled to herself, for she knew that he would let her have a sip of the liquid when no one was looking. She had never cared for the taste of the wine, but the privilege was sweet indeed . . .

"Going, going, gone!"

Melissa blinked, coming back to the present, as the gavel again banged the wood of the table. Another treasure gone.

"And now, ladies and gentlemen, we have a very special treat for you!" The auctioneer bared his teeth at the audience in a false smile, and motioned toward the young man who was coming toward him carrying a square box, or chest.

The lad placed the box on the table in front of the auctioneer. With a lurch of dismay Melissa saw that it was her music box, the one which had belonged to her mother, and which her mother had passed on to her, just before her death.

The box was simple but beautiful, made of glowing mahogany. Its only adornment was a carved rose, which crowned the lid, and which served as a handle to remove the lid when the box was to be played.

Inside the box was a wondrous mechanism, made in Germany, that could play any piece of music for which a disc was available. Melissa's mother had possessed six discs, each one a marvel of tiny holes and gleaming metal. Each one, catching the metal fingers of the mechanism, played a different tune.

Melissa felt her face flame, then grow cold. Simon Crouse had promised her that she could take her personal possessions, and this, surely, was one of them. She took a step toward the auctioneer, as he raised the lid of the box, then stopped herself. What could she do? Could she shout out, "No, that's not for sale!" in front of all these people? No, she would not humble herself before them!

She felt her lower lip start to tremble, and bit down on it with her upper teeth to still the telltale movement. She could feel tears coming to her eyes, and blinked resolutely. She would not weaken. She would *not* show her emotions in front of these . . . these pigs!

She half-turned away and saw that Luke Devereaux was staring at her appraisingly. As their glances met, Devereaux smiled slightly and inclined his head. Melissa faced around again.

"Made in Germany," the auctioneer was saying, as he tilted the box forward so that the crowd could see the interior workings of the box. "And there are six discs, which can be changed so that the music box plays six different melodies. Six, imagine that! Think of how beautiful it would look in your parlor, ladies and gentlemen! Think of the entertainment. Think of the enjoyment it can bring to your family and friends. Now, what am I bid for this musical marvel?"

A thin woman with a parched, narrow face and cold eyes stepped forward. Melissa could see that she was well dressed in what appeared to be new clothing.

The new clothes probably meant that she was either the wife of a carpetbagger, or one of the town shopkeepers who had cooperated with the Yankees.

Oh, how could she bear to see her mother's precious music box go to this crass woman! But she must, she must!

Melissa concentrated on trying not to weep, as the woman signaled her bid. It was embarrassingly low.

"Come on now, folks," the auctioneer coaxed in his crow's voice. "This is a work of art. Won't somebody with a real appreciation of music raise the bid?"

He looked around the crowd hopefully, and then, as Melissa felt certain that the music box would go to the woman, a man raised his hand. It was Luke Devereaux.

With a start of surprise Melissa realized that he was doubling the bid.

The auctioneer's glance went to the woman in the new clothes. He said hopefully, "Ma'am?"

She sniffed audibly, clamped her lips together, and shook her head.

The auctioneer looked around at the other faces. "No more bids on this great bargain?" He sighed, and poised the gavel over the table. "Going once! Going twice! Sold, sold to the gent in the brown hat!"

Melissa felt her heart thump irregularly. She was glad that that awful woman hadn't gotten the music box, but was this much better? What on earth did this man want it for? A gift perhaps, for his wife or sweetheart? Well, it didn't matter. The music box was gone, like all the rest. She must face it, must learn to live a new life. But it was hard. Oh, it was hard!

The rest of the items were auctioned off one by

one, but the details were only a haze for Melissa, who watched but did not see.

At last the final bid was made, and as the auctioneer counted the money he had taken in, and then doled it out to those who had a claim on it, Melissa turned and walked slowly into the house, and into the parlor.

Her footsteps echoed on the bare wood of the floor. Stripped of the rug and furnishings, the room looked huge and shabby. Without its dress of possessions, the small damages done by the passing years were apparent: the peeling wallpaper, the stained plaster, the fading paint. It was like seeing an elderly woman in dishabille, caught without her hair dressed and her face tended. The tears which Melissa had managed to control while watching the auction now slid down her cheeks, as a great, hurtful swelling of pain and anger filled her chest.

"Miss Huntoon?"

At the sound of the male voice behind her, a cry escaped Melissa, a soft, wounded sound that seemed to hang in the air of the great, empty room.

The sound of footsteps approached, but she kept her back turned, trying to regain control of herself. She must not be seen like this!

"I am sorry if I startled you, Miss Huntoon, but I wanted to talk to you before I left. I wanted to give you this."

Melissa, her back still turned, recognized the voice of Luke Devereaux. "What can you have to say to me, sir? And what can you possibly wish to give me?"

"This," he said softly. "But you will have to turn around to see it."

Hastily, Melissa scrubbed at her eyes. Why couldn't

they leave her alone? Hadn't they done enough? Well, she would not have him believe that she was afraid to face him.

Knowing that traces of her tears were still visible, she made her expression calm as she finally turned to face him.

He stood before her, framed with a halo of light from the open door, and despite herself, Melissa was struck by the solid strength implicit in his tall, well-set-up body. In his hands he cradled the music box. He held it out toward her.

"I would like you to have this, Miss Huntoon. I could see, at the auction out there, that it meant something very special to you, and I . . ."

His voice trailed off, and Melissa, despite her churning feelings, could see that he was ill at ease.

"I realize that it's presumptuous of me," he went on. "After all, we don't really know each other, having just been introduced, but these are exceptional circumstances, and I hope that I will be forgiven. Please take it. I bought it just for you."

Melissa could only stare at him, completely mystified. Why on earth was he doing this? What did he hope to accomplish? Was he like the Carpetbagger? Did he want her in the way that men wanted women? Did he think that he could *buy* her in this manner?

Her expression must have mirrored her thoughts, for he said quickly, "I hope you don't think I have any other motive than friendship in mind. I assure you, there are no strings attached to this gift. If you knew me better, you would know that I am a man of impulse, and I had an impulse to keep your beautiful music box out of the hands of that woman. An idiot could tell that she would never appreciate it."

16

He smiled, his teeth startlingly white against the tanned skin of his face, and Melissa found herself close to responding. But the situation was so alien to her, and she was too wounded and confused to sort out her feelings. Yet there was one thing she knew. She wanted the music box, and wanted it badly. As she hesitated, Devereaux stepped forward, just a step, and held out the box.

"Please take it. It belongs to you. If you don't accept it, I don't know what I will do with it. I have no place to keep it."

Suddenly she nodded. His smile widened, and she noticed that his eyes crinkled charmingly at the corners. "Good!"

He placed the box on the floor at her feet. "May I . . ." He hesitated. "May I take a further liberty, and ask what you will do now? Where will you go? Do you have any friends or family in Natchez with whom you can stay?"

The cold reality of the question was like a slap in the face. "I don't know," she answered stiffly. "But Amalie and I will manage. We will survive!"

His smile faded as he stared at her, and there was an unreadable expression in his brown eyes. "Yes," he said. "I somehow believe you will."

As he turned away, the shape of his tall body dark against the light of the doorway, Melissa experienced a moment of panic. This was the first person to offer kindness, the first person who seemed genuinely to care, in such a long time. She almost wished that she dared call him back. What would she say if she did?

As he reached the door, Luke Devereaux turned. "If you should for any reason need to get word to me, I'll be staying in Natchez for the next week at least. Crouse will know where."

Melissa stiffened at this. She had forgotten that he was in some way associated with the Carpetbagger.

He doffed his hat with a slight bow. "Good day to you, Miss Huntoon." He stepped through the doorway.

Melissa stared after him, bemused. Finally she looked down at the music box at her feet. It was all she had left, that and Amalie.

Leaving the music box on the floor behind her for the time being, she walked slowly out onto the veranda to find out what money, if any, would be coming to her, after the creditors had all been satisfied.

Chapter Two

"And after the creditors are paid off, how much will I have left?" Melissa asked the question in a matter-of-fact manner, not wanting to reveal her need to this sly-faced hawker of other people's belongings.

The auctioneer grinned, showing worn yellow teeth. "Well, after all them owed have been paid, and my own fee deducted, this is what's left you."

He shoved toward her a small pile of bills and silver. The amount was pitifully inadequate for her needs. Trying not to show her disappointment, Melissa scooped up the money and stowed it in the small hanging purse tied about her wrist.

"Oh, there's the *Natchez Belle*." He snickered. "Seems nobody has a hankering for her. Couldn't even raise a bid, so I reckon she's still yours."

Melissa, deep in her own miserable thoughts, at first did not comprehend. "The *Natchez Belle*? What's that, for heaven's sake?"

"The old boat. The steamboat. She's tied up at Natchez. Maybe you could get her into working order again, and start yourself a thriving little business. Yessir. You just might try that." He snickered again.

Melissa gave him a withering look. Everyone, even she, knew that many of the steam packets were slowly but surely being forced out of business by the railroads. But what she hadn't known was that her father had even owned a steamboat. Of course, there were many things she had not known about her father's business dealings. Unfortunately, he had been like most men, and thought that women should not bother their heads with business affairs.

So she owned a boat. A steamboat, named the *Natchez Belle*. Of course, it was worthless, the auctioneer's snicker had already told her that, but still, owning *something* was better than owning *nothing*. Yet was it really hers, or did it, like the house and the land, now belong to Simon Crouse?

Crouse and Luke Devereaux were standing beside a high-sided wagon, into which the items Crouse had purchased at the auction were being loaded. Melissa, after a moment's thought, headed toward them. She saw Amalie coming down the veranda steps. She waved, and motioned toward the wagon.

The two women reached the wagon at almost the same moment, and Crouse turned from supervising the loading to face Melissa. His expression was smug, as he glanced from her to the load of pictures and furnishings, and Melissa felt the dislike and aversion she had for him rise in her throat. Still, she strove to keep her expression neutral.

"Miss Huntoon, is there something I may do for you?"

"Yes, Mr. Crouse. I have a question. The auctioneer has just told me that one item was not sold. A steamboat, called the *Natchez Belle*. He—he told me that the boat belonged to me."

Crouse smiled in evident satisfaction, clearly pleased that she had come to him as a supplicant, no matter in how small a degree. "And you wish to know?"

"I wish to know whether or not this boat still belongs to me."

Crouse's face grew thoughtful.

"Or does it," Melissa went on, "belong to you, along with the house, the land, and everything else?"

Crouse laughed. "No, my dear. A steamboat was not included in the estate that I acquired. If such a thing does exist, it is entirely your property. I have no use for it. Does that answer your question?"

"It does. I am obliged to you for your time, sir."

Melissa started to turn away, when Crouse's voice stopped her. "A moment, Miss Huntoon. Since you would not accept my prior offer, I have another for you."

Melissa stopped stock still, suddenly afraid of what he was going to say next, remembering what his "prior offer" had been. She felt the warmth of Amalie's hand on her shoulder, and leaned into the strength of the other woman.

Crouse's smile had become a smirk. "Since, as I said, you refused me one request this day, I hope that you may be persuaded to grant me another. In its place, as it were."

Melissa, still standing frozen, was aware that Luke Devereaux had approached and was listening intently. Strangely, there was something reassuring in his mere presence.

"And what is that, please?" Melissa asked in a voice

scarcely above a whisper, which was the loudest sound she could produce.

"You still have one item of value left," Crouse said, never taking his gaze from hers. "And I am prepared to pay you handsomely if you will turn it over to me."

Melissa felt confused. What could he be talking about? She said coldly, "I don't understand you, sir."

"Why, I am speaking of your maid." He nodded toward Amalie. "I have heard that she is a capable worker, experienced and knowledgeable. I am in need of a woman to manage my household, a housekeeper, someone who is personable as well as efficient. I am prepared to offer you the handsome sum of five hundred dollars for her. It should help you over a difficult time."

Melissa felt her body grow cold, then flush hot with anger. She stiffened with the effort necessary to control her emotions, as Amalie drew in her breath with a hiss. Melissa felt the other woman's fingers tighten almost painfully on her shoulder.

"I'm afraid that you've made a mistake, Mr. Crouse," Melissa said carefully. "I have no power to *sell* Amalie to you. Amalie is my friend, almost like a mother to me. She has never been a slave, and even if she had been, you Yankees just won a war that freed the slaves, if you will remember. So how could I possibly sell her?"

Crouse's smile did not quite reach his eyes. "Why, who spoke of selling, or buying? I simply offered you five hundred dollars to make up for your loss of her services, as it were. Your friend would receive good wages, have a supervisory position, and comfortable quarters. How can you offer her this?"

Melissa turned her head to look into Amalie's eyes.

22

Her face was familiar and very dear to her, and always a cause for wonder. Amalie was so beautiful, even now, even though she had to be nearly forty years old. Smooth skin the color of *café au lait*; brilliant, black, slightly tilted eyes under brows shaped like delicate wings; thin but sensuously molded lips, pinker than those of any white woman; and under it all the marvelous bone structure that would always remain, even when the flesh sagged and the skin wrinkled.

Melissa turned back to confront Crouse, and caught him unaware as he stared at Amalie with the same hot look he had bent upon her, Melissa, earlier on the veranda.

She felt her stomach contract. The reason Crouse wanted Amalie had nothing whatsoever to do with keeping his house. How could men be so base? Were women nothing to them but objects upon which to vent their desires? He had wanted her, but since she wasn't available, then he would take Amalie. Was that the way it worked?

On the other hand, Melissa thought, she could offer Amalie nothing but hunger and hardship. Perhaps Amalie would *want* to go with him.

When she turned to speak to Amalie, her voice shook. "Amalie, I can't force you to stay with me. Mr. Crouse can offer you a good home and a comfortable life. If you want to go, don't let me stand in your way. I will understand."

Amalie's smooth face did not change expression by so much as the flicker of an eyelash as she looked at Crouse, but Melissa saw the man nonetheless take a step back. "Why, I'm afraid that I'm too set in my ways, Miss Melissa, to go changing them now. I'll just go on doing what I've always done, taking care of you. But I do thank you, Mr. Crouse, all the same. I know it was an offer made out of the kindness of your heart."

Crouse's lips thinned, and he said harshly, "Well, suit yourself. But I hope you won't be sorry, Miss Huntoon, when that bit of money you just pocketed is gone, and you have nowhere to go, no place to stay. Good day to you, madam."

Abruptly, he whirled away toward his carriage, and the driver of the loaded wagon reached for the reins and made ready to go.

Luke Devereaux had listened quietly to the exchange. Now he smiled as Crouse stomped off. He dipped his head, and said in a low voice, "Stick to your guns, ma'am." Still smiling, he turned to mount the black horse, and sent it trotting after Crouse's carriage.

Silently, Melissa and Amalie watched as the entourage moved off down the driveway in a cloud of red dust.

Amalie muttered something under her breath, and Melissa had the suspicion that it was something unladylike. In a swelling of affection, Melissa squeezed her arm. "Oh, Amalie! I'm so glad you stayed. I thought it might be better for you, even if he . . ."

Amalie gave a bitter laugh. "Even if he? Ah, yes. You are learning about life, little one. You sensed that a housekeeper was not all that he wanted." She shook her head. "Ah, but he is evil, that one. We will hear from him again, you may be sure. But he will not have us. Not you, not I. We will escape his clutches, and we will survive."

Melissa felt some comfort in the words, the same

brave words she had used to Luke Devereaux, but still she could not help but wonder how they would survive.

"Come. We will go upstairs." Amalie's voice roused Melissa from her thoughts. "I have made your room comfortable for us, and I have a nice supper ready to lay out."

Melissa began to smile. "Amalie, you are a marvel! A 'nice supper'? Now just how did you manage that?"

Amalie laid a finger alongside her nose. "Why, many of the guests brought picnic baskets, did you not notice? Large baskets filled with much food, which they placed in the shade while they attended the auction. They were quite full, the baskets. Far too much food in them. In this heat, it is unhealthy to eat so heartily. That is common knowledge, is it not, little one? And so I did them a favor, by lightening their baskets."

Melissa envisioned Amalie sneaking among the picnic baskets, "lightening" them. She dissolved into helpless laughter. "You *are* dreadful!" she managed to gasp out. "But I don't know what I would do without you."

Amalie smiled, her eyes dancing. "Yes, I am dreadful. That is true. But sometimes it is the only recourse." Her smile widened. "When one walks among thieves . . ." She shrugged, and reached for Melissa's hand. "Come. You must be starved, little one. You have had nothing all day except the small egg I stole from the hen's nest. And do not feel so badly about the poor townspeople whose baskets I lightened. I took the most from Mr. Crouse's basket. He is a serpent, that man, but he has good taste, that I must admit."

Feeling lightheaded and giddy, Melissa hurried toward the empty house, holding Amalie's hand. Amalie pulled her along at such a pace that she did not have time to brood over the empty rooms, or worry about the days to come. Breathless and laughing, she ran into her own room, and stopped short with surprise.

Amalie had spoken the truth. Despite the absence of the canopied bed and other furniture, Amalie had managed to save more than Melissa had dared to hope.

Two sturdy feather bolsters lay on the floor, one on each side of the room, separated by the small Persian rug that had lain beside Melissa's bed. Melissa shook her head, as Amalie lifted the spreads to show what was underneath. Each bolster had a fat pillow in a white embroidered case, and a blanket, which would not be necessary in the summer weather, but would be useful later.

"Amalie, sometimes I believe that you are a witch!"

A strange expression crossed Amalie's smooth features, then gave way to an impish grin. "It has been said so."

Melissa spun about, her troubles forgotten in her surprise at all the things Amalie had somehow managed to salvage. Her large trunk, the leather one with the paintings on the sides and the brass handles, stood in one corner.

"Your clothes are inside," Amalie said, "and all your personal things, your silver mirror and brush, and a few knick-knacks."

Upon the chest sat the music box, rescued by Luke Devereaux, and a large wicker hamper.

Amalie motioned toward the hamper. "*Voilà!* Our

supper. Now seat yourself upon a bolster, and we shall dine."

Melissa, aware now of her gnawing hunger, did as she was bid, arranging herself comfortably on the bolster, with a pillow behind her.

Amalie took a checkered cloth from the hamper, and spread it out on the Persian rug. She began to lay out what looked to Melissa like a feast.

There was a loaf of crusty white bread, fresh from someone's oven just this morning. Melissa inhaled the yeasty aroma and felt her stomach contract. "Oh, was there ever such a smell!" she exclaimed.

"Just wait," Amalie said, as she took out a jar of strawberry jam, half of a large cheese, a roasted chicken, a brown-crusted pie, with berry juice oozing from it, a small crock of butter cradled in water that had once been ice. Several ripe peaches, and two bottles of what looked to be very good wine, completed the feast.

Melissa clapped her hands together in delight. "Oh! So much, so much!"

Amalie said, "We will eat well tonight, little one, and then I'll put what remains in the springhouse, where it will keep cool until tomorrow. Now eat, and thank your kind Monsieur Crouse for his generosity."

Melissa reached to tear off a chunk from the crusty loaf of bread, and soon the only sounds in the room were those of two hungry people eating and drinking. When Melissa finally could eat no more, she sank back upon the bolster, her hands clasped over her stomach.

Amalie watched her with a slight smile on her lips. She was so young! So young, and so vulnerable. So ill-equipped to take her place in this new world now that her old world had been destroyed.

Amalie sighed as she gazed at the flushed young face. She felt toward Melissa as she would feel toward her own daughter, if she had one; and she would do for Melissa what she would have done for her own child. But would that be enough?

Although she was careful not to show her feelings to the younger woman, Amalie had grave fears for their future. They would have to leave this house shortly, and where would they go? And how would they live when they got there?

By herself, Amalie knew she would have no problem. There was always work available for willing hands, and Amalie had never been afraid of work. Also, she had relatives and friends in New Orleans who would take her in until she got on her feet, but she couldn't ask them to take in a white girl, especially a white girl who had been raised in wealth and privilege, and knew nothing of the ways of the world. If they remained together, and she had no thought of deserting Melissa, she would have to educate her, and she would have to do it quickly.

Amalie sighed again, and began to gather up the remaining food. The springhouse was cool, and with any luck the cheese and bread would keep for several days. There was another loaf of bread in the basket, and additional fruit. The rest of the pie would keep, and they would have the remainder of the chicken in the morning.

As she closed the lid to the basket, Amalie looked again into Melissa's sleeping face.

What a lovely child she was! Her lips, slightly open in sleep, were plump and delicately modeled, giving her a slightly pouting expression that was childishly appealing, but the chin was strong, and the bones were good under the rounded cheeks, which were as pink as if they had been rouged. The eyes were closed now; they had soft feathery lashes, several shades darker than the mass of curls, which glowed with all the lights of pure copper; but when Melissa's eyes were open, they were intelligent and serious, their deep blue color darker than expected, their gaze level and intent.

As Amalie watched, Melissa gave a slight snore, and flung one arm out to the side. Amalie smiled.

Across Melissa's nose marched a small parade of red-brown freckles. Melissa hated them, and had tried repeatedly to bleach them away with lemon juice, but they always came back. Now Amalie looked at the freckles with a mixture of love and sadness. Brave little freckles, so determined and alone on the delicate bridge of Melissa's nose; they seemed to represent the girl herself, courageous but unknowing, having no idea of where she was going, but marching proudly.

The sun was starting to go down behind the huge oaks, and the air was cooling. Gently, Amalie removed Melissa's worn shoes and stockings, and loosened her bodice. Lifting Melissa's feet, and turning her on the bolster, Amalie drew the side of the coverlet over her legs, and left her to sleep.

The light was fading, as Amalie carried the still-heavy basket down the winding staircase, and she hurried so that she could get the food stored in the springhouse before it became too dark to see her way.

The springhouse was cool and damp, and she shivered slightly as she placed the basket on a shelf, and covered it with one of the large napkins, which she first soaked in the cool water. Then she closed the door behind her and locked it carefully. There were hungry animals, as well as hungry men, abroad in these hard times, and she had to take care of her own.

The light was almost gone now, the last glow fading behind the great spreading arms of the giant oaks. Amalie's heart was heavy. Great Oaks had been her home for twenty years, ever since Jean-Paul Huntoon had brought her here as a young girl, to serve as personal maid to his new wife, Mariette.

The two young women had found much in common, for Amalie, although of mixed blood, was not a slave. She was a Creole from New Orleans, the daughter of a well-to-do French tradesman and his wife, a woman of Spanish and black blood.

If her father had not fallen onto hard times, Amalie probably would have lived a life of comparative ease in the city that she loved, no doubt making a good marriage, so that now she would have been a matron of some means, with her children around her, in a stylish house in the heart of town. But her father's fortune failed. Unable to stand the shock and the shame, he had sought solace in the bottom of a bottle, hardly seeming to notice when her mother sickened, wasted, and died. And so Amalie, who had been taught to be frugal and to manage a house, sought honest work.

That was not the only option open to her, however. In New Orleans, women of mixed blood but from good backgrounds, particularly if they were beautiful, were in great demand as mistresses for the wealthy white gentlemen of the city.

So, it would have been easy for her to have chosen from among the many interested men who desired to keep her, like some exotic pet, in a fine house, bought for just such a purpose. It would have been an easy life, perhaps even a pleasant one, but Amalie had seen the pretty dark girls on the arms of aging white men, seen the looks they were given, heard the scornful laughter and the ribald remarks. Pretty pets, that was all they were, for all the fine clothes and the jewels. Decorative pets, to be pampered for a while, used to satisfy aging lusts, then cast aside when their owners tired of them. Amalie did not want that kind of life. Her pride, an integral part of her character even then, demanded that she be her own person.

And so when Jean-Paul Huntoon, a gentleman and not a man to demean the pride of others, even black people, had come to New Orleans looking for a maid and companion for his young wife, Amalie had accepted the job. And she had never been sorry. She had always been treated as a member of the family, and when Mariette had died, she had automatically stepped into the vacuum Mariette's death had left in the life of her daughter, becoming mother, sister, and companion for the young girl whom she had grown to love as her own.

Amalie made a small sound of weariness as she turned away from gazing at the darkening sky behind the trees. And now they were alone, she and Melissa. What was to become of them?

As she walked toward the house, lifting her skirts from the grass already dampened by dew, Amalie heard a stealthy rustling sound behind her. Startled, she whirled, and found herself imprisoned by a man's strong arms. She caught a whiff of tobacco and rum, before a rough sack was pulled down over her head and arms, and she was lost in the dry smell of corn, and blackness. Ropes were lashed around her, binding her arms tightly to her sides.

31

Her attacker said not a word, but Amalie could hear his raspy breathing as he lifted her bodily and threw her into what, to Amalie's muffled senses, seemed to be a carriage. She heard the slap of reins and the blowing of horses, and then she was thrown hard against the back of the seat as the vehicle lurched into violent motion. She struggled against the confines of the sack, but she was too firmly bound, and she could get no purchase against which to struggle.

The ride seemed interminable, but when she had collected herself enough to think coherently, Amalie listened attentively, attempting to gauge where they were and where they were going. Soon she heard the sound of other hooves clattering over brick, and that and other city sounds told her that they had to be in Natchez—there was no other town this close. For God's sake, what was going on? Why had this man abducted her, and where was he taking her?

She thought of Melissa, alone in the empty house at Great Oaks, and prayed that she would not awaken to find Amalie gone, or that one of the wandering night marauders, all too frequent these days, did not enter the house and find the girl unprotected.

At last the movement of the carriage ceased, and Amalie was hauled out and made to walk up stone steps and through a door. All the while her captor had not spoken a word, pushing her along with rough hands.

The door slammed behind her, and she heard a mutter of male voices, before she was propelled up yet another flight of stairs, and into another room. Again the voices muttered, then one set of footsteps sounded on the wooden floor, and the door closed.

Amalie felt hands undoing the bonds around the sack, and then the rough fabric of the sacking was raised. She held herself ready for anything, as the sack was whipped over her head.

Then she stood, blinking in the light, staring into the face of Simon Crouse. Amalie saw that they were in a bedroom.

Crouse had a sneering, self-satisfied smile on his face, and Amalie went tense with outrage. How dare he do this to her?

Her anger must have shown in her face, for his smile grew wider. "I gather you don't care for the treatment you've received, eh? I've heard that you New Orleans quadroons are a feisty lot, full of passion and fire. Well, I like my women with a little fire and spit to them, so just boil away, my high-toned *lady*."

By the high flush on his cheeks and the glaze in his eyes Amalie knew that he had been drinking heavily, and from the bulge at the front of his trousers she could tell that he was sexually aroused, and in no condition to listen to reason. Losing control of her emotions would gain her nothing.

"Why have you brought me here, Mr. Crouse?"

He threw back his head and laughed mockingly. "Why do you think, woman?" He made an obscene motion with the lower part of his body. "See if you can guess."

"Why me?" she said, still calm. "Surely there are others here in town, much handier, and likely quite willing. Why spirit me away at night, and bring me all this distance?"

Abruptly the laughter left his face, and his reddened eyes glared at her. In a snarling voice he said, "Because you refused me, you black-blooded bitch! I

33

offered you a fine house, a good position, but you elevated that fine nose of yours, just like you were a real lady, and you refused me! Well, now we'll see what good *that* did you!"

He reached out, seizing her shoulder in a cruel grip, and pulled her toward him. His breath was sour with stale liquor, and his lips were hot and wet against hers. She made a sound of revulsion, and he cuffed her carelessly with his open hand.

"Do not draw back from me, slut!"

Again he pulled her close, and this time Amalie remained still in his grasp; her mind worked furiously, walling herself off from this indignity. She knew it would be a waste of breath to scream. Even if, by the wildest chance, someone came, they would do nothing when they saw who and what she was.

Did Crouse mean to keep her here, a prisoner? Or did he just want her this one night so that he might satisfy his frustration and lust? This had happened a few times before in her life, but it had always been a matter of an hour or so, and she had learned to endure it. But a longer period was a different matter . . .

Crouse's mouth slid away from hers, and he staggered slightly, weaving his way toward a bed on one side of the dimly lighted room. As soon as his hands left her, Amalie bolted for the door, only to find the knob resistant in her hand. It was locked. She had expected as much, but it had been necessary to find out.

Crouse's cruel laughter battered at her ears. "Yes, it's locked, and there is no one here except myself, and one servant, to hear you if you bother to scream. You might as well resign yourself to my company, for we are going to be *very* close for the rest of the night."

More quickly than she would have thought possible, considering his state of intoxication, he pounced, clamping his hand around her wrist. He hauled her toward the high bed, and threw her across it with some force, so that she lay sprawled awkwardly, her skirts up above her thighs.

As she scrambled to pull down her clothing, Crouse fumbled his trousers open, and exposed his organ. It was engorged and throbbing, and he held it toward her as if to threaten her into obedience with his maleness.

Amalie gazed upon it with little emotion. It was not that different from many that she had seen before. She knew that she could very likely wilt it with her laughter and derision, for she had used this trick often before. However, with Simon Crouse it might be dangerous to do so. It was possible that he would vent his frustration in even crueler ways.

The next instant he was upon her, his hot hands ripping away her blouse, and roughly squeezing her exposed breasts. His breath was sour in her nostrils as his lips, unpleasantly soft and hot, again covered hers.

Amalie tried to think of other things. He might violate her body, but he could not reach her soul and spirit. It was something she had learned which had helped her to retain her sanity through other such episodes.

As Crouse pushed aside her skirt and jammed his swollen member into her, Amalie could not help thinking that it was very strange indeed that this act should be called the act of love, when so very often love had little indeed to do with it. And it was stranger still that this same act could be either heaven or hell. When there was love and sharing, it could be an experience that transcended the purely sexual, a joining of soul, mind and body; and without love, without caring, with hate, it could be an act of the utmost degradation.

Amalie wondered briefly if men also knew this. She was certain that all women did.

The man atop her pounded away, his breath rasping in and out with what seemed to be sounds of pain. His fingers were digging into her shoulders, and she knew that tomorrow her body would show the marks of this night's assault.

Then Crouse gave a straining cry, arching his back like a man who had been stabbed. He thrust into her once more, and then again, as his breath sobbed out with the agonizing pleasure of his climax.

In a sort of cold horror, Amalie realized that it had been pleasurable for him. Despite her lack of cooperation, despite the mental barrier she had erected, detaching herself from the proceedings, it had been pleasurable for him!

She sighed as his inert body collapsed upon her. It was over. At least for the moment.

Almost at once, Crouse began to snore. She waited a few moments, until she thought that he was deeply asleep, then carefully rolled him aside. He flopped onto his back, his mouth open and his face lax.

Slowly, Amalie inched her body away from him, and then paused to study his face for a long time, memorizing every line and plane, her own face expressionless.

Crouse did not move as she rose from the bed, pulling her disordered and torn clothing around her as best she could. On a stand in one corner of the room she found a basin of water and clean towels. Using them, she washed herself methodically, erasing every

36

trace of Crouse's touch, every vestige of his ardor. When she was finished, and her clothing and hair arranged, Amalie delicately searched Crouse's pockets until she found the key to the door.

She discovered the simple-witted serving man on the porch, smoking a pipe that sent noxious fumes spuming into the night. He appeared somewhat surprised to see her, but did not question her statement that his master wanted her returned to where she had been picked up. "He is asleep, you know?" She shrugged expressively.

The man grinned, and eyed her body boldly, accepting her implication that he knew how it was with men once their appetites had been satisfied.

On the ride home, Amalie thought of nothing, and of many things.

The sky was not yet light when the carriage let her out in front of Great Oaks, and she stole quietly up the stairs to the room where Melissa still lay asleep. Grateful that Melissa apparently had not awakened and found her gone, Amalie barred the door. She lay down on the other bolster and closed her eyes; yet it was some time before sleep came to her.

How would Crouse react in the morning when he found her gone?

She realized that the events of this night had been in revenge for Melissa's spurning of him, as well as hers. Crouse had not quite dared to abduct Melissa. Even if she was alone and relatively unprotected, she was white, and a lady of the Southern aristocracy. The knowledge that Crouse had dared take *her*, because no one would really care, was bitter; but Amalie had come to grips with the injustice of the world long ago.

Her main concern was whether or not Crouse, having taken at least a measure of revenge, would now leave them alone; or whether he would come after her again, or perhaps attack them both in some other way.

Amalie knew that, no matter what, they must leave Great Oaks as soon as possible!

Chapter Three

The sun awoke Melissa, falling across her face, warm and golden through the uncurtained window. She awoke slowly, feeling pleasant and relaxed, for a moment not thinking of time and place, and then slowly rousing to the consciousness of reality.

She had slept well, for the first time in weeks, perhaps because she had gone to sleep on a full stomach, an event which had become a rarity in her young life. Sitting up, she gazed down at herself, and saw that she was still dressed. She must have fallen asleep right where she sat last night, and Amalie must have covered her.

She looked affectionately at the other woman, who still lay sleeping on the other bolster, one hand curved near her cheek. As she watched, Amalie's mouth opened, her brow contracted, and she moaned softly in her sleep.

Melissa turned away in embarrassment, feeling as if she had been caught spying on her friend. It bothered her, somehow, that Amalie should appear even the least bit vulnerable. Amalie had always been the strong one, the one who could take care of things. Melissa's thoughts veered away from the subject. She didn't really want to think about such things.

She reached down beside the bolster and picked up her shoes, looking at them with distaste. They were so worn. She badly needed new ones, but there was little chance of that at the moment.

She yawned widely and stretched, hearing her shoulder bones pop, then bent over to put on the shoes. She was hungry again. Just knowing that they still had plenty of food made her mouth water.

Carefully, she stood up, and on tiptoe crept past Amalie. Opening the door very quietly, she closed it behind her without a sound. Trying not to look at the ravaged house, she went down the broad staircase, down the hall, and out into the back yard. It was a glorious morning, fragrant and dew-damp, with a promise of heat to come.

She inhaled the scent of the flowers from the overgrown garden, and then headed for the springhouse. She would bring breakfast up to Amalie; or perhaps she shouldn't wake her, but let her sleep. Amalie had worked so hard, and she had looked so tired this morning, her face much too pale against the white pillowslip. Besides, it was too beautiful a morning to eat inside. They would eat on the huge granite boulder under the great oak tree behind the house.

And then they must make plans.

As she thought this, Melissa experienced a moment of panic. What were they to do? Where were they to go? Then she dismissed her doubts. They would think of something. They simply had to.

She filled a pitcher of water in the springhouse, and

washed her face and hands in the cool liquid, drying herself with a linen handkerchief from her pocket. Then she picked up the basket of food, and took it outside to the granite boulder.

She was about to be selfish and yield to her hunger, eating without waiting for Amalie, when a thought struck her. The music box! She had a sudden desire to hear the tunes her mother had played so often for her as a child, and that she had played for herself when she was older.

Yes, she would have music with her meal!

She crept back upstairs and into the room where Amalie still slept. The trip back down was slower; the music box was quite heavy.

Outside, she set it carefully on the surface of the flat boulder, and wound it tightly. The disc already in place on the device was the record of an old German song, with a tender melody that Melissa loved.

Releasing the catching device, she listened as the clear, tinkling sound filled the morning air. As the first few bars played, she only listened, but as the melody repeated itself, she began to dance.

The grass was damp and stuck to her shoes, but she raised her feet high, and holding her skirts out, she whirled and glided over the ground. Above her she could see the branches of the great oak, sheltering her like protective arms.

Moving in time to the music, Melissa felt a mixture of emotions that she could not have described. There was fear there, and sorrow, but also a kind of excitement, a feeling that this destruction of her old life had somehow freed her to find a new, perhaps better life. She felt tears come to her eyes, and did not know why.

When the disc had played through to the end, and the music stopped, Melissa was startled by the soft clapping of hands. She whirled around to find Amalie watching from beneath the tree. Flushed with embarrassment, she wondered how long the older woman had been watching. She laughed nervously. "Amalie! I thought you were asleep. I guess I looked like a perfect fool, didn't I? Cavorting on the grass, all alone . . ."

Amalie smiled warmly. "No, little one. You looked quite fetching, like the spirit of spring. I had almost forgotten how well you dance. It's been so long . . ." She came forward to take Melissa's hand. "Never apologize for doing what you wish to do. It is good to express one's self. And it is a lovely idea. Breakfast with music. It will give a good start to our day."

"And now," said Amalie, when breakfast had been cleared away, and the basket put away in the springhouse, "we must talk about what we plan to do."

Melissa nodded. "I know. Father used to say that in any difficult situation, a person must take stock of his assets, and review his options, so that he might act logically."

"That is still good advice," Amalie said with a smile. "So, let's take an inventory of our assets. You must tell me if I overlook anything. We have the chest, with your clothing and personal articles. We have the bolsters, linen, and blankets. We have the Persian rug, the music box, enough food for another day or so, and the magnificent sum of two hundred dollars in bills and silver."

"And the *Natchez Belle*, don't forget."

"The *Natchez Belle*?"

Melissa nodded. "A boat, a steamboat. It must be in bad repair. No one bid on it at the auction, and the auctioneer told me that since they didn't, it still belonged to me. I even verified it with Simon Crouse, to be sure it should not go to him."

She grimaced, as she mentioned Crouse, and she noticed a strange expression pass over Amalie's face.

"A steamboat! And where is this boat?"

"Docked in Natchez-Under-the-Hill. I've been thinking about it, wondering how we might make use of it. Even if it is in disrepair, perhaps we could live on it. I mean, we don't have anyplace else to go, nowhere to live. If the boat isn't a total wreck, well, perhaps we could stay there. At least for a while."

Amalie nodded thoughtfully. "Perhaps. It is, at any rate, worth considering. We will leave here tomorrow, for today there is something I must do. Also, I have a surprise for you."

Melissa brightened. "A surprise?"

"Yes. It is in the stable."

Melissa shook her head in disbelief. "What is it?"

Amalie smiled mysteriously. "Have you thought of how we are to get our meager belongings to Natchez? Few as they are, they are far more than we two could carry, *n'est-ce pas?*"

Melissa's expression grew serious. "I have thought about it, yes. And I have no answer."

"Well, my surprise is going to get us there."

Melissa jumped up. "Are you teasing me, Amalie?"

"No, little one. Come."

Amalie led Melissa to the stable building, which lay back of the main house at some distance.

As they entered the dark, cavernous building, which had long been empty except for mice and rats, Melissa heard a loud hee-haw. A moment later her hand flew to her mouth, and she watched in total surprise as Amalie led into the light a small mule with muddy eyes and a dejected air.

"Here, hold it," she said, handing the rope to Melissa. "And see there, we have a cart, too. It's not much, but it will be sufficient to get us to Natchez."

Melissa followed the woman's pointing finger, and gaped at the small, frail-looking cart in the next stall. "How did you manage to keep the mule hidden?" she asked.

Amalie's smile widened. "Everyone knows that Great Oaks had no stock for the past year. I knew that they would not even look here."

"Oh, mule! Lovely, lovely mule!" Melissa cried, throwing her arms around the startled animal's neck. "I never thought I'd be so glad to see a plain mule!" She turned back to Amalie. "How on earth did you manage to get him in the first place?"

Amalie placed a finger alongside her nose, and assumed a mysterious look. "A little trading," she said. "I traded the grandfather clock for him, several days before the auction.

"Now, let's tether him outside, so that he can get some sun and crop some grass. We must treat him well, for he is important to us."

After the mule was tied off to graze, Amalie said, "You return to the house, Melissa. I shall be along shortly."

Buoyed by what she had learned, Melissa went along, leaving the older woman to her own devices. Amalie often went off by herself for long periods of time, and something had warned Melissa not to question her disappearances.

44

Melissa stopped at the springhouse for the music box. On impulse she pulled open the drawer that housed the discs. She made her choice—a gay melody to fit her lightened spirits—and put the disc onto the mechanism, wound it tightly, and released the catch.

The disc started turning, and the first few notes sounded. Abruptly the mechanism jammed. Melissa stared at it in consternation.

Oh, no, she thought; *it can't be broken! Not now!*

Gently, she shook the box. There was a slight rustling sound, and the disc began to turn normally again, the music spilling out clear and without distortion.

Much relieved, she smiled happily, as she touched the smooth wooden sides of the box in a caressing motion. It was all right. Perhaps this was a good omen for them. Perhaps things would be all right now.

Amalie stood quite still in the near dark of the small shed adjoining the stable. A criss-cross of thin bands of light patterned her face and body, as they came through the narrow cracks between the boards and illuminated the old wooden table in front of her.

On the table was spread an odd collection of objects: the body of a fat toad, long hairs clipped from the mule's tail, and several small piles of dried herbs.

Now, from her pocket, Amalie took the stub end of a black candle and a flint box. A few quick strokes of the flint against the steel brought forth a spark that ignited the piles of dried herbs, causing them to flame high for a moment. Swiftly, she set the candle aflame, then blew on the herbs and wedged the candle upright, as the burning leaves subsided and began to smoulder, sending up a white, pungent smoke.

Holding the body of the toad over the smoking herbs, Amalie recited a few words in a language so old that she did not even know its origin. Then, taking up the mule hairs, she bound the body of the toad tightly, reciting as she did so. Among the foreign sounds, the name of Simon Crouse was repeated again and again. Last, she pulled three hairs from her own head, and bound the toad once again, always holding it in the smoke from the herbs. When the toad's body was completely bound, she placed it in a small box, and sealed the box with the drippings from the black candle.

This done, she blew out the candle, and put the box in her pocket. It must now be buried, but she had to make certain that Melissa did not see her do this. As close as she and Melissa were, this was one thing she knew Melissa would not understand.

"Are you staying, Devereaux?" Crouse's voice was polite, but underneath it Luke Devereaux could sense the driving greed of the man.

Luke looked again at the cards in his hands, his face expressionless.

He had a full house, queens over tens, and he didn't think anyone at the table could beat him. He just wished he could be sure, because the last of his money was there in the pot.

"Will you accept my note?" he said casually.

Crouse hesitated for just a moment, then gave his thin smile. "Why, of course. We're all gentlemen here."

He motioned to his house servant, who hovered nearby. The man handed Luke a slip of paper on which to write the note.

As he signed the note, Luke experienced a moment

of misgiving. If he lost this hand, it would not only clean him out, but he would also be in debt to Crouse. However, there should be no real problem. The money from the cattle deal he had recently completed in Texas should be arriving at the local bank within the next few days. There would be enough to cover the note and ample left over to live on until he completed the land deal he was working on here. He had nothing to worry about.

"I call." He placed the note on top of the pile of money on the table.

Crouse smiled coldly. "All right, my friend, let's see what you have."

Luke lay down the full house, and the other two players shook their heads dolefully and folded, but Crouse's smile did not falter.

"Too bad." With an extravagant gesture, Crouse spread his cards face up on the table, showing a king-high straight flush.

Luke's first feeling was an enormous chagrin, followed by a spurt of anger. He prided himself on his ability to remember which cards had been played, and he was reasonably certain that there was no honest way that Crouse could have held those particular cards.

In the seconds that he stared at Crouse's cards, alternatives flashed through his mind. He could call Crouse on it, and perhaps a counting of the cards would prove Luke correct, but it was Crouse's house, and these were Crouse's friends, and Crouse was a crucial figure in the land deal Luke was putting together.

No, it would not be wise to challenge the man. Not now. He would have to accept his loss with surface good grace, but he determined to keep his eye on the slippery bastard after this. Luke didn't mind being diddled once by a man—in his business you could expect that and you could put it down to an error in judgment—but if you let him diddle you a second time, you were a damned fool, and deserved what you got!

"Well, it looks like the hand is yours, Simon."

"Yes, it does, doesn't it?" With a smug smile Crouse raked in his winnings. "How soon will you be able to make good your note?"

Luke forced a smile. "Why, by the end of the week, I should think. Some funds are being wired to me here from Texas. The money should arrive any day now."

Crouse nodded. "Good. I trust you, you know that, but I do like to get business details attended to promptly, so that I don't have items continually pending, as it were. You understand, I'm sure."

"Oh, absolutely," Luke said dryly. "Well, I'd best be on my way." He rose, and plucked his coat from the back of the chair.

Crouse rose also. "Won't you stay and have a bite of supper with us? The others are staying."

Luke shook his head. "No thanks, Simon, I have plans for the evening. I'm late as it is."

"I understand."

Both men nodded cordially, and Luke shrugged into his coat. Picking up his hat, he turned again to Crouse. "I'll see you later in the week, then."

"Surely."

Another nod, another half bow, and Luke left the house, hat set jauntily on his head. No one, observing

48

him, could have divined that he was seething with anger inside.

Maybe he was making a mistake, having business dealings with Simon Crouse. If he would cheat at cards, how could he be trusted? True, some men didn't consider cheating at cards to be *really* cheating. But in Luke's view, a cheat was a cheat.

As he mounted his horse, Luke took out his pocket watch. The bank was closed now, but he would check with them the first thing in the morning. Crouse was not the only one who wanted to get the matter between them settled as soon as possible. Luke didn't want anything hanging fire between them when they got down to taw on the land deal.

He was staying at the best hotel in Natchez. It was expensive, but he was not a man to stint himself as long as he had the price of comfort. His room was large and comfortable, with wide windows opening out on the street. He opened those windows now, and let in the humid, fragrant air, and the street sounds.

He removed one of the thin brown cigars that he favored from the silver case he carried with him at all times. The case was engraved with the word "Lucky," inscribed in a flowing script. In the bend of the Y, a small but perfect diamond glittered.

Drawing on the cigar, he gazed at the case, his face, for the moment, going soft, and musing. It was the only thing he had left to remind him of his mother. She had given him the case on his twenty-first birthday, and had died six months later.

He turned the case so that the setting sun caught the diamond facets, and watched the play of light. His mother, Rose Devereaux. She had been quite a woman.

Some people might call her a bad woman—in fact, many had—but Luke knew better. He knew that for a woman with no money, no family, and no training, there were only two ways to earn enough money to support a child, and his mother had chosen what she considered the better way.

She had run a clean respectable house in Galveston, patronized by the very best and richest men in town, and as far as Luke knew, she had never sold her own favors—only those of the girls who happily worked for her, for she had treated the girls more like daughters than like the salable merchandise that so many madams seemed to consider them.

Luke ran his fingers over the lettering on the case. She had always called him Lucky, ever since he could remember. She had raised him to recognize the harsh realities of life, and had taught him how not to grow bitter in the process.

He was very young when he first learned that money could buy perhaps not everything, but a great deal. It could buy comfort, it could buy respect, it could buy power, and it could even buy other people.

He learned that society, particularly women, more specifically wives and "nice" women, sternly disapproved of such pursuits as prostitution, gambling and drinking, and while the men paid lip service to this code, most of them indulged in these pleasures every chance they got.

Luke also learned that while physical love might be bought and sold, a person's inner self was not so easily bartered, and could only be freely given. He found nothing degrading in sex for hire, because it seemed to him that often married women did the very same thing—except that they sold their sexual favors for a man's name and a house, instead of for cash.

Yes, Rose had taught him to be realistic, but she had also taught him to follow her own code: to be fair, unless the other fellow tried to cheat you; to be kind to those less fortunate than you, if you have the wherewithal; to stand by a friend or a member of your own family, unless *they* diddled you; and to hurt no other human being, unless it was strictly necessary.

Rose had been some lady. She was twenty-five when her husband, a merchant seaman, died, and only forty-eight when she had succumbed to the sickness that had been slowly eating away at her for two years. She had left all that she had to Luke—a not inconsiderable sum—and of course the house. Having no desire to run the place himself, he had sold it, and invested the proceeds in several ventures, some of which had paid off, and some which had not.

Then the war came along, and even though he had grave reservations about putting himself in such a position of jeopardy, in good conscience he couldn't stay out. Although a native Texan, and Texas had chosen to side with the Confederacy, Luke had abhorred slavery, so he had enlisted in the Union army, and served with distinction. He had been under General Grant's command at the siege of Vicksburg. The months-long siege had given him time to become acquainted with the Mississippi, and Luke knew that, no matter how far he roamed, he would always come back to the river.

So now here he was, back on the river, trying to put together a deal which would get him back on his financial feet again. But why the South? Why not farther north along the river? Why here in the South, where he could be lynched if it was learned that he had been a Union soldier? At the very least they would refuse to do business with him. It wouldn't faze Simon Crouse, a Northern carpetbagger willing to do business with the Devil himself if there was a profit in it. But it would be different with the Southerners.

So, why here?

Luke had asked himself that many times, and had finally decided that he was plain curious. His curiosity had been aroused by these men who had thought that their way of life was right, just as he thought his was. They saw no evil in possessing slaves; on the contrary, their lives and fortunes were built upon this foundation. They seemed to him an exotic breed, and he was curious about what their world was like.

He realized now, of course, that it would be almost impossible to know how it really had been, for the war had destroyed their way of life, leaving only a shambles behind. Still, out of the wreckage, one could pick up clues. Like yesterday afternoon, for example. God, that had been sad—that pretty child in her patched dress with her pert little nose elevated to show her disdain of the crowd that had picked over the remains of her estate like so many birds of prey.

He had seen the anger and confusion mirrored in her blue eyes—such a dark blue that a person had to be close to her to be certain of their color. Such a brave little thing. She had a quality a man couldn't miss, like a well-bred racehorse. Perhaps there was something in family background after all!

She had stood up to Crouse, too, turned him down flat, when accepting his offer could have brought her a life of ease, but she had been wise there. Life with Simon Crouse would have cost her something, perhaps more than the life of poverty she now seemed destined for. It would certainly have snuffed out that flashing pride.

Luke turned toward the sideboard where a decanter of port stood on a silver tray, and poured himself a glass.

Holding the ruby liquid up to the failing light, he thought of the look on Melissa's face when that music box had gone up for auction. He simply hadn't been able to help himself, even though he had known that she might refuse to take it, proud as she was; never mind the fact that it was an extravagant gesture that he could ill afford.

But she had fooled him. Se had accepted the music box, and his statement that there were no strings attached to the gift. He raised his glass and took a swallow of the mellow port, his smile spreading as he thought of her face when she . . .

His thoughts were interrupted by the sound of a gunshot below. He leaned out to peer down into the street. Although Natchez was an old city and considered civilized, the war had left bad blood in its wake, and a rough element inhabited Natchez-Under-the-Hill, so Luke would not have been greatly surprised to see a gun duel in progress. That rough element sometimes boiled up over the bluff. He relaxed with a grin as he saw a lone citizen weaving his way down the street, waving a pistol around.

He stepped back into the room, thoughts returning to Melissa Huntoon. He raised the glass in a toast, thinking of her brave eyes, and the sweet young curves beneath the clean but worn dress. She was a lovely creature, and she stirred him, he admitted; but he knew that was not the only reason he had made the gesture. It was partly for her courage, and partly a gesture against Crouse's bullying of her.

As far as his own feelings went, well, she was what his mother would have called a "good" woman, and "good" women wanted marriage, a family, and a husband who stayed home, preferably tending to a successful business, and he was ready for none of these things. In fact, he doubted if he ever would be.

He tossed off the last of the port, and reached for his coat. He was hungry, and he had best get to the restaurant downstairs before all the best tables were taken.

As Luke started past the desk in the foyer, the clerk, a small, fastidious man, called to him and beckoned.

When Luke approached the desk, the clerk held out a sealed envelope. "Mr. Devereaux, this came for you this afternoon. I must have missed you when you went up, earlier."

Luke accepted the letter, and gave the man a generous tip. Since it was so late, he did not stop to read it, but stuffed it into his pocket, and went on into the dining room.

It was not until he was almost finished with his meal that he remembered the letter, and pulled it out to read it with his *café au lait*.

The letter was from Martin Barnes, the man who had been his partner in the Texas cattle deal. It couldn't be, or shouldn't be, the draft, since that was supposed to be sent directly to the bank. He lit a cheroot and opened the envelope. No, no draft.

He began to read: "Friend Luke: I do not know how to tell you this. I would rather cut off my right arm than to have to do it, but I cannot let you find out only when the bank draft does not arrive in Natchez . . ."

Luke closed his eyes briefly. His stomach muscles had suddenly clamped around his recently eaten dinner, which now sat there like a lump of cold iron. He sighed, opened his eyes, and resumed reading.

"I know we thought everything was all set with the cattle, and that nothing could go wrong. Well, we were right, except for one thing. Luke, those cattle were on their way to the stockyards, just lined up there, ready to be herded onto the train, when they began dropping like flies. I was there and saw it with my own eyes, and found it hard to believe. It was terrible.

"We sent for a horse doctor, and he said it was anthrax. Well, I guess I do not need to tell you what that meant. They had to kill them, Luke. Every dad-blamed one of them, and I had to stand there and watch it, watch our money falling to the ground, just so much dead meat.

"I expect that by now you are feeling pretty bad, and I reckon I know how you feel, because that is how I am feeling too. I hope you have some dinero stashed away somewhere, partner, cause this pure-dee wiped us out. Minnie and me are going back to Kansas and the farm, until I can get me another stake together.

"Wish you the best, and hoping that you do not take this too hard. Your friend and partner, Martin Barnes."

Luke let the hand holding the letter drop to the table. Wiped out. The words were final and bitter in his mind.

He had lost money before, God knows, and he had

shrugged it off and gone on, but somehow this seemed harder to take. Maybe he wasn't cut out for this wheeling and dealing after all.

He sighed deeply, and swallowed the last of his coffee. His mind, trained by bitter necessity, started sorting debits and credits. He owed a week's room rent at the hotel, and several other small debts around town, and, damnit, the debt he had incurred at the poker table this afternoon.

On the credit side, he owned an excellent wardrobe, several pieces of fairly expensive jewelry, personal articles, and his horse, saddle, and gear. Yet, even if he sold it all, the total wouldn't pay his current debts.

For a moment, he thought wistfully of the grand gesture he had made at the auction yesterday afternoon. That's what he got for being so damned gallant! It crossed his mind to go to Melissa Huntoon and make an appeal. He dismissed the thought at once. His price was just as strong as hers, damnit!

The hotel knew him and would wait, and his other debts in town were not that pressing. The land deal, of course, was dead. Without the money from the sale of the cattle, he had no operating capital. And then there was the matter of yesterday's note to Simon Crouse. Perhaps Crouse would wait for the money; but it galled Luke to think of being in debt to the Carpetbagger. Still, they were operating under the gentleman's code, and he knew that he must tell Crouse that he could not pay the note immediately.

Damn it all! Why now, when things had been going so well, did Lady Luck have to desert him?

He took out the cigar case, and ran his thumb over the engraved letters. He said aloud, "Mother, it could well be that you misnamed your son!"

Chapter Four

"Damn!" Simon Crouse threw the letter that had oc-casioned his outburst onto the desk, and scraped his chair violently backward.

Why did this have to come up *now*?

The letter was from one of his employees, Roy Davis, who managed Crouse's plantation north of New Orleans. The war might have put an end to the use of slaves, but there were plenty of hungry families willing to crop on shares, and Davis had been doing very well with the three hundred acres or so that com-prised Riverview, the plantation Crouse had taken over less than a year ago.

But now Davis wrote that he was having "trouble," and he wanted Crouse to come down to Riverview and help him straighten things out. It sounded serious, and Crouse felt that he should go. However, this was a most inconvenient time. He had Great Oaks in his possession now, and he had to find a good man to put in charge, so it could start turning a profit. There was the land deal with Luke Devereaux to be concluded.

Then there was a personal matter—the quadroon and Melissa Huntoon.

Crouse had taken great pleasure in subjugating Amalie to his will. The passion that her lush golden body had aroused in him, and the fact that he had possessed her against her will, gave him great satisfaction. He looked forward to having her again while the two women were still at Great Oaks, where he could reach Amalie.

He scowled, weighing that against the urgency of Davis's letter. He pushed the letter aside with a forefinger, and rested his elbow on the desk and his chin on his hand. The women would be at Great Oaks until the end of the week—Crouse considered it generous of himself to give them that much time. But even when they left Great Oaks, where could they go? He was confident they would not go far, but remain in Natchez or the vicinity. He would have Jake keep an eye on them, find out where they set up lodgings, and when he returned, he would take up where he had left off.

Crouse smiled, not realizing that he did so, as he thought of thrusting between the quadroon's golden thighs. Abruptly, the image in his mind shifted to that of Melissa.

Melissa would be delicate and virginal, her body white and tender beneath her full petticoats. He would be the first to breach her maidenhead, he felt certain. He imagined how she would struggle beneath his hands, like a plump white bird. How she would cry out, as he took her round breasts in his mouth and stroked them with his tongue, savoring their hot sweetness.

He felt the pressure of a beginning erection pushing

against his trousers, and he moved to arrange himself more comfortably.

Yes, the girl would be very different from the woman Amalie. Amalie was a ripe and experienced woman, musky and exciting, while the girl was dewy fresh, as tempting as a peach ready for the picking. He had eyed the round swellings beneath the material of her dress, and knew that she had generous breasts and, he imagined, a firm bottom and full thighs.

His erection was now a painful pressure and he could feel his pulse pounding. By God, he'd have them both, that he would, before he was done! Perhaps at once. He laughed aloud. Yes, both of them at once, in the same bed; one body golden and sinuous, one body white and young.

His erection now as hard as the wood of his desk, he turned toward the door. "Jake!" he called loudly.

The door opened, and the lanky Jake stuck in his unkempt head. "Yes, Mr. Crouse?"

"Tell that new maid, what's-her-name, the light brown one, to get her tail to my room upstairs immediately!"

"Yes, indeed, Mr. Crouse." Jake did not attempt to hide his leer. He was used to such requests and knew what they meant. He knew that the boss was a man of strong appetites—a "horny little bastard" in Jake's own vernacular—and it was a matter of pride to him that among the serving men of the other gentlemen of Natchez Crouse was known as a cocksman.

The new maid, light brown, with a bottom you could set a plate on, was a tasty little piece, and Jake vowed that he would toss her himself, when the boss was done.

Ella Louise, the maid, showed only resignation

when Jake gave her the order, and followed him docilely enough up to Crouse's bedroom. After she went inside, closing the door behind her, Jake lingered awhile, ear pressed to the door, listening to the sounds coming from inside. Slowly, a lewd smile spread across his face. Mr. Crouse was giving it to her good, that he was!

"That's her. That's the *Natchez Belle*, or what's left of her!" The wharf lounger pointed a dirty finger to a large boat that was grounded below the landing. It sat at a crooked angle, flat nose dug into the bank—an ungainly beast with its back broken.

Melissa let her breath go with a sigh of disappointment as they walked along the bank toward the *Natchez Belle*. The boat had once been white, but time and lack of care had turned her into a sort of light gray, marked with stripes and smears of darker dirt.

Along the railings of her four decks, patches of scrollwork were missing, and her ornamented railings sagged and gaped where they had broken. The *Natchez Belle* looked like an elaborate birthday cake that had been carelessly dropped in the dirt.

Melissa turned to Amalie, shoulders drooping in disappointment. "Oh, Amalie! She looks so awful!"

Amalie managed a smile. "She must not be so bad, little one. Perhaps the damage is only on the outside, and that can always be fixed if she is still sound underneath. Come, let us go aboard. That is what we have come for."

Melissa shrugged helplessly. She didn't feel that going aboard the boat would do any good. It was obviously a hopeless derelict. But still, as Amalie had said, it was what they had come for, and even if the boat looked pretty disreputable, they might be able to live there for a time.

Also, she would be glad to escape the gazes of the denizens of Natchez-Under-the-Hill, who had been watching her and Amalie since they had come down below the hill. Natchez-Under-the-Hill was widely known as the cesspool of the South, inhabited by roughnecks, gamblers, whores, thieves, murderers—the roughest element imaginable. It was said that *anything* could be bought here, if you had the price, and Melissa could well believe it. She was sure that she and Amalie were the first decent women to dare venture down here in years.

The long stage plank, which protruded from the bow of the *Belle* like a narrow tongue, slanted down to the muddy bank from the lower deck. The wood was rotten and badly in need of paint, and the boards underfoot creaked as Melissa placed her feet gingerly upon them. She hurried over the quaking bridge quickly, fearful that it might collapse under her weight.

Once they were on board, the dilapidated condition of the boat was even more apparent. Melissa and Amalie walked the length of the lower deck, avoiding piles of wood and other debris. In the stern, they both leaned over to look at the giant paddlewheel that was suspended from the rear of the boat. Strangely, the wheel itself seemed to be in fair condition; only one of the large wooden paddles was broken.

As they turned away from the rail, Melissa saw a large shape covered with rotting canvas in the middle of the rear deck. "What do you suppose that is?" she asked, walking toward it.

Amalie followed. "Probably the calliope. Someone has wrapped it to keep it out of the weather."

"Someone should have wrapped the rest of the boat," Melissa said sadly. "And why *just* that, I wonder?"

"Here now, you can just stop bad-mouthin' the *Belle* that way. She may need a little paint on 'er, but she's sound underneath. 'Sides, that ain't no way to discuss a lady, particularly in her hearin'!"

Melissa spun about to see a strange figure standing behind them. Tall and bean-pole thin, he had a craggy face, with a jutting nose, deep-set eyes of indeterminate color, and a raggedy brush of gray hair. He wore a boat captain's uniform, patched and tattered, but the brass buttons wore a high shine. Melissa drew in her breath as she noticed something else—where his right foot should have been was a wooden peg.

"Who are you?" she whispered, as Amalie stepped up beside her.

"I'm Captain Jubal King, that's who," he said with some pride, "and I look after the *Belle* here. Now, who might you be?"

Melissa relaxed a trifle. The man had a right to be here then. "I'm Melissa Huntoon, and this is Amalie Dubois, my friend."

Jubal scratched his head. "Huntoon? Any kin to Jean-Paul Huntoon?"

She nodded. "Yes, I'm his daughter. I just found out that Father owned this boat, and we've come here to . . . well, we've come to see if something might be done with it."

Jubal stared at her quizzically, looking surreptitiously but carefully at her clothing, then switched his gaze to Amalie. "Well, there might be . . . that is, if you brought along some Yankee dollars. Like I told you, she's sound underneath, but there's considerable work needs to be done on her, and that'll take money."

Melissa tried not to let her disappointment show, but she could see from Jubal's eyes that he had noticed her reaction. He was not a fool, whatever else he might be.

"How now. Why am I standin' around askin' you ladies questions when I know you must be tired and hungry? Come on inside, and I'll have the missus fix you somethin' to eat and drink."

Without waiting for an answer, Jubal turned and led them the length of the boat, wooden leg thumping with each step. In the bow he went up a curving stairway to the next deck. Melissa and Amalie followed him up the stairs, which Melissa noticed were clean, but badly in need of paint.

The stairs opened into what had clearly been the grand saloon, a large room that ran the length of the boat. Doors lined both sides, and Melissa surmised that these opened into passenger cabins. The walls and the ceiling of the saloon were ornate with fretwork, and the magnificent carpet underneath was not quite concealed by the accumulation of grime and the wear it had been subjected to. Above the tiny cabins, which were roofed over some feet below the ceiling, light was admitted to the saloon through a row of high windows, which also were thick with grime.

Melissa could see that the saloon had once been beautiful and gracious. Like Great Oaks; and a weary sadness possessed her at the thought.

Jubal King was thumping on ahead, and there was

nothing to do but follow him, so Melissa put the thought away, and moved forward.

And then they were at another stairway, curved and graceful despite its worn red carpet and dusty bannister, that divided to both left and right. The followed Jubal up the wide curve of stair to the next deck, and down a corridor toward the rear of the boat.

Almost at the end of this corridor, Jubal opened a door, and turned for the first time to see if they were following. With a beckoning motion of his head, he went into the cabin, and Melissa and Amalie trailed after him.

The cabin was a pleasant surprise. Clean, neat, and bright with fresh paint, it seemed to welcome them. It was a large, windowed, gracious cabin, with comfortable looking couches, a writing desk, a small table upon which some embroidery was set out, and a rocking chair.

In a trumpeting voice Jubal King said, "Melissa Huntoon has come to visit, Martha. Jean-Paul's little gal."

A slender, smallish woman was standing by the rocker, and she came toward them as they entered. She had pale blonde hair touched with gray, and an intelligent, no-nonsense face. She took Melissa's hand and looked into her eyes. "You're the picture of your mother, my dear. The very picture. Come in, come in! Make yourselves comfortable!"

Melissa let herself be guided toward one of the couches after exchanging looks with Amalie. This was certainly a warmer welcome than they had expected, considering they hadn't expected anyone at all to be on board the *Natchez Belle*.

She asked, "You knew my mother, Mrs. King?"

"My land, yes, child. We were girls together here in Natchez. My pa worked for yours. My land, this is a surprise!"

"Yes, it certainly is." Melissa felt thrown off-balance by the fact that she was known to this woman, yet she liked her already. She had the feeling that if she asked Martha King questions, she would always get an honest and direct answer.

"'Course I've been out of touch with your folks these past twenty years, since I took to the river with Jubal," Martha said, as Amalie sat down beside Melissa. "I don't need to ask why you're here. I heard about the auction. A terrible thing. It must have been hard and hurtful for you both."

Melissa nodded. "It was. But that's all behind us now, and we have to find some way to make a new life, don't we, Amalie?"

Amalie smiled, first at Melissa, and then at Martha. "And that is the reason we are here," she said. "We found out that Melissa still owned one thing, the boat, and we came to look at her."

Martha nodded, and pursed her lips. "Well, she's seen better days, no doubt of that. Jubal was her last captain, you know, and when the boat was wrecked, your father gave Jubal permission to live on board the boat, so that he could look after her some. Though without the money to fix her up, there wasn't a lot we could do."

Melissa could not stop herself from stealing a quick glance at Jubal, her glance sliding down to his peg leg; and then, in embarrassment, looked quickly away.

Jubal grinned wryly. "Don't be bashful, little lady. I'm sure you're curious as to how I got this." He gestured to the leg, then thumped it with his knuckles.

"Well, like Martha said, we were both wrecked, me and the *Belle*. With me, it was the leg, and with the *Belle*, it was a hole in her side.

"You see, it was one a them dark, foggy nights that we get now and then, when the old Mississip' don't even show a sparkle so's you can get a bearing off him.

"We was just about five leagues above Natchez, when it began to fog over. We was comin' down from Vicksburg with a load of molasses, cotton and sugar, and an almost full passenger list.

"I was in the wheelhouse, tryin' to spot somethin' familiar out there in the fog, when sudden-like I felt somethin' scrapin' underneath her. It was a sand bar, where there shouldn't've been one, and I really commenced to fret.

"Well, we cleared the bar finally, but in another minute the *Belle* rammed into a reef, which was plump out of place, accordin' to my recollection." Jubal swiped a big hand down over his face.

"I'll never forget it, long as I live. It was like some kinda nightmare. I still dream about it now and again. You see, I know this old river like the back of my hand. I've been travelin' on it for nigh on twenty years, and suddenly it was like I was in another place, on another river. I tell you, it gave me a cold feeling in my guts."

"Now Jubal!" Martha said sharply. "You forget yourself! There are ladies present."

"Oh, sorry, ladies, guess I did forget myself there." Jubal grinned sheepishly. "Anyways, I started feelin' cold and fearful deep down inside, and I tried to steer the *Belle* away from that reef. Finally we got her loose, but in so doin', we backed her smack dab into some logs." He shook his head woefully.

"Now I don't know how much you ladies know about steam packets, but they ain't the sturdiest vessels afloat. It don't take a whole lot to punch a hole through her bottom, and if you hit a bunch of snags, like we done, well, you're shippin' water before you know it.

"By that time the passengers knew somethin' was amiss, and they was millin' about and yellin'. I turned the wheel over to the night pilot, and hurried down to the lower deck, to see what there was to be seen, hopin' to find some way we could get her off whatever she was hung up on.

"When I got down to the lower deck, everybody was runnin' around and hollerin', but I just shoved 'em aside, and went over to look at the place we was stuck.

"I had the men hold lanterns over the side, and I saw a big hole, part above the water line and part below. A big tree, a sawyer, with arms about four feet across, was jammed into the hold, and was a-keepin' us fast.

"I rang up the wheelhouse for us to stand by, and to watch for my signal, and then two of the crew and myself went over the side to see if'n we could get that old monster of a sawyer to let loose of the *Belle*.

"Well, I tell you, ladies, it seemed like 'twas hours we was down there, a-pushin' and a-pullin' at that old tree, with the water whooshin' by, mean-chucklin' like the devil himself.

"Finally, after we were close to tuckered out, she moved, and then she moved some more. The *Belle* was freeing herself. I sent the other two men up the rope, and just as they reached the deck, a sudden surge of water swung the *Belle*, turnin' her, and my leg was trapped between the boat and the tree. Yessir, that old sawyer smashed my leg tight against the *Belle*, as if he was punishin' me for tryin' to cheat him out of his prey. If I hadn't of had a rope tied around my waist, I woulda been catfish bait. The *Belle* started to move away again, and that old sawyer finally let go. But my leg was useless by then. I couldn't feel a thing in it, and I sure couldn't move it. The men had to haul me aboard like a dad-blamed fish!

"We made it out into clear water, with the *Belle* threatenin' to sink every foot of the way. Then the sun came up, and we could see what had happened to the river, and why we had gone aground like that.

"That night, old *Meschebe* had decided that he wanted a shorter channel, and so, like he does now and then, he just lopped off a good twenty miles of river, just forged himself a new route, and that was why there was sandbars and reefs where there shouldn't've been. It was a new bed. It happened so fast that I hadn't even heard about it. The *Natchez Belle* wasn't the only boat to go aground that night, either!"

Jubal shook his head dolefully, and Melissa interjected, "And your leg?"

He shrugged. "It had been crushed flat by that sawyer, and it was beginning to mortify before I could get to a doc. He said it had to come off, or it would do me in for good and all. So both the *Belle* and me was laid up permanent-like. No good, either one of us."

"But why didn't they repair the *Natchez Belle*?"

Jubal spread his hands. "They hardly ever fix up a steamboat that's been stove up bad, Miss Huntoon.

Ain't worth it. It's easier to build another, just strip the old one of her boilers. That is, if they haven't blown up. Pick her clean of a few other useful parts, and build another. The *Belle* wasn't stripped, 'cause your daddy was too busy long about then to worry about buildin' another boat, what with the war comin' and all. Of course she would have been picked clean by the river rats long ago except for the fact that we been watchin' over her. I kept thinkin' that some day I'd get enough money to fix her up, and get her afloat again.

"At any rate, she's given us a home durin' the war years, and now she can do the same for you. Still, it's a pity the *Belle* can't be doin' what she was born to do. If she's like me, she still has an almighty hankerin' to be back on the river, but ain't nobody wants a one-legged pilot. Yup, we're a pair, the two of us." He pulled a long face, thumping the wooden leg. "Nobody can find a use for either of us."

Martha slapped his shoulder with her open hand, and said crossly, "Well, at least it kept you out of the fighting. You're still alive, which is more than I can say about a lot of our boys and men. But that's enough of tale-telling for now." She faced Melissa squarely. "Now that you've seen the *Natchez Belle*, what are you planning on doing?"

The directness of the question caught Melissa off guard, and before she could get a grip on herself, tears filled her eyes. Angrily, she blinked them back, hoping that the older woman hadn't noticed. "Why, I don't rightly know. We were thinking that—"

"Since Melissa owns the boat," Amalie broke in smoothly, "we had thought that we might stay here, at least until we're settled on what course we are going to take. Our funds are limited, and we can't afford to pay for lodgings."

Martha nodded, a bit subdued. "Why, of course. That's the only thing to do. It belongs to you. We'll clean out one of the other cabins for you, the one across the passageway. Jubal and I, we'll move on whenever you say—"

"Oh, no!" Melissa said swiftly. "I won't hear of it! We can share, can't we? It seems to me there's plenty of room."

"My land, yes, child, there's all kinds of room." A smile blossomed on Martha's face, and her relief was plain to see. "I have extra bed linen you can use."

"That won't be necessary. We have our own bolsters and linen," Amalie said. "But we will be grateful for your help in cleaning the cabin. Thank you for your kindness."

Martha blushed. "Why, it isn't anything. After all, in these hard times we all have to stick together. If we don't, there won't be anything but carpetbaggers left in Mississippi."

Amalie leaned forward. "Speaking of carpetbaggers, do you know of one Simon Crouse? He has a house in town."

Martha made a face. "We certainly do, don't we, Jubal? In fact, I would imagine that everyone in Natchez knows Mr. Simon Crouse, one way or another. I know him as a cold, hard man, bent on gobbling up everything as fast as he can, although there are some, ladies mostly, who seem to think that he's a proper gentleman!"

"Hah!" Jubal snorted. "That's women for you! Blind to a man's faults if he has a fair face and money in his pocket." He looked at Melissa. "I understand he's the one owns Great Oaks now."

Melissa nodded. "Yes, and I hope that it brings him nothing but sorrow."

"Do you know if Mr. Crouse is in Natchez at present?" Amalie asked.

Martha stared at her. "As a matter of fact, I happen to know that he isn't. He just left this morning for New Orleans. I happen to know because I saw that simple-minded manservant of his, Jake I think his name is, delivering him to the station with his suitcases."

Amalie smiled in relief. "That is nice to know."

"Why do you ask, Amalie?" Melissa was curious at her friend's question.

Amalie gave a shrug. "I think Simon Crouse wishes us great harm. I would just as soon he not know where we are."

Martha smiled. "Well then, you've got your wish, at least for the time being. Like I said, I saw him leaving town. Now, let's get at that cabin, so you can bring your things onto the *Belle*."

The large cabin, with three pair of hands working on it, was soon clean, and except for the faded drapes and worn rug, it looked quite comfortable.

"These were the suites," Martha explained. "The most expensive cabins on board, where the rich folks stayed. You might as well have the best you can get, I always say."

Melissa's and Amalie's things were brought on board, including the mule, who was stabled on the aft deck so that he would be safe from the derelicts of

Natchez-Under-the-Hill, and by late afternoon their quarters were ready for use.

Both women had a good wash and a change of clothing, and for the moment Melissa felt almost content. They had a place to stay and enough money to sustain them for a while, if they were careful. Not having a place to go, no roof of their own to shelter them, had been Melissa's greatest fear. This boat, damaged though she might be, offered them that, and she felt very grateful, both for the boat itself and for the Kings.

They had supper that evening in the dining room, where the Kings had curtained off one table from the rest. Martha King cooked the meal—the gumbo had been simmering for hours—in the boat's galley, which was nearly intact.

They sat down to a fine meal of shrimp gumbo rich with okra, corn bread and butter, all topped off by a golden caramel custard for dessert. Melissa ate heartily—so much that she feared she had made a glutton of herself. Wiping the last bit of custard from her lips, she glanced up to see Martha smiling indulgently. Melissa said apologetically, "It was all so good, I . . ."

Martha waved away her words, and smiled widely. "A good cook always likes to have her meals appreciated. Besides, the weather's just getting hot, so that custard wouldn't have kept overnight anyway. I'm just happy you enjoyed it."

Amalie, who had also eaten well, pushed her plate away. "Pardon my forwardness in asking, but do you always eat this well? The reason I ask is that I wish to know how you earn your living here. Miss Melissa and I must find some way to augment the bit of money she received from the sale of her property at the auction, and we would be interested in knowing what sort of opportunities there are for a woman to earn a livelihood."

Jubal took a blackened pipe and a tin of tobacco from his pocket. As he filled the pipe, he glanced quizzically at his wife.

"It's quite all right," Martha said cheerfully. "My land, I'll be glad to tell you how the two of us make out. I do fine sewing for the town ladies, while Jubal works at whatever he can get, handyman work mostly. We aren't getting rich, but we manage to put food on the table, and tobacco in Jubal's old smelly pipe."

Jubal had his pipe going now, great clouds of white smoke swirling about his head. He took up the conversation. "Like Martha here says, there's work to be had, but precious little of it is for females. Fine sewing, yes, but if you'll pardon me, ma'am, it seems wrong for a fine lady like yourself to be sewin' for other ladies, who are of a lower quality than yourself."

Melissa looked at him seriously. "I have to live, Jubal. I have to eat, just like everyone else. I may come from quality, but that doesn't mean much to an empty stomach. And I'm not too proud, as long as it's honest work."

Amalie said, "*I* could find work, could I not, Mr. King?"

Jubal took his pipe out of his mouth, and nodded. "Yes, you could find work easy enough, Miss Amalie, since you're . . ." He broke off in some confusion, his face reddening.

Amalie only smiled, and said calmly, "Because I am a woman of color, yes? Well, do not be embarrassed, for it is surely so. If I can find work so that I may earn enough to keep us, I will be content."

73

Martha studied her guests thoughtfully. "How long do you plan on staying in Natchez? Do you plan to remain, or are you on your way to somewhere else?"

Amalie shrugged. "I am not sure. It was in my mind that we might go to New Orleans, but it is not possible now. I think we are in position of having to wait to see what transpires. However, I do think we should leave Natchez eventually, if it is at all possible."

Martha said shrewdly, "Because of Simon Crouse?"

Amalie, surprised by the woman's astuteness, answered truthfully, "Yes, Mrs. King. I think it would be best if we were far, far away from that gentleman."

Melissa, drowsy from the day's activity and the good food, roused herself enough to look questioningly at Amalie. Why was she suddenly so concerned about Simon Crouse? True, he was an unpleasant man, and he had embarrassed and insulted them both by his so-called offers the day of the auction, but he was no real threat to them. How could he be?

Amalie smiled at her in reassurance, but Melissa sensed that there was something that her friend was keeping from her, and it made her uncomfortable, and just a bit angry. She scraped her chair back from the table.

"If you all will excuse me, I think I'll take a turn around the deck to walk off some of this dinner."

"Sounds like a good idea," Jubal said, getting to his feet. He stumped over and offered an arm to his wife. "Come along, Martha. You and Amalie, too. It'll do us all a deal of good."

The promenade deck had a wonderful view of the river, and as they watched, the setting sun lit the sky with swirls and flames of red, gold, and purple. The reflected sun's rays turned the usually muddy brown water a gray-blue color. The river was fairly low, and traffic was sparse. Only a few small keelboats and tugs were anchored at the landing.

As they watched darkness come on, flares, like firefly lights, sprang up along the banks of the river; a fleet of shanty boats was tied up to the bank, and their occupants were lighting their lanterns against the growing dark.

Upriver, Natchez-Under-the-Hill was coming alive as night fell. Light spilled out from the saloons, and red lamps were lit in the brothel house windows. Raucous shouts and coarse laughter poured out, rebounding like an echo against the towering bluff. If you ignored the rowdy sounds and listened closely, Melissa thought, you could hear the chuckle of the river and the cries of the river birds as they settled themselves for the night.

She heard Jubal sigh, and say sadly, "I still can't get used to how quiet it is, except for the cesspool up there. Why, I recollect when this landin' was so crowded you couldn't find a place to tie up. Steam packets, barges, tugs, everythin' that would float used to be in and out of here by the hundreds. Now, what with the railroad and all, it's like a ghost landin' eerielike."

"But I think it's beautiful," Melissa said sincerely. "I love the river. It's . . . well, it's . . ."

"Like a livin' thing," Jubal interrupted. "Like she's kind of a livin' creature. Female creature, cause she's always a-changin'." He chuckled. "Proper speaking, it's a he, not a she."

His wife hit him on the shoulder with the flat of her hand. "Now, Jubal, you just hush up. You got company, remember?"

They were just about to turn away from the rail, when they heard the whistle, booming up the river and breaking over their heads like the call of some primeval beast. It came again, echoing off the river bluffs.

"Steamboat around the bend!" Jubal exclaimed, his voice rising. "I'll be dad-blamed!"

And then the calliope started up, a wheezing, brazen sound that clanged on the ear like a hammer on metal.

"Why, it's 'Down on the River'!" Melissa cried. "Amalie, hear it? They're playing 'Down on the River.'"

Amalie placed her hands over her ears. "How can I not hear it, little one? It hurts the ears."

Around the bend of the river came a wondrous sight. Larger than the *Natchez Belle*, glittering like a frosted palace, lanterns glowing, calliope bellowing, came a huge steamboat. Flags flying, she steamed grandly toward them.

Chapter Five

"My land!" Martha said, putting her hand to her cheek. "Why, I haven't seen a showboat in here for I don't know how long. Just look at her, will you?"

And indeed they all did. Melissa realized that her mouth was hanging open and closed it quickly. She had seen such a boat only once before, before the war, when she was a child. She had kept a memory of it; now, seeing this floating fantasy come toward her was like reliving a dream.

The forward deck and the long stage plank were crowded with performers in bright costumes, waving and calling as the calliope squalled its noisy music into the evening dusk. On the tip of the stage plank, Melissa could see a man in blackface doing a cakewalk, kicking high and doffing his straw hat; and on the main deck, she saw an animal—a bear, it appeared to be— huge on its hind legs, swaying and moving along the deck as if it were dancing.

She drew her breath. "Oh, Amalie! It's beautiful!"

Amalie smiled at the younger woman's pleasure, yet

her own eyes brightened at the spectacle and the infectious sound of the calliope.

"They used to come in here all the time," Jubal was saying. "Used to compete something fierce to see who would get here first and put up their handbills." He shook his head in wonder. "This here's the first one since the war. She sure looks good. A big one, too."

As the big barge came into the landing, between where the *Belle* was beached and the sorry straggle of buildings that was Natchez-Under-the-Hill, Melissa could see the tug behind it, a structurally smaller version of the barge, except for the double paddlewheels and the smokestacks. Together, they almost looked like one huge boat, for they were equally white, furbelowed, and tiered.

The barge and the tug were soon docked, and the performers, prancing down the stage plank, were pouring onto the bank in a regular parade. Then the calliope stopped its clamor, and a fair-sized band, all in red uniforms with tall yellow shakos, began playing, as three young women started to dance on the stage plank.

Melissa clapped her hands together. "Oh, Amalie, can we go watch? I would love to see them up close!"

Amalie looked at Jubal, and he nodded, a wide grin creasing his face. "Why, I don't see why not, little lady. It don't cost nothin' to look. Let's go."

By the time they had fetched their wraps and reached the landing, the area was crowded with townspeople, all chattering and milling about. The denizens of the town below the hill had been attracted as well. Melissa was surprised at the way they all mixed in together, their differences apparently forgotten in the excitement of the arrival of the show-boat.

When a large enough crowd had gathered, the music stopped, and a tall gentleman in a black suit and top hat, his shirt front starched and glistening white, got up on a crate and waved his hands for quiet. When the noise subsided, he commenced speaking in a deep, oratorical voice. "Ladies and gentlemen! I am proud to be able to bring you the *Star of the South*, floating palace, menagerie, and grand opera house! We will be giving our first performance tomorrow evening at 7:00 P.M., and we hope that you will all come to see us. There will be a special price for the ladies, and I assure you that there is nothing in our performance to offend even the finest sensibilities!

"There will be acrobats, dancers, and vocalists to entertain you, and in addition a full-length, stirring performance of *The Old Homestead*. Tell your friends and neighbors, so that they too may see this wondrous show which we have put together for your delectation. Now, if there are any among you who would like to earn a ticket putting up handbills . . ."

As the man held aloft a sheaf of handbills, Jubal King, who was close to the crate, stepped forward, and from his great height reached up and plucked the sheets from the man's hand. "I'd be right pleased to post these," he said cheerfully. "I can guarantee to get 'em up good and high so's everybody can see 'em."

The showboat spieler nodded, and handed Jubal another batch of handbills. "Very well, my good man. You're hired. Anyone else?"

Dozen of hands were raised, as Jubal triumphantly turned back to his little group of women. "Well, here we are, ladies. These are as good as a ticket to the show. Martha, can you see our guests back to the boat? I'm goin' to get these posted right quick, and scoot back for another batch."

Martha nodded. Melissa looked after Jubal longingly as he thumped away. She wanted with all her heart to see the show, but she knew that they could not afford the money for tickets.

"Oh," she said longingly, as Jubal disappeared into the crowd, "at times like this I wish I was a man!"

Amalie put her arm around Melissa's shoulders. She did not speak, but only squeezed the girl's shoulders in understanding.

Melissa smiled at her. "It's all right. I'm just being foolish, since I know we can't afford to go. It's just that it's been so long since we've had a chance to see *any* kind of entertainment!"

"I know, *chérie*, I know. Now, the performers are going back on board the showboat. We had best go home, yes?"

Melissa nodded, and with Martha in the lead, the trio started back toward the *Natchez Belle.*

Melissa slept well that night. She woke once to the sound of footsteps, which frightened her until she realized that it must be Jubal King returning to the boat. Once she had recognized the strange thump-bump pattern of his gait, she sank back into sleep, feeling snug and secure.

When she awakened, it was late in the morning; she could tell by the slant of the sun through the cabin window. Amalie's bed was empty, and Melissa, embarrassed by her laziness, hurried into her clothes, and went in search of the others.

She found them in the dining saloon, sitting over *café au lait* and calas. The smell of the little fried cakes was fragrant, and suddenly she felt terribly hungry.

As she approached the table, she saw that while Jubal King was absent, there was a new face at the table—a large, broad-shouldered woman with irregular features and a thick twist of salt-and-pepper hair piled atop her head. She was wearing a coarse, rather short skirt, shirt and sweater, and her feet were attired in gumboots.

Melissa stopped, nonplused, as the woman stared directly at her. There was a quality of challenge in her gaze.

"Oh!" Melissa said. "I'm sorry I'm so late. I—"

Martha, just coming in from the galley with a fresh pot of coffee, laughed. "Nonsense! It's not that late, Melissa. My land, you were worn out and needed the sleep. You're just in time for fresh coffee, and the calas are still warm."

Amalie pulled up another chair and patted it. "Come, sit down and meet the Kings' good friend. Mollie, this is Melissa Huntoon, daughter of Jean-Paul Huntoon, of Great Oaks. Melissa, this is Mollie Boom, captain and pilot of the *Sprite*, which you can see moored alongside the showboat at the landing."

"Glad to meet you." Mollie stuck out a large, red-knuckled hand, and Melissa, who was not accustomed to women shaking hands, took it somewhat gingerly.

As Melissa sat down, she glanced through the window, and indeed there was a small steam packet moored at the landing. The boat looked serviceable and sturdy, with little ornamentation and plain lines. She suppressed a smile. The association of the name

Sprite with the practical boat, and the even more practical-looking Mollie Boom, struck her as incongruous.

"Don't take any passengers," Mollie said, taking note of the direction of Melissa's glance. "Mostly cargo. She's a good boat, the *Sprite*. Me 'n her get along just fine."

Melissa studied the woman curiously, trying not to appear rude. She had never heard of nor seen a woman riverboat pilot, and she was intrigued.

Mollie grinned lopsidedly. "Cat got your tongue, girl? Don't suppose you ever saw a female captain before. Well, there's not too many of us, that's for sure. Only a couple more that I know of. We're a rare breed, we are."

Mollie's grin was so infectious that Melissa could not help but answer in kind. She decided that she liked Mollie Boom. "I have never seen a woman captain, that is true," she said. "But I think I'm pleased to know there *is* one."

Mollie's laughter boomed out, and she thumped the table with her hand. "That's good enough, youngster. That's good enough. This girl's got spirit, I like that," she said, turning to the table at large.

Amalie reached for the pot, and poured coffee and warm milk into Melissa's cup. "It is good to see women in such roles," she said gravely. "Perhaps some day we will be allowed into other fields as well. I have often thought that women would make excellent doctors, much better than any man!"

Martha looked shocked for a moment, and then smiled. "It's an outrageous idea, isn't it? Do you suppose that it will ever happen? No, it's impossible!"

Mollie drained her cup, and reached for another calas. "I don't know. That's what they said when I first tried to get my papers, but I plumb wore them down. I don't see why it won't work in other fields." She glanced around. "By the way, where's Jubal?"

"He's already out and doing," said Martha, refilling Mollie's cup. "Still putting up handbills for the showboat."

Mollie shook her shaggy head. "Don't that beat all, the showboat? It's sure good to see one of those floating palaces again. Folks can sure use some entertainment. It's been a long, cold time, and folks are hungry for a little fun. Are you all going to show tonight?"

Melissa looked quickly at Amalie, then away. "We would like to, but we can't afford the money for tickets."

The big woman smiled, and exchanged a look with Martha. "Well, maybe something will turn up so's you can still go. Now, I'd best get back to the *Sprite*. Got some unloading to take care of. Glad to have met you two ladies."

She waddled off, and as she disappeared, Amalie said, "She is an amazing woman."

Martha smiled. "She is indeed. Her manners may be rough and some might say unladylike, but her heart is pure gold. She makes a good friend. Now, what would you two ladies like to do today?"

"I must look for work in town," Amalie replied.

"I'll go with you." Melissa put down her cup.

Amalie said firmly, "No, Melissa. It would be best if I go alone."

Melissa could feel her cheeks flush. "I know that I'm not experienced, like you are, but these last few years at Great Oaks, I've had to work. It would only be fair for me to work, too, and that way we could earn twice as much money."

Amalie put her hand on Melissa's, and again shook her head. "It's not as simple as that, little one. Yes, you are capable of working. You are a bright, strong young woman, but it is unheard of for a lady of your background to go into service. The wives would be horrified. They are used to hiring colored people or, on occasion, lower-class whites. You would not be hired, and would only embarrass yourself to no purpose."

Melissa knew that her cheeks were flaming now, and she felt angry and close to tears. Why was the world so unfair? It had taken from her all she cared about, made her poor as the poorest in the land, and yet it would not allow her to work, so that she might earn her keep. "What do they expect me to do?" she said in a low, angry voice.

Amalie patted her hand. "It is hard, I know. But the realities must be faced. Now I must go, while it is still early. I am sure that Mrs. King can use your help today, here on the *Belle*. Is that not so, Mrs. King?"

"My land, yes," Martha said briskly. "With the two of us, we'll get the work done in no time. Then perhaps we can walk up the landing to the *Star of the South* and watch the goings-on."

Melissa said unsmilingly, "I'll be glad to help you, Mrs. King. It's the least I can do."

Melissa felt that she was being treated like a child, shunted aside from the important things, shielded from Amalie's "realities," and yet she realized the logic behind Amalie's words, and could not dispute their merit.

Through the window she watched Amalie leave the

boat and start up the road toward the landing. With a sigh she got up from the table, and began to clear away the dishes. At least she could be useful here.

It was growing uncomfortably sultry, and Melissa moved the palm leaf fan briskly back and forth in front of her face, her chin elevated so that the moving air could reach her neck. She had been sitting on the cotton bale for over an hour, watching the comings and goings on the *Star of the South*, catching glimpses of the bear, as the animal strolled around the deck, and hearing the sounds of the band practicing.

She sighed heavily. Oh, how she wished they could attend this evening's performance! The fact that they could not, coupled with the morning's disappointment, had put her into a gloomy mood, which had not eased all day.

At noon, Jubal had returned to the *Belle* for a quick meal, and had gone out again, but Amalie had not come back.

After the noon meal dishes were washed, Martha had pronounced the day's work finished, and informed Melissa that she was free to do what she wished. And so Melissa had come up to the landing to watch the showboat activity.

She shifted her parasol around so that her face was shielded from the sun, and sighed again.

"That's a mighty unhappy sigh, young miss. Surely things can't be that bad?"

Melissa, startled by the resonant voice so near her ear, jumped, and glanced around to see a small, slender man observing her with sharp blue eyes.

He smiled winningly, and doffed his tall hat to

show snow-white hair. He bowed from the waist. "Nehemiah Prendergast, at your service, m'lady."

Melissa was disarmed by his courtly manner, and she inclined her head in acknowledgement. The little man was rather a curious sight, since he was dressed in clothing that showed much wear, yet everything was neat and obviously well cared for. He wore gaiters on his small, delicate feet, and he carried a black, silver-headed cane, which he continuously flourished dramatically; and yet because of the worn condition of his clothing, the whole effect of Nehemiah Prendergast on the eye was rather strange and out of balance.

"May I join you, young miss? I took note of the fact that you are watching the *Star of the South,* and apparently appreciate the spectacle. I too appreciate the theater, and would be enchanted with the company of a like-minded person such as yourself."

Melissa, somewhat taken aback by the outpouring of words, did not quite know what to do; but the little man certainly seemed harmless enough, and so at last she nodded, and moved over so that he might share the cotton bale.

She couldn't be certain of his age, for although his hair, beard, and moustache were white, his face was not heavily lined, and his manner, as he hopped up beside her, was sprightly. Still, the hands that he folded atop the silver head of the cane were veined, and the skin was stretched thin, as it often was with age.

She said, "I'm Melissa Huntoon."

He dipped his head. "I am enchanted, Melissa Huntoon." He motioned with the cane. " 'Tis a wonderful sight, is it not? The showboat?"

"Yes, it is," Melissa said, still studying him out of the corner of her eye.

"Pray tell me, will you be attending the performance tonight?

She shook her head. "I'm afraid not."

"A pity. But you would like to, would you not?"

"Oh, yes! It's just that . . ."

"I understand perfectly. I am in the same position myself. Many are in these difficult times." He sighed. "I would dearly love to see the performance. It's been so long. I was in the profession myself, you know, up until the war."

Melissa faced him fully, unable to conceal her delight at this news. She had never met an actor. To her they were an exotic breed, glamorous inhabitants of another world.

"Did you—have you ever performed on a showboat like the *Star of the South?*"

He smiled at her excitement. "I have indeed, my dear. In fact, that is where I spent much of my career, on the showboats. Why, I've acted in every town along the Mississippi, from St. Louis to New Orleans, and in every play from *Uncle Tom's Cabin* to *East Lynne*. Yes, it's a way of life I shall never forget."

"But why *should* you forget it? Don't you still perform?"

His smile was melancholy. "No, my dear. If I did, I wouldn't be existing in the state of poverty in which you see me now. Unfortunately, my career came to an abrupt end when the war began. The blockades, the river fighting, the towns under siege, put the showboats out of business for the duration of the war, and now that they're finally starting up again . . . Well, let's just say that I'm not as young as I once was.

87

"My specialty was playing romantic leading men, you see, and I have become a trifle long in the tooth for that. Also, the competition is fierce. There are only a few showboats now plying the river, and ever so many hungry actresses and actors. However, I do keep trying." He motioned with the cane, a gesture that somehow managed to convey both sorrow and acceptance of his fate.

Melissa was touched by the old man's speech, and could identify with his feelings. He, like her and Amalie, was a victim of bitter circumstances. He was being denied a way of life which he knew, and in which he felt secure.

"Have you talked to the captain of the *Star of the South*?" she asked. "You still have a wonderful voice," Nehemiah smiled at that, "and I'm sure there are parts you could still play."

He nodded. "I have indeed talked to Captain Smithers, but they have a full complement, including a senior character actor. The captain did promise to keep me in mind, if he has any openings. Now how many times have I heard *that*?" His smile was wry. "But come, we have talked enough of me. What about you, young miss? What brings a young lady of such obvious quality to such a nefarious site as Natchez-Under-the-Hill?"

Melissa briefly told Nehemiah Prendergast the story of her eviction from Great Oaks. When she was finished, he shook his head dolefully. "Ah, these are difficult times, difficult times indeed! The world has turned topsy-turvy."

He gazed thoughtfully downriver at the *Natchez Belle*. "The *Natchez Belle*, an inspired name, and she seems to have been a good little packet in her day," he

88

said musingly. "Actually there doesn't seem too much wrong with her that couldn't be fixed with nails, new planking, and paint."

"There's a gaping hole in her side," Melissa said, "but Captain Jubal says she *could* be repaired if we had the money."

"Ah, well. Money, there's the rub, isn't it?" Nehemiah shook his head. "Isn't that true of so many things nowadays?" His expression turned wistful, and he sighted along his cane at the *Belle*, then began to sketch patterns in the air, as if tracing the outlines of a boat. "You know, my dear Melissa, if she was fixed up, she would make a grand little showboat, that she would!"

Melissa could not help but laugh. "Oh, come now, Mr. Prendergast! She's small. Just look at the size of the *Star of the South* by comparison. The *Belle* is only half that size!"

Nehemiah said, "You are in error, my dear, to think that size alone is necessary for a riverboat theater. True, the *Star* is very large, that I won't deny, but she carries animal acts, a full band and other assorted attractions. Many of the showboats are not so large, indeed they are not. In fact, if you play the smaller rivers and tributaries, such a great size is a disadvantage. For the smaller rivers, you need a small boat, and there are many towns and villages that are just as hungry for entertainment as Natchez and New Orleans.

"All you really need is a small troupe of players, made up of versatile people. A male and a female singer, who can double as dancers. A man who does comedy roles, who can also double as villain if necessary. A character actor and actress. A handsome leading man, and a girl to play opposite him. And a piano player, to be sure, who can play the calliope. Not everyone can, you know. If you have good people, people who are multi-talented, you can get by with these few. I've traveled with troupes even smaller than that, and we've put on grand shows. All it takes is good direction and a creative mind. A good seamstress is also a help, for costumes and stage scenery. Yes, my dear, it can be done, and truthfully it has long been my dream. If I had a nice little craft like the *Belle*, sound of course, and a man to captain her, I could put together a fine troupe. I could take her to all the small towns, and turn a tidy profit. I could indeed!"

Nehemiah roused from his soliloquy with a start, and smiled apologetically. "Sorry, my dear, to have run on so. An old man's dream, nothing more."

Melissa instinctively reached out to touch his hand. "We all need dreams, Mr. Prendergast. I guess that's all that sustains most of us in these difficult times. Indeed it is."

He laughed at her use of his pet phrase, and then glanced at the sun. "Would you have any idea of the time, my dear? Since I was forced to sell my watch, I never seem to know the time."

She shook her head. "No, sir, I don't, but I do know that I've been here quite a long while, and I must be getting back to the *Belle*."

The old man's face lengthened at her words, and Melissa felt as if she were abandoning him, as she got up from the cotton bale and gathered up her things to leave. He looked so forlorn, sitting there with his short legs dangling, that she acted on impulse. "Why don't you have supper with us on board the *Belle* tonight?"

A startled expression flitted across Nehemiah's face, and his eyes lit up. "That is very kind of you, my dear, indeed it is! It *would* be nice to have dinner with good company again. I must confess that I do grow tired of dining alone. My dear Miss Huntoon, I should be delighted."

Melissa, now that the invitation was issued, was wondering if she hadn't been hasty. After all, she was not providing the food; still, the little man looked so thin, and the gleam in his eye at the mention of supper probably meant that he went hungry much of the time. She gave a mental shrug. There was nothing for it now—she had committed herself. She said, "Mrs. King serves supper at six o'clock."

Nehemiah bowed low with an elegant, sweeping gesture. "I shall be there promptly, you may be sure."

Fortunately, everyone was in a good mood that evening. Amalie had found a temporary position in a dress shop, filling in while one of the regular employees was ill; and Jubal, flushed and swollen with a secret which he said he would not reveal until supper, was beaming with good will. So no one scolded Melissa for inviting another mouth to the table.

Nehemiah was prompt to the minute, which caused Melissa to wonder how he had managed it without his watch. He was so washed and polished that one could almost forget the threadbare condition of his clothing. The silver head of his cane fairly gleamed, but at that, it did not match the brilliance of his smile when he was introduced to the rest of the group.

During supper, he regaled them with tales of the showboats, and it was a merry gathering indeed that sat around the table in the corner of the dining room on the *Natchez Belle* that evening.

Melissa even forgot her earlier gloom, and her unhappiness at not being able to attend the performance tonight. Having Nehemiah Prendergast with them was almost as good as seeing a show. After supper, he sang a song for them, "Goodbye, Little Girl," in a big, mellow baritone that seemed far too robust for his frail body. After the song he performed a few dance steps, capering gracefully on his short legs, ending by grasping the cane between his two hands and dancing completely around it, holding the cane stationary.

They gave him an enthusiastic round of applause when he finished, and he beamed as he wiped his sweating face with a clean but shabby handkerchief. "It would have been much better with a piano," he said, "but one must make do with what one has."

"You have a fine voice there, friend," Jubal said, leaning back in his chair as he filled his pipe. "Really a shame that you're not able to practice your chosen profession. It purely is."

"Thank you, kind sir," Nehemiah said. "Appreciation helps ease the pain, indeed it does."

"Well now, Jubal. Just what is this surprise that you've been teasing us with? Come out with it now!" Martha smiled fondly as she questioned her husband.

Jubal beamed back at her, then at the rest of the group. "Surprise? Did I say I had a surprise?"

Martha shook her head, and gave a knowing glance to Amalie and Melissa. "Listen to him! There he sits, as full of himself as a tick with blood. Come on now, you'll burst something if you don't get it out soon!"

"Well then!" Jubal put the palms of his hands down flat upon the table. "What would you all say if I told you that we were *all* goin' to see the show aboard the *Star* tonight? What would you say to that?"

Melissa clapped her hands to her mouth, and turned toward Amalie, who shrugged, as if to intimate that she had known nothing of Jubal's plan.

"Yessir! I tacked up handbills half the night, and most of today, and in return I was able to get four tickets. It helped that the tickets for females is going for half price. Now, what do you say to that?"

Martha beamed at him proudly. "Why, I'd say that you are a good and kind man, Jubal King, and that you've made three ladies very happy tonight."

Jubal's grin stretched his cheeks. "Well now," he said slyly, "it's not the way I *used* to make three women happy in one night, but seein' as how I'm gettin' on in years, I reckon I'll have to settle for that."

"Jubal!" Martha was scandalized. She hit her husband on the upper arm with her closed hand. "We have company. My land, you are a terrible man!"

Jubal said smugly, "But a man who can make three women happy in one night."

All of them burst into laughter. Although Melissa was not quite certain just what was so humorous, it did not seem to matter. She was going to see the show! They all were. That is, all except . . .

She sobered. "Oh, Mr. Prendergast. I hope you won't feel too left out."

"Now, now, my dear. Don't worry over it for a minute. I have my own ways of accomplishing things, and I may yet see the performance. Don't you fret, Miss Huntoon. Just go and enjoy yourself. It will be an evening to remember, I can promise you. It will indeed!"

Chapter Six

As the calliope's strident music announced the opening of the showboat to the public, Melissa, Amalie, and the Kings strolled through the menagerie, which was housed in a long room in the stern of the *Star of the South*. Most of the animals were not unusual, but they did have a small ocelot, a pair of mongooses, and a seal, which cavorted in a small tank. A hand-lettered sign promised that the seal would perform in the evening's show. There was also a museum of sorts, which contained some Indian artifacts, the dried body of what was claimed to be a small mermaid, and the actual sword used by General Robert E. Lee.

It was strange and wonderful, and Melissa's head was fairly spinning from the crowds and the excitement. Inside the *Star of the South*, elaborate carpeting covered the floors of all the rooms save that of the menagerie, and gilded scrollwork ornamented the walls and ceiling. The drapes were red velvet, tied back with red silk cords, ending in elaborate tassels. It was incredibly luxurious, particularly to people who had not seen luxury in a long time. There were many sighs and expressions of appreciation as the customers roamed through the elegant rooms.

Then it was time for the stage performance, given in the grand saloon, the most elegant room of all. Every seat was taken. The play, the main attraction, was to be *The Orphan,* but before the play was shown, there were several other acts: a juggler; a bevy of dancers in shockingly short skirts that almost showed their calves; a young couple who sang a romantic duet; and the seal, who played "Dixie" on a row of trumpets.

Melissa enjoyed all the acts immensely, but the play was what she really wanted to see. She had only seen one play, and that had been in Natchez, with her mother and father, when she was a child; but she had an instinctive love for the theater and the special magic it wrought. Tonight, she was hungry for the escape that such make-believe offered; and apparently the rest of the audience felt the same, for they all began to applaud when the master of ceremonies announced the opening act of the play.

The piano player, resplendent in a red coat and white trousers, began the introductory music, and the curtain rose on the first act.

Melissa was almost mesmerized by the performance. While the curtain was up, and the actresses and actors played their roles, their world was real and alive, and Melissa lived and participated in it along with them.

There was great participation from the audience as well. Everyone cheered the hero on to noble efforts, and hissed the villain. At last virtue triumphed, villainy was punished, and the spectators cheered lustily as things fell into their proper order and the play reached a happy ending.

Melissa, who in her mind equated the villain with Simon Crouse, cheered along with the rest. It would be nice, she thought, if in real life things worked out as neatly. It had been very satisfying to hiss and scorn the villain for his behavior, and it was reassuring to see wickedness punished; but in real life, villainy seemed too often to thrive and prosper.

She gave a deep sigh and turned to Amalie. "Wasn't it lovely?"

Amalie nodded, smiling. "Indeed yes, little one. It was very enjoyable."

Martha leaned across Amalie. "It was a grand evening, wasn't it? I don't remember when I've enjoyed myself more. My land, did you see that funny little seal playing those horns? It was just like a clever child!"

"A durn sight smarter than some I know," Jubal grumbled.

Melissa and Amalie laughed, while Martha chided him for his "contrariness."

They left the showboat and walked back toward the *Belle* through the warm darkness, with the sound of the river chuckling in their ears.

Melissa, who was often given to examining her feelings, noted that for the first time in longer than she could remember she felt relaxed, happy, and unconcerned about the future; and this struck her as strange, since their situation had not changed all that much. They still had very little money, and almost no prospects, but at least they had a place to sleep and, she felt, good friends, and they had just spent an evening full of excitement and entertainment. It was odd, she thought, how much outside things could affect the way one felt.

As they passed the lantern post that marked the edge of the landing, there was a movement in the shadows, and Nehemiah Prendergast emerged, coming toward them, swinging his silver-headed cane.

"Good evening, my good friends. Did you enjoy the show?"

"Oh, yes, Mr. Prendergast!" Melissa exclaimed. "It was wonderful. I'm sorry you had to miss it!"

He smiled gently. "Well, it just so happens that fortune favored me, and I was able to see the performance. One of the young men from the cast was kind enough to say that I was his uncle, and so obtained a pass for me. It was a small falsehood, to be sure, but one which I think that the Great Spirit above will forgive him, since he did it for a good cause."

"Oh, good!" Melissa said happily. "Did you enjoy it? Wasn't the play grand? Particularly in the second act, when the old man was pleading for his granddaughter? I could hardly keep from crying."

"It was quite good, yes. But you must remember that I view a performance with slightly different eyes than those of you not in the profession. I would have, for instance, played that part a bit differently, if I had been doing it. But no matter. It was, all in all, well done, and it did bring pleasure to the audience, indeed it did."

"It certainly did," said Martha. "A good play like that certainly takes you out of yourself. My land, yes!"

The little man made a half bow. "Well, I'd best let you good people get to your beds. Again, let me thank you for the lovely supper. Perhaps I shall see you again. I will be spending some time here, at least as long as the *Star of the South* remains in Natchez. Perhaps we shall meet again."

Jubal cleared his throat. "Uh, Nehemiah, where are you staying, if you don't mind my askin'?"

Nehemiah smiled. "No, Mr. King, I don't mind. I'll be staying wherever I can find a corner to shelter me from the night dew. Not comfortable lodgings, to be sure, but of the type shared by many in these difficult times."

Jubal exchanged glances with his wife, and then leaned down toward Melissa. "Do you suppose, Miss Huntoon, that it would be all right to invite Nehemiah here to spend the night aboard the *Belle*?"

Melissa felt a surge of affection toward the captain. What a kind heart he had, despite his occasionally gruff exterior. "Of course," she said quickly. "It will be more than all right. I can't bear to think of him sleeping somewhere on the cold ground, or in some alleyway."

Jubal turned back toward the waiting Nehemiah. "Uh, Nehemiah . . . we'd be right pleased to have you spend the night with us, on board the *Belle*. There's plenty of empty cabins, Lord knows, and the wife and I could let you have some beddin'. What do you say?"

"Why, I say thank you, and I should be delighted." Nehemiah beamed. "You are all extremely kind, indeed you are!"

Despite the lateness of the hour, Melissa found it very difficult to sleep that night. Her mind, feverish with the images she had seen on the stage, would not be quiet, but kept going round and round, playing and replaying scenes from the evening's entertainment.

How wonderful it would be to be a part of such a troupe of actors! She imagined that their life must be filled with excitement and glamor. She thought of the ingenue, certainly no older than she, who had performed so capably in the play, and then sung so beautifully in the olio.

At some time during her hours of tossing and turning, she thought of Nehemiah Prendergast's remark that the *Natchez Belle* would make a good showboat. At the time she had dismissed it as impossible. Yet wouldn't it be wonderful if such a thing *could* happen? If some miracle would enable them to fix up the boat, hire a troupe of actors, and take to the river! Melissa knew she was dreaming, but hadn't she told Nehemiah that dreams were what made life bearable?

Such fancies kept her restless almost until daybreak, and when she did finally fall into a troubled sleep, she continued to dream of the beautiful, elegant showboat and its glamorous crew.

Again, Melissa slept late, and found everyone else already at breakfast, when she rushed into the dining room. Nehemiah Prendergast was sitting with them, neat and clean in his worn suit, and they were all laughing and talking with one another as if the good mood of the night before had carried over into the new day.

They all wished her a good morning, and Martha set before her a plate heaped with crispy, brown fried mush, covered with golden syrup.

Melissa attacked the food with good appetite, and washed it down with several cups of *café au lait,* before she contributed much to the conversation.

Finally, she turned to Amalie and the Kings, her chin set in determination. She knew she ran the risk of being ridiculed for what she was about to propose, but the general mood of good will encouraged her. "I didn't sleep too well, because I kept thinking of the show last night."

"My land, yes," Martha King said. "I know just what you mean. My head was fairly whirling all night long."

Melissa took a deep breath, and plunged ahead. "Yesterday," she said, "yesterday, Mr. Prendergast said something that caused me to think."

Nehemiah blinked. "And what was that, my dear?"

"You told me that you thought the *Natchez Belle* would make a fine showboat!"

"Indeed I did, and so she would," Nehemiah said stoutly. "She would make a fine river theater to steam up the tributaries and into shallow landings where the big barges like the *Star of the South* dare not venture. It's a pity that the *Belle* is not operational, indeed it is."

Melissa placed her elbows upon the table, and fixed Jubal with her stare. "Jubal, how much money would it take to fix the *Belle?*"

Jubal frowned in thought for a few moments. "I'm not exactly sure, maybe somewheres in the neighborhood of a thousand dollars, give or take a couple of hundred."

"A thousand dollars," Melissa repeated, trying to hide her dismay. Even if Amalie would approve of her, Melissa, working, they could *never* save that sum!

She gnawed her lower lip. "Well, I wish that I had the money," she said defiantly. "I'd have her repaired and hire you as a pilot, Jubal. Then I'd hire a troupe

101

of players. *You* could hire them, Mr. Prendergast, and you could be the director, and the character actor, *and* sing in the olio. And I, well, maybe I could learn to act. You could teach me, Mr. Prendergast, and then I could be the ingenue!"

Martha King laughed, but not in derision. Instead, caught up in the spirit of the game, she said, "Yes, and I could be wardrobe mistress, and help with the scenery as well!"

"And Amalie could be the leading lady," Melissa said eagerly, well aware that she was playing up to Amalie, hoping to enlist her support. "She's beautiful enough, and she can sing and dance, too! Oh, that would be wonderful!"

Amalie gently placed her hand over Melissa's. "It is a lovely dream, *chérie*." Her expression was wistful and sad. "And one that I wish might come true."

Melissa could hear the warning note in Amalie's voice—she was to consider the idea only a dream, a fantasy, to be enjoyed as such, and then put aside and forgotten.

"But maybe it *is* possible," she said stubbornly. "Maybe we could get the money. Maybe we could borrow it."

Jubal looked doubtful. "To get a loan, specially in these times, a person needs security. What could you offer?"

"Why, the *Natchez Belle* herself. If she was fixed up, she would be worth more than the thousand dollars."

Martha leaned forward, her eyes bright. "It's possible, Jubal, don't you think?"

"Well, it's possible." He added bluntly, "But I don't think it very damn likely."

"But I could try!" Melissa said, a plea in her voice.

"I reckon you could, girl. Tryin' don't cost nothin' except your time, and if'n you're willin' to risk that, well . . ."

"Oh, Jubal!" Melissa cried, jumping up from her chair. "If I get the loan, you *will* take charge of repairing her, and you *will* pilot her?"

Jubal's smile was wry. "Now that I surely will, young lady. That's the very best offer I've had in a month of Sundays. You get the money, and I'll be right there, rarin' to go."

Melissa realized that Jubal was just humoring her, and that he had no belief that anyone would loan her the money, but she didn't care. He had agreed to her plans, if she could get the loan, she knew that he would stand by his promise.

She also knew that, logically, her chances of raising the money were negligible, but despite this, she had a strange sort of feeling that the *Belle* would sail again. A hunch, woman's intuition, call it what you would. As long as the others would go along with her, even if it was just to humor her, well, that was all she could ask.

She could feel Amalie's accusing gaze on her, but she studiously ignored it.

"Let me get this clear, Miss Huntoon. You wish a loan of a thousand dollars, to repair your steamboat, the *Natchez Belle*, and you offer as security this very same steamboat, which you intend to put into service as a floating theater. Have I got everything straight?"

Melissa nodded stiffly. The banker, Mr. Udall, was an unattractive man, corpulent and red of face, with pale blue eyes that seemed to be covered with an opaque film, so she could not help wondering if the man could even see—poached-egg eyes, Melissa thought to herself.

He was going to refuse her the loan, she knew; just like all the others. How many was it now? She had lost count. But for some reason of his own, he hadn't yet told her outright. Melissa wished, wearily, that he would get on with it, so she could make her escape.

"It is very unusual," he said pompously, "for a woman to come seeking such a loan, and particularly such a young, and, mmm, if you will pardon my saying so, such a beautiful young woman."

"Yes, I suppose it is unusual," Melissa said listlessly. "You have not given me your answer, sir."

The banker waved his hand at her. "All in good time, madam. All in good time. Your father, if I am not mistaken, was Jean-Paul Huntoon, was he not? Of Great Oaks?"

Melissa nodded. "Yes, sir. That is true."

"And you are now all alone in the world. How sad." He gave her a sideways glance that, it appeared to Melissa, traced the outline of her body like a dirty finger. She suppressed a shudder. Why didn't he give her his answer and be done with it?

The banker strolled to the window, his back to her, and gazed out into the street. "A young girl like yourself, so well reared and of the quality, should not be concerning herself with such matters as loans and steamboats. You should be taken care of, Miss Huntoon, looked after and sheltered from the hardships of life."

"That may well be, sir," she said with some asperity, "but as you yourself made clear only a moment ago, I am alone now, and have no family to look after me. So I have little choice."

"Ah, but that's just it, my girl!" Udall whirled away from the window, and faced Melissa. His red face was even more flushed than it had been, and his eyes had a hot glitter. "You *do* have a choice! You have no family, true, but there are other people who would be most pleased and happy to look after you, to give you a comfortable home, pretty clothes, fine food and drink. Everything your heart desires!"

Melissa eyed him apprehensively. He seemed to be having trouble with his breathing, and his bulging, milky eyes were protruding alarmingly now. She did not know quite what he meant, but instinctively she knew that he was leading up to something personal, and whatever it was posed a threat.

He edged closer to her, perching on his shining mahogany desk and smiling down at her. She shrank back in her chair, but he only leaned nearer.

"If a young woman such as yourself were to find a protector, for instance, a gentleman of breeding and generous nature who took a personal interest in your welfare, why, such a gentleman might take care of you. He could give you a nice little house, paying all expenses. Do you understand?"

Melissa thought she was beginning to, and was swept by a feeling made up of almost equal parts of anger and revulsion.

The banker was going on, "And in return, all you would have to do, would be nice to your protector . . . if you take my meaning."

"I believe I understand all too well," Melissa said, pushing back her chair. "About the loan, Mr. Udall, what is your answer on that?"

He frowned. "Why, a loan in such a situation as yours would be out of the question. But surely you must have known that?"

Melissa stood up slowly, clutching her small purse tightly so that she would not strike him. "No, Mr. Udall. Whatever you might think, I came here in good faith, with an honest request. And now, as your answer is no, I shall take my leave."

She started toward the door, but he reached out to seize her arm. "Wait! About what we were discussing, perhaps you did not understand!"

Melissa tore her arm out of his grasp. "Oh, I understood, all right, Mr. Udall, but my answer, too, is no! You see, it so happens that I am not that kind of girl."

Leaving the banker staring after her open-mouthed, she left the building and hurried along the road leading down to the landing below the hill. She was trembling with outrage, and on the verge of tears. She felt soiled and somehow diminished. How could he approach her with such a proposal? How *could* he?

The *Natchez Belle* was empty when she got on board, and Melissa was glad of this. She felt too depressed to face any of her friends, and explain to them that she had been refused again.

Udall's bank had been her last chance, for it was the only source of a possible loan that she had not yet been to. She had practically forced her way in to see every wealthy individual in Natchez. It was time to face the truth. Her dream had been foolish and impractical, only a girl's impetuous fancy. Amalie had warned her of what to expect. They had all tried to tell her, but no, she had been too stubborn to listen. She had relied on her feeling that somehow her goal could be accomplished.

Flinging herself upon the narrow bed, Melissa gave way to the tears she had been holding back. It was so unfair! The people she had gone to had more or less openly laughed at her, and Udall had not been the first to hint at an impropriety, although the others had been more subtle in their approach. If she had been a man, and had come to them with her idea, they might have turned her down, but they would not have insulted her into the bargain!

The hot tears burned in her eyes, and she twisted and turned on the narrow bed as the image of Banker Udall, his poached-egg eyes staring, moved across her inner eye; and then it was followed by the image of Simon Crouse, his eyes hot as he gazed at her with barely concealed lust.

Melissa knew that all men were not like these two. Her father had been a strong, gentle man, sensitive and caring; and her grandfather had been one of those gruff but kindly men, who appeared to be all noise and demands, but who had a soft side for their womenfolk and loved ones, much like Jubal King. Why couldn't she meet a man like that, a kind and handsome man? And then she thought of the handsome stranger, Luke Devereaux, who had bought back her music box. He had been good to look on, certainly, and he had been kind—the music box was proof of that.

She turned again upon the mattress, feeling feverish now that her tears had almost stopped. Her eyes burned, and her head throbbed. She could not help but wonder how she would have reacted, if the banker had been Luke Devereaux instead of Udall.

She replayed the scene in her mind with Devereaux in the role of the banker, and it *was* different. Instead of the revulsion and fear, she felt almost *pleasant* fear, a rush of feeling that made her cheeks hot and her body tingle.

But then, she really didn't think that Luke Devereaux would approach her in such a way. He would probably be more gentlemanly. Oh, he might try to kiss her, but it would be very romantic, not sly and ugly like Udall's approach, and not blunt and pushy, as Simon Crouse had been.

Lying there in the warm cabin, Melissa drifted into a daydream in which Luke Devereaux, gallant and courteously flirtatious, bandied light conversation with her and then, gently, stole a kiss.

At the thought of the imagined kiss, Melissa stirred restlessly. It was silly and wicked, dreaming of such things!

Feeling guilty and not a little angry with herself, she jumped up from the bed and found the music box. Choosing a disc, she put it on the spindle and wound the box. She would listen to some music, to calm herself, and then she would go to the galley and peel the vegetables for supper, so they would be ready when Martha returned from marketing.

Melissa released the catch and stepped back, waiting for the delicate, chime-like sounds to fill the cabin, but almost immediately the mechanism caught somewhere inside, and the clockwork began to whir.

Alarmed, Melissa quickly tripped the release and stopped the machine. She remembered the other time that the box had not functioned properly. As she had done that time, she shook it briskly, then tried it again. However, this time shaking did not set it working. The mechanism remained jammed.

Almost in tears again—would *nothing* go right?—she

opened the bottom door that gave access to the working parts and reached inside, feeling for anything that could be stopping the clockwork parts.

Almost at once, her probing fingers encountered a thick wad of paper. What on earth could it be? Angrily, she began to pull it out.

There, at last it was free!

She brought the wad of paper out into the light, and stared in stunned amazement. In her hand was a large bundle of bank notes!

Dumbfounded, she sank down on the bed and with trembling fingers peeled off the bills one by one.

When she was finished, she counted them again, unable to believe it. There in her lap was exactly two thousand dollars in money, Yankee money!

Chapter Seven

Simon Crouse was in a foul mood. Things had not gone well during his visit to Riverview Plantation. He had solved the original problem, the matter for which his overseer, Davis, had summoned him, but then something else had come up, and then one problem after another, until he had been forced to spend a good deal more time away from his affairs in Natchez than he had originally intended.

And now that he was finally back, bad fortune was still dogging him. There were problems with the land deal he was working on, there was some kind of difficulty with his bank, and the business of putting Great Oaks back into profitable operation again was going much too slowly to suit him. It was as if his luck, which had always been good, had suddenly turned sour.

Crouse emptied his wine glass, and with an oath flung it against the wall, leaving a purple stain on the wallpaper. No matter; let Jake clean it up.

And that brought another matter to mind, which

angered him even more. Jake had done his bidding and had kept an eye on the two women from Great Oaks. He had followed them to Natchez and to the wrecked steamboat, where they had settled in with Jubal King, the one-legged ex-river pilot. That would have been just fine. Living there in poverty with the Kings, who were equally poor, they would have been vulnerable. He could have found some way to get at them. But now, according to Jake, from some mysterious source they had obtained a sum of money, and they were involved in the task of repairing the *Belle*.

Crouse swore again, and poured himself another glass of wine. Obviously they were not going to the expense of repairing the boat with the idea of staying where they were. Word was that they would be finished with the repairs by the end of the week, and that they had advertised for an engineer and a black gang. Once they were afloat, Crouse knew that he would lose them. And what in the name of all that was holy did they intend to do with the boat once they were afloat? There wasn't a lot of river traffic nowadays—the trains had seen to that. True, there were still some steamboats carrying merchandise and produce, and some passengers remained loyal to steamboats; but that hardly seemed a likely career for two women, one barely more than a girl. He would have to collect more information before he could plan what he was going to do.

Abruptly, he strode to the door and bellowed for Jake, cursing when the man didn't answer immediately. "Goddamnit, Jake, where the hell are you?"

"Here, Mr. Crouse. Downstairs. I came as quick as I could, I was outside when you called."

"Well, now that you're finally here, send up the

wench, Emmy, or whatever her name is. And tell her to be quick about it."

"Ella Louise, Mr. Crouse. Yessir, I'll send her right up."

By the time the serving girl came upstairs, Crouse had finished another glass of wine, and was slumped into a chair, glaring angrily at the door.

Ella Louise came into the room slowly, neither hurrying nor lagging back. Her face was expressionless as she stared at Crouse with black eyes that reminded him of those other black eyes, Amalie's black eyes. Damn and blast the woman!

"Come here, girl," he said, his words slurred.

Obediently, Ella Louise came to stand in front of him, staring at a spot somewhere over his head.

"Now strip to the skin," he snapped, "and do it slow. I want to watch!"

Without protest, Ella Louise began to unbutton her rough dress, doing it slowly, as Crouse had ordered.

Crouse watched avidly, hand resting in his lap as his desire mounted, pulse leaping as she removed each garment. As her large, rather drooping breasts swung free, he licked his lips; and as she unfastened and dropped her skirt, he began to rub himself unconsciously.

She wore nothing under her outer clothing, and soon she was naked to his gaze. She showed no expression as his lustful glance traveled over the curves and hollows of her body, and his breathing quickened.

"Here!" he commanded, his voice thick. "Over here, bend down over the arm of the sofa!"

A silent twitch of her lips was the only reaction Ella Louise gave. It was an indication of her contempt for this man, and under different circumstances would have enraged Crouse, but he was too inflamed by passion to notice. Ella Louise stepped to the rounded sofa arm, and leaned over it in the subservient position Crouse had requested, so that her upper body lay on the sofa, and her buttocks were raised and exposed.

Crouse gave a raspy grunt and rose from his chair. As he freed his engorged member, a feeling of savage joy filled him, a sense of power. Approaching the girl from behind, he stood for an instant, prolonging the delicious moment, staring at the smooth roundness of her bottom. She was his to use as he pleased, and it pleased him immensely to be able to bend someone so to his will!

With a snarling sound in his throat, he thrust into her roughly, jolting her body forward. But Ella Louise did not cry out as the force of his lunge sent her sliding across the rough horsehair of the sofa. In fact, she welcomed the pain, for it helped distract her from what was happening to the rest of her body, as he pounded into her again, and again, and again.

Luke Devereaux emptied his pockets of what money he had, and fanned it out atop the dresser. One hundred dollars, a fraction over. Not bad, but not good, either.

Since the letter had arrived from Texas, Luke had been living from day to day, always on the edge of success or failure, for he had been keeping afloat by gambling.

It was a risky life at best, and Luke did not enjoy it all that much, but it had been the only alternative to penury, and it *was* a profession in which he did have some experience.

Simon Crouse had been out of town for the past few weeks, and so there had been no immediate confrontation over the money that Luke owed him; but Crouse was due back any day, and the time of reckoning would be upon him. Luke was hoping that before that day, he would be able to pyramid his small stake into enough to take care of his debts. So far, at least, he had managed to stay ahead of the game to the tune of his food and lodging.

Now he gazed down at the bills, stroking the smooth metal of his cigar case, running his fingers over the diamond, thinking: *Lady Luck, you had better be with me tonight; I really need you in my corner.*

As he pocketed the bills and the case, Luke smiled at his own superstition. He had heard that a love boat had arrived at Natchez-Under-the-Hill only this morning, and was open for business.

The euphemistically named "love boats" were actually floating brothels, which also provided gambling and drinking on the side. Luke knew that the novelty of the love boat would draw a large crowd of males from the town, and there was a good chance that he could find a lousy poker player with a fat poke.

He could always cheat, and he was clever enough at cards to get away with it, but there he drew the line. He was a damned good poker player, and if that wasn't enough to solve his money problems, so be it.

It was early evening, and the light was just starting to go when Amalie started down the hill from Natchez proper. She was tired; it had been a long day, but she had earned extra money, and the sound of it made a satisfying jingle in her pocket.

Below her she could hear the sounds of Natchez-Under-the-Hill awakening for the night's revels. Amalie sighed. It was good that they would soon be away from this place. Simon Crouse had returned to Natchez last night; she had learned that fact from a housemaid this morning. She wanted to be well away from here before he found out where they were.

As she reached the bottom of the hill road and walked along the narrow street, Amalie instinctively pulled her shawl close around her shoulders. This was an evil place. Evil and ugly. Saloons, brothels, gambling halls of all descriptions and sizes sprawled along the river bank. Pigs rooted in the piles of garbage, and starving dogs darted about. The stench was awful. Later, the din would be frightening, but right now there were only a few drunken shouts to be heard, and the sound of an off-key piano, playing a ragged, minor melody.

She pulled aside her skirts as a shambling figure lurched toward her, almost knocking her down, then staggered away, mumbling drunkenly to himself. It was dangerous for a woman, a decent woman, to be abroad here after dark, and she should not have stayed so late upon the hills, and would not have, except for the extra money to be earned. Despite Melissa's windfall, they still needed all the money they could get, and so Amalie kept her job in town, leaving the others to work on the *Belle*.

It was amazing, like a miracle, the finding of the money in the music box. They had talked about it, wondered about it, and finally came to the conclusion that Melissa's father had somehow managed to obtain the money, and put it into the box for his daughter. Still, to Amalie at any rate, this was not an entirely satisfactory explanation. Where could Jean-Paul Huntoon have obtained such a sum, and in Yankee dollars at that? It was all a mystery, but the money itself was real enough and was now being used to pay for the repairs and outfitting of the *Natchez Belle*. And it was an explanation that Melissa had eagerly embraced, made happy by the notion that her father had, after all, provided for her.

Amalie smiled to herself. All of them, herself included, had thought Melissa's idea only a pleasant dream, a make-believe, and yet it was coming true. More than that, it was a practical idea. People *were* hungry for entertainment, and would pay to see it. Certainly it was a chance, a hope for them to make their own way, a means of escaping Natchez—and Simon Crouse. With a little more luck, it could come to pass.

In front of her and to the right, she could now see the *Belle,* shining with new white paint. But what was that other boat moored alongside? It hadn't been there when she left this morning. It was a long, low flatboat, with a two-story structure taking up most of the deck.

Amalie walked a little faster, curious now. There were sounds of merriment coming from the flatboat: piano music, a woman's voice raised in strident song, men's coarse laughter.

As she drew closer, Amalie heard the clinking of glasses and the rattle of coins. A sign, somewhat battered and worn by the elements, proclaimed that the boat was the *Melon Patch*. A half-drunken slattern, wearing only a pink chemise, came bursting out of a door, followed by a man in nothing but his trousers, who proceeded to chase her around the deck. Amalie realized with dismay that the barge was one of the floating brothels that occasionally cruised the Mississippi, offering liquor, women, and gambling as entertainment for the rivermen and anyone else who cared to patronize them.

The man had caught the woman now, and the drunken pair, locked together, were stumbling back through the open cabin door.

Amalie sighed again, with a fatalistic shrug. She made few judgments on the way other people lived, but the pleasure boat would be a noisy and irresponsible neighbor, attracting all sorts of river scum. Before, the *Belle* had been isolated from most of the activity of the waterfront; now, a good deal of this activity would be going on right next door to them. She only hoped that the love boat would leave soon and drift on downriver to the next town.

As Amalie walked up the stage plank onto the *Belle*, Melissa came running to meet her, her face ablaze with excitement. It was good to see her charge looking so well and so happy. As each day's work on the *Belle* proceeded, Melissa seemed to grow happier, her beauty glowing more brightly; but tonight she was positively aglow. *What could have happened?* Amalie wondered.

"Oh, Amalie!" Melissa cried. "It's almost done!"

Amalie put her arm around the excited girl's shoulders. "What is almost done, *chérie?*"

"Why, the *Belle!* The repairs are nearly complete. Jubal finished patching the hole today, the railings are fixed, and the new curtains are about done. In

118

just a few more days, she will be ready to float. That is, if we can get an engineer and a gang to fire the boilers, but Jubal says we shouldn't have any trouble there, what with all the men who are looking for work."

Amalie squeezed Melissa's shoulders. "That is wonderful, little one, simply wonderful."

The women stood at the railing, looking down at the awakening beast that was Natchez-Under-the-Hill, and the love boat moored alongside the *Belle*.

"*That* arrived this morning, after you left," Melissa said in disgust, pointing to the barge. "It seems to be some kind of saloon, or gambling den, or *something!*"

Amalie said dryly, "I believe the 'or something' is the most apt."

Melissa glanced at her friend with a shake of her head. "Amalie, you're so tolerant. You never say wicked things about people, like I do. How can you be so patient with people?"

Amalie shrugged. "Someone once said that 'to understand all, is to forgive all.' Perhaps, in some small way, I do understand all. But I realize that the *Melon Patch* is not going to be a good neighbor. It will be noisy, and will attract all sorts of undesirable people."

Melissa leaned over the railing, frankly gawking, as a young woman, with hair of a brilliant yellow that could never have been conceived by nature, came out onto the deck of the barge, with a male companion. The woman was attired only in her corset and black hose, and right there on deck, in plain sight of anyone who cared to watch, she embraced the man and kissed him on the mouth!

Melissa gave a shocked gasp, recoiling. "How can they do that, Amalie? How could a woman sell herself

119

for money to just anyone who wants her? How can they do that and retain any self-respect?" Her voice was cold and accusatory, and her expression was stiff with disapproval.

Amalie hid a smile. "I don't really think that most of them choose it, *chérie*. I think, perhaps, that the life chooses them. You must realize that not everyone has been brought up as you have, with money and family."

"But the war took my family and the money!"

"That is true, but still, you had all the advantages of being brought up as a planter's daughter. Most of the girls in the brothels here and on the barge were raised in the worst kind of poverty, knowing little else. Their only goal has been to keep body and soul together, and they have only one thing of value, one thing to sell—themselves. So you should not judge them too harshly, but feel some degree of sympathy for them."

Melissa shook her head vehemently. "I can't. I would scrub floors first, do the lowest menial work, before I would do *that*!"

"And if there were no floors to scrub, no one who would hire you, what then?"

"Well then, I'd starve to death," said Melissa flatly.

Amalie laughed. "That's a little dramatic, isn't it, Melissa?"

"I don't care, it's the way I feel." Suddenly, she pointed. "Amalie, who's that man just going onto the barge? Isn't it . . ."

Amalie followed the direction of her pointing finger. "Why, yes, it's Mr. Devereaux, the gentleman who accompanied Simon Crouse on the day of the auction."

Melissa, her expression scornful and her eyes dark,

turned her back on the love boat. "And I thought he was such a gentleman! I even accepted my music box from him. And now I see that he is like all the rest, visiting those women. No real gentleman would do a thing like that!"

Without another word she marched up the steps leading to the deck above.

Amalie stared after her thoughtfully. So! The child was interested in Luke Devereaux. Well, she could have chosen worse for her first infatuation, in Amalie's estimation. He appeared to be a gentleman, despite what Melissa might think, and he seemed kind. His gift of the music box was proof of that.

Amalie looked again at the barge. Devereaux had gone inside now, and the approaching darkness was softening the details of the squalid love boat.

She sighed softly. Melissa had so much to learn—about life, about herself. Sheltered as she had been, first by her family and then by Amalie, she knew nothing of the real nature of men or women. She had no sympathy for a man's needs, because she had not yet experienced her own physical awakening; but there were signs that she was beginning to. There were strong passions in Melissa, of that Amalie was certain, for she had the blood of her father in her, and he had been a lusty man, ready and eager for all that life had to offer.

Amalie knew of this firsthand, for after the death of Jean-Paul's wife, she had taken her place in his bed, as well as with Melissa. It was a place that she filled quite naturally, for she had been in love with Jean-Paul since that day in New Orleans when he had offered her the job as companion to his wife, although she had never shown her love until after Mariette's death.

Yes, one day soon Melissa would learn about the desires and passions of the flesh for herself. Amalie could only hope that it would be with someone like Luke Devereaux rather than a pig like Simon Crouse.

It was good that they were nearly ready to put the *Belle* into the water. Amalie had the feeling that the sooner they were gone from here, the better. Although the air was humid and warm, she shivered and huddled into herself. Yes, let them be quit of this place!

Luke Devereaux hesitated for only a moment as he opened the gate leading up the walk to Crouse's house. Luke felt ill at ease and at a disadvantage, and he disliked feeling this way. He was a man who liked to be on top of things, in charge of any situation; and now, because of an ill-advised card game and the death of a herd of cattle back in Texas, Crouse had the whip hand, and Luke was certain that the man would push it to the limit. It was embarrassing and demeaning, but Luke knew that he must not admit to these feelings in front of Crouse. He consciously arranged his features into an expression of confidence as he knocked on the front door.

Crouse's man, Jake, admitted him, and then he was left cooling his heels for at least fifteen minutes, before Crouse appeared. Well, he wouldn't let the man get to him. That was the only thing he had left at the moment. So when Crouse came into the room, he found Luke relaxed in a comfortable chair, smoking one of his thin black cigars.

Crouse crossed at once to the liquor cabinet and

took out a large, cut-glass decanter that sparkled in the light from the window. "Some sherry, Luke?"

"Thank you, Simon."

Crouse poured two generous glasses of sherry and gave one to Luke. "And so you have come to pay me my money, have you?"

Luke took a swallow of sherry before he answered. "As a matter of fact, I haven't," he said easily.

Crouse turned a cold eye on him. "You are joshing, I trust."

Luke smiled, and took another swallow. It was excellent sherry. "I'm afraid not, Simon. I seldom josh about anything as serious as money. The long and short of it is that the money I was counting on from the sale of my cattle in Texas did not come through, and I am temporarily without funds, as they say."

Crouse did not take his gaze from Luke's face. "You *are* serious."

Luke nodded. "Oh, I'm serious, all right. In fact, I'm downright depressed. But I'll survive. I've recovered from worse setbacks."

Crouse tilted the decanter and refilled his empty glass without offering Luke any. "I'm sure you will survive, but the question now is how you will repay the money you owe *me*. Have you any ideas about that?"

Luke looked down at his cigar. "Well, as I see it, there are three alternatives. One, that you allow me time to get the money to repay you, and I'll admit that right now it appears that it might take a spell. Two, you let me go to work for you until the debt is paid. You have many holdings, many types of operations, and I have considerable experience in a number of fields where I am certain that I could be of use to you. The third I'd rather not contemplate, and since we are both gentlemen, I'm sure that you would not stoop to such a measure—that you would bring charges against me for failure to repay my debt to you. This last would gain you nothing, and make *me* acutely uncomfortable!"

Luke looked up at Crouse quizzically. "So it's up to you, Simon. Which shall it be?"

Crouse stared at him for a long moment, eyes unblinking, and then suddenly he smiled, although the smile never quite reached his eyes.

"Well, as you pointed out, alternative number three will gain me nothing. Number one, well, let us say that I am not a patient or a trusting man. I prefer to have my debts settled as quickly as possible. And so, that appears to leave alternative number two. It just so happens that the overseer of Riverview Plantation has been having problems with the workers there. I have straightened matters out temporarily, but the problem hasn't really been solved, and I have doubts about the man being capable of handling it. Have you had experience running a plantation, Luke?"

Luke nodded. "I was overseer for a spell back in Texas."

"Do you think you could handle this problem for me?"

"I'd be willing to give it a try."

"Well then, it's a bargain. Shall we discuss terms?"

"By all means."

It took another half hour for the two men to come to an arrangement, but finally they agreed upon the rate at which Luke's debt would be paid off.

"But you understand," Crouse said, "that this will go only part way to repaying what you owe."

"At least it's a start. Maybe my luck will change meanwhile, and I can win a pot or two."

Crouse was refilling the sherry glasses. "Let's drink to our new association, shall we?"

Crouse had been furious at the beginning, when he learned that Luke Devereaux was broke, but now his mood had changed. Devereaux seemed a cool and competent man, strong and sure of himself. He could be very useful. Also, the fact that the man was in debt to him, in a sense in his power, pleased Crouse, now that he had given some thought to it. He felt better than he had in weeks. Thoughtfully, he put down his glass.

"There's a love boat tied up below the hill. I understand that they have a bevy of girls. Would you care to join me there for some sport, Luke?"

At the thought of women, a flare of anger revived in Crouse, as he remembered what had happened with Ella Louise last night. The stupid black bitch! It had been her fault! What he needed was some professional attention from a woman who had her heart in her work, who knew what to do with a man, instead of being as docile as a milk cow. Yes, he needed a woman to blot out the anger left by last night's failure!

Luke Devereaux was speaking. "Yes, I know about the *Melon Patch*. I played a little poker there last evening. But I can't go tonight, Simon. I have another engagement."

Crouse shrugged. "Very well, suit yourself. I shall expect you here on Monday. I will explain in detail what I want done at Riverview."

"I'll be here," Luke said.

Crouse watched the tall Texan as he went down the

walk and out into the street. Yes, Devereaux was clever and strong, and he could be put to good use. The situation at Riverview should keep him busy until Crouse could decide just where he could be put to further use.

And now to the *Melon Patch* and the juicy wenches he would find there. Perhaps he would sample two this time, one fair and one dark, one mature and one very young. By God, he might just do that!

He rubbed his hands together in gleeful anticipation.

Chapter Eight

Word had spread about the *Melon Patch*, and there were many customers aboard that evening, partaking of the pleasures offered. Rawboned keelboat men stood elbow to elbow with town swells at the gaming tables in the saloon, and one man's money was as good as another's when it came to the purchase of a woman's company.

Simon Crouse stopped in the doorway and smiled. Times might be hard, but men could always find money for gambling, drinking and wenching. It was a good night for the house, and although few knew it, the house belonged to him.

Crouse's smile widened. Yes, his interests took in many things, and it was his money that backed the *Melon. Patch*, although everyone thought that Ephriam (Bear) Smith, the black-bearded giant who ran the boat, was the owner, which was just what Crouse wanted them to think.

Crouse stood to one side for a little, deciding which one of the girls would best suit his mood and his needs this evening. Since there was such a crowd, he finally decided to settle for just one tonight, so as not to take another girl out of circulation when she could be getting paid for her labors.

He finally picked Sweet Sally, a buxom little blonde about the age of the Huntoon girl. The decision made, he pushed his way through the noisy crowd to the table where Bear was playing cards with four men.

When Bear saw Crouse he smiled—a brief parting of the black brush he called a beard. Bear Smith was a giant of a man, as hairy as his namesake, and one of the ugliest men Crouse had ever seen. He loved a brawl, and had been in so many that his face—the little that showed outside the beard—was a lumpy mass of scar tissue. His nose had been repeatedly broken, and most of his teeth were missing. It was rumored that he had killed at least six men along the river, and all with his bare hands. Withal, he was shrewd, and it took a man with his mean nature and fighting ability to keep any kind of order on a boat like the *Melon Patch*.

Now Bear lay down his cards, spoke briefly to the men at the table, and came over to Crouse. "Mr. Crouse, sir. Glad to have you aboard tonight. What's your pleasure?"

Crouse nodded pleasantly. "You're having a good night, Ephriam. I think Sweet Sally takes my fancy tonight. Afterward I'll meet with you in the office for an accounting."

Bear nodded ponderously. "Of course, Mr. Crouse. Just go along to your usual cabin, and I'll send Sally right in. Enjoy yourself, Mr. Crouse."

Crouse smiled thinly. "I fully intend to, Ephriam. I fully intend to."

His usual cabin was a fairly well-furnished one set aside for the wealthier, more fastidious customers. It contained a comfortable bed, two chairs, and a small liquor cabinet.

Once in the cabin, Crouse undressed, then poured himself a stiff drink of bourbon. He thought of Sweet Sally with anticipation, letting his imagination dwell on the remembered lushness of her body, and her willingness to please. Not for nothing was she called Sweet Sally! Not like that sullen brown slut Emma Lou, or whatever she called herself.

Anger filled him again as he thought of last night. He had been pounding away at the wench, driving himself deep into her, glorying in the feel of her warm buttocks under his clutching hands, when suddenly his manhood failed him. Just like that! Try what he might, he could not attain his ultimate satisfaction. Although she had remained expressionless, Crouse had been sure that she was laughing at him. He would have to tell Jake to get rid of her.

This had never happened to him before, and it enraged, humiliated, and frightened him. That was the reason he had come here tonight, to prove to himself that it was her fault, not his. And surely he was right, for now, as he waited for Sweet Sally, his member stood proudly at attention, growing more tumescent by the moment.

Sweet Sally swept into the cabin, dimpling prettily. She was a short, rather plump girl, with a pleasant face and guileless blue eyes. Her hair was bleached a bright yellow, yet the simplicity of her face counteracted the garish color, giving her a look of raffish innocence.

As soon as she entered the cabin, Crouse grunted and shuffled toward her. As he moved, she dropped her chemise, the only garment she was wearing, and held out her arms to him.

"How you been, dearie?" she said mechanically.

"Don't talk," he said, his voice husky.

He motioned curtly toward the bed, and she shrugged, covering the distance to the bed slowly, with much wriggling of her plump hips. She arranged herself on the bed for him, open and inviting, and in a moment he was upon her, driving into her, eager for the release that had been denied him last night.

As the floating whorehouse rocked gently on the motion of the river, Simon Crouse pounded his frustration into the willing flesh of the girl, who encouraged him with appropriate movements and sounds; and then, just as he was about to achieve the relief he ached for, his organ went limp, failing him again.

"'ere now!" said Sweet Sally. "Wot's this now? You never done that before, Guv'nor! Wot's wrong?"

Crouse turned on her savagely, hand upraised. "Shut up, you dim-witted limey, and get yourself out of this cabin!"

Sally hopped off the bed in a huff. "Ain't no call to blame it on me!" she said nastily. "I did my part. It was you who couldn't do your duty."

Trailing her chemise behind her, she flounced out of the cabin, slamming the door.

Baffled and frustrated, Crouse gazed down at his offending organ. What *was* wrong with him? Getting up from the bed, he went to the door, opened it, and howled for Bear Smith.

When the big man appeared, he found Crouse clad in a robe, downing a hearty drink. Ephriam said worriedly, "Didn't Sally please you, Mr. Crouse? Would you care for som'un else?"

"No, she was *not* satisfactory," Crouse snarled. "Not satisfactory at all. Send me someone else. A black girl this time. One who knows how to please a man."

Bear Smith nodded. "Of course, Mr. Crouse. Anything you like. You know we aim to please."

Crouse glared at him suspiciously, searching for mockery, but the bearded face was expressionless. The big man went back down the passageway.

Crouse managed to down another drink before the second girl came into the cabin.

This one, a lithe young black girl, looked primitive enough to have just come from the hold of a slaver's ship. Tall and well-muscled, she wore her hair short, cropped close to her fine skull, and she had hot, slanting eyes.

Crouse was pleased to note that his flagging manhood had also responded to the woman's exceptional good looks, and was again at the ready. Surely, this time things would go right.

Slightly weary now, he motioned to the girl that she should take her position on top, which she did with such skill and superb muscular control that she soon had him ready to burst.

As he strained upward, only seconds away from the peak of pleasure, once again satisfaction was denied him.

It couldn't be happening! Not again! But it was.

For a moment Crouse felt that he might weep, and then a terrible rage seized him. Used to controlling everything about his life, he could not abide this baffling inability to control this one small part of his body.

In a frenzy of rage, he wrecked the cabin, flinging furniture and bottles against the walls, and cursing steadily and vilely. At last he collapsed onto the bed, panting, his head in his hands. He mumbled plaintively, "Why? What has happened to me? *Why?*"

The girl had watched his behavior calmly. "Don't feel bad," she said now. "It happen to men sometime that way."

Crouse, his anger exhausted, said, "Not to me. Never before to me, dammit!"

She shrugged, reaching for her wrapper. "You done someone bad?"

His head came up. "What?"

"I said, you done someone bad? You have, then maybe that someone made bad gri-gri agin' you."

"What? Gri-gri? What sort of gibberish you babbling, girl?"

"You can't make little man stay up. Sometime people get obeah woman to make gri-gri to do this. Only way to get undone is fo' man to see obeah woman, and get it undone."

Crouse glared at her, and the girl got off the bed and scampered from the cabin.

Crouse did not notice. He was thinking over what she had said. It was all nonsense, of course. But suppose it wasn't? Had he done someone bad? He smiled wryly. Hundreds, probably. Then he sobered, for there was one name and face that came immediately to mind. It had to be Amalie Dubois.

Feverishly, his thoughts raced back over the past few weeks. The letter from Riverview had arrived the day after he had Jake bring the Dubois woman to his

132

house, and since then, it seemed that everything had gone wrong for him, culminating in this . . . this humiliation. She *had* to be responsible!

Well, she would pay! That was certain. He thought of her now, only a skip and a jump away, on the *Natchez Belle,* she and the Huntoon girl.

A knock on the door interrupted his thoughts. "What is it?"

A girl's voice answered, "Mr. Crouse, Bear wants to know if you're ready to go over the accounts with him. We're leaving day after tomorrow, you know. He said to remind you."

"Yes, yes. I'll be right there. I'll see him in the office."

As he began to pull on his clothes, Crouse's thoughts returned to Amalie Dubois. And then it struck him. The love boat was leaving. What if Amalie Dubois left with it?

He stopped dressing, and laughed cruelly to himself. Jake had told him that the woman had a job up on the hill. He would have Jake find out what time she returned to the *Belle* every day, and have her snatched on the landing. When the *Melon Patch* embarked, she would be on it, she and her spells or whatever it was she used against him. Once she was away from here, he was certain that the curse, or whatever she had put upon him, would be gone!

Not only would she be gone, she would be earning money for him, for Simon Crouse!

He struck his open palm with the fist of his other hand. It was too bad that he couldn't send Melissa Huntoon along to keep her company, but that would be taking too much of a risk. There might be a hue and cry if *she* turned up missing; but who would make a fuss over a missing black wench, except perhaps Melissa herself?

Crouse grinned wolfishly. It was a fitting way to get back at the pair of them. Losing her friend and companion would hurt Melissa, and would leave her vulnerable when he next approached her.

In better spirits now, he pulled on the rest of his clothing and went down the passageway for his business talk with Bear Smith.

Melissa leaned on the rail of the *Belle*, and watched the spot where Amalie would appear if she followed her usual path back to the boat.

Melissa was tense with excitement. Jubal had just told her that he had found an engineer to run the engines of the *Belle*, and that the engineer had hired the stokers and deck hands they needed.

As Jubal had said, in these times many men were willing to work for food and a place to sleep. Jubal had told the men that they could not offer more than this at the present, but that when they began to earn a profit, the crew would receive a share. They had been more than happy to accept these terms.

So now they were about ready to put the *Belle* into the water. In a day or so, they would be afloat, and on their way to New Orleans, where Nehemiah Prendergast was going to find the performers needed to make up their troupe.

Fixing up the *Belle* had taken a good portion of the money Melissa had found in the music box, but they still had enough left to operate for a month or so. And by that time, hopefully, they would be earning some money with their show.

It was so strange about the money in the music box.

Like a miracle, really. It *must* have been her father who had hidden it there; but why hadn't he told her so?

Martha King said that perhaps, in the last stages of his illness, he had forgotten it, but that was hard for Melissa to believe. She shivered when she thought of how close she had come to losing the box and the money at the auction.

She shook her head to clear it, and searched the pathway for Amalie, trying not to look at the ugly bulk of the love boat, which she thought of as "that place."

It was impossible for her to comprehend. How could those women live like that, being kissed and mauled by any man who had the price? Ugly men, old men, men who didn't bathe too often!

Melissa had lived on a plantation and had observed the farm animals in their natural matings but, she thought, surely it must be different between men and women. There must be more to it than that!

Feeling herself flush, she stole a look at the offending barge.

The denizens of the love boat were just beginning to stir as they made ready for the evening's influx of customers. Several of the girls had come out onto the deck to stretch and get a bit of air.

"What had *he* been doing there?" Melissa whispered aloud. Luke Devereaux had seemed a gentleman, a cut above the rough river types, and yet he had gone there, just as they did.

She forced herself to turn away. It was none of her affair what Luke Devereaux did for amusement. He was nothing to her. Why was she thinking about him, anyway?

135

Determinedly, she turned her thoughts to the showboat, trying to recapture her feeling of excitement.

Martha, with Melissa's help, had been making costumes, and working on stage scenery under Nehemiah's guidance. The old actor had made out a repertoire for them, listing the shows, and then carefully writing out all the parts. He had an amazing memory, and could remember everything word for word. In the evenings, he had been tutoring Melissa in the ingenue roles, and working with her on singing and dancing. Nehemiah said that they would have to purchase a piano when they reached New Orleans, and that he would teach her to play, as well as sing. Oh, it *was* exciting!

But where was Amalie?

Anxiously, Melissa scanned the road. It was late, the sun was going down. Where *was* Amalie?

Amalie was weary. She was not accustomed to working for anyone except the Huntoons at Great Oaks, and there she had received special privileges. The woman for whom she now worked, Mrs. Thomas, treated her well enough, yet she was demanding, and expected long hours for the modest sum she was willing to pay.

Soon, however, possibly within the next day or so, the *Belle* would be ready to float, and they would be gone from this place which was making Amalie increasingly uncomfortable.

Ever since she had learned that Simon Crouse had returned to Natchez, she had been ill at ease. In placing the binding-spell upon Crouse, Amalie had used some of herself, and in doing so had put herself into a kind of psychic jeopardy.

She had learned her occult skills in New Orleans, when she was a girl; and up until now, had always used them for good. It bothered her considerably that she had used the ancient arts for a negative purpose. No matter that Crouse deserved any mischief she might do to him. Amalie felt as if she had taken an irretrievable step when she had used her powers against, rather than for someone. Also, she knew that the use of such powers sometimes carried a penalty. At any rate, she would feel much better when Simon Crouse and Natchez were behind them.

The sun was already down, the shadows beginning to gather, when she reached the bottom of the hill and started down the narrow street. Thinking of a nice bath and a warm meal, she hurried past the doorway of a vacant, crumbling building. Her ear caught the sound of movement from inside.

Quickly, she sprang away from the dark opening, but she was not quick enough. Rough hands grabbed her and hauled her inside the building before she could cry out; and almost before she realized what had happened, she found her mouth gagged with a foul-smelling cloth, and her hands lashed together behind her back. The last indignity was a blindfold, tied roughly over her eyes; and then she was pushed down onto what seemed to be a pile of burlap, or some other rough material.

Amalie lay where she fell, not moving. Her hearing was the only sense left open to her, and she strained to hear what she could.

She could hear the sound of whispering, coming from a little distance away. The voices were male, rough and profane. Was this Simon Crouse's doing again? She tried to recognize Jake's voice, and could not.

Then she heard a grunt, and the noise of a heavy object being dropped to the floor beside her. The next moment she was lifted by her arms and legs, and placed inside a confined space. A large wooden box, she was sure, since she could smell the pine.

She heard a lid being fastened over her, and for an instant she had to battle panic. But the air remained pure, and she could only conjecture that the box was vented. At least they didn't mean to smother her.

As she felt the box lifted, her heart began to beat wildly. She tried to cry out, but the gag muffled any sound. And now they were moving. Amalie was thrown back and forth against the sides of the box, and she could hear the sounds of the landing.

Where in God's name were they taking her, and why?

Simon Crouse must be the instigator. There was no one else who wished her harm. Was he taking her to his house again?

But then she could hear the sound of water, the river, and now the voices of men and women, of music, and the noise of glasses clinking, and they were no longer on the street. There was the sound of planking under the feet of the men carrying her. A boat. They were taking her on board a boat, but which boat, and why?

She was carried along for a few more minutes, and then the box was placed—almost dropped—on the floor. Amalie drew in her breath. Evidently, they had arrived at their destination.

She heard the sound of the men's footsteps retreating, and Amalie was left alone. Now all she could hear were the chuckle of the river and the distant sounds of revelry.

Her arms and legs were growing stiff, and she began to struggle against her bonds; but before she could make any headway, she heard footsteps again, and the lid of her prison was being removed.

"Ah, well, she's a pretty one, ain't she?" The voice was rough and deep. "Here we go now, my beauty. We'll have you out of there in a jiffy, that we will."

Amalie felt strong hands in her armpits, and in a second she was lifted bodily out of the crate, and in a moment more was carefully placed onto a bed.

"We'll get those rags and things off you, and see what you really look like."

Amalie moaned in relief as the pungent gag was removed. The edges of her mouth felt raw, and her jaw was stiff from being held in one position. She blinked her eyes, trying to adjust them to the light, as the man who had taken her from the box untied her wrists and ankles.

Her eyes now adjusted, she could see that he was a huge man, well over six feet and correspondingly broad, with a massive head covered with a wild tangle of black hair that continued down his cheeks and chin to form a full, brushy beard that concealed most of his face.

She recalled seeing him on the deck of the love boat, and she quickly glanced around the cabin. "Where am I? And why am I here?" she asked as steadily as she could, anticipating the answer.

The big man laughed heartily. "Spunky little piece, ain't you now? Well, beauty, you are on board the *Melon Patch*, which is what you might call a 'pleasure boat,' and as to what you're doing here, well, you're going to sail with us in the morning. After that, well, I guess you'll have to earn your keep just like all the other dollies on board earn theirs, on your back." He broke into a roar of laughter that hurt Amalie's ears.

"Who had me brought here?" She had to shout to be heard over the roar of his amusement.

He finally ceased laughing, knuckling his eyes with a huge fist. "I brought you here, beauty, that's who. None other than myself, Ephriam Smith, better known as 'Bear' to them I call friend, and I hope that you'll be calling me that soon. You are indeed a fine looking wench. He said you were." He reached out a sausage-fingered hand and touched her cheek.

Amalie willed herself not to flinch away. "And who is *he*?" she asked calmly; but a look of sly cleverness crept into the big man's eyes, and she realized that he was not as simple as she thought.

"He? Did I say he?" he said innocently. "That must have been a slip of the lip, so to speak. I been watching you, beauty. I've seen you go back and forth up the hill to your work, and I've taken a fancy to you, that I have. And what I fancy, I usually get.

"Now, it's almost time to get things underway for the evening, and since it's our last night, it's going to be a busy one, I'll wager. I'm going to lock you in here. As you can see, I've closed the shutters on the window. You can go ahead and holler all you like, but none will think anything of it, even if they should hear you over the noise of the customers." His roaring laughter sounded again. "Lots of screaming on the *Melon Patch*, as I reckon you've noticed.

"Later, when things get settled down a mite, I'll maybe slip back and pass some time with you, so that we might become better acquainted, so to speak."

140

He reached out his big hand, and placed it over Amalie's breast. It covered her breast completely. Amalie did not move, and he gave the breast a squeeze, just hard enough to make her wince.

"Yep, you and me, we're going to be good friends. Just you wait and see."

He was laughing again as he left the cabin, and she could hear the rumble of his laughter as he bolted the door from the outside.

Amalie remained standing in the middle of the cabin, feeling as if a huge weight had come down upon her. Why did they have to happen now, when things were going so well, when they were almost ready to leave Natchez? The awful irony of it was that Melissa and the Kings would be looking everywhere for her, everywhere but right next door to the *Belle*.

The weight turned into despair. Perhaps it was a punishment visited upon her for using her secret powers to harm someone.

What was she going to do? What *could* she do?

There was no doubt in her mind what fate the man called Bear had in store for her.

Chapter Nine

As Luke Devereaux approached the *Melon Patch*, he thought of Simon Crouse and his offer of the night before. If there was one thing he did not want, that was to become further indebted to Crouse; and also, he could think of no one he cared less about spending time with. There was something about the man that soured Luke's stomach. It was a hell of a thing that he had allowed himself to get into debt to the man in the first place. At the moment he might have to let Crouse call the moves, but at least he didn't have to accept his hospitality.

Luke didn't really enjoy going to the *Melon Patch*, but on his last visit, he had found two well-heeled, very bad poker players from Upon-the-hill, and they had arranged a game for tonight on board the love boat.

Well, this would be the last time. The barge would be leaving tomorrow. Luke hoped that tonight he would be lucky and manage to win a few dollars. He had given up the idea of winning enough to pay

Crouse's debt, but he still needed money to live on while he worked off his indebtedness.

The boat was its usual noisy self, the sounds of merrymaking well under way when he arrived.

Luke went directly to the small table in the back of the saloon, where he was supposed to meet the poker players. One of them was already there, but the other man had not arrived yet, and so Luke and the early bird had a drink to pass the time.

The man from the hill, Dupar by name, watched the half-naked tarts with an ill-concealed desire. It was plain that he itched to get the game over with so that he could get on to the real business of the evening. That should make him easier to take, Luke thought.

As Dupar ordered another drink, Luke saw Moline, the second man, accompanied by a stranger, coming down the saloon toward them. Now they could begin.

Moline introduced the stranger, and Dupar called for a fresh deck of cards.

While they waited for the cards, Luke looked around the saloon at the girls who paraded back and forth with a bold strut. It had been some time since he had been with a woman. Maybe after the game, *if* he won, he would look them over. A man couldn't stay celibate forever. His friends often taunted him for being too particular. Could be they were right.

As he eyed first one, then another, Luke's thoughts, for some strange reason, turned to Melissa Huntoon. What a beauty she was! She made the girls here look like a flock of crows.

He wondered how it would be to make love again to a woman who was not doing it for the money. How long had it been since he'd had a woman he really wanted or cared for? Longer than he cared to admit. It was far easier to satisfy urges with a woman whom you could pay and then forget, a woman who would have no illusions about you, no claims upon you. Yet he *was* particular, and the women he saw here not all that appealing.

"Forget her, forget Melissa," he told himself angrily. She would mean nothing but trouble, nothing but pain. If there was something missing in sex for money, if there was no real tenderness, no sharing, that was the price a man had to pay for his freedom.

Hell and damnation, what was he doing, maundering on like this?

A waiter slapped down the fresh pack of cards, and Dupar broke the seal.

As he did so, there was a commotion at the entrance as two hulking men came in carrying a large wooden chest, somewhat wider and shorter than a coffin. One of the men Luke recognized as Bear Smith, the proprietor of the *Melon Patch*. Shouldering people out of the way, they disappeared down a hallway that led to the small cabins in the back of the barge.

"Cut for deal," Dupar said.

Luke turned his attention back to the table. "Here goes nothing," he said, and turned up a king of diamonds.

They had been playing for about two hours, and Luke was ahead by several hundred dollars, when he felt the need to relieve himself.

Waiting until a new hand was to be dealt, he excused himself, promising to return momentarily, and headed toward the rear of the barge, the part farthest out into the river, which was the customary place to take care of such matters. As he walked along the out-side deck, he was brought up short by the sound of a woman's scream.

On boats like the *Melon Patch*, voices were often raised, and a woman's scream in a feigned abundance of feeling was not unusual; but this cry did not have the right ring to it. It sounded like a woman in pain, or one who was very frightened.

As he paused, listening, the scream came again, a shrill knife slicing through the good-natured hubbub. It seemed to come from the cabin next to him, but since the wooden shutters were drawn and barred, he could not be sure. It was probably none of his business, but he couldn't let it go by without investigation.

With a sigh he went back into the passageway. He found what he thought was the right cabin, and when a third scream came from behind the door, he was certain.

As quietly as possible, he tried the door, and found it bolted. After a slight hesitation he hammered on it with his fist. "What's going on in there?"

A man's harsh voice answered, "None of your damned business, mate! Just go about your own af-fairs!"

Luke could hear the sounds of a struggle, and then the woman cried out again, weaker this time, but he could make out the words. "Help me! Please help me!"

Luke hesitated no longer. Planting himself firmly, he raised his right leg, and kicked in the flimsy door, charging into the cabin after it.

As the door hit the deck, Luke saw a huge bearded man rear up from the bed. It was Bear Smith. A honey-skinned woman, her clothing in disarray, was sprawled across the bed. She looked familiar . . .

That was all he had a chance to see before the big man was upon him. Before Luke could set himself, he had received a stunning blow to the side of the head. He was sent reeling back against the wall. Bear was terribly strong, and Luke knew that he would be done for if he let the man get a grip on him.

Bear, off-balance from his first blow, staggered into Luke's powerful right to the face. Luke felt the shock all the way up to his shoulder socket, but he had scored—blood spouted from the big man's nose. Before Bear could recover, Luke followed up with a fist to the solar plexus, and then a neck chop that put the giant down and out, at least temporarily.

Breathing heavily, Luke turned to look at the woman, and received a shock. Although he had only seen her once, she was not the kind of woman a man could forget easily. He knew now why she looked familiar: the woman on the bed was Melissa Huntoon's companion. How in God's name had she gotten here, and what had happened to Melissa?

He stepped quickly to the bed. Bear would not remain unconscious long, and Luke wanted to be off the love boat before the big man came to.

"Miss Dubois, isn't it? Do you remember me? Luke Devereaux?"

She nodded, and tried to pull the remains of her torn clothing around her.

"We've got to get the hell out of here," Luke said.

He looked around the cabin, and saw a red shawl draped over a chest of drawers. Tossing it to her, he stepped to the doorway and looked out, but no one seemed to have taken notice of the commotion.

Turning back, he saw that Amalie had put the

shawl around her and was on her feet. On the floor Bear stirred, moaning.

Quickly, Luke took her arm and led her out of the cabin and down the passageway to the back of the barge.

Outside, he put his arm around her, and bent his head to hers, as if they were deep in conversation. No one took undue notice of them as he shepherded her to the front of the barge and down the stage plank.

When they were at last on solid ground, he started to lead her toward the road going up the hill, but she held back.

"No, Mr. Devereaux. You can take me home."

He turned a puzzled face to her. "Home? What do you mean?"

She pointed to the lights of a sternwheeler which was raised up on blocks, back from the water's edge. "To the *Natchez Belle*," she said. "They'll be waiting for me."

Suddenly, things fell into place. The *Natchez Belle*. Wasn't that the name Melissa had mentioned to Crouse the day of the auction? A wrecked steamboat that no one had wanted?

He looked at the boat again. Was Melissa staying there as well? He wanted to ask, but did not wish to show his interest.

He took Amalie's arm again, and hustled her along in the direction of the boat. "I thought that the boat was a wreck," he said, as they walked.

"It was. We have repaired it."

At that moment, a bellow of pure rage sounded behind them. Without looking Luke knew that it came from an aroused Bear Smith. Hastily, Luke pulled

Amalie behind a stack of cotton bales. There were still quite a few people on the landing, and the night was dark. He didn't think Bear had seen them.

Peering back between the cotton bales, he saw Bear standing on the river bank, looking in both directions. A mist hung along the river now, making visibility poor. Finally, Bear Smith turned his face up to the night sky, and bellowed like an animal deprived of its prey. Then he turned and stomped back on board the love boat.

"Come," Amalie said. "My friends will be worried about me, and I'm sure they will wish to thank you for what you've done."

Luke followed her, feeling uneasy, out of his depth. Rescuing damsels in distress was not his usual role. And there were three poker players waiting for him . . . No, he'd better skip that. Bear Smith didn't know him, but that one glance in the cabin had probably been enough so that the man would recognize him the next time.

He sighed, and followed Amalie Dubois, his mind seething with questions. Why had she been on board the *Melon Patch*? Obviously, it was not of her own free will.

Amalie seemed to sense his confusion. "We will talk when we are safely aboard the *Belle*. Come. I am sure you want to meet the others.

Did the "others" include Melissa? All of a sudden, Luke very much hoped so. The thought made him uncomfortable, but he could not turn back now. Wondering why he was so nervous, he trailed Amalie up the stage plank and onto the *Natchez Belle*.

When Amalie still had not returned at full dark,

Melissa was almost sick with worry. Martha tried to comfort her; but Melissa could see that Martha was just as worried as she was, and so her reassurances were of slight comfort.

Jubal had gone out and prowled the entire length of Natchez-Under-the-Hill, and had seen nothing of Amalie. Then he had gone into town and inquired at Amalie's place of employment, and was told that Amalie had started for home before sundown.

The fear in the back of all their minds was the same—that one or more of the ruffians or derelicts haunting the landing had assaulted Amalie, or killed her for the meager contents of her purse.

They ate an unhappy meal in the dining room, and then returned to the deck to continue their vigil. When the mist started coming in from the river, they finally gave up and went inside.

"Your getting the grippe, Melissa," Martha said, "won't help Amalie when she gets back."

Inside, they huddled cheerlessly in the renovated parlor on the Texas deck, which they had designed for the use of the "family," as they now referred to themselves. The bright cheerfulness of the room merely made them feel more depressed as they thought of the glowing plans they had discussed only that morning at breakfast.

Martha had just risen from her rocker, preparatory to fixing a pot of coffee, when they heard footsteps coming up from the lower deck. Melissa grabbed the arms of her chair with her hands, and hope caused her heart to beat faster.

Then, in a concerted rush, they all dashed for the door and the stairway outside; Jubal was in the lead, thumping along madly, and Nehemiah brought up the rear. Before them stood Amalie, wrapped in a garish red shawl, her hair disheveled and her face pale. Luke Devereaux stood next to her.

Jubal halted his headlong flight by ramming his wooden peg onto the deckboards.

Martha clucked. "I wish you wouldn't *do* that, Jubal. It ruins the decks!"

But no one, least of all Jubal, seemed to hear her. Melissa, with a flashing, astonished look at Luke, ran to her friend and took her in her arms. "Amalie! What happened? What has he done to you?"

Amalie shook her head. "No, no, *chérie*. Do not leap to such hasty conclusions! Mr. Devereaux has done nothing to harm me. *Au contraire*, he is my rescuer, my hero."

She spoke the last with wry amusement, and Melissa felt a touch of some emotion that she did not want to recognize as jealousy; however, she did have the grace to blush, and then, angry because she had, she said, "Well, seeing the company that Mr. Devereaux keeps, and then seeing him on board *that* boat next door, it was only natural that I would assume—"

"Now hush, little one, hush." Amalie placed her finger over Melissa's mouth.

Then they were all hovering over Amalie, shouting questions, and hurrying her inside, and Melissa, feeling gauche and chastised, trailed after them into the parlor.

Inside, Amalie introduced Luke Devereaux to Nehemiah and the Kings, while Martha bustled about brewing the coffee she had started to make earlier. Amalie, promising to return shortly and tell them the whole story, went to her cabin to wash and put on fresh clothing.

Melissa glanced up, found Luke staring at her, and quickly looked down at her hands in her lap. She could not remember when she had felt so ill at ease.

"Mighty glad that you brought Amalie back to us, Mr. Devereaux," Jubal said, lighting his pipe. "We was all pretty worried, I can tell you."

"That is true," said Nehemiah. "Mr. Devereaux, we owe you a debt of gratitude, indeed we do. When we put on our first show in Natchez, you will be welcome aboard, free of charge."

"Please, gentlemen, call me Luke. I'm not a formal man by nature." Luke looked puzzled. "But as to what you just said—may I call you Nehemiah?—concerning what you just said, I gather you're going to open some kind of a theater here in Natchez?"

Nehemiah Prendergast laughed, shaking his head. "Indeed not, not in Natchez proper, but on the *Natchez Belle!*" he trumpeted. "Sir, you are now sitting in the parlor of the showboat *extraordinaire*, which will shortly be performing up and down the length of the Mississippi, the Missouri, and all the tributaries. We are all but ready to take to the water, indeed we are!"

Luke shook his head as if to clear it, and glanced inquiringly at Jubal.

Jubal nodded, grinning. "Yep, the little feller's right. We're rarin' to go, and it was a terrible surprise when Amalie didn't show up this evenin'. Sure took the edge off our pleasure. But now everythin's all right again, thanks to you."

Luke looked about curiously. "Miss Dubois told me you had fixed the boat up, but I had no idea." He shook his head again. "Now that I take the time to notice, she does look like new!"

Jubal and Nehemiah both beamed proudly.

"Ain't she a wonder?" Jubal said. "And now that Amalie is back safe and sound, we can get her into the river, tomorrow some time."

At that moment Amalie returned, looking fresh though still pale and weary, and seated herself upon the settee next to Nehemiah.

"I feel much better," she said.

Martha, just coming in, smiled and put down the loaded tray. "And you'll feel even better when you get some of this hot coffee into you, along with a good slice of this saffron cake. I'll wager you missed your supper."

Amalie eagerly accepted the proffered cup and plate of cake.

Melissa, aching to hear the explanation of what had happened, felt awkward and tongue-tied. Everyone else was chatting and eating, and there she sat like a lump. What on earth was wrong with her?

"Now!" Martha said briskly, after Amalie had drunk her coffee and eaten most of the slice of cake. "Let me fill your cup again, and then you tell us what happened before we waste away like the cat from the curiosities. My land!"

Amalie put down the empty plate, and wiped her lips with her napkin. "It was strange, sudden, and very frightening. I was walking past that old empty building, the one on the far end at the bottom of the hill, and I was grabbed, blindfolded, and stuffed into a wooden box. I could not see, but I could feel that I was being carried on board a boat. When I was released, I found that it was the love boat next to the *Belle*."

Melissa gasped in shock. "Why did they take you there?"

"I'm not too sure," Amalie said. "A brute of a man called Bear Smith is the only one I spoke with. He said that the boat was leaving in the morning, and that I would be going with them."

"You would have been gone, and we wouldn't've known where you were!" Melissa said indignantly. "What kind of a person would want to do such a thing?"

"White slaver, that's what the scoundrel is!" Jubal was up and thumping back and forth. "This Bear Smith, he's known along the river as a mean'un. Sell his own mother for a gold piece, that he would!" The peg leg thumped angrily. "The filthy poncel Man like that's an insult to a decent woman!"

"Now Jubal," Martha scolded, "watch your language. There are ladies present."

"I do not believe that was the real purpose behind it," Amalie said. "Nothing so simple, I fear. I do not underestimate my own charms, you understand. But I am past the age considered suitable for such a profession. No, I believe that whoever was responsible wanted to get me away from here, and perhaps wanted to punish me as well."

Her eyes were thoughtful, and Melissa sensed that her friend knew more than she was telling. Annoyance filled her. If Amalie knew something they didn't, why couldn't she come right out and say it? After all, they were all friends, except for Luke Devereaux, and the others all seemed to be terribly taken with *him*, although she wasn't fooled for a moment. After all, what had *he* been doing on that boat?

"How did Mr. Devereaux know you were on the boat? I mean, how did he happen to be there to rescue you?" she asked bluntly, and was astonished to see Amalie blush.

"I . . . I was in a difficult situation," Amalie said slowly. "The owner of the boat, this Bear, was attacking me. I screamed, and thought no one would hear, or even care if they did. But Mr. Devereaux heard, and he cared. There was a fight. He subdued this Bear, and got me off the boat. I asked him to bring me here."

Amalie's chin was up, and her gaze was clear as she told her story, but Melissa realized that she was embarrassed to be relating such an experience in front of the men, and she was sorry now for her blunt question.

Martha broke the strained silence by leaning across to pat Amalie's knee. "Well, now it's all over, and all but forgotten. In the morning, hopefully, the love boat will be gone, and soon after we will leave, too. We are so grateful, Mr. Devereaux. I only wish there was something we could do to repay your kindness."

Luke hesitated only a moment as an idea popped into his mind. It was an impulse, but some of the best things in his life had come about through following just such impulses. He said, "Well, there might be a favor you could do for me."

"Well, my land! What is it? If it's at all possible, I know we'll try to do it."

"I agree," Nehemiah said. "What you have done for our dear Amalie cannot easily be repaid."

"Well, it just so happens that I am in need of transportation to New Orleans. Now, you say that you're about ready to put the *Belle* into the water, and if you

155

happen to be going downriver, then I would much appreciate passage with you kind people. I am willing to pay, of course."

Jubal struck his thigh with his open hand. "Now don't that beat all! New Orleans just happens to be where we're headed. We've got to find some playactors for our troupe, and Nehemiah here says there're lots of hungry performers in N'Orleans. Why, we'd be pleased as punch to have you aboard, wouldn't we? And as for payin' passage, we wouldn't hear of it. We ain't a passenger boat." His grin was prideful. "The Belle, she's a showboat!"

There was a chorus of agreement to which Melissa did not add her voice. She was experiencing a mixture of feelings, none of which was comfortable, and then Luke Devereaux turned directly to her, and with that funny, crooked smile, asked, "How about you, Miss Huntoon? Is it all right with you if I sail to New Orleans on the Belle? I understand that she is your boat, after all, and if I am not welcome . . ."

They all stared at her with varying expressions, but she was too flustered to read them. "Why, ah, of course. I mean, you did save Amalie . . ."

And then the others were all talking and laughing, and Melissa felt like a fool, and when she looked up, Luke was staring at her again with that half-smile, smoke curling up from his cigar.

It actually took three more days before the *Natchez Belle* was ready to put into the water.

A long row of logs set parallel to one another had to be put down, and then the *Belle* was pulled forward by ropes over the logs, which acted as rollers. The paddlewheel was removed during this maneuver.

It took a good crew of men to pull the heavy boat, and it was a nervous time for all of them. The Kings, Nehemiah, Amalie, and Melissa stood to one side, each in his own way appealing to both God and the forces of nature to be kind. Amalie had been prevailed upon to quit her job, so she would not have to walk alone up the hill.

It seemed that most of the denizens of Natchez-Under-the-Hill had turned out to watch the procedure, and there was a holiday atmosphere about the proceedings, despite the tension. Melissa knew that she would never forget the sight of the bare-chested men, sweating and straining in the hot Mississippi sunshine, towing the *Belle*, stately and rather dignified, as she slowly slid down the bank and at last splashed into the water.

When the blunt bow hit the water, Melissa held her breath. Would she remain afloat? The others must have done the same, for when the *Belle* stayed on top of the water, they let out a collective sigh.

And then came the shouting and the back-slapping, and the tears as well, but they were tears of happiness.

The *Belle* was tied off to trees on the bank, so that she would not drift, and then the huge paddlewheel was rolled down, and after much maneuvering was bolted back into place. Wood was lugged on board, and Jubal, the engineer, the boiler tenders, and the deck hands went on board, and the boilers were fired.

Soon, wisps of steam could be seen drifting from the tops of the tall twin stacks, and at first tentatively, and then with assurance, the great paddlewheel began to turn.

A cheer went up from those on the riverbank, and

for the first time Melissa felt a feeling akin to fondness for Natchez-Under-the-Hill.

The docking ropes were released, and the boat plowed out into the river, where it turned majestically about, and with a series of echoing, mournful toots on the whistle headed back into shore, bow first, the deck hands lowering the long stage plank, as if they had done it a thousand times before.

Melissa, Amalie, Martha, and Nehemiah hurried up the stage plank to the accompaniment of cheers from the onlookers. As Melissa proudly walked up the sturdy plank her gaze fell on the empty space that had been occupied by the love boat, and her thoughts turned to Luke Devereaux.

Immediately, some of her good feeling left her. He had asked to go with them, but they had not seen him since that night. Now they were ready to depart. Jubal had said they would embark early the next morning.

The thing that disturbed Melissa the most was the ambivalence of her own feelings. Part of the time she wanted Luke to make the trip with them, and part of the time, she did not. Every time she thought of him, she felt strange—nervous, apprehensive! What was wrong with her? Luke Devereaux was just another man!

By late that afternoon, when they were all sitting out on deck drinking after-dinner coffee and admiring the sunset, Melissa had just about concluded that he was not coming, and found herself unaccountably depressed. The rest of the group were very lively, in the best of spirits, and did not seem to notice Melissa's pensiveness.

And then, when they were just about ready to head

for their cabins and bed, they were hailed from the bank. There on the landing, a large bag at his feet, stood Luke Devereaux.

Jubal gave a shout of greeting, and the deck hands lowered the stage plank so that he could come on board.

All of a sudden, Melissa felt in much better spirits. She told herself that the appearance of Luke Devereaux had nothing to do with this, but in her heart she knew differently.

They had been on the river for two days and were now tied up along the bank to pass the night.

Since they had only one pilot, Jubal, they could only travel during the day. They wouldn't make as good time as if they had the normal supplement of pilots, yet as Jubal pointed out, they were not in any great hurry. "This is a trial run, so to speak. We have to take it slow and easy until we see how the old girl bears up."

Jubal had explained to Melissa, who was fascinated by the high wheelhouse, that normally a steamboat carried two or three pilots; they worked in shifts, keeping the boat running day and night. In addition, there was often a cub, or apprentice pilot, who was learning the art of river navigation.

The captain of a riverboat was the authority on everything that did not have to do with navigating the river. Some captains, like Jubal, were also pilots.

"Yep. Looks like I'm the whole kit and kaboodle on the *Belle*," said Jubal, laughing. "It would be a good idea, though, to find us another pilot. There'll be times when we may need to travel durin' the night, and times when, the Lord forbid, I might come up ailin'. Shouldn't be no trouble hirin' another one. There's plenty of good pilots beggin' for work these days. We'll see how she works out."

Martha, after the first day afloat, had already made one firm decision. She was going to hire a cook. She didn't mind cooking for what she called the immediate family, but with the engineer, the tenders, and the deck hands to feed, cooking took up all her time.

"My land, I'll never have time to work on costumes, or a minute to myself this way," she told Jubal. "When we get to New Orleans, we'll look for a good cook who can manage large groups."

And so the days passed quietly enough. The *Belle* was functioning well; no problems showed up in the boilers, or in the repairs to the hull.

Melissa was finding their passage downriver endlessly absorbing. The water was low and relatively calm, and the *Belle* slipped over it smoothly. Melissa loved the sound of the water going by, and the thunk-thunk of the huge paddlewheel as it dipped into the muddy water, sending dazzles of spray into the hot summer air.

The calliope still stood shrouded on the rear deck, for Jubal had suggested that they wait until they reached New Orleans before attempting to get it cleaned and serviced. Melissa longed to see it uncovered, bright and glittering with polish, gusts of steam escaping from the pipes, sending its raucous music across the water. But they would have to dock in New Orleans without the benefit of its clamorous announcement.

"It will be better," Martha told her, "to use it when we make the landing for our first performance. It will be special that way, something we'll never forget," and Melissa agreed reluctantly.

And now the *Belle* was nosed peacefully into the river bank after a long day's travel, supper was over, the dishes washed, and the family and crew were scattered over the ship attending to their various duties and personal chores.

Melissa was standing at the railing on the hurricane deck, looking out over the swiftly flowing river. By moonlight, the normally brown water had a silvery glint.

She recognized the fact that she was in a strange mood, and she could not tell whether she liked or disliked it. She felt both fragile and expectant, as if the moonlight had opened a door into a special, magic world where everyday rules did not apply.

She felt lonely, and yet happy to be alone. There was a certain pleasure in being alone with the night.

Leaning over, the better to see the water, Melissa thought of the day just passed. It had been fun, the most fun she had had since before the war.

The *Belle* rode the river like a queen, and Melissa had hardly been conscious of the movement of the boat. She had worked on her costumes, studied her role in *The Little Violet Seller*, which Nehemiah had decided would be their first play, and practiced her singing. It had been a busy, fruitful day, and she had scarcely even though of Luke Devereaux, although she had noticed that he seemed to be avoiding her.

Of course, that was fine with *her*. She still wasn't at all certain whether or not she approved of him. But it did seem strange.

Now, part of her pleasant melancholy seemed to have to do with the fact that although he was on the

161

Belle, she had not really seen him since the night they departed.

She sighed and raised her head as a night bird cried out along the river bank, the sound sad and evocative in the night air. Perhaps she would take a turn around the deck before retiring. She wasn't at all sleepy, however. This new life was so different from what she had known, each moment so exciting, that it seemed a shame to waste time sleeping.

Slowly, she started around the deck, keeping her gaze upon the almost hypnotic flow of water rippling in the moonlight, rather than on where she was going, confident that she was the only person on the hurricane deck.

And then she discovered that she was not. She collided with a dark figure, careened to one side, and would have fallen into the river but for the high rail.

"What in the Sam Hill! Oh, forgive me, Miss Huntoon. I didn't know it was you."

Melissa's heart began to pound. It was him. It was Luke Devereaux, and she had run straight into him, like some daft child, not looking where she was going.

"Oh, I'm sorry, Mr. Devereaux," she said breathlessly. "It was my fault. I was looking at the river."

"Well, no harm done, I reckon."

His cigar glowed, and she could just see his face in the faint light. Despite his words, he looked angry and not at all pleased to see her.

"Well, if you will pardon me," she said somewhat stiffly, "I will continue my walk."

She began to move ahead, but his voice stopped her. "May I accompany you?"

Her throat was dry, and she felt terribly young. "Of

course, if you would like. It's pleasant, isn't it, watching the river at night?"

There, that sounded right. She desperately wished to appear cool and poised. She would *die* if he knew how upset and confused she really was.

"Yes. But then to me the river is always beautiful."

Struck by the sensitivity of his remark, she looked up at his face. He *was* very handsome, and his annoyed expression seemed to have abated somewhat.

Encouraged, she tried to keep the conversation going. "I am sorry if I seemed ungrateful when you brought Amalie safely home the other night. It was just that I had been so worried, and . . ."

"No apology necessary, Miss Huntoon. Your feelings were entirely understandable." He was smiling down at her. "I am only happy that I was able to be of some service."

"If I may ask, what is it that you will be doing in New Orleans?"

"Of course you may ask. I'm going there on business. I'm going outside of New Orleans, to be strictly accurate. I am going to manage a plantation for a time, trying to get it into working order. As a sort of troubleshooter, I suppose."

Melissa felt almost calm now. The conversation, now going along easily, was like a life raft—something she could cling to so that she could float along smoothly, on top of things, ignoring the strange riot of emotions that she felt underneath. All she need do was to keep the conversation going, and everything would be fine. It was as simple as that. She almost felt relaxed.

"Do you know New Orleans, Mr. Devereaux? Have you been there before?"

"Yes, several times. Is this your first time?"

She bobbed her head. "Yes, and I'm really looking forward to it. I hesitate to admit this, but Natchez is the only town of any size I've ever seen. First, I was too young, and then the war . . ."

"There's no need to apologize. It's understandable. The war took a big chunk out of all our lives. With you, well, it robbed you of your growing-up years, the pleasures of dances and beaux, of going to cities like New Orleans for shopping and such."

Melissa felt a sudden warm surge of feeling. How understanding he was! She had never thought she would meet a man like this, a man who could see into the secret places of a woman's mind so well.

"You'll like New Orleans, I can safely promise you that," he was saying. "It's a city like no other on earth, and—"

His words were cut off abruptly as Melissa fell against him.

Chapter Ten

Melissa's foot had struck a coil of rope that one of the deck hands had left in the way, and feeling the sharp pain and that awful feeling of helplessness that presages a fall, she reached out blindly for the nearest stable object—Luke.

Luke, reacting instinctively, turned and grasped her in his arms. Melissa, startled by her near fall, found herself held gently but firmly in his arms, her body tight against his, her face only a fraction of an inch from his face, her lips only . . .

Such a warm riot of feeling boiled through her that she felt as if she were temporarily bereft of her senses. She had never swooned in her life, and thought it an affectation; but now she felt that she might do so at any moment. Her knees felt weak, her heart was palpitating, she was at once removed from and aware of everything about the situation and conscious of every place their bodies touched.

Part of the feeling was fear, but it was fear of herself rather than him. *My God!* she thought. *Was this*

*what falling in love meant? If it was, how could peo-
ple stand it? It was so deliciously, excitingly terrible!*

And then she heard Luke groan—a sound of anguish, not of pleasure, and as she registered this, their
lips were no longer a fraction of an inch apart, but
were touching; and the warmth and the sweetness and
the thrill that coursed through her body were beyond
her experience.

Dimly, Melissa perceived that she should tear herself away. She knew that she was allowing him an unprecedented intimacy, yet she could not move.

Slowly, gently, his lips parted hers, as his hands
pressed her ever closer, closer, until their two bodies
felt as one. The hot sweetness of forbidden pleasure
washed over Melissa, leaving her without will. She
was conscious of the pressure of her breasts against
his chest, and they ached to be even closer. Her skirts
were too thick to feel the contact of their lower bodies, but the very knowledge that those two parts of
their anatomy touched, even through layers of cloth,
was fantastically exciting, and set her senses aflame.

Luke groaned again, as if he were in pain, and his
right hand, which had been pressing against her back,
moved around her side and then cupped her breast.

Melissa, awash in the tumult of her own feelings,
suddenly released from long repression, was lost.

She made no objection as he pulled her into the
shadow of the stairway, and made no outcry as he unbuttoned her bodice and stroked her breasts until
they tingled and throbbed. Her only thought, her only
desire, was that he not stop. That he never stop, that
he keep on doing this forever.

The throbbing of her breasts was echoed by an

even more urgent pulsing in the center of her being. She wanted him to touch her there, to ease the hungry feeling that was growing in her. She was so far gone in passion that this thought did not even shock her.

She could hear his breathing; he was panting as if he had been running, and the fierceness of his ardor was catching. Melissa made no protest as he led her to the stairs, and up to the Texas deck. She did not even worry that her bodice was unbuttoned, that someone might see her; she simply followed him blindly.

He guided her to what was evidently his cabin—they were already inside before her dazed senses registered this fact. And then they were lying down, their bodies touching from head to toe, and his mouth was again upon hers, forcing her lips open. His tongue, so hot and alien inside her mouth, was touching her tongue, and at the contact, a terrible need rose in her, greater than that which she had felt before.

Melissa writhed and moaned under his stroking hands. Quickly, not taking his mouth from hers, Luke unfastened the clasp of her skirt, and then, pulling away from her briefly, tugged the garments down over her legs and feet.

As he moved away again, Melissa experienced the most dreadful emptiness, and an embarrassing need. She wanted him close again. She wanted . . .

And then he was close again, as close as her own skin, as they lay body to body with nothing between them.

Her breasts were tight against the warmth of his muscular chest, and between her thighs she felt the hard maleness, a delicious pressing. Oh, dear God!

Now he was moving over her, separating her thighs,

and she had no thought of resisting. He touched her gently, tentatively, in the center of her passion, and her body spasmed.

The next feeling she was aware of was pain, sharp and quick, that made her try to draw back, but she could not really move, since his weight had her pinned down, and then he was inside her. For a brief moment, a panicky reality threatened to invade the sensual haze in which she was floating, but as Luke began to move inside her, a blinding pleasure blotted out the memory of the hurt, and her own body began to move in unison with his. She could hear their mutual sighs and gasps, as they strained together toward something . . . something she knew she wanted but could not have put a name to.

Faster and faster their bodies moved, Melissa's moving in counterpoint to his, lifting so that he penetrated her deeply, so that the pressure of his thrusts increased the intensity of her rapture. Melissa heard herself cry out with the effort of reaching, reaching for—

Like an explosion, her body contracted and spasmed in a sunburst of ecstasy that was almost painful. As she moaned in the grip of this terrifying yet wonderful seizure of feeling, she felt his pace accelerate, and then he too was crying aloud his ecstasy. As her own wave subsided, Luke's body still shuddered and contracted upon her.

Now Melissa felt very tired, very relaxed, and very satisfied, as if she had been scoured clean of all other emotions. She felt a great swell of tenderness for this man who had brought her so much pleasure.

So this was making love! So this was the thing that happened between men and women. No wonder they kept it shrouded in secrecy! No wonder society frowned on it without the sanctions of marriage. Otherwise, why, everyone would be doing it all the time. No work would be done. No houses would be cleaned. It was the most glorious pleasure she had ever known.

Melissa smiled to herself, amused by her thoughts, yet sensing that she had just stepped over the threshold into a new world.

She reached up and looped her arms around Luke's neck, to hold him to her; but as she did so, he rolled to one side, to lie beside her, face up. She turned toward him, wanting to tell him how much she loved him; but his expression was set in bleak lines, showing no trace of the happiness she felt.

"Luke?" she said shyly.

He would not meet her eyes. "I'm sorry," he said unevenly. "I'm really sorry, Melissa."

She looked at him in astonishment. He had wanted it to happen, she knew; he had experienced pleasure, she could tell. So why was he now telling her that he was sorry?

"I don't understand. Sorry for what?" she said finally. "It was one of the most glorious experiences of my life!" She swallowed. "I felt . . . I felt as if this was what I had been waiting for my whole life! Now, are you trying to tell me you're sorry it happened?"

He turned his face to hers and stared deep into the dark blue of her eyes. His face reflected misery. "Melissa . . . tell me. What do you expect of me now? What do you want of me?"

Melissa was taken aback. Why was he acting like this? "I . . . I suppose I . . . I don't know! I don't know what you're talking about!" Yet, in her heart she knew very well what she wanted of him—she wanted this pleasure every night. She wanted to be with him, to touch him and hold him. She wanted to marry him.

"I'll tell you what you want, what you expect!" he said explosively. "You expect the same thing every good woman wants. Marriage!" He groaned. "I didn't want this to happen. God, how I tried to keep it from happening!"

Melissa felt a terrible cold creeping over her at the implication of his words. "I still don't understand!"

Abruptly, Luke sat up and put his head into his hands. Melissa, pulling the sheet around her, sat up also, and stared at him through the tears gathering in her eyes.

"Of course you don't understand," he said in a low voice. "The way they bring you up, how could you?" He turned then, facing her, and took her hands. "Melissa, you are an intelligent girl, so I am going to be candid with you. I'm simply not the marrying kind. I doubt that I ever will be."

Melissa shook her head sharply. "But you . . . you liked me. You liked making . . . You liked being with me. I know you did!"

He sighed. "Of course I did. It was wonderful. I loved every minute of it. I've wanted to make love to you from the instant I saw you standing there so proud and independent on the veranda of your dadday's plantation. The thing you don't understand, Melissa, is that with men . . . Well, to put it bluntly, to a man, making love to a woman does not always mean that he wants to marry her. Do you understand at all what I'm trying to say?"

Melissa tried to hold back the tears that threatened to overwhelm her, but they flowed out despite her efforts: two clear cascades of salty water down the soft skin of her cheeks.

Luke went on doggedly, "Melissa, I could have told you lies. I could lie to you now. I could have made all kinds of promises, and then when we get to New Orleans, I could simply walk away, and you would never see me again.

"I haven't been dishonest with you. You must realize that much. There were no promises given or received!"

Melissa swallowed, and blinked against her tears. He was right. He had logic on his side, and she was honest enough with herself to admit that. She had made no protest when he had first taken her into his arms, first kissed her. On the contrary, she had urged him on by her very submissiveness. The fault was hers as well as his. He had promised nothing. It was just that she thought that a gentleman always married a lady if . . . if such a thing happened between them. It was part of what she thought of as the code of honor of a Southern gentleman.

Clearly she had been mistaken! That wasn't the way it was in the outside world. Of course, Luke was a Texan; maybe they had a different code.

All that she was sure of was that she felt a sense of terrible loss and betrayal. It was too cruel to find love, and then lose it, all in one brief night.

She bowed her head and then raised it defiantly, as she gathered her pride. If he didn't want her, she certainly would not beg.

She choked back a harsh laugh, remembering her thoughts of a moment ago. If tonight marked a step over the threshold into maturity, it would appear that it was too soon—she wasn't prepared for the brutal

171

realities of the adult world. Maybe she could step back . . .

Melissa realized, without knowing how she knew, that it was too late for that.

"It's all right," she said stiffly. "I'll be all right." Holding the sheet close to her body, she snatched up her clothing and began to dress.

When she was presentable, she fled the cabin, not looking at Luke, not wanting to see the sympathy and sorrow in his eyes—if he felt those emotions. All that had been so wonderful before, all that they had done, now seemed somehow furtive and shameful.

Quietly, clinging to the shadows, she hurried to the cabin that she shared with Amalie. Once inside, she undressed and crept into bed, moving quietly so she would not wake Amalie.

But Amalie was awake, her eyes wide in the darkness. There was a sorrowing smile on her lips. She knew Melissa too well. She had no need of words to sense the girl's unhappiness. Something had happened to wound her, and Amalie had the intuitive feeling that this was one time when she would be unable to comfort her in any way.

New Orleans, born of a swamp, nourished by the mighty river, was the acknowledged queen of the river cities, and the gateway between the Mississippi Valley and the outside world. The little group aboard the *Natchez Belle* all looked at the city through different eyes, shaded by different experiences, but all of them saw one thing in common: it was an exciting town, colorful, exotic, mysterious, and rich in history. Even Melissa, hugging her anger and hurt to her like a hair shirt, was stirred.

Natchez was the largest city she had seen, prior to this, and she was overwhelmed by the crowds and the activity of New Orleans. It seemed to her that the populace never slept. There were people on the streets at any hour of the day or night.

Since the night she had spent in Luke's arms, she had existed in a strange sort of vacuum, pulled in tight around the center of herself, like an egg. Hiding her emotional wounds as if they were physical hurts that needed time to heal.

She had avoided Luke Devereaux during the rest of the trip. The only times she had seen him had been at the communal table, and there she had laughed and chatted with the others, avoiding his eyes, eating little or nothing, but hoping that her frantic chatter and appearance of good cheer would keep anyone from noticing. She was confident that she had succeeded, except perhaps with Amalie. A time or two she had caught Amalie gazing at her with a look of compassion, yet the older woman said nothing.

And now they had landed at New Orleans, and Luke had left the *Belle* with his black bag, and as far as Melissa knew, without a backward glance. She had made a point of being in her cabin when he departed.

So now it was over. She thought resolutely, *That's the end of it; I'll forget him.*

But the brave thoughts did little to ease the terrible ache she felt inside. He had stirred something in her, awakened something, and had then gone on his carefree way. It was difficult for her to realize that for Luke the experience had not been the same as it had for her. They had experienced great rapture together, but clearly he had no wish to do so again, and he did not want to be with her always, as she wanted to be with him. Men were so strange. However was one to understand them?

She must go on as before. She must not let the others know what had happened. Melissa knew that she could not abide the embarrassment if they should learn that she had given herself to a man, and then had been rejected.

There was another worry, too. Her monthly was due in a few days, and she prayed every night that it should arrive on schedule. During that sweet madness that possessed her while in Luke's arms, she had given no thought to the possible result of her folly.

Now, all of the frightening warnings and tales came back to haunt her. What if she should be with child? It was a horrifying thought. What would she do? How could she face the others? How could she face the shame?

She would have to run away and hide from them, she decided, if it happened. It would be the only thing she could do.

And so, in a mood of anger, guilt, and fear, Melissa gazed out upon the town she had been so eager to visit, seeing the excitement and activity, but taking no pleasure from it.

Luke Devereaux, riding in the back seat of a hired carriage, sat slumped with his chin on his chest.

He had never felt so low, so dissatisfied and angry with himself. Why hadn't he stayed away from Melissa, as he had sworn to himself to do?

True, it was she who had literally bumped into him on the deck, but it was he who asked if he might walk with her, and it was he, when she had tripped and fallen into his arms, who had kissed her.

174

He swore. Good Christ! He was an old hand at this sort of thing, he certainly knew what women to stay away from; and the "good" women, the quality women raised and trained to be wives and mothers, raised to expect marriage from a man if he so much as kissed their cheek—these were the ones to stay away from. The ones he always *had* steered clear of.

But he hadn't this time. By God, it had started out as an innocent stroll around the deck. Who would have thought that it would lead to . . .

He turned his face and stared unseeingly at the colorful French Quarter they were passing through, thinking of Melissa so soft and warm in his arms. Damnit! He had to stop this, or he would drive himself crazy. What was done was done, and there was no rolling time back. But he wasn't ready for marriage, he did not want marriage, and he was not going to pay that price for one mistake.

The only thing he could do now was to take himself as far away from her as possible, so that she could forget him and he could forget her. She was young, she was beautiful, and God knows there would be plenty of other men courting her.

At this thought the cold hand of jealousy squeezed his vitals. Angrily, he struck his knee with a fist. What was he, some kind of a dog in the manger, who didn't want her himself but didn't want anyone else to have her either? By God, he had thought he was a better man than that!

Of course, he *did* want her, that was the crux of it; he just didn't want to marry her.

Well, at Riverview he should find enough to keep him busy so that his mind wouldn't dwell on Melissa. From what Simon Crouse had told him, it would be a difficult task; and right now he welcomed that thought.

"I wish you good luck and success and much happiness, Melissa Huntoon," he said aloud, "wherever you may go, and whatever you may do."

Nehemiah chanted, "*One* two three, *one* two three. No! No, my boy! Keep in step. Lift up your knee!"

Melissa, watching from the corner near the piano, had to put her hand over her mouth to stifle her laughter. The poor young man up there on the stage was ludicrous in his too-short trousers and jacket, and his tall, ungainly body going through the steps of the dance looked much like that of a stork parading before its mate.

Nehemiah motioned curtly. "That's fine. That's enough, young man. Thank you."

Melissa sighed as the young man gangled ungracefully down from the stage, his face set in a look of disappointment. She felt sorry for him; indeed, for all of the ones that Nehemiah had sent away.

For two days now, they had been auditioning performers, and the number who had replied to the flyers Jubal had put up all over New Orleans was phenomenal.

Nehemiah had been right. There were a great many out-of-work show people in New Orleans, and in addition to the professionals, they had attracted every young person who longed for a career in the theater.

Some of the latter category, like the young man just leaving the stage, had little or no experience, and it was painful watching them attempt to perform; but then there *were* the professionals, thank God, the performers who had talent and experience; and Melissa had learned a great deal just watching them audition. The sad thing was that they could use so few of them.

From the ranks of the professionals, Nehemiah had chosen a handsome, mature woman, with heavy dark hair, and a narrow, sensitive face. She sang and danced well, and was an accomplished character actress. She was also no taller than Nehemiah, and would be able to play opposite him without looking ridiculous. Her name was Mary McGee, but she used the stage name of Linnea Longfield.

Melissa, who had thought that Amalie could play opposite Nehemiah, had mentioned this hope to him. She felt a hot flush stain her cheeks now as she recalled the incident and his reaction.

A rather strange look had passed over Nehemiah's face at her question, and he had looked away, clearing his throat. Melissa had always found the little man to be honest and forthright, and she was puzzled. He obviously was embarrassed. At that moment, Amalie came in, and Nehemiah grew more ill-at-ease.

Impatiently, Melissa repeated her question, looking first to Nehemiah and then to Amalie for an answer.

Amalie smiled sadly. "It is impossible, *chérie*."

"But why is it impossible?" Melissa demanded. "You can sing, you can dance, and you're much more beautiful than Mary McGee. Why can't you play the parts?"

Amalie shook her head. "It is a matter of color, Melissa. It is not allowed for a person of color to perform with a white troupe. The townspeople would not come to see such a performance."

Melissa's mouth fell open in shock. "Whyever not? That is the most ridiculous thing I have ever heard of!"

177

Amalie said chidingly, "Come now, little one. Do not be naive. You know how it is, how it has always been. You know how most people in the South feel about persons of color."

"But that's unfair! What does it really matter?"

Amalie shrugged. "It may not matter to us, to you and to me, and to Nehemiah and the Kings, yet it matters a great deal to a great many people, and I am afraid that there is nothing we can do to change it."

"But the war?" Melissa said.

Amalie's smile was wry. "The war freed the slaves, *chérie*, but it has not yet made us acceptable, or equal to the whites."

Melissa had looked to Nehemiah for confirmation, and had found it in his eyes.

Melissa still found the idea that Amalie would not be acceptable to audiences hard to believe; but since there was obviously little she could do, she had tried to resign herself to it.

In addition to Mary McGee, Nehemiah had hired a piano player, a stocky man of medium height, with flaming red hair and a face peppered with freckles. He had merry blue eyes, a clown's mouth, and supple fingers that moved over the keyboard as if they had a life of their own.

His name was Charles Mallard, but he preferred being called Chuck. He was an excellent pianist, and could play anything from the classics to the latest popular tunes; but what was almost as important, he could play the calliope, which was now being repaired by an expert in New Orleans.

"A calliope," Nehemiah had explained to Melissa, "is an odd instrument, and although it has a keyboard similar to that of a piano, the touch is so different, many pianists cannot manage it at all. It takes considerable strength of the hand and fingers to play a calliope, indeed it does!"

Nehemiah's voice jolted Melissa out of her reverie. "All right, next please!"

She turned her attention to the stage as the next performers, a husband and wife team, came forward.

They approached the stage with easy assurance, a youngish couple, probably in their thirties: he was tall and well set up, with a slender, dancer's body; and she was almost as tall, a good-sized woman, with a tiny waist and a shapely ankle, which showed beneath the hem of her costume.

They were attired in complementary outfits which were evidently meant to represent German folk dress. She had long yellow braids hanging to her shoulders, and wore a very full blue skirt over many petticoats, a tight black bodice that laced up to emphasize her tiny waist, and a full-sleeved white blouse. The man had on short leather trousers that came to his knees to be met by long stockings, a white shirt, black vest, a string tie, and a funny little round leather hat with a feather in it.

They introduced themselves as the LaSalles, and the man reached over and handed the piano player their music.

Chuck played a few introductory bars, and then the two appeared from the wings, the woman in front, the man close behind her, their arms spread out, smiles upon their faces, their feet moving, heel and toe in time to the music.

They sang:

179

"Vill yu be mine little struddle?
Ya, I'll be your little struddle.
Vill you be mine kugel noodle?
Ya, I'll be yur kugel noodle."

Their movements, which accompanied the song, were funny—awkward, like the movements of dolls, or marionettes—and Melissa found herself smiling and tapping her foot to the contagious beat of the nonsense song.

When the couple had finished, Nehemiah called them over, and talked with them in low tones for several minutes.

Melissa wished that she could hear what they were saying. She hoped that Nehemiah would employ them. They were very talented, and, she felt, would add something bright and amusing to the troupe.

She noted with relief that Nehemiah did not send them away, but had them wait to one side while he continued with the auditions.

Only one more person remained to be cast—the hero, who would play opposite Melissa. He had to be tall, attractive, able to sing and dance, and capable of performing other roles when necessary.

So far, the applicants for this role had been a sorry lot. There had been dozens of young women applying, but relatively few young men capable of playing a lead. They were either too short, too fat, not handsome enough, had high voices, and/or little or no talent.

It was beginning to look hopeless, and Melissa had about resigned herself to the fact that they would have to settle for a third-rate leading man, when *he* arrived.

He was of medium height, sufficiently taller than Melissa so that he would look well with her, but not so tall that he would dwarf Nehemiah. He was handsome—fair, with heavy, wavy blond hair, a bit on the long side, and a fine, full moustache. His shoulders were good, and his body well-proportioned. When he got up on stage to sing, Melissa could see the expression of hope on Nehemiah's face. If this young man was at all good, he could be just what they were looking for.

The newcomer spoke a few words to Chuck at the piano, giving him the name of his song, "Flower Queen," and his voice was deep and resonant.

Melissa sighed. It was one of her favorite songs, quite new, and very popular.

Chuck started the accompaniment, and then the young man began to sing:

> "Tender as the violet,
> That shelters 'neath the tree,
> Sweeter than the rose's scent,
> Which beckons forth the bee,
> Lovelier than the lily,
> In her nest of softest green,
> Are you, my dearest sweetheart,
> My lovely flower queen."

Melissa drew in her breath and then held it, afraid to let it out. He had a really fine voice, full and rich, and an excellent presence on stage.

When he finished the song, Nehemiah motioned him impatiently forward. As with the LaSalles, their conversation took several minutes.

Then Nehemiah turned to those performers still

waiting, and told them they could go. "The auditions are closed, but we wish to thank you all very much for coming."

Melissa, not wishing to see the disappointment on their faces, turned toward the three just hired.

The young man, whose name she did not yet know, met her gaze squarely. Melissa felt the impact of his personality as their glances met. She shivered slightly. He *was* very attractive, but after her experience with Luke Devereaux, she certainly did not want to get involved with another man.

Thinking of Luke Devereaux made her feel depressed, as usual, even though one worry had been relieved. Yesterday, her monthly had arrived, putting to rest her greatest fear, but she still experienced a feeling of loss and betrayal.

Perhaps it wasn't logical, under the circumstances, but she could not forget that night: the feeling of Luke's body next to hers, the touch of his hands upon her skin, and the wild, hot sweetness that his kisses aroused in her. As always, when her thoughts took this turn, a longing would build in her to experience it again. Her nipples would become sensitive against the material of her dress, and the once-inviolate sanctuary of her womanhood would tingle and hunger for a touch that never came. This physical arousal embarrassed and shamed her, and yet it was becoming a secret, painful delight.

Now, turning away from the attractive young actor, a blush heated her face, as she wondered how *he* would make love. How *he* would touch her. Oh, she was shameless! She didn't really want that! She did not want to find that wonderful closeness again, and then find out that it was only spurious, a one-time thing.

Also, her pride still smarted from Luke's accusation that she wanted only what all good women wanted—marriage. Of course she hoped for marriage. All women did; but Luke had acted as if she had tried to trap him, trick him into marriage with her body. He had acted as if a woman's perfectly reasonable desire to have a husband and home was somehow suspect, and it had confused and upset her.

No, she was not going to get involved again romantically, not until she had sorted things out to her own satisfaction.

Nehemiah's voice roused Melissa from her introspection. "Melissa? My dear, come up here, will you? I would like you to meet the new members of our little troupe."

As she went toward the stage, she could hear him explaining that they hoped to be ready to depart in approximately a week's time, and that that time would be spent in rehearsing the plays and fitting costumes.

When Melissa reached the stage, the young actor reached a hand down to help her up. His hand was strong and warm, and she decided to ignore the fact that he held her hand longer than was necessary once she was upon the stage.

"Melissa," Nehemiah said, "this is Beau Vermillian, who will be performing opposite you. Our stalwart hero, yes, indeed! And this handsome couple are Mr. and Mrs. LaSalle. This is Melissa Huntoon, owner of our floating theater, and our ingenue lead."

Melissa did not really hear the rest of his words. Close to Beau now, she could see that he was even

183

nicer looking, and he did not seem to have the conceited and arrogant manner common to many handsome men. He was a few years older than she, Melissa judged, but evidently far more worldly than his years, for he bowed over her hand with considerable aplomb, and looked into her eyes with a smile that was self-satisfied but not cocky. Despite her resolve not to be attracted, she felt herself drawn to him, and it would have been rude not to return his smile.

Again, he held her hand longer than was necessary, but Melissa was lost in his intense green eyes, as if mesmerized, and she felt herself even swaying toward him.

With a start she snatched her hand from his, and turned to welcome the LaSalles to their troupe, but she could still feel the tingling sensation in the hand that he had held so long.

Chapter Eleven

When Beau Vermillian saw the line of performers waiting to be auditioned, his spirits plummeted. The flyer had stated that Nehemiah Prendergast, well-known actor and director, was auditioning talent for the showboat *Natchez Belle*, and that the auditions would be held starting Monday, and would continue until a full troupe had been assembled.

Beau had not seen the flyer until today, and it was now late Tuesday afternoon. He rushed down to the docks the instant he saw the flyer. Fortunately, he was decently dressed, since he had been on his way to a social event when he saw the flyer. He could only hope that the pianist would know at least one of his songs.

The *Natchez Belle* proved to be a medium-sized sternwheeler, new-looking, and shining with white paint. His heart beating rapidly, Beau hurried on board and to the grand saloon. This could be the answer to his dream, a dream he had held ever since he could remember.

Beau had never performed on a showboat. His limited experience had been in local theaters in small parts; always he had received good notices and much encouragement, but little real chance to advance himself. The theaters of New Orleans were pretty much dominated by older, well-established actors, who were not anxious to have younger performers in the cast who might overshadow them. Also, the town was full of talent, with too few places, and too little opportunity, to perform. Some ended up performing on street corners down on Bourbon Street, or in Jackson Square, something which Beau had not yet brought himself to do; although in time, if he got any hungrier, he might be driven to it.

Beau was twenty-two years old, and for at least ten of those years he had wanted to be on stage. The war years he remembered only as a bad dream; the pain of losing both his older brothers in battle; the sorrow of seeing his mother, unaccustomed to the hardships and privations the war caused, waste away and die; watching his father, escaping the war because of age and illness, become a broken man when his older sons died and his small plantation was taken away.

Beau, too young to fight, watched it all, and decided that the real world was a terrible place. He took refuge in daydreams and fantasies, and from there it seemed that it was only a step or two to the life of an actor.

His father, who once would have protested such a path for his son, was too tired and broken to care. There was little money to be made anywhere, so what did it matter what the boy did?

And so Beau had gone to New Orleans, and there he managed to find odd jobs to keep body and soul together while he stormed the bastions of the theater. It was difficult, but his good looks and fine figure earned him a few small roles, and despite his lack of experience, he had a natural aptitude for the career he had chosen and a quick and retentive mind that helped him to learn his lines. But now, after two years in the city, he seemed to be stuck forever at this same level. The flyer from the *Natchez Belle* was a godsend!

However, as he waited his turn in the grand saloon and saw the line of hungry actors and actresses grow, his good feeling deserted him. There were so many of them! Some he recognized and knew were good. But he decided that as long as he was here, he might as well take his turn.

Resignedly, he waited among the other hopefuls, and watched as one performer after another displayed his talents on the stage.

As the auditions dragged on, Beau's confidence returned. Most of the hopefuls were pretty bad. He began to relax and look around, observing his surroundings more closely.

Nehemiah Prendergast, the director, seemed to know what he was doing. He was a small man, but he had a large presence, a quality which Beau had learned to recognize. He had a marvelous voice for such a small man, and a strong, confident manner.

Beau nodded to himself. Confidence. That was the key. You had to seem to be sure of yourself, in control at all times, even if you were not.

His attention was captured by someone else—a girl. She was sitting in the fourth row of seats, and didn't appear to be involved in the auditions, unless she had already been chosen. It was difficult to see her from where he stood, yet Beau had the feeling that she was beautiful. Her hair was, at any rate, and when she moved her hands or head, her gestures were graceful. He wondered who she was.

The auditions continued. The only person Nehemiah Prendergast had selected since Beau's arrival was a piano player, a stocky young redhead who, Beau had to admit, was very good.

Now that the line was shorter, Beau managed to get a closer look at the girl in the fourth row. She *was* beautiful, more beautiful than he had dreamed, and she had a lovely figure; even sitting down that was obvious. Was she Prendergast's daughter, or a member of the troupe?

There was a couple on stage now, very talented, a husband and wife team, doing a specialty dance, a catchy German comedy routine. Prendergast huddled with them when they were finished, and Beau took this to mean that they were being considered.

There were only a few performers ahead of him now, and he straightened his vest and smoothed back his hair. God, he hoped that the piano player knew some of his music! He was feeling a bit more encouraged now. There had been comparatively few young male performers who could possibly have played leading men—the position that Beau was hoping for. Most of them had been wrong for that kind of thing, and Beau, since he knew without undue vanity that he was good-looking and that he could sing well and dance passably, began to have real hope.

And then it was his turn.

He leaned over to the pianist, and said in a low voice, "Do you know 'Flower Queen?'"

The redhead nodded, and without a word began the opening bars of the song.

Beau took a deep breath, smiled down at Nehemiah and the pretty girl in the fourth row, and began to sing.

When he was done, there was applause from the director, the pretty girl, and his fellow thespians. Beau felt good. He thought he had sung well, but he knew that meant little unless Nehemiah Prendergast liked his style.

He gazed down at the little man, who was striding toward him. Beau's heart was hammering furiously, but he tried to appear nonchalant and unconcerned.

Prendergast crossed the stage, seized his hand and pumped it vigorously. "I think you might just do, young man, indeed you may! What is your experience?"

Quickly, and as calmly as possible, Beau told him his credits, building his experience up somewhat, but not too much.

The little man nodded. "Well, you *are* a bit short on experience, young man. However, I sense possibilities in you, and you are a good physical type to act opposite our ingenue, Melissa Huntoon."

With this, Prendergast motioned to the young woman in the seats, and Beau felt his heart leap. This was much more than he could have hoped for.

The speciality couple came out of the wings, and Prendergast began telling them what they could expect; that at first they would be working for their room and board only, but as money came in, they would be paid a share of the profits. He went on to explain that they were going to remain a small troupe for various reasons, and that they would all be ex-

189

pected to perform in whatever capacity and in whatever parts were necessary.

Before this speech was concluded, the young lady approached the stage apron, and Beau hastened to be the first to offer her a hand up onto the stage.

Close up, she was even more stunning, with almost translucent skin and eyes of a dark and unusual blue. The touch of her hand was like an electric current to Beau, and in that moment, Beau Vermillian fell in love with Melissa Huntoon.

While Nehemiah was busy auditioning performers, Jubal King was also interviewing prospective employees. He was looking for two more deckhands, and at least one additional pilot. The deckhands were no problem, since the docks swarmed with men seeking work, but the pilot was another matter.

Although there were a number of qualified pilots around, few were eager to accept employment where the only wages they could expect had to come from anticipated profits. There were some willing to take the risk, but a good many of these had some sort of personal problem, such as a fondness for the bottle, that made them less than desirable to Jubal's eyes.

And then, just when he had begun to despair, Mollie Boom came to see him.

Looking more tattered and battered than ever, her face set in a fierce scowl, she trundled in one morning just as Jubal was turning down yet another applicant—a tall, thin man, who had wrecked his last three boats because of his drinking problem.

"Mollie!" Jubal bellowed. "What on earth are you doin' in N'Orleans? You're a sight for these old eyes, that you are!"

Mollie grinned, a sight almost as frightening as her frown, and clasped Jubal's hand in hers, giving it a hearty shake.

Jubal said, "Whyn't you tell me you'd be here?"

Mollie scowled again. "'Cause I durned well didn't know I was. I lost the *Sprite* just outside of Memphis. The water's getting so low that I had to take a new channel, and a bunch of drowned trees hung me up, then tore the bottom right out of the *Sprite*. She went down in less than ten minutes. Didn't even have time to save the cargo."

"Oh, Mollie!" Jubal's voice rang with sincerity. He knew well how it was to lose a boat to the river, that constant loved one and enemy. "What you goin' to do now?"

She said mournfully, "I don't know. What can I do? I ain't got the money to build another boat, and all I know is piloting. What with the way money is, and the trade slowing down, and them dad-blamed railroads stealing away our business, I just been staying afloat, so to speak. I came to you 'cause I saw your notice about needing a pilot. The plain truth of it is, Jubal, that this ain't no social call. I'm looking for work, and you're about my last hope."

Jubal's mouth dropped open. "You, Mollie? *You* want to work on the *Belle?*"

She glared. "Well, you don't need to go acting like that's some kind of a seventh wonder of the world! Hell, I'm a good pilot, and you know it, and you need a pilot. Seems clear-cut to me."

Jubal closed his mouth, his mind working at top speed. Why not? As Mollie said, she was a good pilot, one of the best. "Would you be willing to work for shares and room and board? That's the way we're goin' to have to do her for a bit."

She nodded. "Ain't got much choice, the way I see it. Not many want to hire a lady pilot, not that I'm laying claim to being a lady." Suddenly she grinned. "Besides, I'd be with friends. That's got to be worth something."

"Sure is," Jubal said heartily as he shook her hand. "Welcome to the *Belle*, Mollie!"

Well, now their crew was complete. As soon as Nehemiah got his troupe together, they could get out on the river and start earning back Melissa's investment.

The night was very humid. Perspiration ran down Simon Crouse's forehead and dripped into his eyes, making them burn.

Jake, in front of him, tripped over something and set up a great crashing, accompanied by guttural curses that sounded unnaturally loud in the steaming darkness.

"Be quiet, you clumsy idiot!" Crouse hissed.

They were a mile or so out of Natchez, in a section that was inhabited entirely by black people; and it was not the kind of area in which a white man would be well received, most particularly not at night.

The name of the obeah woman and the location of her shack were written on a slip of paper in Crouse's pocket. The place should be somewhere near where they were now, but why wasn't there some sort of light? Even as Crouse thought this, his eye caught a brief gleam of yellow off to his right. Reaching forward, he grabbed Jake's belt, and turned him so that he could see the faint glow.

As silently as possible, they crept through the jungle of vines that hung like ropy cobwebs between the trees, until a small shack loomed into view, a flickering light visible through one small, grimy window.

Crouse wiped his face with his already soaked handkerchief. He felt ridiculous. What the hell was he, with all his money and power, doing crawling through the bushes like any ignorant savage, coming to beg the help of this Granny Jingo, this obeah woman?

The answer, of course, was simple. He was going to her because the bitch would not come to him. This old black woman with her supposedly ancient powers was not impressed by Simon Crouse's name, or even his money. He had been told, almost rudely, that if he wished the help of Granny Jingo, he must come to her, and he must come bearing something special: something that he valued, not just gold, particularly not paper money; but something of worth that had a personal meaning for him.

He fingered the heavy gold ring in his pocket. It was the first thing that he had purchased when he made his first large amount of money. At the time, it had been an important symbol to him of his success. It still was, in a sense, but since he had purchased it his tastes had changed, and now the large stone struck him as a trifle garish and out-of-place on a gentleman's hand. Yet it did mean something to him, something special, and he hoped that it would suffice. He had been warned that what he brought along must have real value, and the towering black man who had conveyed the message looked as if he could follow through if the offering was not fitting.

And so here he was, with one serving man allowed him, thrashing through the humid night on his way to a conjure woman. The fact would be amusing, if he could take it a little less seriously, but the truth was, Simon Crouse believed!

He was not a Southerner, but he had been in the South for some years now, and had seen at first hand some of the things that were attributed to those who possessed the "power." Also, what had been happening to him was so outlandish, so unbelievable, that black magic was the only way to explain it.

At any rate, he was committed. Wiping his face again, he shoved Jake ahead of him into the clearing that surrounded the shack, and stood up to face a huge shadow in the shape of a man.

Crouse's heart lurched painfully in his chest, and Jake let out a strangled cry, and then Crouse recognized the man as the large black who had arranged the meeting with Granny Jingo. Her bodyguard, or assistant, Crouse surmised.

The big man turned, and without a word walked toward the rickety shack, and Crouse, giving Jake another push, followed.

Then they were at the door, which the big man opened without ceremony. As the weak light from inside shone on the black man's face, Crouse's nerves strummed. It was a fierce, cruel face, impassive as that of a carving; showing no feeling, no life, except for the black eyes, the whites shot with red, which held an unreadable expression.

Crouse hurried into the shack, glad to escape the scrutiny of those eyes, and there he found himself facing not the ancient black woman he had expected, but a relatively young woman with glistening black skin and a proud face. She was not dressed in the usual garb of the black woman, but wore an ancient, red silk ballgown, and her head and shoulders were cov-

194

ered with a brightly embroidered Spanish shawl that accented the strong lines of her face.

Crouse, taken aback, could not decide whether to nod or bow, such was the woman's presence.

Her dark eyes flickered as she motioned for him to seat himself opposite her.

Crouse cautiously sat upon one of the low wooden stools, the only seats in the room, and stared at the woman expectantly. Despite the heat, there was a large iron pot bubbling over a bed of coals in a stone fireplace; the fumes from its contents made Crouse swallow, and swallow again. The stench was vile.

"You have brought the offering?"

Her voice was husky and guttural, and at any other time it would have aroused Crouse's carnal nature, but at the moment that was the last thing in his mind.

He nodded quickly. "Yes." He fumbled in his pocket and produced the ring, holding it out to Granny Jingo, who took it with long brown fingers that felt warm where they touched his hand.

She examined the ring carefully in the wavering light from the strangely shaped candle that was centered on a wooden box. Finally, she tucked the ring away out of sight in the bodice of her gown, and turned her strange eyes upon him. "What is your problem, white man? What brings you to Granny Jingo?"

Haltingly, Crouse told her, leaving out nothing. Strangely, he did not feel embarrassment before this woman—instinctively, he semed to know that nothing in this world could surprise or shock her, that there was nothing she had not seen or heard.

When he finished, she nodded, motioned for him to stay seated, and rose from her own stool. He watched as she rummaged in a low chest across the room, removing some objects which he could not see. She then returned to her place near the fire, and threw onto the coals some substance which produced a great cloud of smoke that rapidly filled the room.

Crouse began to cough, and his eyes flooded with stinging tears. He could hear the woman's voice crooning strange words, repeating them over and over. He continued to cough and rub at his eyes with his handkerchief. The room seemed to have grown even warmer, and soon perspiration was running off Crouse like rain.

Just when he thought that he could not stand the smoke and the heat for one more moment, her chanting stopped, and the air began to clear. Soon the interior of the shack was visible again, and he saw Granny Jingo holding two items toward him. One was a squat white candle, seemingly made from some kind of tallow; and the other was a coarsely carved spool, bound with white thread.

"You do have a curse upon you, white man," she said. "Someone has made bad magic against you, the binding spell, I think."

Her voice was matter-of-fact, but Crouse shivered to hear the corroboration of his worst fears. "Can you remove it?" he whispered.

She nodded. "Take these two things. Each night, before you go to bed, you must light the candle; and each night, you must unwind a bit of thread from the spool, and while you are doing this, you must recite the words that I shall give to you.

"You must do this every night for seven nights, and on the morning of the eighth day, you will be free of the curse."

Crouse reached out and accepted the spool and the

196

candle. He felt oddly disappointed. "Is that all there is to it?" he asked.

Granny Jingo's full lips parted, showing strong white teeth. "The power is in the words. On the eighth day, you must burn the paper with the words upon it. If you do not do this, the curse will come back! Do you understand?"

Crouse nodded, intimidated despite himself by the menace in her voice. She handed him a folded piece of paper, small enough to put into his watch pocket.

He stood up, gazing down at the objects in his hand. "And if it doesn't work?"

She gave him a sleepy look, and turned away, yawning. "It will work, white man. It will work. Just do as I have told you. Now leave. I am tired."

Crouse put the candle and the spool into his pockets and turned toward the door. He was not certain that he had not been made a fool of.

At the door he turned for one more look at the obeah woman, and his heart jerked, his breath catching in his throat like a peach stone. There was no one in the room but himself! He was quite alone.

Hurriedly, he disengaged the latch and stumbled out into the black night. He heard Jake's voice, "Mr. Crouse, can we be going now?" The black man was nowhere in sight.

"Yes," Crouse muttered, as anxious as Jake to be quit of this place.

They set off in the direction from which they had come, almost stumbling in their haste. *Damn it all,* thought Crouse; *this had better work. It had better be worth it!*

And it was. For seven nights Crouse did as he had been instructed by the obeah woman. Feeling the fool, he nevertheless lit the candle, unwound a bit of thread, and said the words, which lay oddly and uncomfortably upon his tongue.

On the morning of the eighth day, he awoke in breathless anticipation, and called to Jake to send up the girl Ella Louise. Jake shouted back up the stairs, "You had me fire her, Mr. Crouse! Don't you recollect?"

"Then send me whoever is available, I don't care!"

He waited impatiently for the pad of bare feet outside his room. His thwarted member was ready, as it had been for weeks; but that meant nothing, as he well knew. The test was in the culmination.

In a short while Ella Louise's replacement, a woman a few years older and much more frightened of Crouse, slid quietly into the room. Bidding her strip, Crouse quickly set himself to the task, taking no time for niceties, but pushing the woman onto the bed and falling upon her.

As she lay in silence, he pounded at her in a frenzy, until at last he achieved the satisfaction which had been denied him for so long.

Falling off the woman, Crouse lay spent and panting, marveling at the obeah woman's powers. They had worked, her powers had worked!

He loosed a shout of exultation, frightening the serving woman who had taken Ella Louise's place. She was sent scurrying from the room. Crouse ignored her, savoring the moment.

Things would be better now. Everything would go well, he just knew it; but he still had a score to settle with that Dubois bitch who had put the trouble upon him.

Now that things were right again, he could begin to

think of ways to revenge himself upon the ones responsible for the wounding of his pride and manhood. Amalie Dubois had escaped his clutches on board the *Melon Patch* through sheer good fortune, when some knight errant had freed her from Bear's cabin, but the next time she would not get away, and neither would Melissa Huntoon. Both women would answer to him, and in a way that would give them as much pain as it would give him pleasure.

He was determined that he should have Melissa Huntoon one way or another, if not as his bride, then as his mistress, and Amalie Dubois should watch him take her. Oh, that would be a fine day!

It would take some planning, now that they were out of his immediate reach. The first thing he had to do was plant his own man on board the *Natchez Belle*. Crouse knew that the boat was in New Orleans now, and his sources had informed him that they were advertising for performers, as well as additional crew members. Yes, it would do well to have someone on board who could report to him, who could keep him informed of their plans and whereabouts. So long as he had that information at his fingertips, he could take his time in figuring out exactly what to do.

Meanwhile, he could create a little trouble here and there, just to let them know how it felt to be thwarted at every turn. And then, at last, he would crush them, and have his revenge!

Chapter Twelve

"Jubal! Watch out for that tug! It's coming right at us!"

Jubal gave a long-suffering, very audible sigh, and Melissa hid a smile behind her hand.

She and the Kings were in the wheelhouse of the *Belle*, watching for a landmark that would tell them they were nearing a small river town on the Bayou Teche.

Martha, now that she had someone else to do the cooking, had taken to spending her spare time in the wheelhouse with her husband. She took an active interest in the river and its myriad forms of life, but unfortunately she also took an equally active interest in the navigation of the *Belle*. Her nervous nature and strong urge to manage drove her to tell Jubal how to pilot. The fact that she knew nothing about piloting did not deter her in the least. While Jubal fussed and fumed, Melissa and the others found Martha's comments to her husband hilarious.

"There she is!" Jubal said suddenly. "That's what

I've been lookin' for. We can't be more'n a mile or so out of town. Melissa, go and tell Chuck to fire up the calliope! We got to come in in style!"

Melissa hurried from the pilothouse, anxious to act out physically the anticipation that had been seething in her since they had left New Orleans two days ago. This was going to be their first stop as a functioning showboat. They were scheduled to give their first performance this evening.

Everyone on the *Belle* had been in a high state of excitement since leaving New Orleans. Last-minute attention to costumes and stage scenery had kept everyone hustling, and rehearsals had gone on long into the night. Now they would have to put it all together, and hope that everything came out right.

She found Chuck standing aft, near the calliope, which had been painted and polished until the brass pipes shone in the sun like gold.

"It's time!" she called out, and Chuck grinned, and hastened to take his seat at the instrument.

As Melissa hurried away, she heard the first notes blast out in the still afternoon air. When she found the others, there was no need to alert them—the piping of the calliope had done that for her.

They were already in costume; and now the decks of the *Belle* were bright with the moving figures of the performers as they hustled toward the bow of the boat, and the long stage plank that protruded forward.

Melissa's place was near the front of the plank, and she was both thrilled and frightened to be standing out there in midair, looking down at the swirling water, and swallowing to keep her throat clear.

Beau Vermillian stood beside her, one hand on her

arm to steady her. Despite the distraction of the moment, she was very conscious of his touch.

In front of Melissa and Beau, right out on the very tip of the stage, Peggy and Martin LaSalle posed, waiting to break into their dance when the *Belle* came in sight of the landing.

"Oh, I do hope the playbills were put up." Melissa had to shout so that Beau could hear over the sound of the calliope.

He nodded. "They will be, don't worry. After all, Jubal told the bill poster that he wouldn't get paid until the *Belle* arrived and he saw for himself that the posters were up. I'm sure the man wants his money."

Melissa nodded back. The calliope blare was too deafening to try to talk over it. But she had heard, back in New Orleans, that rival showboats sometimes tore down playbills of competing show troupes, to put their own bills in their place. Still, located off the main route, and being a small town, this place probably wouldn't be visited by the larger showboats, such as the *Star of the South*. In addition, the water here was low, and the *Star of the South*, with her big, side-paddle tug, would not be able to navigate in here.

Nevertheless, Melissa worried that there would be no crowd to meet them at the landing, no customers to see their play and olio.

The *Belle* steamed on around a curve, the calliope screaming, and the cast standing expectantly on the stage plank. And there, suddenly, was the landing and the town; and there, thank God, were the people, a good-sized crowd of them, standing on the docks and jetties, waving and shouting.

The calliope backed off a bit, playing more softly; and the cast burst into song. The LaSalles began their dance, limited by the space available on the stage, but embellished by high kicks and struts.

Everyone else waved flags, handkerchiefs, whatever they had, and sang at the top of their voices. The sound of the music was punctuated by the deep, melodious sound of the Belle's whistle. It was bedlam, and joyous, and just as Melissa had dreamed it would be.

Jubal maneuvered the *Belle* delicately into the landing, the stage plank was lowered, and to the accompaniment of the calliope, the performers paraded off the *Belle* and onto the landing, and formed up before their audience.

Women in plain sunbonnets and faded dresses clutched the hands of wide-eyed children. Here and there could be seen an affluent planter with his family, or a well-dressed townsman, but for the most part the audience was made up of simple folk who worked hard for a living.

They watched with open-mouthed fascination, yet there was not much smiling or laughing, and Melissa's hopes were dampened. They didn't like the players! They weren't coming to the show, she just knew it!

And then Nehemiah raised his hand, and one of the deckhands set up a large box. The little man hopped up onto to it so that he could be seen.

The calliope had stopped at Nehemiah's hand gesture, and now he began his spiel, his manner and words resembling those of the gentleman from the *Star of the South* that afternoon in Natchez. In Melissa's opinion, Nehemiah's voice was richer and more dramatic.

"Ladies and gentlemen, your kind attention, please!

Here before you, you see the performers of the *Natchez Belle*, actors, actresses, singers, and dancers. The best talent available!

"Tonight, you shall have the once-in-a-lifetime opportunity to see them perform, starting at eight o'clock, in the grand saloon of the *Natchez Belle*. There, in comfort and with great pleasure, you may watch one of the great plays of our day, *The Little Violet Seller*. This will be followed by an olio of superlative excellence, which will include comic songs and dances, tender ballads, and feats of magic. A show the likes of which you will not soon see again. Yes, indeed!

"So, come one, come all, to this evening's performance, where you will see Miss Melissa Huntoon . . ." At his gesture, Melissa stepped forward, her cheeks pink with embarrassment and excitement. ". . . In the role of Madelain, the Little Violet Seller. Mr. Beau Vermillian, in the role of the hero, Andrew Stewart." Beau stepped forward and bowed.

"Myself, I shall enact the role of the dastardly villain, Silas Smythe, and Linnea Longfield will delight you in the tender role of Madelain's mother."

The crowd buzzed with talk as each performer was presented in turn. Melissa was wondering what they were thinking. Did they like the troupe, or did they not? It was impossible to tell from their response.

"Supporting roles," Nehemiah continued, "will be played by Martin and Peggy LaSalle, who will also entertain between acts with their singing and dancing.

"I promise you good people that you will not be disappointed. It will be an evening you will long remember. Come one, come all! Tell your friends, anyone who was not able to get down to the landing in time for our arrival.

"We will be waiting for you, waiting to entertain and delight you! Indeed, we shall!"

Nehemiah bowed low, and was acknowledged by mild applause, and a murmur from the crowd.

The calliope struck up again, and the performers paraded back aboard the *Belle*, while Nehemiah remained behind, passing out handbills.

Melissa felt both elated and apprehensive—elated because she thought that everything had gone off well, but worried because the crowd's reception seemed only lukewarm.

Beau walked up beside her as she stepped onto the deck from the stage. "See, Melissa," he said, stripping off his white gloves so that they would remain clean for the evening's performance, "I told you not to worry. The handbills were posted, all right. We had a large crowd."

Melissa arched her eyebrows and tried to smile, forming an expression that caused Beau to laugh aloud, until she had to laugh, too.

"But they didn't seem too enthusiastic," she said uneasily. "I thought there would be more cheering, more applause."

Beau shrugged. "Oh, I think it's just that these are mostly country people. They don't get much entertainment out here. This is probably the first showboat here since the war began, maybe the first one ever. It could be they were just awed."

"Well, I hope you're right, but I would have felt better if I knew for certain how many were going to attend the show tonight. After all, we must take in some money if you all want to be paid."

"You're right about that." Beau grinned. "Acting for love is all very well, but it would be nice to have a few dollars in my pocket. I'm sure the rest of the troupe won't complain if you pay them a little now and then."

They had been standing near the railing, just a little way from the stage plank, and now Nehemiah strode up the plank, his face stretched in a wide grin.

"You think it went well?" Melissa asked hopefully.

He bobbed his head. "Went fine. Yes, indeed. They'll be there tonight, don't you worry, my dear. Haven't had a showboat here since before the war."

"That's what I just told Melissa," Beau said. "But they do look poor. Do you think there'll be enough with money to pay to see the show?"

Nehemiah laughed. "Oh, they'll pay, all right, but it all won't be in coin of the realm. Indeed not. We'll get a lot of fresh vegetables, fresh fish, a few chickens, maybe even a porker or two. Some butter and cheese maybe. But it's all worth something, and if they pay in food, then that means the less food we have to buy out of our own pocket. There will be some with cash money, never fear. I saw a few well-to-do families in the audience. We'll make out, indeed we will. We may not get rich tonight, but it will be a start, and word will spread up and down the river that we're on the way. Indeed, it will!

"Now, off to your cabins, the pair of you, and get out of those clothes, so you won't dirty them before the performance. I've asked Martha to have the cook fix an early supper, and as soon as we've eaten, I want the whole troupe in the grand saloon."

Nehemiah hurried off, rubbing his hands together, and humming under his breath.

207

Beau laughed. "Well, he certainly seems cheerful enough, and he's the only one of us with experience with showboats, so I'll take my cue from him. Good afternoon, Miss Huntoon. I'll see you at supper."

Melissa made a mock bow. "Good afternoon, Mr. Vermillian. It will be my pleasure."

Her spirits buoyed by Nehemiah's optimism, she went to her cabin to get ready for supper, although she felt too nervous to eat. Her stomach was fluttery.

Tonight was the night. Tonight she would get up before a live audience and speak the lines she had been rehearsing for weeks. She knew them perfectly, had done them a hundred times, yet she knew that speaking them in front of an audience would be a different matter. Maybe she would be terrible. Maybe she would forget her lines. Maybe . . .

She stopped herself. There was no use worrying, no use at all. Resolutely, she continued toward her cabin. Maybe she would forget her songs. Maybe her voice would . . .

The lamps in the grand saloon were all lighted, and torches illuminated the stage plank and the decks of the *Natchez Belle*.

Jubal stood at the top of the plank and collected the price of admission; which, as Nehemiah had predicted, ran as often to food as it did cash. Still, there was a steady parade of customers, far more people than had been on the landing earlier; and Jubal realized that the audience would be gratifyingly large.

The people were dressed in their best—which was often not fancy—and there was a shine of expectancy in their eyes, although their behavior was quiet and well-mannered. But near the end of the line came several rather tough-looking men, who all paid in cash, and who jostled one another, and made coarse jokes about the coming performances, especially that of the women. They struck Jubal as a bit rowdy, yet he couldn't very well turn them away for that. Besides, they *did* have cash.

He contented himself with a cautioning word: "Let's not get too loud now, fellers. All right?" This caused the men to smile among themselves, but they did quiet down, and Jubal figured that his words had done the trick.

Finally, the members of the audience were all in their seats in the grand saloon. There was a great deal of whispering, and examining of the appointments, and much fingering of the velvet draperies, and much admiring of the carved and gilded fretwork. By comparison with a big showboat like the *Star of the South*, the *Belle* was not lavish; but care had been taken with her refurbishment, and she was as fine as Melissa and the Kings could make her with the money they had to work with.

After everyone was seated and had grown quiet, a stocky young man strutted out and sat himself down at the piano. His red head bounced, and his fingers flew, and the huge room filled with music.

The audience sighed and settled back in their seats, prepared to be entertained and mystified, hoping that the events upon the stage would take them for a time out of the drab, workaday world of their own lives, and into another place, into someone else's life; and knowing that after the play, after they had wept and empathized with the characters, they could laugh and clap to the music of the olio, and then go home uplifted in spirit and refreshed.

The lamps were dimmed, and as the piano music changed to a tender and haunting melody, the curtains were slowly drawn back to show the cold, wintry streets of a large city.

The audience let out a collective sigh of appreciation. The sets were good, quite realistic, and near the front of the stage, beneath a street lamp, crouched a slender, golden-haired girl, her bright curls peeping out from beneath a ragged cloak. She turned her wan face toward the audience, and held forth a basket of violets. "Violets? Who will buy my violets?"

A man came striding across the stage, ignoring the fragile girl, who lifted her basket toward him.

"Violets, kind sir? Violets for your lady?"

The audience murmured and sighed in sympathy. A few of the women were already weeping softly for the luckless maiden, although they knew instinctively that the girl would suffer much more hardship and unhappiness and find herself in jeopardy, before the play could end happily.

There were whispers:

"Isn't she lovely, poor thing?"

"An orphan, no kit nor kin."

"Poor child, such a terrible life!"

And for a moment the unhappiness and problems of their own lives were forgotten as they suffered along with the little violet seller and her poor, sickly mother, as they struggled to solve their many problems and find a bit of happiness in life.

As the curtain drew back, and the light from the stage apron struck her face, Melissa's mind froze. Chuck was playing the gentle air that had been chosen for her theme music, and this usually helped to get her into the proper mood of melancholy that was necessary for the opening scene of the play.

But tonight it was different. Tonight there was the sound of whispers, the rustle of clothing, coming from beyond the footlights, and Melissa was acutely aware that there were people, strange people, out there watching her. Her lines, she couldn't remember her lines!

Finally, despite her terror, she found that she could move, and make the gesture that she had rehearsed so many times. She held forth the basket of violets, and spoke her first line, pleading with a cold, cruel world to buy.

Then Martin LaSalle strode by, a passing stranger, and Melissa turned to him with the flowers, and suddenly it was all right. She knew what to do. She remembered all her lines, and the rhythm of the play caught her up, although she still felt somewhat self-conscious, and terribly aware of the audience out there.

It went even better in the scenes with Nehemiah, but his first appearance onstage did throw her off a bit.

They had rehearsed the scene repeatedly, but this time something was different. As Nehemiah came swooping onto the stage, which was now the humble abode of the little violet seller and her widowed mother, he appeared much taller.

Melissa, pondering this, almost missed her cue, but caught it in time, and went on. She had to admit that his extra height was effective, for it enhanced the bits of business that Nehemiah did with his long black cape. Then she saw the reason for the suddenly added height—his shoes. He was wearing shoes with thick soles and heels almost as high as a woman's heels, but apparently much sturdier.

By the time for the second act to begin, Melissa was feeling quite at ease. She had been pleasantly surprised by the size of the audience, and so far their response had been good; they had applauded enthusiastically at the end of the first act. It was as if they had needed a little time to get accustomed to being entertained again, and even more time to show their pleasure. But now they were receptive, and Melissa finally experienced the warmth and affection that an audience can convey to an actor or actress. It was a wonderful feeling, and she was anxious for the second act to begin.

The LaSalles were just finishing up their between-acts dance routine, and then, as they took their bows and left the stage, Chuck began the introductory music for the second act.

The curtain was drawn back, and Melissa, sitting at the feet of Linnea Longfield, looked up and spoke her first line:

"Perhaps, Mother, I should go with Mr. Smythe, as he asks of me. He would then spare our home, and you would not be forced to go to the poorhouse."

A raucous shout came from the back of the theater. "You can come to my house any time you choose, you pretty little thing! I'll make good use of you, you can bet on that!"

The shouted words were followed by loud guffaws and the thunderous stamping of feet.

Melissa flushed with anger. What was this? What was going on? This could ruin the performance!

Loud shushing sounds erupted from the audience, and in the moment of quiet, Linnea Longfield spoke

212

her lines clearly and calmly, as if nothing had happened.

Melissa sighed with relief, thinking that the shout had come from a member of the audience who took everything on stage seriously. She recalled Nehemiah telling of one man becoming so incensed with the villain that he had stormed up on stage and tried to kill him.

But then, as she started to speak her next line, it happened again.

"Come on, dollie! Let's liven things up a little. Why don't you take off some of them raggedy clothes you're wearing, and give us a peek at what you really look like! I'll bet you're really something under all them rags!"

Again the hooting laughter and the stamping of feet were heard, and then more coarse remarks.

Melissa's cheeks blazed with mortification. Why were they doing this? The performance would be ruined, and they would have to refund the ticket money.

She and Linnea gave up any attempt at going on with the play, and stood, peering out into the audience, trying to locate the troublemakers.

Melissa saw Jubal thumping his way toward the back of the saloon, along with three of the deckhands, but before they could reach the agitators, a tall, heavy-set man sitting near them stood up and motioned. Men around him rose, and all converged on the half-dozen rowdies. They waded in, fists flying, catching the troublemakers by surprise. The melee was rough but over with quickly, and fortunately nothing was seriously damaged, except one of the seats in the back row.

Before Melissa could fully grasp what was happening, the offenders were hustled out of the theater. Once they were ejected, Jubal posted the deckhands at the door, and armed them with stout clubs.

Then the townsmen resumed their seats, and waited patiently for the play to resume, which, after a few false starts, it did. Now that the troublemakers were gone, the second act went even better than the first, and the curtain fell on the last act to thunderous applause and whistles of unqualified approval. Melissa and the other players took bow after bow, and were finally let go on Nehemiah's promise that they would be back in the olio.

The olio was as well-received as the play, and when the curtain finally closed, Melissa felt the satisfaction that comes from giving a good performance to an appreciative audience.

After the final curtain, Nehemiah took the stage and made a little speech, thanking the man who had helped roust the toughs. When Nehemiah was through, the man stood up, his face red with embarrassment.

Twisting his hat in his hands, he said shyly, "We'uns been waiting a long time for a little pleasure to come our way, and we plain didn't aim for it to be ruined. We paid our money to see a show, and I didn't mean for no rowdies to stop me from seein' it. I'd like to thank y'all for a fine show that me and my folks will remember for a long time to come, and I hope that y'all will give another show tomorrow night, 'cause there were some who couldn't come tonight, and some who I know are comin' from out of town a ways, hopin' to see your show."

At the finish of the man's speech, Nehemiah called for a round of applause, and the man ducked his head

214

right and left, clapped his hat on his head, and hurried off the boat, followed by his wife and four children.

Melissa, still in her costume and makeup, watched the customers file out, eavesdropping on the nice things they had to say about the play and the performers. She felt keyed up, intoxicated with excitement.

The rest of the troupe seemed to feel the same. They congratulated one another and milled about backstage, as if reluctant to take off the trappings of the make-believe world.

Finally, Nehemiah got them settled down by telling them that a late supper was being served in the dining room, and that they had better hurry and partake of it or Martha King's feelings would be hurt.

Melissa was certain that she couldn't eat a bite; but she went to her dressing table to remove her makeup. She had just begun scrubbing the rouge from her cheeks, when Amalie appeared beside her, her face glowing with pleasure.

She gave Melissa a kiss and a hug, smoothing back her hair. "Oh, I was so proud of you, *chérie!*" she exclaimed. "No one could have guessed that this was your first public performance. The ladies in the audience, they wept when you appealed to the wicked moneylender, and when you tried to sell your violets in the cold streets!" She threw up her hands. "*Alors!* Such weepings I have never heard! But I do think that tomorrow night a little less rouge, little one. You looked too healthy. You must look wan."

Melissa stared up into her friend's eyes. "It *was* all right, wasn't it? Everyone was fine? No one forgot their lines, or anything?"

Amalie nodded vigorously. "Everyone was excellent, especially Nehemiah, with that wonderful voice of his, and did you notice," she laughed, "how he suddenly grew a few inches?"

Melissa joined her laughter. "Oh, yes. It startled me so in my first scene with him that I almost missed my cue. But he looked marvelous, didn't he?"

"Indeed he did. Now, I will leave you to get on with your toilette."

"I'll see you at supper shortly."

Amalie hesitated. "Well, no, *chérie*. I will not be present at supper. You see, I have an engagement."

Melissa dropped the square of linen with which she was removing the cream. "At this time of the night?"

Amalie blushed. "Yes, at this time of the night, my nosy little one."

Melissa, looking at her own face in the mirror, saw that she was gaping, and closed her mouth. "But with whom?"

Amalie said chidingly, "May I have no secrets? Must you know everything?"

Melissa smiled. "You know everything about me." But as she spoke the words, she thought of Luke Devereaux, and the lie caused her embarrassment. She was certain that Amalie, who missed little, noticed it, but the older woman was going on as if she had not.

"But if you must know, my curious little friend, I am going to visit with Amos Johnson."

"The chief engineer?" Melissa's curiosity was piqued. She had never known Amalie to have a man friend, or a suitor; and although she often wondered why, considering Amalie's beauty and intelligence, Melissa had been content to think of Amalie only as a surrogate mother and friend.

Now, the idea of Amalie and a man both disturbed and pleased her. "I don't know as I approve," she said with mock severity. "After all, I haven't even seen this man, this engineer. I only know that Jubal hired a man named Amos Johnson. Is he handsome?"

Amalie hesitated, then nodded slowly. "Yes. At least I find him so. Also, he is a strong man, yet very kind and gentle."

Melissa wiped off the last of the makeup. "Why don't you bring him up to supper?"

Amalie shrugged. "The supper is mostly for you, for the performers, and I think he might feel out of place."

Melissa thought this seemed rather odd. Why should the man feel out of place? The engineer of a steamboat held a respected position; it was not as if he was just a plain deckhand. Oh, well. It wasn't really any of her affair.

"I'll miss you at supper."

"Well, I'll wager that young Mr. Vermillian will be most happy to keep you company." Amalie smiled teasingly. "He seems quite smitten with you, little one."

Melissa blushed redder than the rouge she had just removed. "Oh, Amalie! You're awful." She glanced up, and grinned. "But he is handsome, isn't he?"

Amalie nodded. "And he seems a very nice young man. Well, I'd best go now. I will see you in the morning."

Melissa threw her a kiss, and began to get out of her costume. She wondered if Amalie was right. Did Beau Vermillian like her? What was more important, did she like him?

As she smoothed the bodice of her dress down over

217

her breasts, she looked at herself in the glass, thinking of Beau's hands following the path that her own were taking, and her face reddened again.

What had Luke Devereaux done to her? Why had he awakened her to forbidden pleasures, and then left her to suffer in frustration? Did she really care for Beau, or was she attracted simply because he was a man, and available? Was she going to turn into one of those women who went from man to man, drawn only by the thought of physical pleasure? She didn't want to be, and yet the memory of Luke's hands on her body could still keep her sleepless through the night, and now thoughts of Beau were beginning to do the same.

She tore her gaze from the mirror. This was not the time for such thoughts. She must hurry up to the other deck, they would be waiting; and she knew that Martha had gone to considerable work to plan the festive supper.

Amalie, pulling the shawl close around her shoulders, walked aft on the boiler deck. Amos would be waiting there for her, she knew. He probably would be smoking his pipe, calmly gazing at the stars, standing there big and solid as one of the granite boulders that occasionally jutted out from the river bank. She had never known a man so in command of himself as Amos Johnson.

She had cared for no man as she had for Jean-Paul Huntoon; the men she had known since Jean-Paul had not mattered to her beyond the pleasure of the moment. But now, she felt that she might come to care for this big, gentle man with the slow smile and the easy wit; at least he had roused feelings in her that had lain dormant for a long, long time.

Amalie smiled to herself as she thought of Melissa's reaction to her announcement that she was seeing a man. Melissa had been pleased, but also somewhat upset. It was not good that she relied so much on Amalie. It had been necessary in the past, but now Melissa was a woman, and it was time for her to learn to stand alone. Not that Amalie did not intend to be there as a friend and supporter, if needed; but in this life one never knew what would happen next, and one must be prepared to face life alone, if the necessity arose.

Amalie threw back her head and looked up at the gibbous moon shawled with wispy clouds. She had thought that something could be developing between Melissa and Luke Devereaux, but clearly a rift had come between them that night on the way to New Orleans. Devereaux had left the *Belle* abruptly in New Orleans, and it had taken many days before Melissa was her normal self again.

But now there was a new young man, this Beau Vermillian, young, handsome, charming, and seemingly sincere—at least his feelings about Melissa seemed clear enough. But would he be good for her? Ah, well, in any relationship between a man and a woman, who could answer that except time itself?

Of course, he was a boy, as opposed to Luke Devereaux, who was a man. Also, Amalie had to admit that she favored Devereaux, for his maturity would offset Melissa's youth. Melissa could learn from Devereaux. With Beau Vermillian, they would be like two babes in the woods.

But what was she doing fretting over Melissa's love life? She had her own man waiting for her, and at the thought a warm wash of feeling pervaded her. Oh, it was good to have someone to care for again!

She was on the boiler deck now, and she could see the tall shadow that was Amos Johnson, leaning on the rail, staring out over the moon-painted river.

He faced around as he heard her footsteps. "Amalie?" His voice was very deep and resonant, deeper even than Nehemiah's.

"Yes."

He opened his arms wide, and she could see the gleam of his teeth in the moonlight. Eagerly, she stepped into his embrace, and felt his warm, muscular arms draw her tenderly to his broad chest.

He tilted her head back, and their lips met in a kiss that was more than a touch of flesh against flesh. It was, to Amalie, as if something passed between them as their lips met, an essence, the feeling of love; whatever it was, it made the kiss more than just a physical act, and Amalie knew that she did, indeed, love this man.

He took his mouth from hers. "I thought you weren't coming," he said.

"You should know better than that," she chided. "I had to congratulate the players. They are having a supper, a kind of celebration, in the dining room. Would you like to be there?"

He shook his head. "I would rather stay here with you, alone. We have so little time together."

"I knew you would say that. That's what I told Melissa," Amalie said, placing her head against his chest.

"You're very close to Miss Melissa, aren't you? You

220

have been like a mother to her." His words were a statement, rather than a question.

She raised her face. "Yes, that's true. I told you how I have raised her, since her natural mother died."

He looked away, and Amalie sensed a tension in his big body. "How do you think she will feel toward me, to the relationship between us?"

Amalie did not answer immediately, for she had thought on this subject herself and knew what he meant. Melissa was a young woman of fine instincts and a good heart, but she was a child of her era.

Amalie well knew that Melissa did not really think of her, Amalie, as black, or colored. This was partly due to Amalie's very light color, and partly due to familiarity. And since Melissa, essentially, thought of Amalie as white, how would she react to Amalie's love for a black man? For Amos Johnson was indeed black, his blood little diluted by the white masters who had owned his ancestors.

It was unusual to find a man of color in a position such as that of engineer; but then, Amos Johnson was not an ordinary man. He was of great size, six-feet-four at least, with broad shoulders and muscular arms. His thighs were the size of young trees, and his neck could not be spanned with a man's two hands.

Despite this appearance of brute strength, Amos was, first of all, an intelligent man. To those who looked into his eyes, this fact was obvious. He had a handsome face, with a high-bridged, rather long nose, that ended in two flaring nostrils that sometimes gave him a look of disdain which had no relation to his real feelings. His eyes were compelling, large and dark, with clear whites and thick lashes, and his mouth was wide, with rather thin lips.

Amos had been fortunate in life, and he realized it. For in addition to his formidable physical presence and bright mind, he had had the good fortune to be born to parents who belonged to an enlightened plantation owner, who had not believed in the fallacy that it was necessary to keep his slaves ignorant in order to control them.

The planter had, early on, glimpsed the potential in the boy Amos, and had arranged for him to attend school, along with his own children, in the schoolhouse on his own property. Amos was not the only black child in the classroom, for the planter offered the same opportunity to any child on the plantation who showed the desire and will to learn.

Amos had early shown a great ability with machinery, and after he had graduated from the classroom, he began to take care of the machinery on the plantation. The planter had also owned a small steam packet, and had taken Amos aboard so that he might learn about the engines. From there it was only a few steps, with the permission of his owner, to becoming an engineer.

As far as Amos knew, there were only two other black engineers on the Mississippi, one working on a tug, and the other on a packet that steamed out of New Orleans.

Amos had worked on his owner's steamboat, the *Nancy June*, until the war and the blockades had ended most river traffic. Now the war was over, but his ex-owner was long dead, and with the slackened river traffic, he had seen little chance of working at his chosen craft, until the *Natchez Belle* came to life, and he had read the notice advertising for engineers.

Amos thanked his lucky stars for that day, for it

proved that he was still being watched over. In one swoop he had found a good job with nice people, and he had met Amalie Dubois, who was everything that he had ever dreamed of finding in a woman.

He said, "It won't . . . You won't let Miss Melissa come between us?"

Amalie still hesitated, her hand gentle against his chest. "It will not come to that, my love. She will understand."

"Hmmmm." The questioning sound made his chest rumble. "I hope so. I surely do. Because you mean more to me than anything else in this world, honey babe, and now that I've found you, it would kill me to lose you!"

She stood on tiptoe and fiercely pressed her mouth to his, and felt his body stir in answer. She laughed throatily.

Easily, as if she were a child, Amos scooped her up in his arms, and strode with her toward his cabin.

Chapter Thirteen

In the dining saloon the supper party was in full swing. Martha and the cook had outdone themselves, and the performers, hungry after their night's work, set to with gusto.

Melissa had been sure that she was too excited to eat, but when she smelled the food, she found that she was ravenous. Looking at the food spread out on the table, she didn't know where to start. "Where did all this come from?" she asked Martha, who was across the table from her.

Martha smiled widely. "A lot of it was taken in tonight for admission. You might say that tonight we are eating up the profits. Literally!"

Everyone within earshot laughed, and Melissa helped herself generously to the rice and crawfish ragout, then to hush puppies and greens.

Beau was was sitting beside Melissa, on her right, and Martin LaSalle was on her left. Feeling relaxed and happy, Melissa chatted with them both, discussing the evening's performance, and the trouble from the toughs in the audience. In the mood she was in, everything they said sounded witty and amusing. It was a wonderful party to climax a wonderful evening.

As Melissa was finishing her brandied peaches and demitasse, she felt a pressure against her left leg. Turning slightly, she saw that Martin LaSalle had crowded his chair close to hers. It had to be his leg she felt.

He was turned away, talking to Peggy, who sat on his other side, so Melissa assumed that his touch must be accidental.

And then the pressure was increased, as his knee moved against her leg. Melissa sucked in her breath, puzzled and a bit shocked. Was he doing this deliberately? If so, why?

She moved her leg away, trying not to be too obvious about it, and scooted her chair to the right; but this then brought her close to Beau, who looked at her in question, smiling.

Melissa found herself flushing. What on earth was she suppose to do now?

Martin's nearness, the insistent pressure of his leg against hers, was not all that distasteful. He was a very attractive man, but until this very moment Melissa had never thought of him in intimate terms. After all, he was married, and to Melissa that meant that he was not a person to be thought of as a man, but as a husband, as part of a pair. Now, by his actions, Martin had made himself seem a separate person, a male person, and Melissa did not know how to deal with the situation.

Fortunately, just as Melissa thought she would have to excuse herself from the table, Chuck went to the piano that Jubal had installed in the dining saloon, and struck up a merry dance tune.

At the sound of the first chord, Beau jumped to his feet, extended a hand to Melissa, and requested the first dance. Melissa gratefully accepted, happy to escape a potentially embarrassing situation.

Beau was an excellent dancer, and as he swept her out onto the small space that served as a dance floor, Melissa forgot everything but the pleasure of the moment . . . no, not quite everything, for she was very conscious of Beau's arm around her waist, and the scent of his Bay Rum was heady. He *was* very handsome, and he was looking at her with undisguised admiration. She wanted him to ask to hold her closer, although she knew that it would be bad manners. In fact, she wanted . . .

She gave herself a mental shake. No! She must not think about that. It was wrong, and beside she did not want to go through what she had gone through with Luke Devereaux. She would not think of it. She *would not!*

And then the dance was over, and before Chuck could begin another, Martin LaSalle was at Beau's shoulder, tapping it gently, and Beau, with a half-angry look, reluctantly released her into the arms of the other man.

The music started up again, a lively tune, and Melissa's heart was beating as rapidly as the music. She kept her eyes cast down as Martin swept her into the dance, only looking up when he spoke to her.

He had brown, very intense eyes, and they looked into hers with an insistence that made her again look down.

"You look very lovely this evening, Melissa."

"Thank you," she murmured. And then, desperately: "And so does your wife."

"Yes," he acknowledged suavely. "It is fortunate that we have two such beautiful women in our troupe. By the way, if I haven't already complimented you, you performed very well tonight. It was hard for me to believe that this was your first time before a real audience."

She chose what she hoped was a safe answer. "Why, thank you. I was frightened silly at first, but as we went on, I forgot about being on stage, and started to *be* the character."

He nodded, and held up his arm for her to turn under. "That is the way it goes with a good performer. There is half of you in the character, and half of you watching the audience, so that you can modify your performance, if necessary."

He brought her close to his body in a dipping movement, and she instinctively pulled back.

Then, in a riffle of chords, the dance was over, but before releasing her hand, Martin pulled her close again. "Melissa, let's stroll awhile on the deck. It's very warm in here, don't you find it so?"

Melissa, thinking of Peggy, was just opening her mouth to refuse, when Beau appeared and took her arm. "Sorry, LaSalle, but Miss Huntoon has promised to promenade around the deck with me for a bit of air. Oh, by the way, I think your wife is looking for you." Beau gave a slight bow, and then turned and led Melissa out of the room onto the deck outside.

Beau seemed rather stiff, and Melissa wondered if he had overheard Martin's invitation. Her question was answered when he turned to her.

"Did he annoy you? If he did, let me know and I'll

teach the scoundrel to pay attention to his own woman, and leave decent young girls alone!"

Melissa knew that she had to smooth things over. She certainly did not want this evening spoiled by unpleasantness, and a quarrel between the players at this stage could destroy the harmony of the troupe. "No," she said quickly. "No, Martin was only being friendly. I'm sure he didn't mean any harm."

Beau snorted. "No harm. I'm afraid that is your innocence speaking, Melissa. But I am a man, and I know what other men are like. I've seen LaSalle looking at you, don't think I haven't, but I hoped that he wouldn't go beyond that, seeing that he is married, and his wife is along with him. You're too trusting by far, Melissa. You must learn to beware of men of his type."

Melissa, her thoughts touching on Luke, felt her cheeks grow warm. What would this young man think of her if he knew that she was not as innocent as he assumed? She felt ashamed and guilty.

"Well, at any rate, he didn't harm me, Beau, and I shall watch out for him in the future. Now, let's not spoil tonight. It's been so lovely. Everything has gone so well."

She smiled at him, putting considerable warmth into it, but instead of disarming him, to her surprise and dismay he seized both of her hands in his, and said fervently, "I have to tell you this, Melissa. I know it's too soon. I know I should wait, but tonight when I saw you . . . Melissa, I could hardly stand to see you dancing in another man's arms! Melissa, I care for you desperately! As I said, I know this is not yet the time to speak of it, but—"

He swept her into his arms, releasing her hands and

229

grasping her shoulders. She was close against his chest, and as she looked up, too surprised to react, Beau bent his head until their lips were only a fraction of an inch apart.

His breath was sweet and warm, and Melissa felt a yearning rise up in her that swept away all logical thought and all her firm resolves. As his lips pressed upon hers, she welcomed them with her own.

His kiss began gently, but grew more intense with his mounting passion, and Melissa could feel the stir of his manhood as their bodies pressed more closely together. His passion fueled hers, until they were clinging together in an embrace that seemed to have no beginning or end.

They were both breathless when they separated, and Melissa felt shaken and weak, as a hunger filled her, a hunger that she knew would only be satisfied when they came together body to body, with nothing between them, and he . . .

She tried to pull up short, tried to stop the avalanche of feeling that was overwhelming her, but she could not.

He kissed her again and again, each kiss deeper, more probing than the one before. His hands, at first restrained, now touched her and caressed her until they were both in a frenzy of need.

"Melissa," he muttered. "Darling Melissa, I want you so! I need you. Please, come with me to my cabin. If you wish, we'll just lie together and hold one another, nothing more. I just want you in my arms . . ."

Slowly, like some strange, blind, two-headed creature, twined in one another's arms, they made their way to Beau's cabin. Inside, in the dark, their wild, seeking hands stripped away their clothing until there was nothing between them. Melissa sighed as Beau's hard young body pressed hers, and Beau moaned, whether in pain or pleasure, she could not tell.

He was hesitant at first, and gentle; but when her thighs parted to permit him entry, it was as if a violence in him was unleashed, and he plunged into her with a force that was half hurt and half ecstasy. Her own body began to move beneath his as her hands clutched and caressed his smooth, muscular back. Then, all of a sudden, he collapsed atop her with a sob, and pulled away from her.

Melissa, still in the throes of passion, experienced disappointment and dissatisfaction. She made a small sound of entreaty deep in her throat.

Beau raised up to gaze down into her face. "Melissa? Are you all right? Did I hurt you?"

Melissa knew that she was not all right, but how could she tell him that she wanted him to continue? Obviously, it was over for him. She sighed, relaxing some of the tension she still felt. She said faintly, "I'm all right."

He put his arm across her stomach, and pulled her closer. "Melissa . . . I'm sorry. I shouldn't have done this, but I do love you so. We'll get married. It will be fine. I want to marry you."

Melissa felt nothing in that moment but shock. She had come to Beau's bed because she could have done nothing else at the time. She had a feeling for Beau, and he aroused her physically; she had been taught to believe that intimacy between a man and a woman led to marriage, and yet . . .

She was very confused, for her instant reaction to his offer of marriage had been fear and shock. Married? Married to Beau Vermillian?

Beau was kissing her breasts, caressing the tender nipples with his tongue, and Melissa's confusion was drowned by the sensations building in her again. She felt his hard readiness against her thigh. She groped for him, and Beau gasped as she found him.

In another moment, he was again inside her, moving, thrusting deliciously, and all coherent thought fled, as her eager body began to pulse and quiver with the violence of her fulfillment.

Roy Davis, the overseer at Riverview, did not view the coming of the man named Luke Devereaux with pleasure. As far as Davis was concerned, he was doing a good job of managing the plantation, and any difficulties he was having were due to circumstances beyond his control.

True, he had written to Simon Crouse, asking for help; but the help he had wanted was extra men, paid toughs, to keep the sharecroppers and field hands in line. What could one man do?

The whole thing, in Davis's view, was the fault of the times, and the war. These damned blacks now thought they were as good as a white man, and were getting increasingly difficult to control.

In the old days, he would simply have taken a horse-whip to them, and they would have shaped up quickly enough, but now, with all the attention focused on the South and the double-damned carpet-baggers swarming like maggots on a corpse, a man never knew when one of the blacks was going to complain. What was even worse, they could always find some nigger-loving, Northern administrator who would listen, and cause trouble.

Of course, Davis still used what force he could,

without being too obvious about it, yet he needed some men he could trust. Men who would follow his orders to the letter and keep their mouths shut. Instead, he had first gotten Simon Crouse himself, who didn't really object to roughing up the field hands, but who wanted to see results in the form of profits; and, he claimed, damaged workers meant fewer profits. And now he was sending this Texan, this Luke Devereaux, to stick his nose in.

Davis cursed the moment he had written the letter to Crouse. If he had just kept his mouth shut, it would probably all have worked out in the end. Now he had to worry about this Texan, as well as trying to get the work done and the money in.

Maybe if he gave the Texan a hard enough time, he would tuck his tail between his legs and sneak away. It was certainly something to think about.

Luke's first impression of Riverview's overseer was far from favorable. Rarely had he seen a man he disliked so much at first sight—unless it was Simon Crouse. Two of a kind, he thought wryly.

Roy Davis was a tall man, running to fat, with a long torso and short, heavy legs. He had a long head, seemingly too narrow for his beefy body, and his eyes were too close together over a long, flattened nose. Altogether an unlovely sight, as far as Luke was concerned.

Of course the man couldn't help his looks, and Luke had never been one to judge a man on external appearance alone, but the expression in the overseer's small eyes was mean and calculating, and he had an unpleasant, whiny way of speaking that sounded accusatory. It was plain that he was unhappy about

Luke being sent to the plantation as a trouble-shooter, and that he was going to be uncooperative at best, and downright hostile at worst.

Still, there wasn't much Luke could do about the man right now except try not to alienate him too much, until he had time to study the man, the plantation, and the workers.

So he approached Davis with a smile and an outstretched hand. Davis took the hand reluctantly, and did not bother to return the smile.

"Don't know why Crouse thought we needed a trouble-shooter," he said accusingly. "There's no trouble here that I can't handle myself."

"Why, Simon told me that *you* wrote *him*, saying that you needed help," Luke said innocently.

"Mmmph! Well, I reckon that's true, but that problem, well, Crouse helped me take care of it when he was here. I don't know why he thinks I need someone here now. I don't mean to sound unfriendly, but this is our busy season, sugar cane harvest coming up soon, and an outsider will just be in the way!"

He shot Luke a sidewise glance, evidently in an attempt to gauge Luke's reaction to this statement.

Luke, wanting to grin at the man's transparency, said amiably, "I'll try real hard not to get in your way, Mr. Davis. Like you say, there's probably no problem here, and all I'll have to do is put in my time, and then tell Simon that, so you just go on ahead, and run things like you always have. Don't worry or put yourself out on account of me. Just pretend that I'm not here!"

Davis gave him a suspicious look, his small eyes cold and mean. "We'll see. We'll see. I reckon you might as well come up to the main house. The wife's got a room ready for you. She sets a good table, and the house is snug. You'll be comfortable enough, at any rate."

Luke nodded and tried to look properly grateful. He was beginning to enjoy himself. Davis was so patently a villian that it was amusing to try to outwit him. It was obvious that the man trusted no one, and it would appear that his usual view of the world was one of suspicion and dislike. Luke was almost certain that if there was any trouble on Riverview, Davis was the cause of it.

Riverview's main house was a three story colonial, with four tall columns across the front. The exterior needed paint, but the building seemed to be in good repair, and the veranda and the yard were neat and clean.

Someone had taken considerable care with the plantings, and all in all, the house made a graceful and favorable impression, particularly when viewed from the front, for the approach was lined with large oaks, dripping moss. The trees formed an aisle up which carriages and foot traffic could travel in shade and beauty.

The overseer's wife was a complete surprise to Luke.

When Davis had said he was married, Luke had visualized a female version of the man himself—middle-aged, dumpy, dour. The truth could not have been further from this concept.

Elena Davis may have been in her middle years, but she looked much younger, a tallish woman with dark brown hair and blue eyes, broad-shouldered and narrow-waisted still. She looked at Luke with frank interest, and offered a well-shaped, warm hand when they were introduced.

He took her hand, and bowed over it with some feeling of shock. How had this red-necked oaf managed to get a woman of his wife's obvious class and style to marry him? Maybe his stay here wasn't going to be so bad after all, Luke thought. At least he would have something pleasant to look at when he got tired of looking at Davis.

"This is a great pleasure," he said softly, lingering over her hand, which, although it showed signs of hard work, was smooth and clean, with neatly trimmed nails.

Elena Davis returned his smile, revealing a deep dimple in her right cheek. "It is a pleasure for me as well, Mr. Devereaux. We get few visitors here in this backwater, and it is a nice change in the monotony when we see a new face. You must tell me all the news of Natchez and New Orleans."

"I shall be delighted, madam."

Luke released her hand, and straightened to see Davis staring at him narrowly. Oh, oh! Mustn't be too polite to the wife, or he would antagonize the husband. Davis struck him as one of those possessive men who consider their wives mere chattel, yet bristled if another man showed an undue interest. And right now the last thing Luke wanted to do was antagonize the man.

So, reluctantly, he turned away from Elena, and spoke to her husband. "You know, the plantation certainly looks in fine shape. Simon must be pleased with the way you've kept the place up."

"Mmmph," Davis grunted. "The missus here sees to it that the grounds are kept up, anyways. The niggers like her." This last was spoken with a sneer. "And they work real good for her. She coddles them. Just like a female!"

Luke, without seeming to, studied both the man and the woman. The woman showed no reaction to her husband's sneering comments, but continued to maintain a polite expression, as if he had not spoken. The husband spoke with no little underlying anger and desire to wound.

It was Luke's opinion that Davis resented the very traits that made Elena desirable to Luke—her intelligence, her breeding, and, from what Davis had just admitted, her ability to get along with people. An odd couple. When he knew Elena better, Luke decided, he would try to find out why she had married such an obvious piece of horse dung as Davis.

At supper that night, Luke caught a glimmer of the "trouble" that had caused Davis to write · Simon Crouse for help.

Supper was served in the formal dining room—in his honor, Luke supposed—with a well-appointed table, excellent food, and good wine.

Elena Davis looked delectable in a rather low-cut dress of some shiny fabric, in a rich shade of pink. The color brought out her eyes and complemented her fine complexion, and Luke felt a stirring of interest that was far from intellectual. Thoughts of Melissa intruded into his mind, and he determinedly cast them out.

Davis, attired in a white suit that did little to improve his unpleasant appearance, seemed somewhat mellowed by the wine he had imbibed before supper, and the meal showed some promise of being quite pleasant.

It was after the meat course that Hiram, the black serving man, spilled part of a dish of vegetables into Davis's lap, causing the overseer to leap to his feet, cursing, and strike the man across the face with his open hand.

Luke got a good look at Hiram's face as Davis struck him, and for an instant he saw a look of murderous rage, quickly suppressed. It had taken a great effort, Luke felt sure, for Hiram not to strike back, and for a moment tension hung in the air, thick as smoke.

Then Hiram lowered his head. "I'm sorry, Mr. Davis," he said in a low voice that was still tight with anger. "I'll clean it up right away."

"You're damned right you'll clean it up, you clumsy oaf!"

He wheeled on his wife, scrubbing at his ruined suit. "You see what comes of being easy with them? How many damned times have I told you that it doesn't work!"

Throwing down the stained napkin, Davis stalked from the room, heading for the stairs, bellowing for someone named Thomas to come and clean this "double-damned suit" and fetch him a fresh one.

Luke turned his gaze on Elena. Her face was flushed and her eyes bright, but she held her head high.

"You must forgive my husband, Mr. Devereaux. He is a man of quick temper, and there have been difficulties with the workers of late. I fear that his patience is stretched thin."

Luke nodded, and murmured, "Of course, I understand."

He had a hunch that Davis's temper was always stretched thin, that it was the nature of the man.

He looked from Elena to Hiram, who was cleaning up the spilled vegetables. The servant's face was expressionless, but his mouth was a thin line and his hooded eyes were bleak. Luke had a strong feeling that the animosity between master and servant was of long standing, and when Hiram left the room, this was verified by Elena.

When Hiram was out of earshot, she sighed and bit her lip. Looking up and catching Luke's glance on her, she shrugged. "Truthfully, my husband and Hiram have never gotten on well together. But Hiram is an excellent servant, well-trained and capable of taking charge of things without being constantly told what to do. I rely strongly on him to run the household. If only he didn't feel this hostility toward my husband, he would be the ideal servant.

She raised and lowered her hands. "But what can one do? I should fire Hiram, but I truly believe that I could not manage the house and gardens without him. One day, perhaps, Mr. Davis will fire Hiram himself, but until that happens, I try to smooth things over."

At that moment Hiram returned with a tray of desserts, consisting mostly of fresh fruit and melon.

Luke was wondering if Elena ever called Davis by his first name; so far she had referred to him only as "my husband" and Mr. Davis. It had been his experience that this was an indication of a rift between husband and wife. Luke broke his train of thought to select a peach from the dessert tray, and Hiram poured him a demitasse.

It had been an excellent supper, despite the spilled vegetables, and truthfully, Luke welcomed the chance to talk with Elena alone, without the presence of her disagreeable husband.

"You seem to get along with the servants here very well, Mrs. Davis," he said, raising his cup as if in a toast.

"Please," she said, "call me Elena. Thank you, yes, I have little trouble with any of the staff, or even the fieldhands. I listen to their troubles and try to help them when they have problems. You know, it is sad really. They have been freed, but most of them have no real idea of what that means. All of their lives they have been looked after, like children, told what to do, even what to think. Now they have been told that they are their own masters, and yet they have never been allowed to learn for themselves.

"Some, like Hiram, the bright and aggressive ones, will be all right. They have been aware, they have learned, despite us. But the others . . ."

She broke off, throwing up her hands in a charming gesture. "Ah, but I am running on. How about you, Mr. Devereaux? What you think of Riverview? And do you think you'll be able to get things running smoothly?"

Luke took a cigar from his pocket. "May I?"

"But of course."

He leaned across the table to light the cigar from a candle flame. "To answer your question, Elena . . . from what I've seen of it, I think Riverview is very lovely, particularly in the present company. As to whether or not I can get things running smoothly or not, well, your husband tells me there is nothing wrong, that there is no problem, and that I am wasting my time here." He looked at her intently. "Do you agree with that?"

Elena flushed, and her mouth thinned. Then she managed a stiff smile. "My husband, as you have no doubt already gathered, is a proud and stubborn man. He does not wish to have others know that there is a problem. It is natural that he would resent an outsider coming to Riverview to, if you will pardon me, interfere with his job. As another man, you must see this."

Luke nodded. He would certainly quarrel with her description of Davis as a proud man, he would have called him arrogant and stubborn instead, but what can you say to a man's wife, particularly when she is looking at you out of cornflower-blue eyes, and smiling hopefully?

"Of course," he said, "I understand fully." He toyed with his cigar. "You know, I am curious. How did you and Mr. Davis happen to meet? If I'm not being too presumptuous in asking."

She flushed, and looked away. For a moment Luke feared that he had gone too far.

"I met Mr. Davis during the war," she said slowly, as if debating with herself how much to tell him.

"I was a widow. My first husband was killed at the Battle of Champion Hill, shortly before the siege of Vicksburg. It was a difficult time."

She paused, and for a moment Luke thought she was not going to go on, but then she continued. "Mr. Davis was the commanding officer of the Yankee platoon that occupied my husband's small plantation. He—Mr. Davis—showed me exceptional kindness, and saw to it that his men did not destroy what was left of the place. We became friends, and when the war was over, he decided to remain in the South.

"I was unable to save the plantation. I was deeply in debt, and Simon Crouse, newly arrived in Natchez, bought the land and the house. Soon after, Mr. Davis asked me to marry him, and I accepted. He went to work for Simon Crouse, and that is my story. Not quite a romantic novel, I'm afraid."

And not quite all the story, either, I'll wager, Luke thought to himself. Her story, on the surface at least, was a lot like Melissa's. In fact, with those blue eyes and that lush figure, she was much like Melissa physically, or what Melissa would be like given ten or fifteen years time. Ah, Melissa! To think of her was like probing at a sore tooth. Resolutely he put the thought away.

"And you, Mr. Devereaux? Now that you have heard my life's story, what is yours? Are you married? Engaged? Is this the kind of work you usually do?"

Luke grinned. "To answer them in order, no, no, and no. I'm not married, not promised, and although I've done many kinds of work in my life, I've not done this particular kind of thing before.

"My mama, God rest her soul, left me some money and property when she died. She had been a, uh, a businesswoman, you see. I dabbled a bit in property and in cattle, a number of different things. I too was in the war, and found myself adrift when it was over.

"This job, Simon Crouse, is just temporary. At least by God I hope so! When it is finished, Simon Crouse and I will go our separate ways."

She looked at him intently. She was perceptive; she had caught the inference.

Luke was just about to ask Elena if she would care for a turn about the yard for a breath of fresh air, when Davis returned, wearing another white linen suit which showed signs of age. He seemed to have calmed down somewhat, but his face was still red, and his eyes angry.

"Damned, incompetent niggers. They were bad enough when they were slaves, but now there's no controlling them. A few licks from a blacksnake, that's what that buck needs. It's times like this that I think I fought on the wrong side in the goddamned war!"

He pulled out his chair and dropped heavily into it, glaring first at his wife and then at Luke, as if challenging them to dispute his remarks. Luke, choosing the prudent course, drew on his cigar, and blew a smoke screen between them. Davis grunted and turned his attention to the tray of desserts. He selected one, and ran the bell angrily.

This time it was not Hiram who responded, but a short, stocky woman with very dark skin and a tremendous bosom. She was carrying the coffee pot in her hand, and after filling Davis's cup, she left the pot on a trivet on the table.

Davis glared at her the entire time she was serving, but she appeared oblivious of his attention.

Luke glanced at Elena Davis and saw that her face was carefully blank. *God*, he thought, *it must hell for her, married to this boor*, and then he smiled wryly to himself. It certainly didn't seem to take much to arouse his chivalrous instincts. First Melissa Huntoon, and now Elena Davis.

Again the thought of Melissa hurt, and he grimaced. He saw Elena staring at him curiously.

He said, "If you folks will excuse me, I think I'll retire. It's been a long day."

As Luke stood up, Davis merely grunted, not even looking up. Elena nodded graciously. Was that a look of disappointment in her eyes?

"Good night, Mr. Devereaux. I hope you sleep well."

As Luke, candle in hand, headed up the curving staircase, he wondered how it would be to make love to Elena. Very nice, he should think. She was clearly a warm, giving woman, and with that husband of hers . . . well, having a man like Davis make love to you would be like mating with a surly bear.

He scolded himself sharply. He was here to do a job, and he had better keep his mind on that, to the exclusion of everything else.

Chapter Fourteen

Life on the *Natchez Belle* was falling into a pattern. Although the river was low now, the *Belle*, with her shallow draft and rear paddlewheel, was able to go where the heavier, sidepaddle-equipped boats could not. She journeyed from town to town up the river, drawing good crowds and playing to appreciative audiences. They traveled up numerous side rivers, stopping at places never visited by a showboat before.

Much of the payment taken in for admission was still in the form of food or goods, but they received enough cash to pay their operating costs and to dole out small stipends to the performers and the crew members.

Mollie Boom and Jubal shared the piloting, with Mollie taking the night shift—when they traveled at night—because she claimed she liked being alone. But the truth of it was, she took the night shift to get away from Martha King's incessant nagging.

"You may have to put up with her dad-blamed advice, 'cause she's your wife. But she ain't my wife, and

I'm going to hurt her feelings if I have to tell her to shut her yap!" she said to Jubal, who laughed and clapped her on the back as if she were a man.

The performers, strangers only short weeks ago, were adjusting to one another and becoming that beautiful unit, a functioning repertory theater group, in which every actor and actress knew what they could expect from each other. Everyone seemed to get along well, and the spirits of the entire group, performers and crew alike, were high.

After the night of their celebration supper, Melissa had managed to avoid Martin LaSalle, although she sometimes caught him staring at her, and at gatherings he often contrived to be standing or sitting next to her. Still, he made no overt overtures and did nothing to alarm her, and Melissa found the subliminal attention rather flattering.

Nehemiah and Mary McGee seemed to have struck up a friendship, and Melissa was pleased that the little man had found a companion. She also knew that Amalie was spending a great deal of time in the company of Amos Johnson, the engineer, and this did not please her, for it had been the cause of the only unpleasant scene that had never occurred between her and Amalie.

It had happened the week of their opening performance. She had needed Amalie's advice about a costume she was to wear for their next performance, and had gone looking for her. She had been told that Amalie was down on the boiler deck, with the engineer.

Melissa could have waited, but her curiosity was too strong. She had yet to meet this mysterious engineer, who seemed to keep pretty much to himself on the lower decks, so now was her chance to see what Amalie's suitor looked like.

So she tripped down the steps, with a feeling of expectancy, and charged into the boiler room without announcing herself. She saw Amalie deep in conversation with a huge black man of imposing mien. But where was the engineer?

Then Amalie turned and saw her, and her expression changed, just the least bit, but enough to let Melissa know that she was troubled. Didn't Amalie want her to meet this paragon, this Amos Johnson?

"Amalie," she said, speaking rapidly, "I have something to ask you, and Martha told me you were down here. I thought I'd come down and meet your friend, the engineer. Where is he?"

She glanced around expectantly, and almost missed Amalie's slight frown. Amalie took her hand, as if to steady her, and looked directly into her eyes. "This *is* my friend, Melissa. This is Amos Johnson."

Melissa could feel the shock hit her stomach, like a plunge into icy water. This, this black giant was Amos Johnson? This was the engineer, the man that Amalie was spending time with? Why, he was a black man! Could blacks be engineers? And he was *so* dark! Amalie couldn't marry a man that dark. It wouldn't be right. It wouldn't be . . .

Amos Johnson was looking at her steadily, with no expression on his brooding face. He had good eyes. Intelligent eyes. And then Melissa realized that she had been staring, that she had been rude, incredibly so, and her words stumbled one over the other as she tried to make amends, but she sensed that it was too late—the damage had been done. "I'm very glad to meet you, Mr. Johnson. Very glad. Amalie has been

247

just like a mother to me, and I love her very much. I mean, anyone she cares for is important to me, too. I'm terribly glad to meet you."

Melissa smiled and nodded and generally, she suspected, acted like a complete idiot. Amos Johnson smiled sadly, and said that he was glad to meet her too, but she felt that she had disappointed him in some way, and Amalie most of all, and she fled as soon as she decently could, running away with a sense of confusion and embarrassment weighing her down.

Yet it didn't seem right, somehow, that man and Amalie. It just didn't seem right.

Since that unfortunate incident, there had been a marked coolness between Amalie and Melissa, a coolness so subtle that no one else seemed to notice it. Melissa desperately wanted to make things right between them, but she did not know how to go about doing it; and besides, she was still upset, for in her mind she had not yet come to terms with the relationship between Amalie and Amos Johnson. Although she did not realize it, jealousy played no small part in her emotional reaction. Before she had always been first with Amalie, and she resented the fact that Amalie was now sharing her affections with someone else.

However, she did not really have time to dwell on the subject, or on her feelings, for life on the *Belle* was very full, and except for this one slight cloud on the horizon, Melissa had never been so happy. It was as if some spring within her had been released, and now she was traveling at top speed, whirling from one thing to the next with boundless energy and enthusiasm.

After that first night in his cabin, Beau wanted to

be with Melissa every night; and in spite of her attempts to keep the affair on a casual level, she was with him more often than not. It was only the strength and resiliency of youth that enabled them to make love until almost dawn, and then arise and tend to the duties of the day with some alertness.

As for Melissa, she was not quite sure what their relationship was. She adored having Beau make love to her. It was just that she seemed to have lost control over herself, as well as the situation; it seemed to her that the more they made love, the more they wanted to make love. It was like a fever, and appeared to have the same wasting effect, causing a sort of delirium. It was only in her saner moments that she paused to ask herself how she really felt about Beau, and how he felt about her. Did she even *care* where the relationship was going? The answer to that, at the moment anyway, was in the negative, and that troubled her considerably. Still, it was a heady thing, exciting and, to some degree, dangerous, since it was forbidden.

The days went by so quickly that she was scarcely conscious of their passing. She seldom thought of Luke Devereaux, but when she did she found that the pain was still there, so she avoided thinking of him as much as possible.

She tried to dwell on the positive things. For the first time in years, she was content. Everything was going well. The *Belle* was earning a profit, and at the same time they were making people happy.

Oh, there were problems. For instance, it seemed that in almost every town where they played, at least one thing went wrong. In one place, their flyers had been mysteriously torn down prior to their arrival, but even though they had, in effect, arrived unannounced, a large crowd had gathered by the time the *Belle* docked, and they had a respectable house that evening.

In the last town, the trouble had been a bit more serious, for someone had cut the landing ropes, and in the middle of the night the *Belle* had drifted out into the river with no steam up, and no means of control.

Before that, it had been a good evening. The audience had been large and receptive, and the cast had performed *The Miser's End* to great acclaim.

Everyone was in bed and asleep except for Mollie, who because of her usual night schedule had become accustomed to staying up late.

Since she could not sleep, Mollie had gone for a stroll around the deck. She noticed a bit of unusual motion as she climbed from one deck to another, but thought only that the river was becoming a little rough. Perhaps a wind was coming up, or perhaps there had been a sudden hard rain farther north, and the river was rising. She hoped that was the reason, since the river had been getting dangerously low.

But when she arrived on the top deck, she saw, to her horror, that the *Belle* was adrift, moving broadside down the river, with no steam up, which meant there was no control.

Mollie seized the rope that pulled the large brass bell hanging from the eaves of the pilot house, and set it to clanging. Then she raced into the wheelhouse, arriving just in time to hear the engineer's faint voice coming through the speaking tube.

"Hullo? Hullo the wheelhouse! Captain? Are you there, captain? What's the trouble?"

Mollie shouted down the tube. "Amos, that you?

Listen, Amos, we're adrift! Get those men of yours out of their bunks, and get steam up! And do it now, afore we run aground or get our bottom snagged out!"

"Right away, Cap'n," Amos said, and the tube went silent.

Mollie grabbed the spokes of the giant wheel, turning it so that the *Belle* slowly began to change her position in the current. She had to get the durned boat around so that she could see where the devil she was going! Without power and with the *Belle* drifting, it took all of her strength to spin the wheel.

By now, the rest of the crew and cast had been roused, and Jubal, Martha, and Melissa hurried into the wheelhouse.

"What happened?" Jubal's voice was strident.

"Damned if I know," Mollie said, horsing the wheel around another turn. "All I know is that I came up on deck and found us cut loose and drifting crosswise down the river. Jubal, help me wrestle the wheel so's we can get her around. Amos is getting the boilers fired up, and as soon as we get up steam, we'll be all right. Just pray that we get steam up afore we bottom out on a bar, or run into a sawyer."

Jubal took the wheel, and together they finally got the *Belle* facing downriver. "Call down to Amos, see how that steam's coming!" Mollie bawled. "I can handle her all right now."

Jubal used the tube, then looked up at Mollie and shrugged. "He says they're doin' the best they can, but it'll be a few more minutes afore we have any power."

Mollie cursed, and Jubal looked at her curiously. "The man's doin' his best, Mollie. You can't get up steam in a few seconds, you know."

Mollie shook her head. "It's not that. Look out there." She pointed.

Jubal, Martha, and Melissa all peered through the big window, and Melissa's heart sank. A heavy blanket of fog was rolling toward them, like an unfolding quilt.

"Oh!" said Martha. "Be careful, Mollie!"

"I aim to be, woman!" Mollie snapped.

The fog reached them, shrouding them in featureless gray. Melissa couldn't even see the bow. She shivered, hugging herself. She had heard the stories that Jubal and Mollie had related about the whims of the river, and she knew how often steamboats met their end from snags, sand banks, blown boilers, and the fog, which was an ally to the many dangers lurking under the roiling brown water.

She couldn't bear to think of the *Natchez Belle* being gutted on a waterlogged tree, or being crushed on a bar. They had all worked so hard!

Jubal and Mollie both had their hands on the wheel again, their faces tense and pale in the splash of light from the lantern Jubal had lit.

The most frightening thing, to Melissa, was the silence. Usually when they were on the river, there was the comforting pound of the engines below, like the beating of a huge heart. Now there was only stillness, which added a ghostly effect to the tense situation.

And then, all of a sudden, ahead and to their right, a light pierced the gloom, and the craft bearing the light was almost upon them.

Jubal reached for the bell rope and gave it a series of savage yanks. The clang of the bell seemed muffled by the fog, but nonetheless it should be audible to any boat on the river.

"Damned shantyboat!" Mollie muttered. "They know we're supposed to have the right of way. Why in hell isn't he up against the bank for the night?"

Melissa, wondering how Mollie knew it was a shantyboat, peered into the gloom. As she did, a rift appeared in the fog, and she caught a glimpse of a shack on a raft, almost colliding with the port bow, bobbing wildly as the *Belle* swept past. She could hear the squall of rage and fear from the shantyboat owner, and then the raft was gone, swallowed up in the fog.

The speaking tube squawked, and Jubal bent to it. He listened for a moment, a slow grin spreading across his face. Straightening up, he shouted, "We've got steam! Thank the good Lord for small favors!"

Melissa felt the cold in her stomach lessen, but it did not go away entirely. Even though they had steam, there was still the fog to contend with. She had no idea where they were, and wondered if either Jubal or Mollie did.

As the huge engines kicked in, and the paddlewheel took hold, churning the water behind them, the boat slowed its forward movement. "What will you do now?" she whispered.

"Well," Mollie said, "I think I got me some idea where we are, but I'm not sure enough to put the *Belle* into the bank yet. If I misjudge, we could hole her. I reckon we'll just have to creep along, sticking close to the main channel, or at least along where I *hope* the main channel is, and then . . ."

Her voice faded, as the fog abruptly thinned and blew away, like smoke, in filmy strands.

"On the other hand," Jubal said happily, "we might just turn her around and head back to where we were!"

He began to laugh, and the others joined in.

As Mollie slowly brought the *Belle* about, they could hear a loud cheer go up from the lower decks.

Martha heaved a great sigh of relief. "Jubal," she said, "there's still some fog left, you look out for that shantyboat now, and look! My land, there's a barge coming down, there on our left. Now be sure and stay to this side of the—"

The roar of laughter from the others drowned out her voice, and Melissa felt her apprehensions melt away with her amusement; then a small thought in the back of her mind that she had not had time to pursue until now surfaced.

How had the *Belle* been set adrift?

Everyone slept late the next morning; but when they finally woke, the first order of business was the inspection of the ropes used to tie off the *Belle*. Jubal held the end of one of the ropes out to Melissa. It was obvious that the rope had not parted through wear or accident, for the edges were neatly cut across, as if they had been severed with some sharp instrument.

On the bow with them were Amalie, Mollie, and Martha. Melissa looked from one to the other in growing dismay.

"Damn!" Mollie swore and struck her thigh with a gnarled fist. "Some toad-swallowing river slug cut the fool thing! Now, who'd want to go and do a sneaky thing like that?"

Jubal shook his head, and Amalie said thoughtfully, "You know, this isn't the first unexplained problem we've had. First, those rowdies at our first performance, then the handbills being taken down. It seems to me that too many things have happened for it to be just coincidence. So it raises a question. Could someone be behind these misfortunes? Could someone have arranged all these things, including this?" She pointed to the severed rope.

The others looked at her with varying degrees of astonishment.

"Why, I don't see how," Jubal said slowly. "I mean, things like that . . . The other things happen all the time on the river. There's always somethin' goin' wrong. It's the natural order of things. But this now, well, this is a horse of another color. This rope's plain been cut!" He thumped the deck with his peg leg for emphasis.

Amalie spread her hands, remaining silent.

Melissa looked at her through lowered lids. She knew Amalie well enough to realize that something was bothering her, and she longed to go freely to her, as she once had, take her arm, and pester her until she got the information out of her; but because of the recent reserve between them, she hesitated, wishing painfully that she could simply forget what had come between them. It was all Amos Johnson's fault! If he had not come along—!

"Well, what are we going to do about it?" Mollie asked with her customary forthrightness.

"The first thing we're goin' to do is to post a guard at night, so's this don't happen again," Jubal said harshly. "There's no way of tellin' who did the deed, but at least we can see that it don't happen again." He shook his head. "At least nothin' nor nobody was hurt, and no real harm done."

"That wasn't the fault of whoever did it," Martha said. "The person responsible probably meant for the *Belle* to drift onto a snag and rip her bottom out.

That's probably what they expected, and I think Amalie's right. My land, when you think about it, some of the things that have happened have been kind of peculiar. A little too much coincidence, I'd say."

They all looked at Amalie, who shrugged. "I didn't say that someone had caused all these things. I only said that it was possible."

A horrifying thought came to Melissa. "Simon Crouse, I'll bet he's behind it!"

They all stared at her in disbelief, all except Amalie, who nodded slightly.

"Come now, little lady," Jubal exclaimed. "Hell's fire, he's way up in Natchez! How could he be doin' it?"

"I didn't say he was doing it personally. But he could have hired someone, paid someone on board, a crew member, even one of the players, to cause us trouble."

Jubal scrubbed at his chin, and thumped the deck. "But why in tarnation would he go to all that expense and trouble?"

"Because he's that kind of man! Because I refused to—" Melissa broke off, flushing at the memory of Crouse's proposal.

After an extended, uncomfortable silence, Jubal said briskly, "Well, we'd best get busy, if we're goin' to put on a show tonight."

Martha nodded. "Yes. That costume of Beau's, for the second act, has a tear in it. I'd better get to work on it."

At the mention of Beau's name, Melissa blushed, and was angry at herself for doing so. She had been with Beau last night when the clanging of the boat's

256

bell had alerted her that something was wrong, and she was sure that Martin LaSalle had seen her coming out of Beau's cabin. She felt shame that someone should know of her affair with Beau, and since it was Martin, anger as well. She was not sure why.

The next stop on their itinerary was a small town, and the *Belle* was only staying for one performance. The boat steamed into the landing in the middle of the day, giving the troupe ample time to prepare for the evening's show. They planned to take to the river early the next morning, so they could reach the next town before nightfall.

The performance went well—they had done *The Little Violet Seller* again and it had been well received. Melissa was feeling a bit weary. The wild frenzy that had sustained her for the past weeks was losing momentum, and she was beginning to feel the effects of her strenuous schedule.

She knew that Beau was expecting her to meet him in his cabin as soon as the boat settled down for the night; but for the first time, she was not sure she wanted to go. The thought of her own bed, and being alone in it, was suddenly very attractive. On the other hand, she didn't want to hurt Beau's feelings, or make him angry.

She was heading toward her cabin, to freshen up before seeing Beau, when a figure stepped out of a darkened passageway and seized her arm.

She gave a leap of fright before she recognized Martin. She swallowed and pulled her arm away. "Martin, you frightened me, jumping out at me like that!"

"I'm sorry," he said, but with little contrition in his

voice. "You know I wouldn't do a thing like that on purpose. Melissa, you're the last person in the world I'd want to frighten or hurt."

He placed a strange emphasis on the words, and Melissa felt a mixture of feelings that she recognized as anticipation and fear. She swallowed again. "What do you want?"

He was standing very close, and she could smell his shaving lotion, not Bay Rum, but something heavier and sweeter.

"Just to be close to you. Just to touch you. Do you have any idea how I feel about you? How much I want you?"

The intensity of his voice, the pressure of his fingers on her arm, stirred her more than she cared to admit. She tried to pull away. "Martin, you're a married man. You shouldn't be saying things like that to me!"

He drew her closer, until she could feel the fabric of his coat against her bosom. "I'm a married man, true, but not a happily married man. My wife and I don't really care for one another any more, not in the way a man and wife should. I'm lonely, Melissa, and I'm mad about you. Your hair," he stroked her head, and she trembled. "Your skin! So white and smooth!" He caressed her face. "And those lips . . . Oh, God, Melissa! Have you any idea what you do to a man?"

Melissa felt her heart pounding madly, and suddenly her fear overcame any attraction that Martin had for her. "No!" she said firmly, pushing him away. "Martin, I'm sorry, but I've never given you any reason to think that I would welcome your advances!"

He would not release her, but held her to him again. "It's not as if you are inexperienced," he whispered insinuatingly. "I saw you coming out of young Vermillian's cabin. You must listen to me. Whatever he does for you, whatever he makes you feel, I can do more. I am a man, not a boy, and I know what women like. I know how to please you. Come with me, my dearest—"

He stopped in mid-sentence, staring past her, and he dropped Melissa's arm abruptly.

Melissa turned to see what he was staring at, and saw Amalie standing not three feet away.

Martin mumbled something that might have been an apology, and vanished into the shadows. Melissa and Amalie stood staring at one another, without speaking.

A riot of feelings warred within Melissa—shame, anger, outrage, guilt. The expression on Amalie's face mirrored disappointment and seemed, to Melissa, to be accusatory.

She raised her chin defiantly, wanting desperately to explain, yet angry that she should be expected to provide an explanation.

Amalie shook her head sadly. "Oh, Melissa!" Her voice was low.

The sudden realization struck Melissa that Amalie had misunderstood the situation; she had evidently thought that Melissa had been in Martin's arms willingly. Her face flushed with heat.

"Amalie," she said, "how could you think that!"

Amalie stared at her. "How do you know what I am thinking? I know only what I see."

Melissa laughed, and the sound was not a happy one. "Oh, I know what you think, Amalie. I know you too well. The saintly Amalie, always so understanding, has for once misunderstood!"

Amalie's expression chilled. "I do not judge you, Melissa, you know that."

"And you had better not," Melissa said, her voice shaking with sudden, overwhelming anger. "Because if you did, then I might judge you, you and that—that man, that engineer, who's not good enough to—"

Amalie gestured sharply, her voice cutting like a knife when she spoke. "Enough, Melissa. Do not say something you'll be sorry for, and make it impossible for us to remain friends. Amos Johnson is a fine man, and his intentions, which are none of your affair but since you seem so concerned, are most honorable. Amos has asked me to marry him."

Melissa suddenly felt drained, almost ill from sustained anger. "Martin LaSalle came upon me suddenly in the dark, Amalie. He was trying to . . . He wanted to . . . I was fighting him off when you came upon us."

It seemed, even to Melissa, that her words lacked conviction, and she knew that it was because she had, however briefly, thrilled to Martin's advances, and had almost, but not quite, entertained the thought of giving in to him.

Amalie shrugged, and stood stiffly for a long moment. Then her body relaxed. "Of course. I should have realized. It is just that . . . Well, no matter really. You should get to bed now, Melissa. You appear tired."

Melissa nodded. She *was* weary, in mind and body. The two women walked together to their respective cabins. That in itself was an indication of their growing apart. On leaving New Orleans, Amalie had requested a cabin of her own.

Probably to share with Amos Johnson, Melissa thought resentfully.

Amalie murmured a goodnight and slipped into her cabin. Melissa walked on, weighed down with a sense of loss. Amalie was the only real friend she had in this world, but the schism between them yawned wider with every passing day.

Tears starting in her eyes, Melissa stopped with her hand on her cabin door, suddenly remembering that she had been on her way to Beau's cabin when she was intercepted by Martin LaSalle. Well, she was certainly in no mood for romantic dalliance now. Let Beau realize that she wasn't always at his beck and call!

The morning was hot and humid, and Luke wiped his forehead with his handkerchief. After a good breakfast in the cheerful kitchen, he had gone out to look over the fields and the workers. He wanted to see Roy Davis in action, so that he could pinpoint the trouble here, whatever it was.

The fields looked fine. The sugar cane seemed well tended. There were field hands working in the sugar cane, under the scorching sun. At first look, Riverview seemed to be functioning smoothly enough. Perhaps Davis was right; perhaps there was no problem. Then, as Luke turned to make his way back toward the main house, he saw Davis coming toward the field.

Luke stepped behind an oak. He wanted to see how Davis handled himself around the men, and he wanted it to be natural, not staged for his benefit.

Davis, in polished riding boots and carrying a crop, strode around the perimeter of the field, stopping to talk to first one man, then another. Luke was too far away to hear what was said, but the workers' gestures spoke of a thinly veiled hostility toward the overseer.

Davis continued on from one worker to another; and then, as he was approaching a tall, stooped black man with long, heavily muscled arms, the man rose from his half-stoop and swung one of his fists at Davis, missing him, but causing the overseer to step hastily back.

Davis loosed a string of curses, which Luke could hear even from his place of concealment. The rest of the men had stopped working and were staring stonily at the scene. There was tension in their postures.

Davis raised the riding crop and brought it whistling down on the worker's head. The man grunted with pain, and as Davis raised the crop to strike him again, he seized it in both hands and tore it from the overseer's grip, tossing it contemptuously into the stand of sugar cane behind him.

Davis took a step back and, reaching under his long coat, he pulled out a gun and pointed it threateningly at the field hand.

Luke broke from his hiding place and ran at top speed toward the overseer. Was Davis stupid? Didn't he know that if he shot the field hand, every other worker would be upon him within seconds? If that happened, he wouldn't stand a prayer!

Breathing harshly, Luke raced toward them, his feet sinking into the soft earth with every step. He seemed to be running in quicksand. He thought of yelling, but he doubted that Davis, in his rage, would hear him, or even heed the shout.

As he drew near, he saw Davis switch his grip on the pistol and, holding it by the barrel, swing it toward the black man's head. The gun connected with the man's skull, and he dropped to his knees like a stunned steer.

There was a concerted movement among the other blacks in the field, and an angry murmur rose around Luke and Davis like the hum of a disturbed beehive.

Luke dropped to one knee beside the wounded man. The man's eyes rolled loosely, and blood dripped from the broken skin where the gun butt had struck him, but he didn't appear to be seriously hurt.

Aiming an angry glance at Davis, Luke put one shoulder under the worker's head.

"Get on the other side," he told Davis, "and hurry up before the rest of these men realize there are some twenty of them and only two of us."

"They wouldn't dare," Davis blustered. "The war may have set them free, but their asses would still be burned if they raised their hand to a white man."

"That may well be," Luke said harshly, "but right now I don't reckon they're doing much in the way of clear thinking. Now help me, goddamnit, or I'll leave you here to their mercy!"

Davis, muttering, finally bent down to help support and lift the injured man. Together, they walked him toward what had once been the slave quarters.

Behind them, Luke could hear the angry murmurs rise in volume, and his back itched all the way to the small, dilapidated shack that was the man's home.

The cabin had a flimsy, ill-fitting door, which was opened by a young, rather pretty black woman; her eyes flared wide in fright when she saw the three men on her doorstep.

She backed up into the dimness of the room, her hand to her mouth and her eyes apprehensive. She didn't speak as Luke and Davis lowered the man to a pallet in one corner of the room.

When the man was prostrate on the ragged quilt, Luke turned to the woman. "Would you fetch some water, please, and some clean cloths? He'll need the wound washed."

She nodded, and went to do his bidding.

"Are you his wife?" he called to her as she bent to get a battered basin from the floor.

She nodded again, face averted, and scurried out of the room, apparently to fetch the water.

Luke lifted the injured man's right eyelid, and inspected the pupil. He sighed heavily. "It looks as if he'll live, Davis. But what got into you? What the hell did you do that for?"

Davis glanced at him in surprise. "Why, you saw the black bastard. He swung on me. Almost hit me! What did you expect me to do, pat him on his woolly head?"

Luke sighed in disgust. "No. I didn't expect that, but I don't think it was necessary to pistolwhip him."

"Mr. Devereaux, you plain don't understand niggers." He shook his head. "You got to keep them in line, like I told you before. You can't let them think they can get the best of you, or you're dead!"

Luke choked back a heated retort. It wouldn't do any good to talk to Davis on the subject, that was plain enough. The man was obsessed by the notion that the white man was superior, in all ways, to the black.

Just then, the injured man's wife returned with a basin of water and some strips of cloth. She approached timidly. She glanced at Davis with obvious fear, and halted without coming near her husband.

"Don't be afraid," Luke said. "Go ahead, clean his wound."

Cautiously, the young woman inched forward, rolling her eyes at Davis, as if ready to flee if he showed displeasure.

"For Christ's sake, Davis!" Luke said in exasperation. "Will you tell her that it's all right?"

Davis, his face coloring slightly, backed away from the pallet. He did not look at the girl. "It's all right. Go on, do as he says," he said curtly.

The woman, never taking her gaze from his face, approached the pallet, and fell to her knees by the side of her husband.

As she started to tend him, the man moaned softly, and rolled his head back and forth on the pallet.

"He's going to be fine," Luke said. "You take care of him now. I'll drop by tomorrow to see how he is. All right?"

The young woman nodded silently, not looking up as she huddled over her husband.

Luke could not understand it. The woman seemed terrified. Was she afraid of Roy Davis?

Luke had seen other cruel overseers, and knew that some men preferred to control their workers through fear; but now that the Negroes were free, their white bosses no longer had the power of life and death that they had possessed before the war. Davis was rough and brutal—there had been no need to strike the man with the gun. But could he have so intimidated the workers there that they would show the depth of terror that this young woman had shown? Besides, that didn't fit with the fact that the man *had* tried to strike Davis first, nor did it fit with Hiram's attitude.

Luke thought that perhaps he should talk to all the workers, but before he did that, he would have to gain their confidence. Right now, he was a stranger, and they would probably trust him no more than they did Roy Davis. He'd give it a little time, make himself more familiar to them, keep his eyes and ears open, and then he would begin to ask his questions. A little information here, a little information there . . .

He and Davis left the cabin and walked toward the main house. During the stroll back, Davis was uncharacteristically friendly, trying, in his clumsy way, to minimize the incident that had just occurred.

This made Luke more curious than ever. What in the name of heaven was going on at Riverview?

"You must understand, Devereaux, that the only reason I clipped that fellow with my gun was because he's a real troublemaker, always has been. That's not the first time he's raised his hand to me, and I thought, by God, I've taken enough of that bastard's sass! I believe in treating my workers strict, but I'm fair, I'm sure you'll find that to be true. This time, the bastard had it coming to him!

"Well, now! Let's have a refreshing julep on the veranda. Hiram makes a damned fine julep, I'll hand him that, although that's about the only thing he does do well."

Davis laughed uproariously, and looked at Luke as if for approbation. Luke, although he didn't want to antagonize Davis, simply could not bring himself to that point of hypocrisy. However, he managed to mask his hostility.

"That would be nice," he said pleasantly. "It's damned hot out today."

Davis grinned, bobbing his head rapidly.

Luke sighed inwardly. Davis's smile was not much more pleasant than his usual scowl, and it was so out of character that Luke wanted to laugh aloud. Why was the man trying to be ingratiating? Was he embarrassed at being caught out in the role of bully? Or was he afraid that Luke would report the incident to Simon Crouse?

Well, at any rate, Luke decided, he would go along with the situation, awkward as it was.

He grinned derisively to himself. He had little choice in the matter. Either he pounded Davis on the head and drove him into the ground like a stake, which was what he felt like doing, or he played the hypocrite, in the hope that he could uncover the trouble here and then, hopefully, be free of Crouse.

Chapter Fifteen

"What in the blue blazes of hell is that thing doing tied up next to us?"

The raucous voice of Mollie Boom echoed across the dining room, and Melissa, just arrived at her place at the table, leaned forward to see what Mollie was referring to.

There, docked next to them, was a familiar-looking barge. Mollie pointed. "See that?"

Melissa followed the line of the pointing finger. On a small pole atop the barge was a flag bearing the words *The Melon Patch.*

"Oh, no!" Martha said. "Not again!"

The rest of the troupe crowded around the window, and Peggy LaSalle wanted to know what the sign meant, and what was so terrible about it.

"It's a floating whorehouse," Mollie grumbled, "that's what's so terrible about it!"

"Mollie!' Martha cried. "My land, I declare. You're as bad as Jubal. It's a gambling hall, and they offer . . . Well, they offer entertainment." There was considerable laughter at this. "They were tied up next to us at Natchez, and there was some . . . unpleasantness. They caused us some trouble."

"Trouble!" Jubal snorted. "They laid hands on Amalie here, and was goin' to take her off with them. That's more'n just trouble, in my thinkin'."

Amalie was suddenly the focus of all eyes, causing her to blush. She laughed at her own consternation. "It is true," she said. "They are bad people, particularly the man who owns the barge, the man called Bear."

Nehemiah pushed his way through the chattering actors, to Jubal's side. "What do you think we ought to do about this, Jubal? Should we move the *Belle?*"

"Hell, no!" Mollie exploded. "We're here first, and here we'll stay. We'll just double the watch, and keep a close eye on the bastards so's they don't try anything."

"Maybe we should go aboard and have a word with the man in charge, let him know that this time we are not alone and undefended, that we will fight him if he attempts any skullduggery," Nehemiah said thoughtfully. "If he knows we're not an easy mark, perhaps he will consider any attack on us unprofitable."

"Maybe that's a good idea," Jubal answered. "I'll think on it."

"Oh, no, you don't, Jubal King," Martha said, punching him not too lightly on the upper arm. "I'm not having you go aboard that—that—"

"Whorehouse, Martha?" Mollie said helpfully.

The others laughed. The newest members of the troupe seemed to view it as something of a lark.

Beau made his way to Melissa's side, and under cover of the chatter of the others whispered to her,

"Why didn't you come to my cabin last night? I almost went crazy, Melissa, waiting for you."

Melissa worried her lower lip with her teeth. She did not dare tell him the truth, for if she did he would probably call Martin on it, there would be a fight, and the troupe would be disrupted, maybe destroyed.

"I didn't feel well," she said as convincingly as she could. "I was really ill. I went to my cabin to lie down, fell asleep, and didn't wake up until this morning." She smiled ruefully. "Forgive me?"

He nodded. "As if I could refuse you anything, my darling. Just don't let it happen again." He smiled and squeezed her arm, and she tried to smile back.

He peered through the window over her shoulder. "It doesn't look like much, does it, this love boat?"

Melissa shivered. "No, but I hate seeing it again. It can mean nothing but trouble. I wonder if that awful man who kidnapped Amalie is still in charge?"

As she spoke, a tall, slope-shouldered man emerged from the main cabin of the *Melon Patch* and stood on the deck. He had long hair and a bushy beard, and he was staring directly at the *Belle*, seemingly into the window of the dining room where the troupe was gathered.

Amalie said tightly, "It's that awful man. It's Bear Smith."

"Is he the one who kidnapped you?" Peggy LaSalle asked avidly, her eyes bright with curiosity.

Amalie nodded, her eyes cast down.

Melissa could see that she was trembling, and went quickly to her side. "It's all right, Amalie. We will look out for you this time."

Her anger forgotten for the moment, Melissa embraced her friend, and Amalie hugged her back.

271

"Thank you, *chérie*. It is just, to see him like this again . . ."

Upon seeing Bear, Amalie's thoughts had jumped back at once to Simon Crouse, for she knew very well that Crouse had been behind her abduction.

Why was the love boat here, in this particular place, at this particular time? Was it a coincidence, or had Crouse sent them? If so, what was he plotting this time? Did he plan to attempt again to take her by force? Had he discovered that she was the one responsible for the bad things that surely had been happening to him?

She shivered, and hugged herself as if cold.

If Crouse had the sense, or if someone had advised him, to go to an obeah woman, he would have found out the reason for his bad fortune; and since he was not a stupid man, whatever else he was, he would surely guess that the cause of his troubles was Amalie Dubois. If that had happened . . .

No, it was not beyond the realm of reality to suppose that Simon Crouse had sent the love boat to follow the *Natchez Belle,* and cause trouble in one way or another. For that reason, they must remain alert.

For a moment, Amalie leaned against Melissa, taking comfort in the closeness of the girl she truly thought of as her own daughter. The recent coolness between them had hurt Amalie deeply, and she yearned for their relationship to return to its former state. However, she could not push it, she could not make the first move, because this time Melissa was in the wrong, and she must have time to work things out in her own mind before discussion of the subject could do any good.

Amalie was certain that she knew what was bothering Melissa, but the girl, she felt sure, would not admit it, even if she was told what it was. For Melissa considered herself very enlightened, very tolerant; it would be difficult for her to accept the fact that her disapproval of Amos Johnson was based on something as simple as Amos being very dark, while Amalie was light.

So Amalie knew that she must be patient. In time Melissa would come around. She had faith in Melissa's basic fairness; it was just that she could not be pushed, and must come to terms with the situation in her own good time.

She came back to the present with a start as the hairy figure on the love boat made an obscene gesture toward the *Belle*. The group at the window drew back with a concerted gasp. The sound of Bear Smith's laughter was harsh and taunting on the quiet morning air.

Beau, fists clenched, stepped up. "I say that we should go over there and confront this scoundrel! Let him know once and for all that we won't put up with that sort of thing. After all, there are ladies present!"

Mollie Boom snorted. "And *I* say that we all go down there and whale the stuffing out of him. That'll do a durn sight more good than all the jawing in the world!"

Jubal stretched to his full height, and thumped his peg leg. "Whoa there now! I'm captain of this here boat, and because of that I'm in charge. Now, Miss Huntoon here, she hired me, so she's in charge of me. Nehemiah here is the director and is in charge of all you play actors. So why don't you all just settle down and go about your business and let us decide what's to do about Mr. Bear Smith and his love boat?"

There were some mutters of discontent from the rest of the group, mainly from Martin and Beau.

Melissa whispered in Beau's ear. "Behave yourself now, and do what Jubal says. Get along with you."

In a few minutes only the original members of the *Belle*'s complement were left in the dining room, having a "council of war," as Mollie Boom put it.

"Now," Jubal said, when they were settled around the table, "I think that we should be a little foxy with Mr. Bear Smith. I think we should just ignore him, pretend that he ain't even there."

"I agree," Melissa said. "It's plain that he wants to annoy us. If we pretend that he isn't annoying us, well, then we'll have won, and he'll go away."

Nehemiah said doubtfully, "I don't know. The man is a villain. He's dangerous. We'll have to keep a strong watch on duty at all times, indeed we will. I shouldn't like to have a repeat of Amalie's misadventure. What do you suppose the blackguard really wants with us? It seems to me there is something sinister behind this harassment, something more than just mischief on the part of a rude and wicked man."

"Hellfire!" Mollie thumped the table. "I say we should put a hole in that floating sin bucket, and let 'er sink to the bottom of the river, with doxies and customers alike. It's not that I'm against a little fun, but that man takes things to a new low. He and that scummy boat of his are a stink on the river, and best wiped out."

"We'll take a vote," said Jubal. "How many think we should hold off for a bit, keep our guard up, but wait until we see what he's up to before we raise a fuss?"

Slowly, everyone but Mollie raised a hand.

Jubal nodded. "Well, it looks like that's the way we

274

do her for the time bein'. Sorry, Mollie, but we'll do it your way if Bear Smith starts any trouble, or if'n we have reason to think he will."

Mollie snorted. "You'll all be sorry, wait and see if I ain't right."

"You're a fire-eater, Mollie Boom." Jubal laughed, then sobered. "All right. Let's get on with the preparations for tonight's show. We've got a goodly crowd comin', from what I can see, and we want to give 'em a good show for their money."

"Please, sir! Unhand me! I am the wife of another!"

Linnea struggled in the grip of the villain, portrayed by Nehemiah, and then broke away to stand with her arms outstretched against the front of the fake brick fireplace that formed the focus of the parlor set.

Nehemiah twirled the ends of his long black moustache, and laughed a deep, evil laugh. Whirling, he flared his black cape, and faced the audience. "She refuses me now," he hissed directly to them, "but she shall be mine, never fear, when that weak, foolish husband of hers is in his grave. And that will be soon, mark me!"

He leered, and there were hisses and catcalls from the members of the audience, who were, to a man, woman and child, perched on the edges of their seats. "For shame! Shame!"

A voice offstage cried, "Mother! Oh, Mother!"

Melissa, as the daughter, came running on, false blonde curls flying, demure in a plain blue dress, with a ruffled apron which helped to hide her too-adult figure. "Oh, Mother! What has he done to you?" She whirled on Nehemiah. "Begone, you foul bird of prey!

My mother shall never be yours! My father still lives and . . ."

The noisy sound of feet on planking echoed through the theater, and seemed to be coming closer.

Melissa, wondering what was happening, spoke louder. "Mother, I have found Daddy. He is here, outside. He is ill, and needs . . ."

The sound was louder now, and accompanied by drunken shouts and rude laughter.

There was no use trying to go on, for the actors could not be heard above the noise. All action on the stage ceased, and performers and audience alike turned their heads toward the entranceway.

With a great babble of sound, several people were crowding through the doorway into the grand saloon. There was a collective gasp from the audience and cast as one of the men stumbled drunkenly into the first row of seats, and began swearing mightily. It was still light outdoors, and in the light that came in through the open door, the interlopers could be seen clearly. The crowd gasped again, for the uninvited visitors consisted of drunken, half-dressed men and women.

Melissa knew instantly that they were from the love boat; they could be from nowhere else.

Shocked housewives covered their children's eyes, and husbands stood up and raised their fists and voices in anger at this outrage.

Melissa realized that a fight was inevitable, if the intruders were not ejected as soon as possible.

"Where is Jubal?" she said despairingly, and then saw that Jubal was already in the thick of the crowd, trying to subdue a muscular man who was carrying an axe handle and waving it about wildly.

276

Nehemiah, Beau, and Martin LaSalle all leaped down from the stage into the melee, and converged upon the milling throng.

"Out! Out of here!" Jubal was shouting and thumping about on his wooden leg, trying to be heard and trying to herd the intruders back through the entrance, but with so much drunken confusion, the new arrivals managed to stagger into the crowd, and fights began to erupt among the men, as the women and children struggled to get away, drawing away from contact with the painted, half-dressed women.

Melissa had climbed down off the stage, only to find herself being pushed back against the apron by a woman with several children. Melissa tried to crane over their heads in search of Beau. She finally caught sight of him, struggling with a wide-shouldered man, and then she felt herself grasped by both arms, and unceremoniously hoisted back onto the stage.

Angrily, she looked to either side, staring into the grinning faces of two evil-looking men.

As she opened her mouth to scream for help, a hand was clapped over her mouth, and she was dragged into the wings, where a strip of cloth was quickly tied around her mouth and her hands were bound.

Almost choking from the pressure of the gag, she was half-pushed, half-carried out onto the deck, and then along the stage plank to the river bank. She struggled wildly, but her strength was puny compared to that of the two men, and they simply laughed at her as they propelled her on ahead of them, down the bank to the rickety landing plank of the *Melon Patch*.

Dear God! Melissa thought. They were doing to her what they had done to Amalie! But why? The gag bit cruelly into her cheeks, and her arms hurt where the men had seized her. On the verge of tears, she stumbled on board the *Melon Patch*, wondering about her ultimate fate.

On board the barge, the men hustled her inside the long cabin and down the foul-smelling passageway to a large, rather well-appointed cabin in the stern.

Sitting in the cabin, lounging in a large carved chair, was the bearded man they called Bear. As her abductors pushed Melissa in front of him, he smiled, and the thick brush of his beard parted to show large white teeth, like the teeth of a hungry animal.

Melissa found herself trembling.

One of the men untied the gag, while the other unbound her arms. Her wrists burned so that she had to rub them, using the contact of her hand against the bruised flesh to assure herself of the reality of what was happening.

"What—what do you want with me?" she demanded, her voice quivering.

Bear's laughter rumbled. "What do you think I want with you, pretty? What would a man who runs a floating whorehouse be likely to want with a woman?" His voice was deep and resonant, issuing from the cave of his chest in guttural bursts. "I've got a standing order for you, pretty. Got a man who'll pay me dear for delivering you to him. Now what do you think of that?"

"Who? Who would do that?" Melissa asked bravely, although her voice still trembled.

He roared laughter. "Best that be left a mystery, pretty, until you find out for yourself."

He continued to laugh, and Melissa, her thoughts churning, could think of no one who would be so cruel as to pay this hideous creature to abduct her. Who could it be?

A thought nagged at her mind, but was quickly gone as Bear, still laughing, rose and lunged toward her, seizing her right wrist with his powerful hand.

"But he never said I couldn't enjoy you first, now did he? Never said nothing like that!"

He fell back into the chair, holding her on his lap. He began to fondle her, running his big hands over her breasts, and under her dress, squeezing her thighs.

"Aye, a nice, plump, pretty little pigeon, ain't she? Just ripe for the roasting, and old Bear has just the spit to turn her on."

Melissa, almost overcome by the stench of sour sweat, alcohol, and tobacco, felt that she was going to faint if he did not let her go. For the first time, she fully realized how helpless a woman was in the grip of a powerful man; and how easily such a man could do what he would with her.

The thought sent a shiver of fear through her. She had only known two men, Luke Devereaux and Beau Vermillian, and they had both been gentle with her, and had brought her pleasure.

This beast of a man, she sensed, would not be gentle, and her flesh shrank at the thought of having him touch her. His hand on the inside of her thigh was an invasion, and she shuddered in revulsion.

This only made Bear grip her the tighter, and then he bent his shaggy head, and pressed his mouth to hers, the beard wiry and strange against her face. The beard had a stale, musty odor and, strangely, made Melissa think of a moment in childhood when she had found a deserted bird's nest, and buried her face in it.

She twisted her face away, to find herself staring into the fascinated eyes of one of her captors, who was stooping, the better to see what Bear was doing to her.

He was rubbing the front of his bulging trousers, and Melissa felt dizzy with disgust. He grinned at her lewdly, and then began to unbutton his trousers, but Bear, raising his head and seeing him, roared, "Out of here, you river rats, and don't come back 'til you're called!"

When the door slammed behind them, Bear reared up, lifting Melissa in his huge arms, and carried her easily over to the bed.

Dropped upon the lumpy mattress, Melissa tried to scramble away. He cuffed her casually alongside the face. He reached down, and with just two fingers caught in the front of her bodice ripped the fabric of her dress from neckline to hem. Melissa cried out, and tried to cover herself, but with his other hand, Bear batted her hands away.

He stared at her out of the thick tangle of hair that surrounded his face, his mouth open like a large O, as he gazed at her exposed breasts and the triangle of copper hair at the junction of her thighs.

"By God!" he muttered hoarsely. "I don't blame him for wanting you. You're a prime pretty, you are. I think this trip is going to take quite awhile." He chuckled, reaching out a thick hand and touching Melissa's abdomen. "Yeah, this trip will take time. I'll see to it that it does, and I will enjoy you every day, pretty, until the journey's end. Perhaps twice a day if I'm man enough."

Grinning hugely, he stood up, and undid the belt of his trousers. The garment dropped to the floor, and Melissa clamped her eyes shut, but not before she had seen the threat of his manhood jutting out of its nest of hair like a weapon.

In panic and terror, she tried again to roll off the narrow bed, but he dropped atop her, supporting himself on all fours, his organ touching her. Laughing, he gripped her clamped thighs with his hands, and forced them apart, kneeling between them.

Melissa screamed, putting all her outrage into the sound, and he roared with laughter, and shoved himself at her until she could feel the insistent, obscene presence of his organ at the entrance to her body.

She was tense with the effort of rejecting him, and she did not recognize the sound of the splintering door for what it was. It was only when she saw the figures spilling into the cabin that she realized what was happening.

Bear, in one spring, was on his feet and roaring his rage at the intruders. Melissa, snatching the coverlet over her nakedness, felt a welling of gratitude for her narrow escape, a feeling immediately replaced by apprehension for her rescuers. How could even an army of men subdue this monster called Bear?

Jubal was in the lead, followed by Amos Johnson and Beau. The three men confronted Bear with determination. They were not armed.

Bear did not appear in the least dismayed by the three-to-one odds. Melissa did notice that most of his attention stayed on Amos Johnson, as if he recognized the engineer as his greatest threat.

Amos moved first. Catlike on his feet for such a big man, he glided in and struck Bear a mighty blow alongside the head. Bear only shook his shaggy head and roared laughter as Amos danced back out of his reach.

And then Jubal, his long arms waving awkwardly, got in a solid blow to Bear's body. Bear bellowed in rage, and closed in on the one-legged captain, clasping Jubal's lean body in a crushing grip.

The air left Jubal's chest with a loud whummph, and Melissa could hear his vertebrae crack. Jubal yowled in pain, and thumped the floor with his peg leg.

Melissa screamed. The big man was breaking Jubal's back!

Then Amos snatched up a straight-backed chair, and swung it at the back of Bear's head. The chair connected with an unpleasant sound and Bear staggered, releasing his hold on Jubal, who slumped back against the wall.

Bear, still dazed from the force of the blow, staggered out through the open door and into the passageway. Amos and Beau charged after him. Amos was brandishing a heavy brass candlestick, and Beau picked up its mate as he followed Amos out.

Jubal got to his feet, shook his head gingerly, and thumped after the others. Melissa could hear the sound of their struggle as the men fought down the length of the passageway and then out onto the deck.

She heard thumps, shouts and cries of pain, but try as she might, she could not tell from whose throats the cries came.

"Oh, please, dear God," she prayed aloud. "Don't let any of my friends be hurt!"

And then there came a loud, prolonged scream, followed by a tremendous splash. One of them had gone overboard. But who?

Melissa got off the bed and scrambled into her torn clothing, not caring what sort of appearance she made, in a fever to know who it was that had gone into the river.

She ran down the empty passageway, and burst out of the door onto the deck. It was almost dark now, but there was sufficient light to see the customers and girls of the *Melon Patch* crowded on the deck, staring out into the river, where a dim figure thrashed in the current.

The crowd prevented Melissa from seeing who it was, and she pushed and fought her way through the forest of arms and backs with little thought of courtesy.

At last she caught sight of Jubal, and managed to make her way to his side. He looked around, saw her, and put an arm around her shoulders.

"Maybe you'd better not look," he said.

"Why? Who is that out there?"

"Amos knocked Bear into the river, and it appears that Bear can't swim."

Melissa looked at him in surprise, and he caught her look. He added, "Amos Johnson went in after him."

"Oh . . ." Melissa clapped a hand to her mouth.

She had heard Mollie say that the current here was very swift and treacherous, particularly out in the main channel, and then she saw Bear's head and open mouth bob up quite a distance out from the barge. Near him she could see Amos, stroking through the water.

"But why?" she cried. "Why would he risk himself for that—that animal?"

Jubal shrugged. "Seemed the only thing to do, but only Amos had the courage to do her."

"Why can't somebody help him?"

"They're putting out boats."

"Oh, no!" Melissa cried out, as the two forms in the water were swept farther away; and then there was just one head in the water. Whose? Whose head was it?

Melissa gave a start as a hand grasped her elbow. She glanced around into Amalie's stricken face.

"They told me that Amos went into the river," Amalie said. Her voice was thin.

Meilssa, seeing the pain on her face, put an arm around Amalie's shoulders. "He'll be all right, I'm sure."

Amalie closed her eyes and suddenly, for the first time, Melissa saw her as a separate person, not her friend, not her mother, but another woman, with emotions and concerns of her own, a woman who loved a man, a good man, a man who would risk his life to save a worthless hulk like Bear Smith.

Amalie stirred, looking past her. "Where is everyone hurrying to?"

"It's Amos, he's all right, and swimmin' in," Jubal said joyfully. "And they're headin' for the river bank to pull him in."

"They won't—they won't hurt him for what he did, will they? Some of those men are customers of the *Melon Patch*." Amalie's voice was concerned.

"Lordy, no," Jubal said. "They think he's a hero. All they know is that Amos was out there riskin' his life tryin' to save Bear." His expression grew bleak. "Now, I purely hate to rejoice at the death of any man, but in this case, I'd reckon it's good riddance. He was a bad 'un." Shaking his head, he turned to Melissa. "In all the excitement I forgot to ask you, girl, are you all right? Did he harm you?"

Melissa, thinking of how near she had come to

being violated by that gross, hairy animal, shuddered. "Not really, but if you hadn't come when you did—" She grimaced.

Amalie squeezed her shoulder. "Did he say anything to you about why he had you seized?"

Melissa thought back. "He said that he was paid to do it by someone, a man whom he didn't name. He said that he was going to make the return trip last a long time, so that he could . . ." She buried her face in Amalie's shoulder. "Oh, Amalie! I feel so ashamed of the way I've been acting. I've been selfish and cruel. I knew that you really cared about Amos, but I didn't *want* you to! And what's even worse, I don't even know why!"

Amalie tilted her chin up, and looked into her eyes. "Don't you, little one? Be honest now."

Melissa's glance skipped away. "You're right. I do know. I thought he wasn't good enough for you because he was black, and I was a little jealous. You have looked after me for so long that I didn't want to have to share your love with anyone else." She forced herself to look again into Amalie's eyes. "I acted like a spoiled child, and I am truly sorry."

Amalie kissed her cheek. "Then all is well between us once more, *chérie*. Now I must go and see if Amos is all right."

"I'll go with you."

The two women followed the line of people streaming off the *Melon Patch* and along the river bank.

Ahead of them, a shout went up, and a moment later, they could see the tall form of Amos Johnson coming toward them through the dusk, surrounded by a crowd of well-wishers. Amalie laughed, a choked sound of gladness, and hastened to intercept him.

285

Melissa watched as Amos took Amalie into his arms; the expressions on their faces would have touched the heart of the greatest cynic.

Melissa wept freely, delighted to be rid of the unhappy feelings she had been harboring, and happy for both Amalie and herself.

Chapter Sixteen

At Riverview the days slipped by easily, as Luke tried to make himself as unobtrusive as possible so that Roy Davis would go about his work as usual. After more than a week had passed, Luke began questioning the plantation workers, going about it slowly so as not to frighten them; but he found most of them uncooperative.

It was clear from their manner that they had little love for Davis. In fact, in most instances, direct antagonism was evident, yet they still would not voice any open charges against the overseer. Although Luke tried hard to gain their trust and confidence, he made little progress, even when Elena attempted to intercede for him.

Seeing Elena every day, Luke developed a strong liking for Davis's wife. Not only was she beautiful, but she was a good manager and an excellent housekeeper. Davis left her alone a great deal of the time, and it became more and more difficult for Luke to keep his thoughts from straying to her. This temptation was heightened by his growing conviction that Elena also liked him and was attracted to him.

Still, he felt it would be very bad policy for him to get involved with the wife of Riverview's overseer. It could lead to all sorts of problems, not the least of which would be the bungling of his task here. And he wanted to do it right, so he could get out from under Crouse's thumb.

Therefore, he tried as best he could to keep his thoughts on Davis, and the cause behind the hostile attitude of the workers. It wasn't easy—he wasn't learning anything of value, and he was getting bored. He decided it was necessary to change his method and take a stronger tack, so he could finish up.

On one particular evening, Davis, as he did so often, excused himself after supper, saying that he had some paperwork to attend to.

Luke nodded politely as the man took his leave, grateful and at the same time suspicious. There simply couldn't be that much paperwork involved with running Riverview. On the other hand, Davis making himself absent left Luke alone with Elena, and when her husband was not present Elena was an enjoyable, entertaining companion.

Of course, Luke realized that one of these nights he was going to have to follow Davis and see what he was really up to. It could be nothing more than drinking alone in his room; Luke knew that he was drinking heavily, since he could smell liquor on the man's breath at all hours. On the other hand, it could be that he liked Luke's company no better than Luke cared for his.

The problem with following Davis was that Luke would have to find some excuse of his own to leave

Elena. She would be bound to wonder if he disappeared into the night just after her husband had done the same. But one night soon, Luke knew that he would have to risk arousing her curiosity.

But for now, he sat contentedly enough, his feet up on a hassock, a glass of excellent port in one hand and a good cigar in the other, and smiled at Elena.

She looked particularly lovely tonight, he thought, with a special glow to her eyes, and a becoming pinkness to her cheeks. She was dressed in pale blue, and Luke had to keep his thoughts turned to everyday matters to avoided becoming aroused by the mere sight of her.

"Shall we finish our wine out on the veranda, Luke?" she said softly. "It will be cooler out there."

Luke was comfortable where he was, but he nodded, and got up to follow her out onto the wide porch. It *was* cooler outside, and the smell of magnolia and honeysuckle mingled with nightblooming jasmine to create a scent so heady that it almost made his senses reel.

Luke stood for a moment looking out into the darkness beyond the railing, and Elena came to stand near him. In fact, she was *very* near him, he noted with a warm rush of anticipation. His pulse began to pound.

Now she stepped even closer, and he turned his head to meet her eyes. They were very dark in the dim light that filtered through the curtains from inside the house. Elena placed her hand on his arm, and he felt himself tremble. *Damnation!* he thought. *That's what comes of being without a woman for too long a time.*

"Luke?" she asked shyly. "Do you think I'm attractive?"

Luke took the cigar out of his mouth and stared at her in surprise. "Attractive? What kind of a question is that? Elena, you know you are much more than that. You're beautiful, one of the loveliest women I have ever seen."

She caught her lower lip between her teeth. "But am I attractive to *you*? Are you attracted to me as a woman?" She was bold now, the shyness gone. "Luke, would you like to make love to me?"

Luke choked on his cigar, and felt desire blaze through him. What was she asking? Didn't she have any notion of what she was doing to him?

"My God, Elena," he said through gritted teeth. He thumbed the cigar into the night and watched the glowing end fall to earth like a dying firefly. "How can you ask a man a thing like that? I'm sure you've got some idea of how much I've wanted to make love to you since the day I arrived here, so why make it difficult for me?"

Her smile was slow and tender, but her eyes were melancholy. "Then why haven't you made love to me?"

He shook his head in exasperation. "For one thing, because you have a husband. A big, mean sonofabitch, I might add. I've always made it a practice to tread gently where jealous husbands are concerned. And don't try to tell me that Davis wouldn't care if I became intimate with his wife, because I know better. He's a man who likes to keep his property to himself."

She grimaced. "You have that part correct, at any rate. To Mr. Davis, I am a possession, and he would fly into a rage if he knew that you and I . . . that we . . . But why must he know?"

"Elena, I—Good Christ!" Luke set his glass down on

the railing, and with one step, drew her into the circle of his arms.

She felt just as good nestled there as he had imagined she would. She smelled of some heady scent, and her skin was soft and smooth against his cheek, as he pressed her face to his, and then turned his head so that their lips met.

At the touch of her mouth on his, he groaned, and felt his blood run hot and thick. He had tried, damnit! But what could a man do when a lady asked?

She returned his kiss eagerly, her lips pliant and warm beneath his, opening readily as his tongue wedged between them.

She pulled back, and whispered near his ear, "Come, my dear. Let us go to my room."

"But your husband?"

She shrugged lightly. "Mr. Davis will not be back for hours. Believe me. Come!"

Luke wondered how she could be so sure of that, but he was in no mood to quibble. His body felt as if it were on fire, and his need drowned out all logical thought.

When the bedroom door was closed behind them, Elena turned and with a glad cry ran into his arms.

Gone now was the quiet, dutiful, well-mar ered wife; in her place was a frenzied wanton who quickly undressed herself and then Luke, so that in a very few minutes they lay on the four-poster bed with nothing between them, body pressed to body, and she proved herself as hungry as he.

It was difficult, but he restrained his impulse to enter her at once, and instead touched and fondled her full breasts, stroking her body in all the tender, pleasure-arousing places, until she moaned and cried out with pleasure and wanting. Only then did he enter her, slowly, trying to prolong it, but she thrashed beneath him, moving sensuously, voicing her desire, so that he could not control himself, and began to move in rapid, rhythmic thrusts, the sensation so pleasurable that he too had to cry out; and even then, in the arms of this desirable woman, for just an instant, he thought of Melissa, and the remembered pain and regret that this thought engendered made him move the faster in an effort to eradicate the memory of one woman with the body of another.

When at last they lay breathless and spent upon the damp sheets, Luke experienced a deep gratitude and affection for Elena. He kissed her gently on the lips.

She laughed softly in the warm darkness, and raised a hand to touch his forehead. "Thank you, Luke Devereaux."

He tried to see her features in the dark. "What are you talking about? It's I who should thank you. I've wanted you from the beginning, and I probably would have continued torturing myself with self-control, trying to stay away, if you hadn't . . . Well, if you hadn't encouraged me."

She began to laugh, a healthy, rolling laugh that came from the belly. "Encouraged you! Oh, Luke, you *are* a gentleman! I didn't encourage you. I practically seduced you." Her laughter gradually quieted. "And I suppose you are wondering why."

Luke said quickly, "Of course not."

She nodded, laughing again. "Yes, you are, Luke. 'Nice' women don't behave this way, and you think I'm a nice woman. Ergo, you must be wondering. Well, I will tell you."

He kissed her again, marveling at the wondrous if

baffling ways of women. "You don't have to, you know."

"I know, Luke, I know. You ask less of me than any man I've ever known. But I want to tell you. I want you to understand." She settled her head in the crook of his arm. "You must have noticed that Mr. Davis spends many nights at 'work,' as he puts it, and I'm sure you have also wondered how he can have so much paperwork."

"He has a mistress?"

Elena shook her head. "I only wish it were that simple. If that was it, I wouldn't mind so much. I really don't mind the fact that he has other women, since that means that he leaves me alone most of the time. I am a healthy woman with normal appetites, but I would rather languish away than have him touch me."

She shivered. "No, it's not the fact of another woman that hurts me, it's the fact that Mr. Davis forces himself on the women of the plantation workers. On Hiram's wife, and the man in the field, the one that struck him; all of them, even the young girls. The women are not willing, but they are afraid, terrified that if they complain their husbands or fathers will be fired, and then they will have no place to go. And the men, well, they eventually find out about it, and they too do nothing, at least nothing overt, because they also fear for their jobs, and don't want to see their families go hungry.

"Despite the fact that the war is over, and the black man is free, he's still fearful of the power of the white man, and with good reason, certainly in my husband's case."

Luke said thoughtfully, "This had occurred to me,

but I dismissed it since they wouldn't talk to me about it."

"They were afraid. They know that you work for Simon Crouse, and Crouse is known to be a cruel, vicious man. So they have continued trying to pretend that it isn't happening, and only now and then, when the pressure becomes too great, do they lash out. Like that field hand did." Elena made a sound of disgust. "My husband is an animal, Luke. He's insatiable, when it comes to those poor girls. While their men are in the fields, he takes them, and he's cruel to them. When he slips off at night like this, it's usually to someone like Hiram's wife, knowing that Hiram is busy here at the main house. I've tended some of the ones he's forced himself on, and it turns my stomach."

She sighed, and reached over to stroke his chest with her smooth hand. "And that is why the men do not work well at Riverview, and why they do rebellious things. And so your task here is finished, Mr. Devereaux, for you have the answer you sought."

Luke felt a pang at her words. "I could pretend that I've yet to find out," he said, finding her lips with his fingers.

"And let the situation go on?" she said. "Let it go on until real violence erupts, and someone is killed?"

He sighed. "I reckon not. But why did you tell me now, when we have just begun to know one another?"

She said sadly, *"That* is the reason. If I let this go on, I would not be able to tell you, for then I wouldn't be able to let you go."

Her exploring hand had found his member, and it began to pulse under her ministrations.

"Well, I'm not finished here just yet," he muttered

against her breast, and pulled her into a fierce yet tender embrace.

Luke found his parting from Elena Davis to be even more difficult than he would have guessed. His affection and gratitude had prompted him to offer to take her back with him to Natchez.

Elena had refused. "What is there for me in Natchez? You do not want to marry me, and in any event, I am married already. Mr. Davis may be a sorry excuse for a man, but he is all I have right now, and at least he keeps a roof over my head. You are not a marrying man, Luke Devereaux. I have known this from the beginning. And I didn't take you into my bed in an effort to beguile and trap you. I sought pleasure, and I received it. You have given me as much as I have given you. I know you must go and report to Simon Crouse. If he discharges Mr. Davis, he will find other employment. He is aggressive and resourceful, whatever else he may be. Go in good conscience."

And so Luke had gone, hating to leave her behind with her brute of a husband, but realizing that what she had said was true. Divorce was almost unheard of in the South, and a woman's reputation, once soiled by it, could never be restored. Also, as Elena had pointed out, he was not the marrying kind. The words struck an unpleasant pattern in his head, and again he thought of Melissa. But there was no time for that. Best to get back to Crouse and make his report, and then find out what else was necessary to repay the debt to the Carpetbagger.

"Mr. Crouse . . . Boss, Mr. Luke Devereaux is here

295

to see you." Jake put his head inside the study door. "He wants to know if you can see him now, and if not, when you can. He says he's here to make his report."

Crouse looked up from his account books, his expression thoughtful.

After a moment he said, "Tell Devereaux to wait, Jake. I'll see him, but not right away. Offer him a drink and a cigar, and tell him I'll be with him as soon as I have finished what I'm doing."

Jake nodded, and closed the door. Crouse leaned back in his chair, ruminating.

Just yesterday he had received the wire notifying him of Bear Smith's death. The *Melon Patch* was now without anyone in charge, and if he didn't get someone there soon, the girls, the equipment, and the profits would all go up in smoke. He had to get someone there, and quickly.

Bear—damn his hairy hide—did not seem to have accomplished much toward the task he, Crouse, had given him. Perhaps he had tried; perhaps that was why he was now dead. The telegram had been skimpy with details.

Crouse no longer underestimated the two women, Amalie Dubois and Melissa Huntoon, and now that they had a group of people around them they would not be the easy prey he had hoped for. What he needed was someone resourceful and clever. Perhaps Bear had not been a good choice.

But now Luke Devereaux, like a gift from the gods, was back again on his doorstep, evidently having solved the problem at Riverview. Devereaux was handsome, bright, and resourceful. He, far more than Bear, would have a better chance of working his way into the confidence of the showboat people. Of course, he would probably balk at the assignment, for Crouse had recognized that Devereaux fancied himself a gentleman, too good to manage an establishment like the love boat; but Crouse was confident that if he offered to cancel Devereaux's debt as payment for the job, the man would agree.

Crouse rubbed his hands together briskly, and closed the ledger. He liked to keep his callers waiting; it always made them edgy and gave him an advantage, but Devereaux was not a man to be kept waiting *too* long.

As the door to the parlor opened and Simon Crouse strode in, Luke glanced up, but did not rise nor take the cigar from his mouth; and he made no effort to mask the annoyance he felt at being kept waiting.

"Hello, Luke. I'm sorry to have kept you waiting, but I was putting the finishing touches on a business deal."

Luke accepted his outstretched hand but still did not rise. He said dryly, "Some wise man once said that waiting is good for the soul."

"I take it that you have completed your investigation at Riverview?"

Luke nodded. "Yep. You've only got one problem at Riverview, Simon, and that's Roy Davis. The reason for the unrest among the workers is due to his sex habits. He can't, or won't, stay away from their wives and daughters. From what I could gather, he's made free with every woman on the plantation over the age of twelve, and that doesn't make the men—or women—very happy. Despite their release from bondage, they don't quite dare confront Davis directly, so their anger comes out in other ways. Sloppy work, carelessness, accidents. Naturally, all this affects production.

"My recommendation to you is that you get rid of Davis, and give the job of overseer to his wife. She gets along fine with the workers, she's intelligent, and I think she's quite capable of managing your plantation."

"A woman?" Crouse said incredulously. "You must be mad! Get rid of Davis, but put his wife in charge?" He shook his head. "I'd sell the damned place first."

"Suit yourself." Luke shrugged. "I've given you my opinion. It's up to you what you do about the situation." He looked at the smoke spiraling up from his cigar. "At any rate, here I am back again, ready to sweat off the rest of my gambling debt. Do you have anything for me?"

Crouse smiled nastily. "As a matter of fact, I do. Something just came up. It seems that the man in charge of the *Melon Patch* met with a fatal accident, as it were."

Luke squinted at him. "*You* own the *Melon Patch?*"

"That I do. I told you once that I had a finger in many pies," Crouse said expansively. "And I need someone to take his place, and it occurred to me that you'd be perfect for the job."

Luke was already shaking his head. "That's not quite my line of work, running a whorehouse, Simon. You must have something else I can do."

Crouse poured himself a dollop of brandy. "At the moment, I do not think so. At the moment, what I sorely need is someone to take over the love boat, and you're the man for the job. Just to prove my faith in you, Luke, I'll sweeten the pot. I'm willing to wipe out the rest of your debt to me. Do this one last thing for me, and we can call it square between us. What do you say?"

Luke was frowning. He heartily disliked the idea of having to live on board the so-called love boat, riding herd on crooked dealers and a flock of raunchy whores. Still . . . to cancel his debt and get Crouse off his back, it might be worth it. He smiled to himself. After all, he'd had *some* experience in operating a brothel!

He sighed. "All right, Simon. I reckon you've got yourself a man. I'll do it, but I won't like it. Just how long do I have to manage this floating whorehouse before my debt is paid off?"

"Until I find another manager, or six months, whichever comes first. Is it a deal?"

Luke put out his hand. "It's a deal. Where is the barge now, and is there anything specific that you want me to do?"

Crouse smiled, a private, sly sort of look, that made Luke go tense and wary.

"The *Melon Patch* is only a short distance downriver, and there certainly *is* something specific I want you to do. I want you to make life difficult for the owner of a certain steamboat and for her friends. I want you to harass, make trouble for, embarrass, Miss Melissa Huntoon and her companion, Miss High-and-Mighty Amalie Dubois, and every else on that damned floating theater of hers!

"And then, when the opportunity arises—Better yet, make your own opportunity, as it were. I want those two females, Huntoon and Dubois, seized, taken on board the *Melon Patch*, and brought here to me."

Crouse's face was set in cruel lines. "I don't care much what happens to the rest of them. You can sink

299

the *Belle* for all I give a damn. I only want the two females."

Luke had been listening with dismay and growing anger, and now he tried to mask his feelings. It would never do to have Crouse discover that he had come to know the group on board the *Natchez Belle*, or that he cared deeply about what happened to them, most especially to one of them.

"Melissa Huntoon . . . Isn't that the young woman we met out at Great Oaks?"

Crouse nodded smugly. "The very same."

"May I ask why I'm to do this?" Luke said casually.

"You may not," Crouse said coldly. "It is enough that you do as you are told. The main thing is to remember that I want those women. Now, do you think you can do what I want?"

My God, Luke was thinking, *what can I say?* He knew that if he refused, Crouse would get someone else, someone who would actually try to abduct Melissa and Amalie, and perhaps succeed. If *he* took the assignment, he could pretend to comply with Crouse's request, and secretly stall, do everything in his power to protect them.

"Well?" Crouse said impatiently.

Luke frowned, as if thinking hard. "If I do, the debt will be wiped off the slate, even if the six months period is not over?"

Crouse smiled. "Yes. We'll make that a term of the agreement. You'll do it?"

Luke nodded. "Yes, I'll do it." *God help me,* he thought grimly.

Crouse grinned triumphantly, drywashing his hands.

The performance given by the entertainers of the

Natchez Belle, on the night after Bear's death, was very special. Fueled by their pride in defending their own, and egged on by the sympathy and encouragement of the townspeople, they gave a brilliant performance.

Everyone was excited, riding the crest of strong emotion. The performance was free, to make up for the interruptions of the prior night, and the grand saloon was packed with many standees.

Melissa knew that word of the incident would spread up and down the river, as all news of such happenings did, and that it would be great publicity. Everyone would want to see the actors and actresses who had done battle with the denizens of the love boat and rescued the fair maiden; at least that was what Jubal and Nehemiah had told her, and Melissa recognized it was truth.

Tomorrow they would be in the river again, moving north to the next play date. They were bypassing Natchez, for which Melissa was glad. Jubal was sure that the news of the love boat episode would have spread, and they could expect a tremendous crowd in the next town.

Melissa laughed. "But how can the news travel so fast?"

Jubal grinned. "I don't rightly know, girl. I only know that news travels mighty quick along this old river. Just wait and see if I ain't right."

And Jubal was right. When they reached the next town, word of their exploits had preceded them. A huge crowd awaited the *Belle* on the landing, and they had to spend an extra day there so that they could accommodate the demand for tickets.

In the next town it was the same, and in the one

after that. Jubal's strongbox began to accumulate a tidy sum of cash, over and above what was paid to the crew and the performers.

So things were going well, and in addition, the small problems that had plagued the *Belle* and her crew also disappeared. Everything went smoothly; there were no interruptions of performances, no play-bills were torn down. In fact, things were going so well that Jubal announced that he was getting super-stitious about it, and that something bad was bound to happen to balance their sudden good fortune.

It had been just over a week since the incident with the love boat, and they were giving the first of three performances in a fairly large town. Everything had gone well, from the arrival of the *Belle*, to the spiel on the landing, to the first act of the play, which tonight was *A Mother's Heart*.

The second act curtain had just been raised, and Melissa, in her blonde wig, stood poised on the steps of the humble abode that was the centerpiece of the set. She spoke her first lines, and then turned and gazed out over the footlights, preparatory to voicing an aside, which was to be directed to the audience.

Despite the glare of the footlights, she could see the faces of much of the audience, and there, on the aisle in the first row, she saw a face that made her gasp and forget her lines.

She looked again, disbelieving what she saw. It was Luke Devereaux, in a fine, fawn-colored suit, looking content, smiling up at the stage. He motioned with the unlit cigar in his right hand, and winked.

Melissa became conscious of the fact that her si-lence had extended so long that the audience had be-come aware of it, and whispers buffeted her. She hastily spoke her lines, but her mind was not on the words she was saying.

What was *he* doing here? Was it by chance? Did he just happen to be in this town at this particular time, and took the advantage of the opportunity to watch her perform? Or had he come purposely to see *her*?

Melissa went through the rest of the second act, but afterward she could not remember one word of what she had said.

When the olio was over, and they were taking their bows, she looked at Luke again, and their glances met. He nodded gravely, and she felt herself flush scarlet, and she stumbled as she made her bow.

When the curtain came down, she hurried to her dressing room, and slumped down at the small makeup table, staring blankly at her reflection in the mirror until there was a knock on the door. A crewman came in with a message written on the back of a calling card. The card had Luke's name engraved on the front, and the message said:

"Will you grant me a few minutes after the performance? Luke Devereaux."

Melissa turned the card over and over in her hands as the crewman, Bertram, stood waiting patiently.

How dare he come here now, after what he had done to her? Of course she wouldn't see him! It would be foolish of her to do so. If would only rake up painful feelings best left undisturbed. Besides, she did not *want* to see him!

She sighed and looked up at Bertram. "Tell the gentleman to come in," she said in a low voice.

Bertram nodded and left the cabin, and Melissa turned back to her reflection in the glass. Strangely, she felt nothing—no anticipation, no hate, no anger, and certainly no love for this man.

The door was pushed slowly inward, and Luke stood there, behind her in the glass, looking at her quizzically, his mouth quirked slightly in a deprecatory grin. "I was afraid that you might refuse to see me. I was hoping that you would not."

She stared at him without expression. "I thought of saying no," she said honestly, "and even now I don't know why I didn't. I must say you look prosperous, Mr. Devereaux."

He came on into the room, and shut the door. "And you look fantastic, more beautiful than ever, Melissa. I trust you've been well?"

"Very well, thank you," she said coolly. Her fingers fumbled with a small pin box on the dressing table. "What brings you to this out-of-the-way place?" Melissa was proud of the steadiness of her voice.

"Business," he said with a rueful grin that she did not understand. "And you, Melissa."

"Me?" She felt an unwanted emotion stirring in her. "I thought you made it very clear back in New Orleans that you wanted nothing further to do with me."

"Now, that's not quite accurate, Melissa. I only said that I couldn't marry you. I've thought about you a great deal in the time I've been away."

Melissa slammed the pin box down with considerable force. "Well, I haven't spared a single thought for you, Mr. Devereaux! I'd forgotten you completely until I saw you out in the audience tonight."

"Are you happy, Melissa?" he asked unexpectedly.

She narrowed her eyes. "Why shouldn't I be? I've met a very nice young man, an actor with the troupe, who wants to marry me, but I've decided that I am not quite ready to settle down, so I haven't given him an answer yet. Also, our tour has been successful, and we're beginning to make money. Why wouldn't I be happy?"

For a moment, Luke's face was sad, and then his habitual, somewhat sardonic expression was back in place. "I'm glad for you, Melissa. I really am. Now, there was something that I came here to tell you, and I would appreciate it if you would listen to me with an open mind, because it's for your own good—"

A peremptory knock on the door interrupted him. "Who is it?" Melissa called crossly.

"It's Bertram again, Miss Huntoon. I have a message for the gentleman."

"Very well, come in."

The door opened, and Bertram's worried face poked around the side. "Mr. Devereaux, there's some kind of trouble over on your barge. One of the customers is saying he's been cheated or something, and one of the girls has been cut. They want you over there right away!"

Melissa looked at him in disbelief. Barge? Customers? Girls? "Just what kind of barge is this, Bertram?"

Luke started to speak, but she glared him silent. "Go ahead, Bertram. Answer the question."

Bertram squirmed in embarrassment, and ducked his head. "Ah, you know, Miss Huntoon. The one called the *Melon Patch.*" He stepped back into the passageway, closing the door.

Melissa, trembling with anger, turned away from Luke, and began to remove her wig. "I think you had better go, Mr. Devereaux," she said coldly. "It seems that your exployees have sore need of you."

Luke said tightly, "Look, Melissa, it's not quite what it appears to be. Listen to me—"

"Good night, Mr. Devereaux. I believe that we have said all that there is to be said between us, and I would appreciate it if you would not try to see me again."

"Melissa," Luke said through gritted teeth, "you're going to listen to what I have to say!"

"In that you are mistaken, Mr. Devereaux." She raised her eyes to meet his in the mirror. "I've asked you to leave. Don't force me to call for help and have you thrown out."

Luke made a guttural sound of frustration deep in his throat. He locked gazes with her for a moment in the mirror, and she saw him raise his curled hands, and thought that he was going to seize her by the shoulders and shake her. Then he whirled and stalked stiff-legged to the door, slamming it behind him.

Melissa sat white-faced before the mirror, watching the silent tears make runnels in the powder and rouge on her cheeks.

Chapter Seventeen

"Oh, Amalie! What am I to do?"

Melissa huddled at Amalie's feet, her head against the older woman's knees. Amalie stroked the hair back from Melissa's damp forehead, and smiled tenderly.

"This is one time I will not be able to help you, *chérie*. In affairs of the heart one must struggle alone. I can listen, I can even give you advice, but you will not take it unless it is what you wish to hear."

Melissa shook her head. "How could I have been so wrong about him? I thought that he was a gentleman, and now here he is, in charge of that awful boat of—of whores! I might as well say the word! That love boat turns up everywhere we play, in every town. It's as if they're following us deliberately!"

Amalie sighed. "Yes, the townspeople do not like to bring their families to the showboat with the *Melon Patch* tied up right alongside. It will hurt our business, I know."

"But why do you suppose he is taking Bear Smith's place? How could he stoop so low?"

Amalie shrugged and looked away. She had some time ago decided that Simon Crouse owned the love boat, and was behind the attempts upon both her and Melissa. Melissa had guessed, and accurately Amalie was sure, that Crouse was behind the sabotage attempts on the *Belle*, yet neither Melissa nor the others had made the connection between Crouse and the presence of the *Melon Patch*. Amalie did not think it would serve a useful purpose to voice her suspicions, since she had only a feeling to back them up.

Besides, there was nothing they could legitimately do to the love boat. Since there were no laws governing such river activity, they were within their rights to make a landing almost anywhere along the river.

As to why a man like Luke Devereaux was now in charge of the *Melon Patch*, Amalie could not hazard a guess. He seemed to like the people on the *Belle*, and Amalie was certain that he cared for Melissa. Why he was now doing something that, at least on the face of it, seemed to portend trouble for the showboat, and possible harm to Melissa, was very confusing.

From what Melissa had told her of Luke's attempt to talk to her in the dressing room, Amalie gathered that Melissa had not given him the opportunity to explain. Perhaps if she had, things would make more sense.

Amalie had learned long ago that things were not always what they seemed on the surface; and that trouble between a man and a woman was often due to a simple misunderstanding.

She had not been shocked when Melissa confessed that she and Luke Devereaux had been intimate; she had expected as much, and she also knew about Melissa's affair with Beau, which was fairly obvious to

308

anyone close to Melissa, a fact that no doubt would embarrass Melissa if she knew it. It was strange how lovers always thought that their affairs went unobserved by those around them.

"I am afraid there is nothing we can do about the love boat, *chérie*," she said now. "At least not at the moment. We must just continue to ignore them as best we can, and keep a close watch, hoping that we will be able to spot trouble before it develops."

Melissa clenched her fists. "I wish there was something we could *do*. I feel so angry and helpless!"

"I know, little one, I know."

The river was getting very low now, and navigation was more difficult with every passing day. Everyone on board the *Belle* prayed for a good rain, so that the river might raise a little; without it, passage might become impossible to the towns on the side rivers.

When they were on the river, Melissa began to spend more and more time in the wheelhouse, watching the muddy water with Jubal and Martha King, keeping an eye out for signs that denoted snags or sandbars, and listening to Jubal spin his yarns of life on the river.

Beau had chided her for not spending more time with him, but the truth was, she needed to be away from Beau. She wanted time to think her own thoughts.

The presence of Luke Devereaux on the love boat upset her more than she cared to admit, and she found that she thought of him far too much of the time. Listening to Jubal as he told the old river stories in his deep voice somehow comforted her.

"I wish the river had more water," Melissa complained, looking unhappily out the window at the brown water that barely seemed to move as the *Belle* plowed through it.

Jubal chuckled. "Well, it will have, more than you probably will care for, come spring. Did I ever tell you the tale of the *Lucy Ann?*"

Melissa shook her head, beginning to smile.

"Well, it was back when I was just a nipper, a cub pilot under Captain Josiah Quinn. It was early in the month of April, as I recollect, and it seemed like the whole country round here was under water that year.

"Ole Miss'ip' was a-rollin' and a-roilin' along, and every captain and worker on the river was nervous as a long-tailed cat in a roomful of rockin' chairs, just waitin' for the river to bust loose.

"Now the *Lucy Ann* was a stout packet, new built, and this was her first trip down the river, and her captain, this Captain Quinn, was one of them smart-alecky, know-it-all captains, what think their papers come direct from the hand of God, and make them something special, a cut above everybody else." Jubal snorted and thumped the wheelhouse deck.

"Well, like I say, I was just a cub, but I had steamed under another captain afore, a man what knew his business, and if I do say so myself, I was, and am, a quick learner.

"Now Captain Quinn had him a pilot with no more sense than the captain himself, 'cause when the captain asked him to, the durned pilot steered that boat close in shore so that the passengers could see the big water.

"Despite the fact that I was just a cub, a cub not rankin' very high on the river, I couldn't keep my

310

mouth closed. I went up to the captain and told him what I thought, that the water was tricky, and that there were crevasses along the bank there that could cause us bad trouble.

"As you can well imagine, that didn't set so well with Captain Quinn, and he huffed and puffed and told me to mind my own business, or the *Lucy Ann* would be missin' one cub pilot. He said that on the day that I got my license, *then* he would listen to what I had to say, and not afore.

"Well, sir, while he was rantin' away at me, that fool pilot steered the *Lucy Ann* right smack into a crevasse! The *Lucy Ann* quivered and bucked, like a spooked horse!" Jubal chuckled and shook his head.

"I can laugh about it now, but it wasn't no laughin' matter that sad day, I can tell you. There was bells a-janglin', passengers a-running every which way, the firemen were throwin' on wood, and the pilot was spinnin' round and round on his wheel.

"The *Lucy Ann* splashed and bucked, but it wasn't no good. Old Miss'ip' had a-hold of her, and she just went shootin' through that crevasse like an arrow with the force of the river behind her.

"Lordy, lordy, that was one fast ride? The captain was runnin' around the decks shoutin' to the passengers, 'Don't jump! Don't jump!' but the boat was goin' so fast that nobody was thinking about leavin' the deck, I can tell you.

"We went crashin' through the willows, the river makin' its own bed as it pushed us along, and then we shot through another crevasse, and now we're headin' right for a big white plantation house. All I could think was that some plantation owner was goin' to be

311

mighty surprised to find Old Man River knockin' at his door with a steamboat in his hand!

"It didn't take no time at all for the *Lucy Ann* to reach the plantation, where we went bumpin' through the fields and into a sycamore grove near the house. Then we struck an open field with some high ground behind it.

"One of the deckhands, an older man, yelled to the captain to give him a line, and maybe he could pass it around a tree and anchor the *Lucy Ann* when she reached high ground.

"The deckhand jumped out, which weren't no risk to him since the water was only knee deep at that point. He pulled that line around a big sycamore. Then we all threw him more line, and in a few minutes the *Lucy Ann* was fast, and the passengers was taken off in skiffs. Didn't lose nary a one.

"After the water went down, it did look a sight, that big white steamboat perched there on a ridge of dry land ten miles from the river channel!

"O' course, the man what owned the plantation didn't think it was comical a-tall, nor did Captain Quinn when the story got spread around. He was a laughin' stock all up and down the river!"

Jubal laughed heartily, thumping the peg leg.

Melissa asked, "Is the *Lucy Ann* still there?"

Jubal shook his head. "Naw. It took about a year or so, but the darkies used to go up there and carry off whatever they needed for their cabins. A lock here, a door there, planking and the like, until she was plumb gone, stripped down to the bare bones, like a catfish just eaten!

"Yup! The old river is a chancy critter, whether it's

high water or low, and one's about as dangerous as the other."

Melissa smiled, for the moment distracted by the image of the *Lucy Ann* squatting in a hill in the middle of green farmland. She laughed aloud. "I guess we're really pretty lucky so far, aren't we? I mean, we've had no real trouble with the *Belle*."

Jubal nodded emphatically. "You're right as rain, girl. Why, I've seen some terrible things happen on the river. Boilers explodin', the whole bottom ripped out of a boat on a clump of snags, sawyers that cut a boat in half. Yup. We been mighty lucky, you can bet your boots on that."

Melissa worried her lower lip with her teeth. "But I do wish we could get away from the bilge-barge."

Jubal's mouth dropped open. "The what?"

Melissa grinned, and for a moment she looked her usual cheerful self. "Bilge-barge! That's my own name for the *Melon Patch*. I certainly am not going to call it a love boat, and it's not ladylike to say floating whorehouse."

Jubal's loud guffaw rang through the wheelhouse, and roused Martha from a catnap. She flapped her hands and twittered. "My land, what on earth are you two carrying on so about? Jubal, you look sharp now to your right! Don't you see that snag?"

Jubal and Melissa exchanged amused glances.

"Yes, Martha," Jubal said. "I see the snag, I purely do."

Aboard the *Melon Patch*, Luke Devereaux sat at a small table in the saloon and nursed a straight whiskey. He felt surly out of sorts, and depressed—a mood that was definitely out of character for him.

Women could be the most aggravating creatures! He had only taken this damned job so that he could look out for Melissa and her friends, and this was the gratitude he got! Why wouldn't the stupid girl let him explain? He had wanted to tell her the reason for his being on the barge, and set her mind at ease, but she had cut him off like a thread off a coat. Well, to hell with her! Let her stew. Let her wonder why the love boat was following the *Belle*. She deserved to suffer some discomfort for her intolerance.

He threw back the whiskey and motioned to the bartender for another.

It was midafternoon, and business was very slow. The worst thing about this job was the boredom. The bookkeeping was simple, and it didn't take too much effort to keep the girls in line, and the rest of the time there was little to do but see that fights didn't break out, or that some girl didn't take a knife to another in a fit of pique, and to keep the dealers reasonably honest.

Through the window, he could see people coming and going on the *Natchez Belle*. The showboat looked good, he had to admit, and it appeared that Melissa's idea had been successful. *She* looked wonderful, more beautiful even than he remembered, and the sight of her had awakened a whole set of feelings that he had not known he had.

It was ridiculous, that he should be so upset over a mere girl. God knows, there were plenty of them around, and he had never had any difficulty in finding one to help while away the time. For instance, there were over a dozen on the *Melon Patch*, any one of whom would be delighted to pleasure the boss. So maybe they were soiled doves; at least they didn't make a man's brain ache!

Luke stared moodily down into his glass. He had better get his mind off Melissa, and on to the matter of what he was going to tell Simon Crouse, when Crouse found out that he, Luke, had made no move toward the two women. He was bound to catch on soon.

Luke figured he was doing half of his job, at least, for he was also hired to manage the love boat, and that, he decided, he was doing very well—with the help of his prior experience, so to speak.

With a harsh laugh, he hoisted his glass. "Here's to you, Rose!" He took out the cigar case that had been his mother's gift to him and stared glumly at the engraved letters. "I don't know, Rose, right now your only son doesn't feel so damned lucky!"

The memory of his mother and her profession gave him an idea. He knew how he could at least relieve the boredom; he would upgrade the *Melon Patch* into a respectable whorehouse, like the one Rose Devereaux operated—a place where a lonely man could come seeking diversion and not be ashamed. First, he'd spruce the barge up, clean up the girls, maybe even rid himself of the raunchier ones. If the *Melon Patch* had a better image, it would draw a better class of customer, and a better class of customer meant more income. And a stronger income might help to dampen Crouse's anger when he found out that he had been betrayed.

Excited now by his developing idea, Luke pushed

back from the table and went down the passageway to his office, where he began to draw up plans, and figure out how much of the current profits it would take to fix up the barge.

"Well, you will have to admit that it does look better," Beau said with a half-grin.

Most of the performers and crew of the *Belle* were hanging over the starboard rail of the boat, trying for a better look at the *Melon Patch*, which was moored alongside.

The barge had been absent at their last two play towns, and there had been much speculation as to the reason. Melissa had about decided that she had been mistaken in thinking that the love boat was dogging their trail, and she hadn't known whether to be sad or happy about it. Oh, she knew how she *should* feel, of course; she should be delighted that it was gone. But strangely, when the *Melon Patch* did not show at their last stop, she had felt a twinge of disappointment.

But now the love boat was with them again, even if it was looking far different.

Gone was the warped deck—it had been re-planked and hidden under a coat of brown paint. The long structure atop the barge looked as if it had been torn down and another built in its place. It stood four-square now, with a handsome yellow door, white painted sides, and curtained windows. There were even pots of flowers spaced along the side decks.

Over all flew a new flag, one with a brown background, two ripe muskmelons rampant, and the words "The Melon Patch—Fine Entertainment" in red letters.

The door of the main cabin opened, and a woman with bright red hair came out onto the deck. She was

dressed a bit skimpily, but she did at least have all
her clothes on. She saw them and waved in a friendly
manner. Some of those watching on the *Belle* waved
back.

The atmosphere on the *Belle*, to Melissa's astonishment, was almost festive, as if the spruced-up appearance of the barge had diminished any threat that the
dingier-looking craft had posed.

Peggy LaSalle took her husband's arm. "Oh, Martin,
let's go on board. I've never been to a . . . Well, you
know, to a place like that!"

Martin looked startled momentarily, then laughed
heartily as his wife's remark was passed on.

"Yes, let's do it!" Mary McGee exclaimed.

Nehemiah looked at her with something like horror.
"Why, my dear, why on *earth* would you want to visit
a place like that? The fact that it has received a new
coat of paint does not, in any way, alter the nature of
the place, indeed not!"

Mary blushed, but took his arm determinedly. "Oh,
pooh, Nehemiah, don't be such an old fuddy-duddy.
Anybody can see that it's changed for the better. It
certainly can't be as bad as it was before."

"That's right," Peggy said, "and besides, if we go in
a group we'll surely be safe enough. I think it would
be fun. The only things we get to see are the *Belle*
and the landings along the river. What could be dreari-
er? We need a change of pace, we've been working
very hard. I say we all get together this afternoon, and
visit the *Melon Patch*! How many of you want to go
along?"

There was a moment of hesitation, then most of the
group agreed.

"Well, I suppose there is no real harm in it," Nehemiah said thoughtfully. "Maybe we *should* take a look at the competition. A wise man knows what he is fighting, yes indeed! Jubal, what do you say?"

Jubal shrugged his wide shoulders, and turned his head aside to hide a slight smile. "Well, since you put it that way, I guess there's no real harm in it. Martha, what do you say?"

She said sharply, "If you're going, then I'm going, Jubal King! I'm not going to have you wandering around over there by yourself, with all those loose women about!"

One by one all of the performers except Melissa and Amalie agreed to go. Beau took Melissa's hand, and leaned close to say, "Melissa—darling, what's wrong? Don't you think it would be fun, a kind of lark?"

Melissa's lips were tight. "It's a whorehouse, Beau."

Beau arched his eyebrows. "Well, yes, that's true, but it isn't catching."

Melissa raised her chin. "You seem to forget that Amalie and I were both taken onto the bilge-barge against our will."

Amalie stepped close to her. "You do not have to go, *chérie*. I am not going, so you may stay here with me." She shuddered. "My one experience on that boat was enough."

"For one, I don't blame Melissa for being afraid," Peggy LaSalle said, rather loudly. "After all, she did have an unpleasant experience over there, and although I do think it's probably safe enough, now that that awful Bear person is gone, I certainly can understand how she feels."

For some reason, Peggy's rather patronizing manner rubbed Melissa the wrong way. "I am not afraid," she

318

said somewhat primly. "I just don't think there's any real reason to go over there."

"Come along with us, Melissa," Beau urged. "I'll take good care of you, and see that nothing dire happens to you. We'll all be together, what *could* happen?"

Melissa hesitated. She couldn't tell Beau the main reason she did not wish to visit the love boat. He had no idea that she and Luke Devereaux had ever met before Luke took the job of operating the pleasure barge.

"Oh, all right," she finally said, "but I don't want to stay long. We'll just look around and we'll leave. Promise?"

"Promise," Beau said, kissing her cheek. "It will be amusing, just wait and see. After all," he laughed, throwing his head back, "an actress should experience all things. Who knows, perhaps some day you may be asked to portray a doxy in a play!"

Although it was only midafternoon, the saloon of the *Melon Patch* was about half-filled with customers. Card games, a dice table and a roulette wheel were on one side of the room, and a long bar and dance floor occupied the other. A rather battered upright piano was being pounded vigorously by a skinny little man with huge hands. His playing, Melissa thought, while it did not come up to the standard set by Chuck on the showboat, was competent.

The group from the *Natchez Belle* ventured into the saloon with some hesitation and a good deal of giggling, and many whispered comments behind their cupped hands. Most of them had never set foot inside

319

such an establishment, and so there was some embarrassment, and a feeling that they were doing something terribly daring in coming on board the barge.

Melissa, clinging tightly to Beau's arm, tried to maintain an aloof, calm expression. She hoped that Luke would not come into the main room; she prayed that he was busy elsewhere, or off the barge altogether. She felt that she simply could not face him again. Not only would it be too painful, but she cringed away from the thought of that knowing, sardonic grin of his if he saw her here.

The customers of the *Melon Patch*, in turn, eyed the newcomers dubiously, mostly in disbelief, and some were openly angered. It was clear that the visitors were slumming, and the men patronizing the barge's entertainment obviously did not care to be observed at their recreation.

And then, of course, there were the girls—standing at the bar with the men; lounging provocatively against the gamblers' chairs; gathered around the piano, tapping out the rhythm against the wood; and dancing together on the small floor.

The women from the *Belle* kept glancing at them and away, their faces a battleground of embarrassment and curiosity. On the other hand, the men stared unabashedly.

The interior of the saloon was now rather attractive, Melissa had to admit, with comfortable couches and chairs along one wall for those who wished to watch the dancing. The card tables were new, and the bar had been refinished.

A large brass lighting fixture hung in the middle of the room, supporting four brass lanterns, and the whole effect was rather cheerful and even wholesome, despite the things that happened here.

Melissa and Beau strolled from table to table, watching the gambling. They were the targets of angry glances from the men playing. Melissa noticed that several of the men from the *Belle* were taking seats at one gaming table or another. Mostly they were members of the crew, but she did see Martin LaSalle at one of the poker tables, and Peggy appeared quite upset about it.

As Melissa and Beau progressed around the saloon, and nothing untoward happened, Melissa began to relax. Luke was nowhere to be seen. Perhaps their group would see all they cared to see, and leave before he made an appearance. Melissa fervently hoped so, and yet, somewhere deep inside, she knew that she *wanted* to see him.

Martha, dragging Jubal by the arm, sidled up to Melissa and whispered behind her hand, "Aren't these women awful? Just look at the hair on that one. My land!"

Melissa followed her pointing finger to the flagrantly redhaired woman they had seen earlier from the deck of the *Belle*. Melissa nodded agreement, yet her mind was more engaged with the question of how soon she could ask Beau to take her back to the *Belle*.

Then, as her gaze swung to the back of the saloon, she saw Luke Devereaux just coming through the door, and her heart jumped in her breast, causing her to involuntarily place her hand there.

Beau, noticing the gesture, looked at her in concern. "Is there anything the matter, darling?"

She shook her head wordlessly. "No, I just tripped.

Clumsy of me." She smiled at Beau sweetly, hoping that Luke would take note, and not approach them.

But her hope soon died. Luke headed directly for them, and there was no way, short of flight, that she could avoid a confrontation. He was smiling, that maddening, mocking smile. Smoke drifted up lazily from the cigar in his hand.

She held herself steady, waiting with dread. What would he say to her, after the way she had dismissed him in her dressing room?

"Good afternoon, Miss Huntoon," he said with a slight bow. "It's nice to see you. After our last conversation, I had thought I might not have that pleasure again."

Beau shot her a questioning look, and Melissa felt herself flush.

"I thought so, too," she said as calmly as she could manage, "but my friends insisted that I accompany them, so that we might see your new establishment. It would appear that you have made a great many improvements."

He nodded, his smile growing. "Why, how nice of you to notice. Yes, I decided to upgrade the *Melon Patch*. Whatever I do, you see, I try to do to the utmost of my ability, and since I am now being paid to manage this barge, I decided that I might as well make it presentable. Besides, it has been good for business. We're getting a better class of clientele now. Witness for yourself." With a wave of the cigar, he indicated the members of the showboat troupe who were now scattered about the room at the various gaming tables.

As Melissa followed his gesture with her gaze, she noticed one of the *Belle*'s crewmen following a girl's swishing hips out of the saloon toward the back, and she flushed again.

"I hope you will feel free to visit at any time you choose," Luke was saying with mock seriousness. "You do add a touch of class to the establishment."

"We thought that since we are often neighbors, in a manner of speaking, we should pay a courtesy call," Beau said smoothly. "You do seem to spend a great deal of time tied up next to us, an extraordinary coincidence, upon which we have all remarked. I am Beau Vermillian, by the way."

"And I'm Luke Devereaux," Luke said, staring at Beau with a glint in his eyes. "You've noticed that, have you?"

"It could hardly be missed. Naturally, we were all curious to see what you had done with the barge, Miss Huntoon and Miss Dubois having seen it previously under, shall we say, less than ideal circumstances?"

Luke frowned, his glance going to Melissa. "I knew that Miss Dubois was taken aboard the barge by Bear. In fact, I was helpful in getting her off and back to the *Belle,* but I hadn't heard about your visit, Melissa. How did that come about?"

Melissa felt a prod of annoyance, and she resisted a strong urge to rail at Beau. Why did he have to bring that up? She did not particularly want Luke to know that she had been abducted and nearly ravished by the infamous Bear.

"It's not important," she said quickly. "Beau, don't you think it's time we returned to the *Belle?* We do have a show tonight."

Beau looked down at her. "Of course." He nodded to Luke. "Glad to have made your acquaintance, sir."

"Likewise, I'm sure," Luke said, still looking quizzically at Melissa. "I do hope that this will be the beginning of friendlier relations between our two vessels."

Melissa, still upset by Beau's remark, wondered briefly what Luke meant. Was it his hope that he and she would become friends again?

All of a sudden, the anger went out of her. What was wrong with her? Why was she making so much of what Luke Devereaux said or did? What had happened between them was as much her fault as his, and he had never lied to her, or tried to delude her in any way. Now that he was behaving reasonably, could she not, at least, do the same?

"I hope so, too," she said a trifle wearily. "I also hope that you mean the *Belle* no harm, nor any of the people on board, as did Bear Smith." She stared directly into his eyes as she spoke.

"I believe that I can safely promise that," he said slowly. His face was serious, with no hint of mockery in his manner. "In fact, I know that I can."

Melissa nodded, and took Beau's arm. "Thank you, Mr. Devereaux. Shall we go now, Beau?"

"Certainly." Beau offered his hand to Luke. "See you again, Mr. Devereaux."

Luke took the proffered hand and shook it. "Likewise, Mr. Vermillian."

As Melissa and Beau left the barge, she was certain that she could feel the impact of Luke's gaze between her shoulder blades. She felt very tired, and yet in some way relieved, as if some demon within her had been laid to rest.

Beau was silent as they covered the short distance between the two vessels, but once they were on board the *Belle*, he rounded on her. "Melissa, you didn't tell me you knew this Luke Devereaux. How did that come about?"

There was something more than just curiosity in his voice, and if Melissa had not been so weary, she would have resented this, she knew. She said quietly, "I've known him for some time, actually. He came to Great Oaks the day that they auctioned off our things. He was very kind."

"Oh?" The single word seemed to express many things.

"We also saw him later, in Natchez. He saved Amalie, helped her get out of the dreadful situation, when Bear Smith had her abducted and taken on board the barge. Luke—Mr. Devereaux—traveled with us to New Orleans after that, on the *Belle*. And that was the last we saw of him until he turned up on the barge." She gave him a level look. "Is there anything else you wish to know?"

Beau flushed. "Naturally I'm interested," he said defensively. "After all, we *are* more than just friends." He took her hands in his, and looked into her eyes. "You know, Melissa, although we have never actually discussed it, I do intend to wed you."

As he watched her face for a reaction, Melissa stood mute, frozen inside. Why was he bringing this up now? "But we haven't ever talked about this!"

He nodded. "I realize that, that's what I just said. But I'm sure you must know how I feel. I wouldn't have . . . I mean, I'm not an utter cad, Melissa. Surely you must have known that I wouldn't take advantage of you, then just leave you. I love you, darling, and as soon as I'm able to support a wife, we'll be married."

Melissa took her hands gently from his. "There's one thing you seem to have forgotten, Beau."

He looked honestly puzzled. "What is that?"

"You haven't asked me yet."

"But I just did!"

She shook her head in reproof. "Beau, you haven't asked me whether or not I *want* to get married, whether or not I want to marry *you!*"

The shock and amazement upon his face would have been comical in less serious circumstances. "But I thought—I assumed that you knew how I felt, and that you agreed. After all we—well, we have been *very* close."

Melissa felt close to tears, angry, and depressed, all at once. How could men say that women were difficult to understand, and then behave so inconsistently themselves? One man had made love to her, and then told her that he had no intention of marrying her, or anyone else, claiming that intimacy between a man and a woman did not of necessity have to end in marriage; now another man had made love to her, and *assumed* that she would know that this meant that he loved her and wanted her to be his wife! However were you supposed to understand *them?*

Seeing the hurt on Beau's face, Melissa sighed and gave him her hand. "It's just that it's a little sudden, Beau. You see, I didn't *assume* anything, and I had no idea that you had. I'll just need time to think about it for a while, all right?"

He nodded, and squeezed her hand, but she could see that he did not understand in the least.

Quickly, she leaned close to him and kissed him on the cheek. "Now we had best go in. We do have work to do before this evening's performance."

They walked up the stairs, hand in hand, but Melissa's heart was heavy. She knew that in some way she had lost her innocence this afternoon, in a manner quite different than that of loving a man for the first time. Beau's words had made her stop and think, opening up an area that she would have to explore in more detail. She knew one thing for certain—they had slammed the door on the wild, carefree sexuality they had been experiencing, and had opened another, the door to something else.

She felt beset by choices that she was not certain she was prepared to make. She desperately needed to talk with Amalie.

Chapter Eighteen

Although it was only a few minutes past noon, there were already a number of men in the main room of the *Melon Patch*, playing at the gaming tables and drinking at the bar.

At one of the poker tables, Luke noticed, was Martin LaSalle, the actor from the *Natchez Belle*. Luke puffed thoughtfully on a cheroot as he watched the man from the corner of one eye. La Salle had been a frequent customer since the visit by the performers and crew of the *Belle* a week ago, and he was one customer Luke would just as soon not see again.

It had started out innocently enough. LaSalle would come in in the afternoon, play a few hands, win or lose a little money, and then return to the showboat for the evening performance.

But in the past few days, the pattern had changed. Now the man came earlier and stayed later, and he lost, lost more money than Luke would have thought a traveling actor could have, and Luke was beginning to worry.

At the last town, for instance, LaSalle had not only lost a considerable sum, but he had gotten a little intoxicated as well, and caused a ruckus at his table, when he had not been able to pay all of his losses.

Because the man was from the *Belle*, and because Luke did not want to endanger the revival of his friendship with the showboat people, he had written off the loss, but if LaSalle kept losing, Luke knew that he would eventually have to speak to the man, a course he dreaded for it was certain to result in an unpleasant scene.

Luke switched his attention from Martin LaSalle to the showboat anchored next to the barge, a portion of which was visible through the saloon window. Ever since that impromptu visit to his barge, the people from the *Belle* had been reasonably friendly to him, nodding to him when they saw him on the street of a town they were both visiting, or when the *Melon Patch* tied up within hailing distance at a landing.

Even Melissa seemed to be mellowing. At least she would nod to him now and then, and he had the feeling that she no longer felt so unkindly toward him, even if she never said so in so many words.

He did have hopes that in time, when she saw that he was causing no trouble for her, she would let him get close enough to explain the circumstances of his being aboard the love boat. After that . . .

Hell! He didn't rightly know *what* would come after that, if anything at all. He'd certainly like to make love to her again, that was one sure thing. Memories of her soft, magnificent body and eager lips still haunted his dreams, and he longed and ached to hold her body next to his, but he never let his thoughts go beyond making love to her, because when he did, he always ended up totally confused.

The *Melon Patch* was doing well, and he doubled its former profits. He looked upon the additional profits as a hope that when he showed Simon Crouse how much he was taking in, Crouse would be pleased enough to forget some of the anger he was sure to feel when he learned that Luke was not following through with the rest of his bargain.

Daily, Luke expected a telegram from Crouse demanding answers. Where were the women? What was holding things up? And Luke still didn't know what he was going to answer.

While Luke was thinking, he had been edging closer to the table where LaSalle and three other men were playing poker. He looked at the small stack of chips in front of LaSalle, and felt pending trouble give a tug at his gut.

Sure enough, even as Luke watched, LaSalle pushed the remaining chips into the pot in the center of the table, and called. The last player in the pot triumphantly turned up his hand, a full house, and LaSalle slapped his own two pair down with a snarl of frustration.

"Tough luck, friend," chortled the winner as he raked in the pile of chips.

LaSalle, with a muttered obscenity, slammed his hand down on the table and pushed back his chair.

As he did so, he spotted Luke, and a smile bloomed on his face. "Mr. Devereaux! Just the fellow I want to see!"

"Is that right?" Luke said cautiously, stepping away from the table so that LaSalle would have to follow him.

331

"Yes." The smile widened. "I have a favor to ask of you."

Luke, the smell of trouble like a bad odor in his nostrils, drew on his cigar. "All right, let's go into my office. It's more private there."

LaSalle bobbed his head, and trailed Luke down the passageway to the back of the *Melon Patch*.

Inside his office, Luke offered the other man a drink, which LaSalle accepted without thanks.

As LaSalle gulped greedily at the whiskey, Luke could see that it obviously was not the actor's first drink of the day. His eyes had an unfocused look, and he was the slightest bit unsteady on his feet. Being an actor gave a man some advantages, Luke thought ruefully. They could always pretty well hide the things they did not want known, and could pretend to be pretty much what they wished to be.

"Now what's the problem, Mr. LaSalle?"

The other man looked at him coyly. "Problem? Now, did I say I had a problem? I thought I only said that I wanted a word with you. Ask you for a favor, if I recall correctly."

"Yes, well, I have this feeling that your request will turn out to be more than a favor, Mr. LaSalle. I have discovered that is all too often true in an establishment such as the *Melon Patch*." Luke spoke frankly, hoping that his bluntness might inspire LaSalle to cut out the dramatics and get to the point.

LaSalle smiled wetly. "Well, in my case, you're wrong. My request is very simple. It is only that I be allowed to establish a line of credit here, until some funds I am expecting come through. You see? A very simple request."

Luke bit down hard on his cigar. "Not quite so simple, Mr. LaSalle. I am, as I'm sure you know, not the owner of the *Melon Patch*, merely the manager. The owner, I'm afraid, would be mighty unhappy if I started to grant credit to customers to gamble with."

LaSalle stared at him in what appeared to be genuine astonishment. "But of course I know that you're not the owner, my good fellow. Since that is the case, I'm sure the owner won't mind. After all, we both work for the same man, and he'll be getting back out of what he owes me any money I lose here."

Luke was taken aback. "We both work for the same man?" What the holy hell did this fancy-boots actor mean? What did he have to do with Simon Crouse?

Of late he'd had a few casual conversations with Jubal King, and in passing Jubal had mentioned the numerous sabotage efforts against the *Natchez Belle*. Intuitively, his mind made the connection—Martin LaSalle was in the pay of Simon Crouse!

If that was true, Luke knew he had to proceed with caution. He exhaled a cloud of smoke to screen his face, and said carefully, "I still have my instructions . . ."

"Instructions be damned! Simon Crouse owes me some money, and he's usually pretty prompt, I'll say that for him. When it comes, I'll be able to make good any losses here. I don't think I'll need to, for I feel that my luck is about to change. So, now, be a good fellow and do me this favor. You won't regret it. I'll put in a good word to Simon for you."

Any lingering doubts Luke had were dispelled when he heard LaSalle name Crouse as their mutual employer. Rage rose in his throat like a choking lump, and he ached to plant his fist right in the actor's smirking face. He had to admit that one reason for his anger was LaSalle's conspiratorial air, as if they shared a common cause—the destruction of the *Natchez Belle* and all the people there.

Luke swallowed his anger. It would not do to let this man know how he felt. If he lost control and struck LaSalle, the actor would undoubtedly fire off a telegram to Crouse, and bring the Carpetbagger roaring into town. Luke said slowly, "I'll do this much. I'll wire Crouse and ask if it's all right to extend you credit. After all, I only have your word that you work for him."

LaSalle assumed a long-suffering expression, and finished off his drink. "I suppose that will have to do, but I was hoping to play some more this afternoon. No matter, I'll just go back to the *Belle*, and my charming wife." He placed a harsh emphasis on the last two words. "Or perhaps I'll try once again to breach the elusive Miss Huntoon, Miss Handsoff Melissa." He winked lewdly. "A choice piece of femininity, that one, a beauty, a rose just begging to be plucked, but thorny, very thorny." He shook his hand up and down, miming being pricked by a thorn.

Luke, trying to ignore the white anger that blazed through him, said evenly, "You fancy her then, this Miss Huntoon?"

LaSalle smiled wryly, and motioned toward the bottle. "Mind if I have another drink?"

Without waiting for Luke's permission, LaSalle poured himself a stiff drink and held it up to the light. "Fancy her? You might say that, Mr. Devereaux. Usually, you know, I have no trouble with women, they find me irresistible, but Melissa Huntoon . . ."

He drained half of the contents of the glass in a

gulp. "Well, little Miss Melissa spurned me, and what's more, she has the gall to prefer the company and attentions of that callow youth who plays opposite her." His mouth got a twist of bitterness and his eyes were bright with venom. Then he shrugged. "Oh, well! Here's to women and war!" He finished the glass of whiskey. "If we can't have one, we have the other. If you know what I mean. Thank you for the drink, my dear fellow. I'd best go now. Please let me know as soon as you hear from our esteemed employer."

He left the cabin, weaving slightly, and Luke watched him go with relief. His nerves were strung tight as wires, and his muscles ached from the great effort it had required to resist smashing Martin LaSalle in the face.

He turned away with a savage gesture, and poured himself a drink. He sat down behind his desk, pondering his next move. He must see Melissa, and try to get her to listen to him. She must be made aware of the fact that Simon Crouse had a spy on the *Natchez Belle*, and that she was in great danger. Crouse was not a man easily thwarted, and when he learned that Luke wasn't following his orders to the letter, he would likely set LaSalle to the task.

Getting on board the *Natchez Belle* was no problem. They had slackened their vigilance the past week. The man at the foot of the stage plank sent word to Jubal King that Luke wished to see him, and Jubal came at once to welcome Luke on board.

When they were seated in the wheelhouse, and Jubal had plied Luke with a drink and a cigar, Luke began to explain his reason for being there.

Jubal listened quietly, nodding now and then, and

when Luke had finished, he shook his head sadly. "I thought it was almighty funny how that love boat managed to be Johnny-on-the-spot at the same towns we hit, but since I seen funnier things in my time along the river, I didn't think *too* much of it.

"But this actor gent now, LaSalle. By damn, that's hard to take! A river snake is what he is!" Jubal thumped back and forth. "You sure about him?"

"He didn't admit to being behind the 'accidents' to the *Belle,* but it's a logical assumption, since he works for Simon Crouse."

"Yep, 'twould seem so," Jubal agreed glumly. "What kind of a man can this Crouse be, to want to take two innocent women and do 'em harm?" He sighed. "Well, I reckon Melissa and the others ought to be told about this. You see, we sort of got us a democracy here. Melissa, she owns the boat, but the rest of us all have a say in what we do and how we do it. Most times, anyways. I purely don't think that this is somethin' we should keep from the ladies, since they're directly involved. Besides, I never did hold with that foolishness that says women is the weaker sex." He grinned. "People what say that never knew my Martha!"

So Melissa, Amalie, Martha, Nehemiah, and Mollie Boom were summoned to the wheelhouse, crowding the cabin almost to capacity when all were present.

Melissa frowned at the sight of Luke and, on his part, Luke was wondering how she would take what he had just told Jubal. Would she appreciate his warning? Or would she hate him all the more for being in the hire of Simon Crouse?

He let Jubal do all the talking, watching the women's faces as they listened, but avoiding Melissa's gaze.

336

"And that's the story, kit and kaboodle," Jubal finally said. "Now the question is, what are we going to do about it?"

"Humph!" Mollie said. "It seems to me the question is, what *can* we do about it? I say we give Mr. Carpet-bagger a taste of what he's been giving us. Let's march over to the *Melon Patch* and go to work with axes. Put a few holes in her bottom and she won't be *able* to follow us around!"

Amalie shook her head. "No, Mollie, that's not the way. Whatever we do to the barge would not keep Crouse from coming after Melissa and me."

Nehemiah chimed in, "She's right, indeed she is. It would seem that this villain, this Simon Crouse, is set on an evil course against Melissa and Amalie, and that he will not give up until he has done them grave harm, or until he is rendered incapable of doing so."

Martha sighed, and fanned herself with the small palm leaf fan she was carrying. "What I find hard to believe is that that nice Mr. LaSalle is in the pay of such a man, that he's been trying to wreck the *Belle*!"

Mollie Boom snorted. "Hah, pretty is as pretty does, I always say, and I've seen him sneaking around Melissa like a hunting dog after quail!"

Melissa flushed a brilliant scarlet, and Luke felt sorry for her at the same time that he was amused at Mollie's bluntness.

Mollie was going on, "I always say that you can't trust a man who sneaks away from his wife. You're too easy tooken in by his smooth manner, Martha. You've been spoiled by Jubal here. Most men ain't no damned good, and that's the truth of it!"

"Be that as it may," Nehemiah said, "the question still is, what are we going to do?"

"If I may say something?" Luke interjected.

The others nodded, except Melissa, who refused to look at him. She had moved over to a window, and stood staring moodily out at the river.

"When LaSalle reports that I've done nothing toward accomplishing what Crouse wanted me to do, namely abducting you two," he nodded at Melissa and Amalie, "he's going to blow like an overheated boiler, and I've seen enough of Crouse to know that when he gets angry, he does something about it. The first move I'd suggest is to discharge Martin LaSalle, so that Crouse no longer has a spy on board here. Then I'd suggest that you cut short your stay here, and go on to the next town. I also think you should post guards at night, and keep a sharp eye out for trouble. I understand you've relaxed your vigilance since the trouble stopped."

"We thought there was no longer any need for it," Jubal said sorrowfully.

Martha made a clucking sound. "It's hard to believe that a man, this Simon Crouse, can be so set on wickedness. Don't you suppose he might relent after awhile? After all, it must take a lot of time and money to do what he's doing."

"Yes," Melissa said suddenly. "Surely after time has passed, Crouse's anger will fade, and all this will seem more trouble than it's worth to him."

Amalie said strongly, "No, *chérie*, men like Crouse do not forget. They hold their grievances inside them like a festering wound that eats away at their souls. He is like a man possessed. He will not forget us, not Simon Crouse. Mr. Devereaux's advice is sound, and we should follow it."

338

Melissa said, "Nehemiah, will you take care of discharging Martin?" She could feel her cheeks burn as she spoke the man's name.

Nehemiah said, "Indeed I will. And Peggy?"

"They came together, let 'em go together," Mollie said forcibly.

Melissa nodded in silent agreement.

"Mr. Devereaux," Martha said, "I don't recall that any of us have properly thanked you for the many things you've done for us. First with Amalie, and now in this matter. I for one wish to express my sincere gratitude."

Jubal coughed. "That's true, Martha. Luke, we want you to know that we appreciate all you've done."

The others voiced agreement, all except Melissa, who gave him a flashing look and glanced away.

"What will you do now, Mr. Devereaux?" Nehemiah asked. "This Crouse individual is certain to be upset when he finds out what you've done, or, I should say, haven't done. As you pointed out, he is evidently a bad man to cross."

Luke shrugged, smiling. "That's why I'm going right along with you."

"On the *Melon Patch*, you mean?"

"On the *Melon Patch*." Luke grinned. "After all, I've received no word yet from Simon Crouse, firing me, and until I do, I consider the barge still mine to manage as I see fit."

Martin LaSalle stood outside the wheelhouse door, which had not been closed completely. He had not heard every word spoken, yet he had heard enough. His face an angry red, he hurried away from the wheelhouse before they could spot him.

So that sonofabitch Luke Devereaux had told them everything! Well, he would fix the Texan's wagon once and for all.

Without even bothering to detour by his cabin for his belongings, LaSalle left the boat. He had to get to a telegraph office and alert Simon Crouse as to what was happening. Crouse should be grateful enough to recompense him for what few personal things he was leaving behind.

He gave little thought to his wife. Let her fend for herself. He was sick and tired of her, anyway.

From the window of his hotel room, Simon Crouse could see the *Natchez Belle* and the *Melon Patch* tied up side by side. His expression was cold and malevolent.

He watched for a few moments longer, but saw nothing of interest. It was early morning, and both the boat and the barge were still asleep. He dropped the curtain back across the window and turned away.

Crouse deeply resented being summoned here to this one-horse town. He had had to stall important business back in Natchez to hurry here. The trip was costing him dear in time and money, and it was all the fault of that goddamned, doublecrossing Texan! Luke Devereaux was going to rue the day he had gone counter to his, Crouse's, wishes.

Crouse did not like to be thwarted. Once he had set himself on a course, he would not give up until the bitter end, no matter what the cost. His pride was too strong.

In his own mind, this pride was the foundation of his success. This time, where the motive was not personal gain but emotional satisfaction, that still held true. He meant to have the Huntoon girl and the quadroon, and *nothing* was going to stand in his way. In some dark, secret corner of his mind Crouse knew that the blow to his pride administered by these two women would not be eased until he had them both at his mercy, and that should have come to pass before now.

Angrily, he poured fresh coffee into his cup on the breakfast tray. As time had gone by, he had waited impatiently for word from Devereaux, word telling him that the mission had been accomplished, that Melissa Huntoon and Amalie Dubois were his prisoners, but the word had not arrived.

Cursing the slowness of communication, Crouse had stewed in impatience and frustration. Then the telegram from Martin LaSalle had arrived, informing Crouse that Devereaux had betrayed him.

Why had Devereaux allied himself with the showboat people? That question completely baffled him. Surely they couldn't even begin to match the money Crouse was paying. He knew they were doing good business, but not *that* good.

Of course! Suddenly enlightened, Crouse slammed the flat of his hand down on the table. It had to be the women. He should have realized that women as beautiful as that pair would tempt other men as well, and Devereaux had seen the Huntoon girl that day at Great Oaks.

Well, he'd soon even matters with Mr. Luke Devereaux! He would have that blasted Texan on his knees and begging for his life before he was finished with him.

He prowled back to the window, and stared down once again at the peaceful scene on the landing.

Dockworkers were stacking bales of cotton in orderly piles near the river's edge, and a wagon was jolting along the landing, loaded with fresh produce. It seemed to be heading for the *Natchez Belle*.

As Crouse watched, he saw several figures come out on the deck of the *Belle*, and he squinted as he tried to ascertain if any of the women were Melissa or Amalie. He cursed aloud. He was too far away to be sure.

Several men were wending their way toward the *Melon Patch;* they looked prosperous and respectable. Crouse's gaze scanned the refurbished exterior of the pleasure barge. To give the devil his due, the barge looked good. Crouse wondered if Devereaux had been taking in much money. He must make sure to get his money before he had Devereaux stomped.

Crouse's lips curled in a cruel smile as he remembered his brief meeting with Martin LaSalle last night, in this very room. The actor had been puffed up with self-importance as he strutted back and forth, filling Crouse in on Devereaux's treachery. When Crouse figured he had the actor pumped dry, he thumbed a gold piece from his pocket and flipped it to LaSalle.

LaSalle caught it, gaping. "What's this for?"

"That's your pay."

"Now wait a minute! You owe me a lot of money for what I've been doing for you. And I figure," LaSalle smirked, "that my finding out about the Texan for you is worth quite a lot."

"Be damned to what you figure. That's all you get."

"But I did the things you asked!" LaSalle wailed. "I caused all kinds of trouble for the *Belle* and the troupe!"

"Not enough, it would appear," Crouse said harshly, "since they're still in business, and prospering. I don't pay for failures."

"How about Devereaux? But for me you wouldn't have known about him! That should be worth something."

"The gold piece is for that. I would have found out about his treachery for myself in time."

"My job with the troupe, it's gone! Even my personal things are back on the *Belle*. I don't dare go back for them."

"That's your problem, actor." Crouse gestured. "Now, begone with you."

"No, not until I get my due!" LaSalle blustered.

"You'll get your due, a cracked head," Crouse thrust his head forward, lips peeled back in a snarl, "if you don't hustle your ass out of here right now! I've got some rough lads downstairs in the lobby who'll take you apart, if you force me to summon them. Now, begone with you!"

Martin LaSalle, a deflated and beaten man, left the hotel room.

Crouse had lied. There were no roughnecks downstairs, but they were always easy to find in these hard times. That was the first thing he had done this morning, hired a pair of toughs.

The mellow sound of a steam whistle split the still morning air, jolting Crouse out of his reverie. He saw a fair-sized steam packet coming up the river, her tall stacks spewing thick smoke.

As if by magic, the streets of the town suddenly became full of people: women in sunbonnets, children clinging to their hands; shopkeepers, still in their aprons; all heading toward the landing.

Quickly Crouse made ready to leave. Now would be the time to pay a visit to Devereaux, for in the crowd streaming toward the landing no one would take note of him or his "assistants."

Opening the door to the hotel room, Crouse spoke to one of the two men in the corridor. "All right, you two. It's time to do the job."

The taller of the two men, a lumpy-faced brute with a bullet head and no discernible neck, grinned, showing missing teeth. "We're ready, Mister. That we are. But don't forget now, you promised payment right after we do our job. Ain't that right, Jed?"

The other one nodded dimly, his muddy eyes sparkling for a moment at the word "payment."

"Come along then," Crouse said, "and earn your money."

Luke had been expecting a move from Crouse for days. Although Crouse's informer had fled the *Belle*, having gotten the wind up some way, it was well known that the *Belle* made overnight stops at almost every town along the river, so Crouse would have no trouble finding them.

Luke wouldn't have been surprised to see a complete stranger turn up, bearing a message from Crouse to the effect that Luke Devereaux was discharged, and ordered to turn the management of the *Melon Patch* over to the bearer of the message. The one thing he had not expected was the appearance of Simon Crouse in person.

And yet here he was, striding through the door of the *Melon Patch* with two big, ugly bruisers siding him. The saloon was nearly empty, for most of the dealers and the girls had gone on deck to watch the arrival of the packet that had just announced its arrival with a whistle blast. In fact, Luke had been about to go out on deck himself to see the boat come in. Someone had mentioned that it was a passenger packet, carrying mail, passengers, and supplies for the river towns.

But now here was Simon Crouse, a bold sneer on his coldly handsome face, striding arrogantly along between the two toughs beside him. Luke felt his mouth go dry. He wasn't afraid of a fight, God knows, but the odds were prohibitive. He was confident that he could beat Simon Crouse with one hand in his pocket; but these two brutes were another matter. They had the look of hardened waterfront brawlers.

Luke cursed himself roundly for not toting a sidearm. When he took over the barge, he had made the decision to keep order without the use of guns, and he had succeeded. But this was something else again!

He had a choice: turn tail and run, or stand up to them. What a choice!

He moved only to take a cigar from his case and fire it. He exhaled smoke and waited for them, smiling lazily.

He said, "Simon! What a surprise, and an unexpected pleasure."

Crouse's answering smile had all the warmth of an icicle. "Is it now? I should have thought not. Considering all in all."

Luke said innocently, "Whatever do you mean, Simon?"

"I mean," Crouse said slowly, fixing Luke with his glare, "that Martin LaSalle has made me aware not only of your perfidy, but also of all that has transpired between you and my enemies aboard the *Natchez Belle*."

Luke's nerves spasmed. Damn! Somehow LaSalle must have overheard the conversation in the wheelhouse. Well, it was all on the table now, and there was no use dissembling any longer.

He spread his hands. "What LaSalle told you, Simon, is correct. I never had any intention of abducting the women."

Crouse's sneer became fixed, and his eyes narrowed dangerously.

"Wait now," Luke said. "Hear me out. I said that I never had any intention of harming the women, that's not my way, but I *have* held to the other part of our bargain. I have managed the *Melon Patch* well, I think, and she's been making a substantial profit, all of which I have for you in the safe in the office. If you'll check the books, you'll find that I have been turning twice as much profit as Bear Smith did in the same amount of time."

Crouse's eyes glittered like diamond points. "That is all very well, Mr. Devereaux, and I am not hypocrite enough to pretend that I am not pleased at this indication of your industry. However, the most important part of our arrangement, as I most carefully stressed to you, was to obtain the women. Now, if you would care to give me your reasons for not doing so, it will postpone the beating you are about to receive, by the length of time it takes you to tell me. Do you care to

346

proceed, or shall we begin your chastisement at once?"

He put a hand on the shoulder of each of the men beside him, and they grinned with glee and cracked huge knuckles with a sound like pistol shots.

"My reasons wouldn't really interest you, Simon," Luke said tiredly. "They have to do with things like friendship, and a certain code of ethics, nothing you would understand."

"You're right, I don't understand," Crouse said. Then he hissed, "Now! Hammer him into the deck!"

Before the pair of hirelings had taken the first step, Luke was already in motion. He flipped the burning cigar into the face of the man on Crouse's right. The thug yowled in agony, hands going up to his face.

Luke was already on top of the second man. He slammed a fist into the man's broad nose, and felt satisfaction as blood spurted. He hooked a humming left into the soft midsection, and then another hard right to the face, and he felt a flash of elation as his opponent backed up a couple of steps.

If he could render both thugs temporarily helpless, he could then run right off the barge, thus salvaging his pride and seeking the protection of the crowd on the landing.

Luke laughed shortly to himself. What fools men could be—to value pride over a bloody beating!

Even as these thoughts sped through his mind, he was raining telling blows on the roughneck, who gave ground grudgingly, trying to ward off Luke's blows.

Deck him, Luke thought, *and I can stroll right out of here!*

Then he was seized from behind, arms like steel ca-

347

bles wrapping around him. The arms tightened, squeezing, driving the breath from him. He was lifted a few inches from the deck.

Dimly, he heard Crouse's angry screech: "Cripple him! Cripple him for life!"

Luke lashed back against his captor's shins with his bootheels, with little effect. The vise-like grip tightened even more. Luke reached back with both hands, fingers searching for a hold—hair, nostrils, eyeballs, anything!

A sledgehammer drove into his exposed belly, then into his face, and again into the belly. Pain slashed into his side like a hot knife, and he felt a rib go.

Lights danced before his eyes, and his consciousness began to go, as one bruiser held him immobile while the other used his great fists with impunity, raining blows on him from head to groin.

All of a sudden, Luke slumped, blackness taking him.

"All right, that will be enough," Crouse's distant voice said.

The band of pressure around his chest was relaxed, and he was falling free toward a distant star that was a pain-prick of light piercing into his brain.

He hit the deck with a thump, and a boot slammed into his broken rib. Luke screamed silently, but the pain aroused him so that he began to surface through a pain-filled fog. Through swollen eyes he saw a vaguely familiar face swimming before him, eyes wide and mouth agape. Somewhere in his battered mind, Luke recognized the face as belonging to Bertram, a crew member from the *Belle*.

"And what do *you* want?" Crouse snarled. "This is private business!"

Bertram stammered, "I—I was sent to fetch Mr. Devereaux, to invite him to supper on the *Belle.*"

Crouse roared with laughter. "Did you hear that, Mr. Devereaux? You have been invited to supper. Isn't that thoughtful? You really should attend. I feel certain that your appearance will liven the supper hour for your friends aboard the showboat. Yes, I really think you should go, just as you are. Don't bother to bathe and dress. You, my good man, help Devereaux to his feet. He's having a spot of trouble with his legs."

Luke heard Bertram give a low whistle, and then he felt hands under his arms as Bertram attempted to raise him. He struggled to help, but his legs seemed to be made of water instead of muscle and bone, and kept collapsing under him. His body ached and throbbed with pain.

Over Bertram's soft grunts of effort, Luke heard Crouse's laughter, a maniacal sound. "It seems that our Texas friend cannot manage, lads. Why don't you give him a helping hand? Lift Mr. Devereaux, and see that he makes it over to the stage plank of the showboat right alongside the barge.

Luke now felt himself hoisted brutally by hurting hands, and the pain was so intense that he groaned aloud. His eyes were so swollen now that he had trouble seeing anything, and he felt as if he were strangling on his own blood.

He kept fading in and out of consciousness as the two toughs manhandled him out of the saloon to the deck. Luke could smell the welcome fresh air through blood-clogged nostrils, and he could hear the sound of voices on the landing.

He was barely conscious now, clinging to a small

glimmer of alertness through a combination of stubborn pride and sheer force of will. He did not want Crouse to have the satisfaction of seeing him completely down and out.

"That's good enough," Crouse snarled. "Drop him right there."

The cruel hands released him, and his full weight sagged into the arms of Bertram, who staggered beneath it, but managed to remain upright.

Luke even managed to take a few steps on his own. He heard the sound of excited voices around him, and then the icy voice of Crouse slicing through the hubbub: "That's it, Mr. Devereaux. You go on along and keep your supper engagement. Be certain to inform them that I was gracious enough to see to it that you were prompt."

Luke heard Bertram grunt with the effort of helping him up the slant of the stage plank, and then he heard nothing more. He felt himself stumble and fall, down, down, and it seemed that he was tumbling endlessly through a thick, smothering blackness, and then he welcomed surcease from the grinding pain.

Chapter Nineteen

At last Luke was resting quietly. For three days and nights he had tossed in the narrow bed, feverish from the beating, moaning and crying out from the pain in his body and the fancies in his head.

Melissa, who had been by his side almost constantly, had heard him speak her name numerous times, always with passion and pain; she had heard things that made her blush and then grow pale.

Now, she wiped his forehead with a cloth dampened with witch hazel, and gazed down into his swollen and discolored face. Tears burned her eyes. She could not help it. She could not bear to see him like this, broken and in agony; and it was all because of her; or at least because of the *Natchez Belle* and her crew.

When Jubal and Amos had brought him to the cabin three days ago, literally carrying him by the arms, Melissa had thought her heart would stop. At first, she had thought he was dead, but his heartbeat

351

was still strong, despite the cruel damage to his body, and she and Amalie had tended him faithfully, cleaning and bandaging his wounds, trying to make him as comfortable as possible.

When Luke was settled in the bed that day, and they had done all they could for him, she had turned to Jubal. "Simon Crouse?"

He nodded grimly. "He and two thugs dumped him at the foot of the stage plank. Way I hear it, this Crouse came in by train last night. Then, this mornin', he and them toughs went over to the barge, and whomped on poor Luke." His lips thinned. "Somethin' has got to be done about a man like that. He shouldn't be allowed to run around free and easy, causin' people hurt and trouble."

Melissa clenched her hands to still the trembling that had suddenly overcome her. Her nails dug painfully into her palms. "I hate that man, Jubal," she said in a low, intense voice. "I will hate him until the day I die. We *must* do something about him!"

"I know, little girl." He gently patted her shoulder, and met her eyes briefly before looking away. His eyes were wet. "Poor Luke! All this just 'cause he helped us. Terrible, terrible thing."

Amalie stepped up to take Melissa's hand. "Come away, *chérie*. You should rest. I will stay with Mr. Devereaux."

Melissa had refused to leave Luke's cabin, even when Beau, upset over her interest in this stranger, told her angrily that she was foolish to overtax her strength. But somehow, Melissa felt that she *must* stay with him, that she owed it to Luke in some way.

So, except for brief naps and during show perfor-

352

mances, Melissa had been at Luke's side during the three days he was unconscious. Now the fever seemed to have broken, and he was sleeping a good sleep, a real sleep. His face was relaxed and peaceful, and his wounds were beginning to heal, although the bruises were still colorfully in evidence.

On the afternoon of the third day, the cabin door opened quietly and Amalie slipped in, carrying a covered tray.

"I brought him some broth," she said softly.

"He's sleeping. Really sleeping, Amalie," Melissa said happily. "I don't think we'd better wake him now. We'll wait until he wakens by himself."

Amalie nodded. "But *you* must eat, *chérie*. You haven't eaten a decent meal since they brought Mr. Devereaux on board. Come and have lunch with me. I have not seen you to talk to in days. I'll fetch Martha to stay with him. As you say, he is sleeping now. He will be fine. The crisis has passed."

Reluctantly, Melissa permitted Amalie to lead her from the cabin, and to the dining room.

"Here, sit. I will go find Martha, and then bring you a good lunch."

Melissa smiled, feeling tired but happy, knowing that Luke was out of danger now, and too worn out to brood upon her hatred of Simon Crouse.

Amalie soon reappeared with a steaming tray, which she placed on the table. The aroma of the food made Melissa suddenly aware that she was starving. As Amalie uncovered a bowl of bouillabaise, thick slices of fresh bread, and butter, Melissa began to eat ravenously. Nothing had ever tasted so good!

Neither of the women spoke while Melissa was

busy with her food, but when her plate was clean, and she was sipping her coffee, Amalie smiled at her contentment. "Well, little one, you feel better now, no?"

Melissa nodded and leaned back in her chair. With the food in her, she realized how very tired she was, and how much she needed sleep, but right now the effort required to go to her cabin seemed too much. She was content to remain where she was.

Amalie said suddenly, "*Chérie*, I do not wish to interfere in your life, but it seems to me that you care for this Luke Devereaux. Is this not so?"

Melissa gave a start. Then she smiled sheepishly. "I never could keep any secrets from you, Amalie."

"Do you think that when he is well, that all will be right between you two?"

Melissa sobered, and ran her finger around the rim of the china cup that held her coffee. "I don't know, Amalie. I told you what happened before New Orleans. Well, that stands between us, I guess. I suppose I was naive, to think that he would marry me."

Amalie shook her head. "No, no, Melissa, it was a natural thing for you to assume. You are young and innocent of the ways of the world."

Melissa's expression turned rueful. "*Was*, Amalie. I am still young, perhaps, but I am innocent no more."

"You are more innocent than you know. Innocence is more than a condition of the body."

"But I fear that I am wanton, Amalie. There's more. After Luke I—well, there is Beau."

"Yes, I know."

She gave the older woman a penetrating look. "Nothing escapes you, does it?"

"Well, you did not go to any great trouble to hide it, my dear."

"I suppose not." Melissa sighed. "And there's Martin LaSalle . . ." She put down her cup and twisted her fingers together. "With Martin, I must admit that I was not all that angry at his attentions. I . . . I even found him somewhat appealing. When he asked me . . . Well, I was tempted, and thought of going to his cabin. Oh, Amalie, am I a wicked woman? A wanton? Will I go through life like those girls you told me of in New Orleans, the ones who are kept by men in the houses on Rampart Street?"

Amalie shook her head vehemently. "No, no, *chérie*! Of course not! You are your own woman, you may have loved a man, or even two, but you have not been kept by any man. You are a woman of independence, a rare thing, I think."

Melissa's agitation subsided as she considered Amalie's words. "That's true, isn't it? Then you don't think that what I feel is wicked, this need to be held and loved by a man?"

"If that were so, then most of womankind would be so labeled," Amalie said gently. "It is a natural thing, little one, a natural feeling. Men and women were made in this fashion."

Melissa smiled suddenly, and a question that had long troubled her popped to the surface. "You never married, Amalie. Have you been happy?"

Amalie looked taken aback, and her look was probing. "Ever the curious one, aren't you, Melissa? But this time I shall tell you. Yes, my friend, I consider that I have had a good life. I have had many offers of marriage, which I turned down, and I have had lovers

355

who shared my bed. However, there was only one man who captured my heart until now, when, the saints be praised, I have found Amos."

Melissa, her fatigue forgotten, leaned forward eagerly. "Who was the man you loved, Amalie? Please tell me. I have often wondered. I am not just being curious, truly. I want to share it with you!"

Amalie stared at her for a long time. "All right, I shall tell you. I always meant to some day, and perhaps this is the time. But first, are you certain that you wish to know? The answer might not please you."

"I know that I've been intolerant and a prig, Amalie, about Amos and all, but I know better now, really I do. Please tell me."

Amalie nodded slowly. "I shall, *chérie*. The one man whom I loved with all my heart and soul was your father, Jean-Paul Huntoon."

Melissa reared back, and a shocked silence was her only response. Her *father?* Her mind reeled. Her father, and Amalie?

Amalie raised a hand. "Before you think something that you should not, I must tell you that there was nothing, nothing at all, between us until after your dear mother's death. Before that time, I think I may have loved him, but did nothing about it, and he, with his heart full of love for your mother and for you, had no need nor desire to look elsewhere for affection.

"But after your mother died, after a long time had gone by and the numb hurt was beginning to leave him, he was a lonely man. I, too, was lonely, and we came together in mutual need and sympathy. A love grew soon between us. He would have made me his wife, but because of my black blood, I knew he would suffer for it, so I would not marry him. Instead, I stayed as I was, on the surface his servant, and a companion to you; but knowing in my heart that I held a different place in his heart. Can you understand that?"

Slowly, Melissa nodded. "I . . . I think so."

Her first reaction had certainly been shock, and a kind of outrage at learning that there had been someone other than herself and her mother in her father's life; but the longer she thought on it, the idea became less strange and more natural.

Jumping up from her chair, Melissa hurried around the table, and leaning over, put her arms around Amalie from behind. "You are my mother, too," she said softly. "Almost as much as my natural mother. I love you, Amalie, and I thank God that I have had you to look after me all these years."

Jubal came into the room abruptly, to find both women with tears in their eyes. "What's the matter here?" he asked in alarm. "Is our patient worse?"

"No, no," Melissa assured him, laughing at his expression.

"The patient is doing just fine, and we are giddy with relief," Amalie said.

Melissa and Amalie exchanged knowing looks, and began to laugh almost hysterically.

Jubal shook his head in wonder. "Women! You're a strange breed, as hard to understand as Old Man River out yonder."

The worry about Simon Crouse was always in the back of Melissa's mind. After the beaten Luke had been brought on board the *Belle*, some members of their group wanted to untie the showboat and steam away, but Melissa had stubbornly refused.

"I will *not* be driven away by that scoundrel!" she had stormed. "We will honor our commitments! Where we are scheduled to perform, we will perform!"

They had remained for the evening's performance. The performers and crew members of the *Belle* kept the pleasure barge under close surveillance, but everything seemed quiet. In fact, too quiet for comfort. The only action to be seen was the usual: a parade of the town's males on and off the barge.

Simon Crouse was observed twice, either leaving or returning to the barge, but that was all.

Everyone on the *Belle* was puzzled and worried, and there was a meeting held in the wheelhouse that night as they steamed up the river.

"It's like waitin' for a rattlesnake that you know lurks in the bush to rear up and strike you," Jubal said glumly. "Whatever that sidewinder is up to, I wish he'd get on with it. This waitin' ain't doin' my old heart any good."

"Just be glad he hasn't done anything," Martha said tartly. "We've got one man near dead in that cabin. We don't need any more wounded on our hands."

"It ain't like me to say I told you so," Mollie Boom said, "but if we'd done like I wanted, poor Luke might not be in the shape he's in!" She spat through the open wheelhouse window. "I say let's get together and march over there and put a pistol ball through the weasel's head. That'd put a stop to his shenanigans once and for all!"

"Please, please!" Melissa said, holding up her hands. "Stop it, Mollie. I don't want any more violence.

There's been more than enough of that. There has to be another way."

"Easy enough to say, but what?" Mollie grumbled. "I say, direct action is the only thing a snake like that one understands."

"Wait now," Martha said. "I agree with Melissa. We should defend ourselves, but to attack that barge, well, that's going too far."

"Well, leastways," Jubal said, craning his neck to look behind them, "he ain't followin' us tonight. Maybe he'll just be satisfied with beatin' up Luke."

Melissa wanted desperately to believe him, yet in her heart she knew better. Simon Crouse was not so easily satisfied. She said, "Let's hope you're right, Jubal. We'll just have to wait and see. Now I have to go check on Luke." She ignored the hurt look Beau gave her, and went out.

After the evening's performance on the day Luke's fever broke, Melissa slept the clock around. She was astounded to find that it was past noon when she awoke. The *Belle* was steaming upriver, headed for the town they were to play that night.

It was into fall now, the days cooler, the nights crisp. Jubal had told her that when they reached St. Louis they would turn back south, fleeing before the winter's freeze. They had been playing the towns on the east side of the Mississippi; on their way downriver, they would play the west side of the river.

Melissa hurriedly got dressed and hastened down the passageway to Luke's cabin. She went in without knocking, and found him sitting propped up against the wall in his nightshirt, a cigar pluming smoke.

His eyes brightened as she came in. "Ah, my dear Melissa, you are a sight for sore eyes!" He grimaced. "And I am speaking literally."

The coloration of his bruises was fading, but both eyes were still blackened. Otherwise, he looked fine. Hiding her pleasure, Melissa said tartly, "I must say that you seem much like your old self."

"Much of that is due to you, I understand." He put the cigar in a saucer on the bedside table. "I've been told that you have been by my side day and night."

Coloring, she approached the bed. "People on this boat talk too much."

"I appreciate it, Melissa. It gives me hope."

"Hope for what?"

"That you may care for me more than you will admit, even to yourself."

"Don't be too sure of that, Luke Devereaux," she retorted.

"A man can only hope." He grinned lazily, with a self-assurance that infuriated her.

"Have you had breakfast?"

"Breakfast and lunch, and I ate like a pig."

"Then I don't see that there's much I can do for you. I have things to do. I overslept."

She started to turn away, but he caught her hand. He said gravely, "Don't go, Melissa."

She tugged at her hand. "I told you, I have things to do. And there's nothing I can do here."

"But there is." His grin was back.

"What?"

"A kiss. Haven't you heard the old saying, kiss it and make it well?"

"That's for children," she scoffed.

Before she realized it, he had pulled her down across his lap and put his mouth to hers. She started to struggle, then subsided as a warm tide of feeling took her. Despite herself she responded, and as his arms went around her tightly, she snuggled into warmth and love.

His kiss grew more ardent, and his hands began to caress her body. In her haste, Melissa had not put on undergarments, and he soon found the secret places of her passion. She let herself be swept along until she became aware that he was fully aroused.

She tried to pull away. "What are you doing? You're a sick man!"

He laughed softly. "Not that sick, not that sick at all, my dear."

Luke shoved her skirts up around her waist, and positioned her on top of him.

"The door, I must lock the door!" she cried frantically.

Then he was inside her, and it was too late, as that wild, heedless rapture she had known that other time in his arms seized her. She gave herself up to sensation, and they became one, striving toward the culmination of ecstasy.

After the storm had passed and Melissa lay with her head on his chest, the sound of his heart under her ear like a pagan drumbeat, he chuckled, and said with heaving breath, "You see? I'm not too sick. And I'll heal much faster, now that you have ministered to me."

"Oh! You're insufferable, Luke Devereaux!"

She scrambled off the bed and hastily arranged her clothes, but her face, turned away from him, wore a pleased smile. She hurried from the cabin, ignoring his call behind her. Just outside the door, she almost collided with Beau Vermillian.

His accusing gaze took in her flushed, disheveled appearance, and as he looked from her to the door of Luke's cabin, his face tightened with anger.

A week later they learned why the *Melon Patch* had not followed them from the town where Simon Crouse had assumed charge of it.

As the *Belle* steamed into their current stop, Melissa, standing beside Jubal at the wheel, noticed a sternwheeler already tied up at the landing. It seemed familiar, and as they swung alongside, she recognized it. "Jubal, isn't that the steam packet that docked alongside the *Belle* that day Luke was beaten up?"

Jubal, busy watching the crewmen throw out the lines, spared the sternwheeler a quick glance. "Looks to be the same," he said judiciously. "Not a bad lookin' little boat, either."

"But not as nice as the *Natchez Belle*," Melissa said in a mock argumentative tone.

Jubal threw back his head and laughed. "Reckon you're right there, little girl. But she looks pretty fast. Got good lines and she rides high."

"Did you ever see a steamboat race, Melissa?" Mollie Boom said behind her.

Melissa looked around, shaking her head. "No, but I've heard about them."

"It's some sight," Mollie said excitedly. "I was on a boat that raced once. Nearly bought the farm when the boilers came close to exploding."

Martha clucked in disapproval. "It's a silly waste of

time and money, if you ask me. My land, grown men acting like little boys, that's what it is. Seeing who can outrun who. Well, who cares, that's what I say. People getting hurt, even killed . . ."

"Now, Martha," Jubal said, "don't go kickin' up a fuss."

"Melissa?"

Melissa turned at the sound of Beau's voice and found him just behind her. He said, "Could I talk to you for a minute, please?"

His voice and manner were very formal, and Melissa's heart sank. She hadn't spoken to him since he'd seen her come out of Luke's cabin, and she knew that he suspected the worst.

"Yes, Beau, certainly."

Nodding to the others, she followed him outside and to a secluded section of the deck, where he turned and looked at her, all of his pain showing in his eyes. "Melissa, I think that you owe me an explanation, don't you?"

Melissa sighed. "I suppose so, Beau."

"You've stopped caring for me?" he said, the words more a statement than a question.

She was slow in answering. "Beau . . . It's just that . . . Well, I'm a little confused right now, a little upset, and my mind is on other things—"

"Like that Texan, Luke Devereaux?" Beau spat the words. "I've watched you together. I've seen the way he looks at you. There's something between you two, isn't there?"

Melissa, despite her unhappiness at having hurt him, found her temper stirring. "There was once something between us, yes. But that is in the past."

"In the past?" He arched an eyebrow. "How about when I saw you coming out of his cabin earlier?"

"What about it?" she said challengingly. "I've been tending to him, you know that. We owe him that, after what he did for us. Don't you agree?"

"Well, perhaps." His glance fell away. "Was he your lover, too?"

Melissa felt heat rise to her face. "That is none of your affair, Beau Vermillian! Have I asked you about the other women you have known and loved? Have I?"

"It's different with a man," he said hotly.

"That's what men always say," she said evenly. "But no one has been able to explain to me why. I'm sorry if I've hurt you, Beau. I would never do it intentionally."

Her apology did not erase the pain in his eyes. "I suppose that is your answer then?"

She was puzzled. "What answer?"

"Have you forgotten so soon? I asked you to marry me, Melissa, and I've been waiting weeks for your answer."

Melissa felt a rush of guilt. In the excitement of the past few days, she *had* forgotten.

Right now, as of this moment, she wanted to tell him no, in no uncertain terms. She could not marry a man who did not trust her, and yet she knew that such a blunt answer would only antagonize him, and in his anger he might leave the showboat, or perform so badly that the customers would notice. Besides, in all fairness, she was not certain *how* she felt, either about him, or about Luke Devereaux—in spite of what had happened in Luke's cabin earlier.

364

"All of this has been too much, Beau," she finally said. "I have to think about the *Belle*, you know, and the troupe. I have a responsibility to them, and until this matter with Simon Crouse is settled, all my energies will have to be directed to that. Would you be willing to wait until this is settled? Then, I promise, I will give you an answer."

Beau's lips were tight, his manner distant, but he nodded with evident reluctance.

Melissa leaned forward, kissed him lightly on the cheek, and then made her escape with relief. What she had told Beau was true; she could not, with the threat that Simon Crouse posed still hanging over them, think of much else. The stark truth was, she was afraid for them all, for the *Belle* and for the people who made the boat their home.

And then, as she walked along the opposite side of the deck, she saw him, Simon Crouse, standing on the bow of the steamboat next to the *Belle*. His hat was in his hand, and he was standing very still, his reptilian gaze on her.

As she stopped, frozen with horror and astonishment, he smiled coldly, and pointed down to the side of the boat, where a man was swinging in a makeshift cradle, repainting the name of the boat on the side. The painter was working on the last letter of the name, and it leaped out at Melissa in bold black letters, very clear and easy to see: *Revenge!*

With a gasp Melissa fled, running toward the wheelhouse, Crouse's cruel, taunting laughter pursuing her.

* * *

"But why did he go to the expense of buying that steamboat, do you suppose?" Martha asked. —

" 'Cause it's three times faster than the barge, that's why," her husband answered.

— Mollie Boom grunted. "Yep, that's probably it. You know the barge was always tailing us, about twelve hours or so behind, being so big and clumsy, and being shoved along by the tug the way she was. This way, with the packet, Crouse can keep pace with us, even get ahead of us if he wants. Yep, that's what he's got in that black heart of his'n, I'll bet."

Luke sat back in his chair, listening to the others as they debated the question of the *Revenge*, and what to do about her. He had been summoned to the wheelhouse for the conference, his first time out of the cabin since being taken to it unconscious.

He was feeling pretty fit now, and his strength was rapidly coming back. Soon he would be able to stand up to Simon Crouse, but this time, he assured himself, it was going to be on his own terms! No more fights with Crouse's bully boys, thank you. He'd get the bastard alone, and then let Simon Crouse see who was the better man!

Luke was not a man who enjoyed fighting, but this was different. Always before he had only fought in self-defense, but this time he was willing to take the fight to the other man.

"That name, *Revenge*," Nehemiah was saying, "it's a deliberate taunt to us, indeed it is!"

"*Revenge*," Melissa said bitterly. "What can he know of revenge that we do not? It is *we* who should seek vengeance, not Simon Crouse. The audacity of the man!"

"I reckon we'll have to hire some hard cases of our own," Jubal said thoughtfully. "He's got a whole pack of toughs at his beck and call. We're goin' to have to fight fire with fire. No other way I can see . . ."

"If we do that, Jubal, where will it all end?" Amalie said. "If we hire fighting men, then he will get more men, and then we will get more, and more . . . no, that is not the answer."

"Then what is the answer, knuckle under to the scoundrel?" Mollie demanded with her customary bluntness.

"That I do not know, but I suggest that we use our heads, and see if we cannot devise one."

Life aboard the *Belle* now settled into a difficult and confining routine. As they steamed into each show town along the way, the *Revenge* was always right behind them. When Nehemiah attempted to give his waterfront spiel, it was interrupted by jeers, rough language, and often brawling, from the men of the *Revenge*. This succeeded in keeping most of the women and children away, and left little in the way of an audience.

The same thing happened at most performances, and soon word spread that the showboat only brought rowdiness with her, and attendance dropped off alarmingly.

The women were forced to remain on board most of the time, and when they did venture ashore, they had to be accompanied by several crew members. It was somewhat like living in a town under seige, and they all grew irritable with the strain.

Through it all, Simon Crouse swaggered around the

decks of the *Revenge*, like a pirate captain of old, smiling evilly, and arrogantly conveying the impression that he could crush them any time he wished.

Luke helped out wherever he could on the showboat, even to the extent of performing some of the minor parts in the plays when necessary. He was physically fit now, and the scars were fading, but a consuming anger rode him, like a demon on his back. His longing to get even with Simon Crouse was gnawing at him.

Melissa sensed his anger although he tried to hide it, and she was worried for him, but then she worried for them all.

The money they had taken in prior to Crouse's coming on the scene was being used up at a great rate, and very little was coming in. If Crouse and the *Revenge* kept up the harassment, there would soon be no money left to run the boat. Then what would they do?

Also, Beau and Luke, confined on the same boat, were always in one another's way, snarling like two strange cats. Melissa momentarily expected this antagonism to bring them to blows.

Melissa, her emotions in a state of confusion, could not for the life of her decide whether she loved one or the other, or neither. She avoided being alone with either man, and there had been no repeat of the sexual encounter with Luke.

Surely, she thought, Crouse would eventually have to get back to his business in Natchez, but the days dragged on, and he gave no indication of being anxious to leave. He stuck so close to the *Belle* that the *Revenge* might have been a twin to the showboat, tied by the same umbilcal cord, moving when the *Belle* moved, stopping when she stopped.

"I think I will go crazy!" Melissa shouted one afternoon, as the *Belle* lay tied up at the landing in a pretty little town off one of the tributaries.

The *Revenge*, as usual, was tied up right next to the *Belle*, so close that anyone on one boat could see anything that happened on the decks of the other.

They sat disconsolately around the the dining room table, picking at their lunch, staring glumly at the packet alongside.

"There isn't much use even giving a performance tonight," Nehemiah said tiredly. "There was hardly anyone at the landing to greet us when we came in."

Jubal set his jaw. "We can't just give up. We've got to put on a show."

"I don't see why," Mollie said belligerently. "At last night's stop there was, what, fifteen people in the audience? We didn't take in enough to pay for the kerosene we burned in the footlights!"

"We have to *do* something!" Melissa said, her voice breaking.

"Sssh, little one," Amalie said with false cheer. "At least none of us have been hurt, and we are all still together."

"But for how long?" Mollie grumbled. "How long can we keep together, steaming from town to town and not doing any business? Tell me that, will you?"

Luke, who had been very quiet, stood up suddenly, and started out of the dining room.

"Where you goin', Luke?" Jubal said in alarm.

"I'm going to do what has to be done, what I can't

369

postpone any longer. I'm going to have it out with Simon Crouse."

"No!" Melissa cried, jumping up.

"We can't go on like this, Melissa," he said, turning back to them. "If he keeps this up, you'll surely lose the *Belle*."

"But Crouse has probably twenty rowdies on that boat," Nehemiah said. "Even if we round up all the crew, we don't have enough to match them."

"But we'll surprise 'em, that's what we'll do!" Mollie said excitedly. "And I'm going along, by darn I am!"

"Please, please!" Amalie had to raise her voice to be heard. "Listen to me. Please!"

They quieted, turning to her.

"I know how you all feel," she began. "I too feel anger at this man, and I too would like to be avenged against him, and yet I know that violence is not going to solve our problem."

"The only thing that cad understands is violence," Beau said in a harsh voice. "I agree with Mollie and Mr. Devereaux. I say we collect every available man, and storm the *Revenge*."

"And if you win, what then?" Amalie asked softly. "Many of you would be hurt in any fight, some perhaps even killed, and surely the law would have something to say about a direct attack on another boat."

"But just look what he's done to us!" Beau exclaimed.

"That's true," Jubal said, "but nothing has been done direct-like. Mostly it's been things that we couldn't really call the law on. But if we attack them, that *would* be a matter for the law."

"And think if you should be defeated in a fight."

370

This from Amalie. "How do you think Melissa and I would fare then, with no one to protect us?"

"Amalie is right," Melissa said soberly. "As owner of the *Natchez Belle*, I would like to say that I disagree with Mr. Devereaux's plan. It's courageous, but foolhardy."

"I am my own man, Melissa," Luke said tightly. "I don't take orders from you."

Melissa flared, "So long as you're on *my* boat, you do."

"That, by God, can be remedied soon enough," he snapped. "I can walk right off this boat!"

"Luke," Amalie said gently, "please don't do anything rash. You may regret it later."

He glared at her. Then with a slight hitch of his shoulder he turned away, lighting a cigar.

An embarrassed silence ensued which was finally broken as Mollie thumped her fist onto the table. "But we have to do *something*!"

"I agree," Melissa said, "and we should talk about it."

"Hell, talk! That's all we been doing, it seems to me," Mollie said in a grumbling voice.

A thought suddenly came to Melissa. "Luke, would you say that he is a sporting man, our Mr. Crouse?"

He frowned at her in surprise. "He likes to gamble, yeah. Why do you ask?"

"Amalie, you've said more than once that Crouse is a proud man, and so, if he is proud, and if he is a sporting man, perhaps we can get him to agree to a wager with us."

She had their full attention now.

"What kind of a wager, my dear?" Nehemiah asked.

"A steamboat race!" she announced triumphantly.

"A steamboat race?" Jubal echoed. "What on earth?"

"A race between the *Belle* and the *Revenge*. Winner take all!"

"You must be daft!" Mollie growled, leaning forward. "Winner take all? You mean the winner ends up with both boats?"

"That's just what I do mean. It would be a chance for Crouse to get his revenge, and a chance for us to get ours."

"There's a hitch," Luke said slowly. "What makes you think he will agree to such a wager? He's already well on his way toward ruining you as it is. And if, as you say, his main purpose is to get his grimy hands on you two ladies, this wouldn't stop him from doing that."

"You're surely not going to agree to marry him if he wins?" Beau said in alarm.

"Heavens, no!" Melissa said in horror. "I would never agree to that, no matter what. But I think that he will reason that, if he wins, and wins the *Belle*, well, we will have nowhere to go, and will be easy prey for him. It seems to me that he might reason that way."

"Yes, he might," Nehemiah said dubiously. "That might be some incentive for him to agree, yet Luke is right. Yes, indeed! The way things are going, the villain will accomplish the same end, without the risk. Why should he risk a wager?"

"Just a minute," Luke said, his eyes bright. "Crouse *is* a proud man. His pride is an obsession with him. If we should post the challenge in the town, like a playbill, then he might feel honor bound to accept. If he doesn't, then everyone will know, and they will think him afraid of accepting the challenge. I doubt Simon would care for that."

"Oh, Luke!" Melissa said, clapping her hands together. "That's perfect! It will work, I know it. We could even put a notice in the newspaper." She made a frame with her hands. " 'The *Natchez Belle* herewith wishes to announce that she is challenging the *Revenge* to run a race of—' How many miles, Jubal?"

Jubal grinned, obviously beginning to relish the idea. "From here to St. Louis would make a fair race."

"There is one thing you may have forgotten," Amalie commented.

"What's that?" Melissa demanded.

"You had better inquire of Jubal whether or not he thinks the *Natchez Belle* can beat the *Revenge* in a race. If not, all our lovely plans are for naught."

Melissa rounded on Jubal. "Well?"

Jubal, the focus of all eyes, flushed, and thumped the deck with his peg leg. "Hell!" he said. "The *Belle* could beat that boat with half her paddle spokes gone!"

A spontaneous cheer went up. Jubal flushed anew, but Melissa had to wonder if his optimism was warranted.

There was a general movement toward the door. Melissa noticed that Luke was lingering behind.

She crossed over to him, ignoring Beau's black look.

"Luke," she said hesitantly, "I'm sorry I spoke so harshly to you."

"That's all right," he said with a flashing grin. "I probably had it coming."

"Do you approve of the race?"

"Hell, yes! If it can come off. I may try to arrange a personal stake in it."

"What do you mean?"

"A little side bet with Simon." At her look, he added, "I owe him money, Melissa. That's why I took over his," he grinned, "bilge-barge. To work off my debt, that and with the hope that I might protect you and Amalie, where some other gent might have carried out his orders to the letter."

Chapter Twenty

Simon Crouse lounged in a comfortable chair in the ornate grand saloon of the *Revenge* and stared through the side window at the *Natchez Belle* tied alongside.

He was feeling quite content. True, he was away from his business in Natchez, but he was keeping in touch by telegram, and things seemed to be going along well enough without him. Buying the steamboat had been a capital idea, in his opinion, enabling him to follow the *Natchez Belle* with no time lapse, as had been the case with the slower barge.

In a short time, he was certain to achieve his goal of putting the showboat out of business. When that happened, he intended to make his move on Melissa and Amalie, have his band of toughs abduct them, and then he could proceed to the completion of his plan—the sexual possession of the two women.

Part of his goal, to revenge himself on Luke Devereaux, had already been accomplished. He had derived great satisfaction from seeing that cocky Texan humiliated, beaten into the ground by the two thugs, and from all he could ascertain, Devereaux was still suffering from the effects of the beating.

Crouse smiled cruelly. The showboat people were hurting, really hurting, and the more they suffered, the greater was his glee.

The whole thing should be over soon, and then he could return to his business affairs, satisfied that his pride and honor had been avenged.

As Crouse mused, one of his men hurried into the saloon. "Mr. Crouse, have you seen this?"

Crouse accepted the handbill that his man handed to him. The corners were torn, as if it had been ripped down from wherever it had been posted.

"Them things are up all over town," the man said warily, waiting to see Crouse's reaction to what the flyer had to say.

Crouse gazed down at it incredulously. "It is hereby stated that the steamboat *Natchez Belle*, owned by one Melissa Huntoon, and captained by Jubal King, is hereby giving notice that she is challenging the steamboat *Revenge*, owned by one Simon Crouse, and captained by one Phineas Jones, to a race, to be run between here and St. Louis. The stakes are to be— Winner take all! One boat wagered against the other. The *Natchez Belle* is awaiting a reply to this challenge."

Crouse's face tightened, and his head began to throb. He immediately grasped the implications of the challenge, and the fact that someone aboard the *Belle* had thought of such a plan angered him excessively. He suspected the fine hand of Luke Devereaux, and wished that he had had him killed instead of just beaten.

"Damnation!" He crumpled the poster and threw it onto the floor. "They're posted all over town, you say?"

The man nodded. "Yep, and everyone in town is talking about it, wondering what we're going to do. What *are* you going to do, Mr. Crouse?"

Crouse breathed in deeply, his nostrils flaring. "I will have to think about it," he said coldly. "Now get out, get about your business, and leave me."

His fingers opened and closed, and he made a fist. "Damn them all to hell!" Crouse said aloud.

This was the first sign they had shown of fighting back. Crouse knew that he had them on the run, knew that he and his hardcases were ruining their business, knew that it was only a matter of time until he put the showboat out of business. And now this!

Of course, all he had to do was refuse the challenge. But if he did, word of his refusal would soon be all up and down the Mississippi. It would eventually reach Natchez and New Orleans, where most of his business was conducted; and although he might protest that he had not accepted the challenge on the theory that it was a vain and foolish pastime, a city of men raised in the sporting tradition would scorn a man who had refused such a dare. His prestige would suffer, and what was worse, to him, was the fact that he would become the laughingstock of the river.

His fists clenched again at the thought and cold anger poured through him. He decided to go into town and see for himself what the general reaction was.

The flyers *were* posted all over town, as Crouse's man had stated. As Crouse walked the main street of the town, he was greeted by shopkeepers and other

377

local businessmen; they all hailed him in a friendly manner, asking him when the race would take place, and how good he thought the *Revenge*'s chances were. They seemed to take it for granted that he had already accepted the challenge. Steamboat races were commonplace on the river, a popular wagering sport.

Some wagering was already taking place. His anger increased with each poster he saw. He did not want to be forced into such a race, when he was bound to succeed at his plan soon without any additional risk; but when he passed the newspaper office, and saw a copy of the daily paper tacked to the wall, Crouse knew that he would have to accept the challenge.

Right on the front page was an article about the challenge, implying that if the gauntlet was not taken up, Simon Crouse would be considered lacking in sporting blood, and might even be thought a coward by some!

Crouse stared at the paper with burning eyes, his teeth gritted until they ached, and then, suddenly, he relaxed. Why *not* race the *Belle*? The *Revenge* would be sure to win, as it was new, in perfect condition, whereas the *Belle* was older, and had once been wrecked. Also, there were things that could be done to improve the odds in his favor. He began to smile.

When he won, the women would have no place to go. His men could pick them off then, when the troupe of players had scattered, as they certainly would.

The more he thought of it, the more it appealed to him.

The showboat, in her present condition, should be worth something, and the prospect of profit always cheered Crouse up. Not only would he humiliate the people of the *Belle* by winning, he would end up with a tidy profit!

"Simon Crouse agrees!" Melissa waved Crouse's letter. "He'll do it. The race is on!"

Melissa gazed into the faces of her friends and found mirrored there the same mixture of feelings she was certain was on her own face—excitement and apprehension.

Beau, who was standing beside her, took her hand. In a low voice he said, "After it's over, Melissa, and we've won, you'll be free of him. Then maybe you'll give me your answer."

His expression was serious but gentle. Melissa smiled, and squeezed his hand. "Yes, then we can return to normal, and when we do, I promise you that I *will* give you a decision. And whatever that decision is, Beau, I want you to know that you have been very dear to me, and I am grateful for all the love and kindness you've shown me."

Beau motioned uncomfortably. "Melissa, don't talk that way! It sounds so—so *final!*"

"I don't really mean it to," she said, turning slightly away, as she caught Luke's gaze on her, and saw his grim expression. Dear God, it seemed that she could not even talk to one of the two men without hurting the other. It was all such a tangle!

Right now, the important thing was the race.

"We will all have to pitch in during this race," Jubal was saying. "And there is some danger, I won't lie about that. So, if any of you want to bail out, now is the time. We won't think any the less of you for it. In fact, it probably would be the sensible thing to do. We could strike a snag, or a sand bar, or a boiler could blow. It happens all the time. I'm a dadburned good pilot, as is Mollie here, and we'll do the best we can, but there is always the risk. Now, anybody feel like bailin' out?"

There were some uneasy glances exchanged, but no hands were raised.

Jubal grinned, bobbing his head. "Good! Now I'll tell each of you what I expect from you."

As Jubal began giving out instructions, Luke came over to Melissa and touched her arm. "Melissa, could I have a word with you?"

Melissa nodded, and let Luke lead her outside onto the deck, out of sight of the others.

She said impatiently, "Well, what is it, Luke?"

"I've been giving this thing a lot of thought, and I think you should add another stipulation to your wager with Crouse."

Surprised, she stepped back. "Why?"

"The reason for this race is to settle matters between you, Amalie, and Crouse, once and for all. Is that correct?"

"You know that it is."

He shrugged. "And if you win—"

"*When* we win!" she said forcibly.

He gave a grudging smile. "All right, *when* you win, you'll take over Crouse's boat."

"Yes, that's the whole idea." She was more puzzled than ever.

"And you seem to think that winning this race will solve all your problems."

"Well, he will be beaten. He will have lost. His boat will be gone, and he'll have to leave us alone."

Luke sighed. "What makes you so sure he'll leave you alone? What makes you think he won't just buy another packet, and take up right where he left off?"

Melissa's mouth dropped open. "But that would cost him God knows how much! Surely even *he* wouldn't go to such great lengths! Would he?"

Luke spread his hands. "I think it's possible, Melissa. He's a stubborn man. I hate to put a damper on your high spirits, because it's a good plan, as far as it goes."

Melissa looked at him almost pleadingly. "Do you have any suggestions, Luke?"

"I do. Like I said, I think you should add a stipulation to the wager. Demand that Crouse put it in writing that if he loses the race, he will leave you, Amalie and the *Belle* alone, that he will go back to Natchez and cease harassing you. With that signed statement in your possession, it would give him pause if he ever thought of bothering you again."

Melissa thought for a moment. "You're right. That should be a part of the wager. But I see one flaw."

Luke smiled ruefully, and drew on his cigar. "What do we offer in exchange for his agreeing?"

"Exactly. He wouldn't promise such a thing without something wagered in return. What could we offer? The *Belle* is all I have in the world."

"The only thing I can suggest is that we put it to Crouse and get his reaction." He grinned crookedly. "I already sent him a note about that side bet I mentioned to you. If the *Belle* wins, my debt to him is canceled. If he wins, my debt is doubled. He fired his acceptance right back." Luke assumed a gloomy expression. "God knows what I'll do if we lose. Kill myself, I reckon."

She placed a hand on his arm. "Don't worry, Luke, I'm sure we'll win," she said absently, still mulling over his suggestion. "Your idea's sound. I'll get Nehemiah to draw up a legal-sounding document. He has a way with words."

She started to turn away, ready to return to the others, but now she turned back. "Thank you, Luke, for your help . . . for everything, really. For Amalie, and for taking such terrible punishment just for trying to help us. I've been rude and hateful at times, I know, and I'm sorry for that." She smiled, and added wryly, "After all, Jubal says we may blow up or sink. I want to have my conscience clear, in the event that that happens."

Luke shook his head. "God forbid. But I do appreciate your words, Melissa." He grasped her hands in his. "They mean more to me than you probably know. I care about you deeply, even though it's taken me awhile to admit it to myself. You have never ceased to be important to me, very important, and I would like you to know that I have never lied to you, whatever else I may have done to hurt you."

Melissa felt tears forming in her eyes, and did not know the reason. She did not resist as he pulled her to him, and gently placed his lips on hers.

The warmth, the yearning, the feeling that she would like to yield once again to this man, filled Melissa with a warm sweetness, and then she heard a sharp intake of breath, and pulled away from Luke quickly, to see Beau standing behind her, glaring at them in rage.

Melissa's happiness deserted her, leaving her feeling apprehensive and guilty.

Beau's eyes blazed with his anger, and his body was tense as a bowstring. "Devereaux," he said in a low, rough voice unlike his usual clear tones, "you are a cad, sir! I challenge you to a duel. You may choose the weapons!"

It took a moment for the words to penetrate. Melissa took a step toward him. "No! Don't be ridiculous, Beau!"

He refused to look at her, but continued to glare at Luke. "Do you hear me, hero, rescuer of ladies, stealer of other men's women?" he said with weighty sarcasm.

Melissa didn't know whether to laugh or cry. This was all so hurtful, so unnecessary, so foolish! Why did men always want to settle their differences with violence?

Her glance jumped to Luke.

He was calm, perfectly relaxed. "Don't be a fool, Beau," he said softly. "A duel won't settle anything."

"It will rid us of you, once and for all," Beau said, his voice trembling. "I have challenged you, and now I await your answer, sir!"

Melissa made a sound of despair. How rigid and righteous, how angry he was in his pain and wounded pride. This now, now when they all needed to pull together!

"Beau," she said strongly, "this is not the time for personal concerns."

Still he would not look at her.

"Listen to me! This will have to wait," she said more loudly. "We have the race to think of. That comes first. We have preparations to make. If you can't put this aside for now, then I will be forced to ask you to leave the *Belle*."

He finally looked at her, his eyes baffled and hurt, but she forced herself to go on, "I mean what I say. And the same goes for you too, Luke."

Luke nodded. "I understand. And I, for one, will

abide by what you say. I'll forget this until the race is over. In fact, I'd just as soon pretend it never happened."

They both looked expectantly at Beau, who stood rigid for some moments, and then, at last, he nodded stiffly, turned on his heel like a reprimanded soldier, and strode away, his bootheels drumming an angry tattoo on the deck.

Melissa let out a gusty sigh of relief. "Now we had better get that paper off to Crouse. He should have it as soon as possible."

"All right, listen everybody!" Mollie Boom said, waving a long sheet of paper. "This here's the checklist. I'll read 'em off. Fresh water?"

"On board," Nehemiah said.

"Wood?"

"Plenty," Amos said. "Also, I've got ten buckets of grease and pine tar, and there's wood stacked all around the boiler deck."

"Food?"

"I've stored all kinds of staples and as much fresh food as I could get my hands on," Martha said, wiping her hands on her apron.

"Emergency equipment, ropes, grasshoppers, hatchets, fire buckets?"

"All taken care of," Beau said, "as well as medical supplies in case of injury."

"Good, good!" This from Jubal, who had been silently reading the checklist along with Mollie. "We want to be ready for anythin' that might happen, anythin' a-tall. Even then, there's sure to be somethin' we didn't think of. Always is." He looked over at Amos. "Have the engines been checked?"

"Sure thing," the engineer said. "They're in fine shape, running smooth as silk." He looked down at Amalie, standing in the crook of his arm, and smiled.

"And the paddlewheel?"

"The paddle is solid, no breaks or cracks."

"And the hull is sound, I've checked her myself." Jubal glanced up from the checklist. "Appears to me that we're as ready as we're ever goin' to be. Now if Mr. Crouse will only reply to Nehemiah's note, we're ready to race!"

Melissa and Luke exchanged glances. The note, with the added condition to the wager, had been written by Nehemiah and delivered yesterday, but still no answer had been received.

The race was scheduled to start on the morrow, and Melissa was jittery with nerves. Ever since Luke had talked with her, she had lived with the fear that the race would ultimately solve nothing, no matter who won, unless Crouse agreed to the addendum. Why didn't he answer?

Martha voiced a question. "I wonder why that man moved his boat away from the *Belle,* over to that little landing around the bend?"

Jubal frowned. "Appears to me that he did it 'cause he don't want us to see what he's doin' to his boat to get her ready for the race."

"But what could he do that would help him that needs to be kept so all-fired secret?" Mollie asked pugnaciously. "I don't put it beyond that river rat to be planning something sneaky, something to give him an edge."

Melissa looked at Jubal in consternation. "Could he do that, Jubal? Do something to his boat that would make her faster than the *Belle?*"

Jubal bit his lip, looking away. He was pretty sure what Crouse was up to, but he didn't want to tell the others. It would just cause them to worry, and it wouldn't help matters a durned bit. Sure, they could do the same thing to the *Belle*, but then she would have to be rebuilt after the race, and they would lose the rest of the show season.

So he simply shrugged, and said, "I reckon every captain thinks that he has the secret of winnin' a boat race. But as for me, well, I leave it up to my skill as a pilot. That's my secret for winnin' races."

Everyone relaxed and began to talk together, except for Melissa, who had a suspicion that Jubal was being evasive. But before she could confront him there was a loud knock on the outside door, and Jubal thumped over to open it. One of Crouse's hulking crewmen stood there with a scowl on his face, and a sealed note in his fist.

"Mr. Crouse sent this for Melissa Huntoon," he growled.

Jubal handed the note to Melissa, but she shook her head. "You read it, Jubal, please. I'm too nervous."

"I was told to wait for an answer," the messenger said.

"Fine, you just do that, but out on deck. We would like some privacy, if you don't mind." Luke strode forward and slammed the door in the messenger's face and turned back to the group.

Jubal was already unfolding the note. He scanned it quickly, looked up briefly at the waiting faces, and then read it again. His expression was dour.

"What is it, Jubal?" Melissa asked. "What does it say?"

Jubal's lips thinned. "I don't think you want to hear it, girl."

"Come now, Jubal," Martha said crossly. "Whatever it is, we have to know it, so stop being so dramatic, and read it."

He looked in question at Melissa, and after a moment's hesitation, she sighed. "You might as well, Jubal. We have no secrets from one another now, and whatever it is in the note will affect us all, so read it."

Luke stepped up to stand beside her, cupping her elbow with his hand to let her know that he was there, and as he did so, Beau moved to her other side, taking her hand possessively in his. She was too worried about the contents of Crouse's note to fret about them. But she did admit to herself that it was nice to have them there, so close and protective.

Jubal began to read: "I, Simon Crouse, owner of the steam packet *Revenge*, do agree to the terms set forth by Melissa Huntoon, owner of the steamboat *Natchez Belle*; to wit, that the boat race between the *Revenge* and the *Natchez Belle* shall be for the following terms: Winner of aforesaid race to take possession of the loser's boat and all appointments; and also, in the unlikely event that the *Revenge* should lose, I agree to stop and desist from any contact with the owner or employees of said boat, the *Natchez Belle*, and do agree to stop any harassment of said owner or employees."

Melissa let her breath go with a whoosh. He had agreed. There were murmurs of pleasure from the others.

Jubal glanced up frowning. "That's not all," he said. "The scoundrel goes on: 'In addition, the owner and employees of the *Natchez Belle*, in the event their boat loses the race, do hereby agree to turn over to myself, as owner of the winner, not only the craft and all appointments, but also the person of Melissa Huntoon, who will agree to become my lawful wife.'"

There was a concerted gasp from his audience as he finished, and Jubal lowered the note with a dark scowl. "How dare that low-bellied snake demand such terms?"

"It's outrageous!" Nehemiah stormed. "That villain should be horsewhipped, indeed he should!"

Luke's hand tightened on Melissa's elbow. "Are you all right?" he asked softly. "You've gone white as your dress."

She nodded, feeling weak with despair. She had expected Crouse to ask for *something* in return for his agreement, but she had not expected this. "What am I going to do?" she said in a whisper.

"Tell him to go to the devil," Mollie Boom said, her face red as fire.

Melissa swayed, her eyes closing, and Amalie, pushing both men aside, took her arm and assisted her to a chair.

"We can still race on the original terms," Beau said hopefully, "and then deal with Mr. Crouse afterward, if he continues to plague us."

Melissa looked up. "But I wanted this race to solve *all* our problems, not just postpone them." Her glance went to Jubal. "I'm sure we will win, Jubal will *make* us win, but I'm not sure enough to risk having to marry that . . ." She shuddered, covering her face with her hands.

"Nobody expects you to, girl," Mollie said stoutly.

"It's unthinkable," Nehemiah said, "out of the question. We won't even consider it!"

Luke, kneeling beside her chair, said in a low voice, "And I wouldn't allow you to do it."

Melissa raised her head. "Amalie, what do you think?"

But Amalie was nowhere in sight. She had disappeared, and Melissa was not given time to wonder about her absence, for the others were all talking at once, all attempting to voice their viewpoints.

Suddenly Melissa felt very tired. Beau was right, there was nothing to do but go ahead with the original wager. What other way was there?

It was a subdued group who finally gathered around Nehemiah to help him phrase their answer to Crouse. The note stated that since Miss Melissa Huntoon found the additional terms unacceptable, they were willing to proceed with the original agreement.

When they went out on the deck to give the note to Crouse's man, they found him gone. Only Amalie was on the deck, standing by the railing, looking pensively down at the water.

"Amalie," Melissa said, glancing around the empty deck, "where is Crouse's messenger?"

Amalie looked around. Her face was serene. "I sent him back."

"You sent him back! I don't understand."

"I sent him back with a counter offer."

Melissa felt herself go cold with foreboding. "Amalie," she whispered, "what did you offer?"

Amalie took her hands. "I wrote to him that his terms were not acceptable to us, but that if the *Belle* lost the race, I would agree to become his housekeeper' for as long a time as he wished me to fill the position."

"Oh, Amalie! No, no! I won't allow it!"

Amalie smiled sorrowfully. "Do not worry, *chérie*, for we cannot lose. We have the great captain and pilot, Jubal King, do we not, and another great pilot in Mollie Boom. We have a superior engineer in Amos, and excellent deckhands. And surely, God is on our side, for I cannot imagine Him being on the side of Simon Crouse."

"But if we should lose, think what would happen to you!"

"Shhh, little one. It is done. And we cannot lose."

"Look!" Martha cried, pointing. "There comes the messenger back already."

Silently, they watched the man slouch along the landing toward the *Belle*.

At that moment, Amos Johnson shouldered his way through to Amalie's side. "What's this I hear, Amalie? What is this thing you've promised? Is what I hear true?"

"It's true, my dearest." She put her hand on his arm, and gazed up into his smouldering eyes. "It is something that I had to do, Amos."

He swallowed hard, his columnar throat working as if he were swallowing something vile. "And if we lose, what then?"

"If we lose, I shall not keep my promise. Always I have prided myself on the fact that my word is my bond, but in this case, I do believe that God would forgive me."

"But you know the kind of man Crouse is," Melissa said. "He will come after you!"

Amos growled, and pulled Amalie into the circle of

his great arm. "If that comes to pass, I personally will kill this Simon Crouse, before I will allow him to lay a hand on you, my Amalie."

"Hush now." She smiled up at him tenderly. "Always you men talk of killing. At any rate, he has not accepted yet, and he may not."

The messenger thumped up the stage plank, his heavy boots resounding on the wooden deck, and the group moved forward to meet him halfway.

He handed the note to Amalie, an insinuating smirk quirking the corners of his thick lips. Then without a word he turned and moved away.

With trembling fingers Amalie unfolded the piece of paper and read it quickly. She looked up, her face pale.

"He has agreed," she said in a dead voice.

Chapter Twenty-one

The day of the race dawned overcast and humid. The river, under the lowering sky, rolled sullenly, its water low between the high banks.

Melissa, keyed-up and tense, looked at the sky in dismay. Somehow the dreariness of the weather seemed a bad omen.

The *Belle* was ready for the race—as ready as she would ever be. All expendable material had been dumped ashore, anything that might add unneeded weight to the boat. The engines were oiled and in perfect condition, the boilers were fired, and arrangements had been made to pick up additional fuel from barges along the route. Everything that could be done had been done, and they were ready.

The boats were supposed to start at ten A.M., and it was now nine-thirty. Where was the *Revenge*?

The members of the immediate group were gathered in the stern of the *Belle*, staring anxiously toward the curve of the river that hid the small bend behind which Crouse's boat was concealed.

Melissa stared until her eyes ached, hands clenched around the rail. They simply *had* to win! Now, with Amalie's fate a part of the stake, they had to win more than ever. Melissa knew that Crouse, if he won, would come to claim Amalie as his prime prize, and Amalie's vowing to break her promise would not deter him if he got his hands on her.

"There she is!" Mollie cried suddenly.

"Oh, my land!" Martha gasped.

Melissa could only stare.

The *Revenge* was a strange sight. Now she knew why Crouse had arranged to prepare the boat in privacy.

All the glass in the pilothouse had been removed, as well as the steam escape pipes, doors, windows, shutters, and any removable projections. Everything that might offer resistance to the air and cut down on their speed had been removed.

Jubal groaned. "I feared that was what he was up to. He's stripped her down to the buff. Even the anchors, rigging and hoists are gone. She's nothin' but a skeleton of herself!"

Melissa, feeling panic rise in her like yeast, clutched at his sleeve. "Jubal, what does this mean? Will it help him win?"

Jubal nodded glumly. "It'll help him some, I'd reckon. He'll have less weight to move, and less air resistance, but it won't be enough." He brightened, smiling at her. "Don't worry, little girl. We're still goin' to win. We'll just have to try a mite harder, is all."

Melissa swallowed and clung to his arm, wondering if this wager hadn't been a dreadful mistake.

Shortly, the *Revenge* was tied up alongside the *Belle*, with only a single line fastened to the landing.

Near the line, a man with an axe was stationed, holding the axe in readiness.

Luke made a sound of disbelief. "Look at that, will you? He's going to cut the rope so that the *Revenge* can make a faster start."

"Yep." Jubal spat over the railing. "Luke, tell the men to release all the lines but one. We can't arrange for an axe man this late, but at least it will cut down the odds agin' us."

Luke nodded, squeezed Melissa's arm, and went to follow Jubal's instructions.

"I've got to hustle up to the wheelhouse," Jubal said. "Give me a kiss for luck, Martha, that's a good girl."

Martha, standing on tiptoe, gave him a resounding kiss on the cheek. Jubal thumped away, and the group scattered to their assigned tasks. The race was about to begin.

There was a large crowd on the landing, cheering and calling out wagers on their favorite to win. The steam from both boats roiled thick and white into the air, and the boats trembled with the pressure of the boilers, as if they were anxious to be away.

Melissa felt giddy from all the excitement, but her mind was clear.

The starting signal, a shot fired into the air by the town's mayor, sounded, and Melissa saw Crouse's man on the landing swing his heavy axe. With a single blow, the line was severed, and the *Revenge* sprang away like a startled deer.

At the same time, the man holding the *Belle*'s line released it from the boat's stern, and the *Belle* surged away, although not quite as quickly as the *Revenge*.

A roar went up from the crowd on shore, and Melissa felt her heart give a leap. Now it was up to God, Jubal King, and the river.

The brown water splashed and flew from the spinning paddlewheel, leaving a foaming wake behind the *Belle*, and she bucked a bit as she hit a patch of rough water.

The *Revenge*, several boat lengths ahead and to the right, plowed on, her bell clanging, the men whooping from the decks and making obscene gestures at the *Belle*.

In the wheelhouse Jubal and Mollie both wrestled with the huge wheel, watching the river closely all the while. Their faces were tense, for the river, low as it was, could present them with an unpleasant surprise at any time.

Melissa wondered how she would be able to survive the suspense during the three days that the trip would take to St. Louis. Venturing one more look at the *Revenge*, chugging along just ahead of them, she mouthed a silent prayer, and went below to help Martha and the cook with the preparation of the midday meal, for extra men had been hired to help stoke the boilers so that maximum speed could be maintained.

The meal was eaten in an atmosphere of high excitement; an almost party feeling prevailed, particularly among the men. Melissa, now feeling somewhat subdued, watched them. It struck her that men only really seemed to come alive in a situation fraught with danger and excitement.

By late that afternoon, the *Revenge* had managed to increase her lead, and was now well ahead of the *Belle*. The festive mood had worn off, and faces were grim aboard the *Belle*.

Melissa had seen little of either Beau or Luke, but

she had noticed that they seemed to have put their animosity aside for the moment, and were concentrating on feeding the hungry boilers, working side by side.

By suppertime, they were surrounded by a fog as thick as file gumbo, and no one felt much like eating.

Finally, Jubal sent word from the wheelhouse that the *Belle* was going to tie up until the fog lifted. Melissa and the others, gathered in the dining room, greeted this news with dismay.

"But the *Revenge* will have to tie up, too, won't she?" Martha asked. She had been banished, at Mollie's request, from the wheelhouse for the duration of the race.

Jubal, who had joined them after the boat was tied up to a grove of trees along the river, shook his head. "I don't know, Martha. In a fog like this, it's the only sensible course to take, but this Crouse ain't exactly sensible, it strikes me."

"Then he *could* keep going. And if he does . . ." Melissa sighed. "He could get farther ahead of us. We may never catch up."

"Don't talk that way, my dear," Nehemiah said rather crossly. "We must all think in a positive fashion, indeed we must! It is also possible that if he charges on in this fog, he may run aground or hit a snag."

Amalie laughed softly. "I try never to wish bad luck onto other people, but I must confess that I am doing so now."

"Well, you all might as well get some sleep. I know I'm goin' to," Jubal said. "They'll rout me out soon as the fog lifts enough to charge on."

They retired, but Melissa was confident that few of them slept that night. Lying awake, hearing the sad cry of water birds through the fog, she thought hard about her life, and what she would do with it once this race was over, and came to no firm conclusions.

She fell asleep near dawn, waking when the *Belle* took to the river again. She rushed out on deck to see the paddlewheel churning in a froth of water, pink-tinged by a clear, rosy dawn.

The new morning, crystal-clear and bright, cheered the group aboard the *Belle*, but gloom set in when it became clear that the *Revenge* was nowhere in sight. Evidently, the other boat had raced on into the night, despite the killer fog.

Melissa and Amalie, standing in the bow, looked at one another in dismay. "How far ahead do you think they are?" Melissa asked in a subdued voice.

And then as the *Belle* steamed around a bend, they saw her, ahead and slightly to the right.

The *Revenge* was clearly not in motion, and the great paddlewheel was still. Even from this distance, Melissa could see a great deal of frantic activity on the decks.

"The boat is sitting at an odd angle," Amalie said, shading her eyes with her hand. "It's gone aground on a bar, *chérie!*" She began to laugh. "Oh, I am wicked to be so pleased by someone else's misfortune, but, oh, I am glad!"

Melissa burst into laughter, and hugged her.

As the *Belle* steamed past her opponent, Amalie and Melissa performed a little dance on the deck, their music the cursing and shouting of the deckhands on the *Revenge*, as they struggled to free their craft from the sandbar that held her.

* * *

By the afternoon of the second day, the *Belle* was running low on fuel.

Jubal had made prior arrangements for a barge to meet them near the next town, and they prayed that it would soon come into sight. The *Belle* was well in the lead now, and they wanted to keep their advantage.

Finally, late in the afternoon, the barge hove into sight. Jubal steered the *Belle* carefully alongside the barge, and the men immediately began to load the wood and pitch on board, working hard and furiously.

Spirits were high, and most of them felt that they now had won the race. Jubal and Mollie knew better; for only they realized how unpredictable and treacherous old Miss'ip' could be. Right now, everything looked good, but it could change in an instant, and so their pleasure was tempered with caution.

Loading the wood took about half an hour, and by the time the *Belle* was ready to speed up again, the *Revenge* came in sight downriver. A concerted groan went up.

"Don't be so down-mouthed," Mollie scolded. "Don't forget that now the *Revenge* has to stop and fuel, too. It'll take her just as long as it took us, and we'll be well away by then."

But Mollie was wrong. As the *Revenge* steamed toward them, a tug nosed out from the bank. To the amazement of those watching from the *Belle*, the tug steamed up until it was running beside the *Revenge*. Ropes were thrown across, and the tug hands began tossing wood onto the deck of the steamboat.

"Damnation!" Jubal swore, thumping the deck with his wooden leg. "I'd better get up to the wheelhouse and relieve Mollie. This means that we have to run full out again."

Melissa and Martha accompanied Jubal as he stumped up to the wheelhouse, his face set.

Mollie turned around as the door opened. "Don't that beat all? That sure puts a hitch in our lead, don't it?"

Jubal nodded grimly, and took the wheel. "Go and rest a spell, Mollie. You'll need it for tonight."

Mollie slouched out wearily, and Melissa realized that never before had she seen the hardy little woman show fatigue or discouragement. She looked out the side window at the *Revenge*, steaming alongside, almost level with them.

Jubal shouted down the speaking tube, "More steam, Amos! More steam!"

"More steam coming up!" Amos yelled back. The men working at the boilers shoveled and threw wood into the hungry, blazing maws of the big boilers, until the *Belle* shuddered and trembled under the load she was carrying.

Martha placed her hand timidly on Jubal's arm. "Is it safe, Jubal? We aren't going to blow up, are we?"

Jubal said through gritted teeth, "Not if I can help it. I just want to pull ahead, get an edge. We'll be comin' to that big bend off the Riversee Plantation soon. With this old river so low, there should be only one passable channel there, and I want to get to it first."

Melissa pulled Martha back, concerned that the woman's nervousness would communicate itself to her husband.

Sounds of tapping came from the tube, and then Amos's voice said, "I daren't get up more steam, Cap'n! She's starting to shake!"

Jubal glanced out of the side window. They were

pulling away from the *Revenge*—a quarter of a boat length, a half, and now a full length.

"It's all right," he shouted down the tube. "Just hold her there for a few minutes."

The wheelhouse was silent now except for the throbbing of the great engines, and the *Belle* continued to forge ahead, now two full lengths in the lead. The bend of the river was coming up, and Jubal threw the *Belle* into the main channel, with the *Revenge* right behind.

Melissa stood still and tense, a lump of fear in her throat, for she could see the dimple marks in the water that Jubal had once told her were the indications of sandbars beneath the surface; and here and there shaggy tree tops would surface, the dreaded "sawyers" that were the bane of all river pilots.

On the *Belle* surged. They were almost out of the channel now, and then suddenly they were caught, seized and stopped with a jar that made the boat creak alarmingly, and threw them about the wheelhouse.

Jubal, managing to cling to the wheel, swore mightily. Melissa went skidding across the polished wooden floor until she fetched up against the front wall. Before she could get to her feet, Jubal was yelling instructions down to the men through the tube.

As Melissa stood up, checking herself for damage, she could see the deckhands hurrying with the "grasshoppers," the long poles that were used like giant legs to "walk" a boat off a sandbar.

Behind them, the whistle of the *Revenge* screamed loudly, again and again. Melissa knew, from what Jubal had told her, that with the *Belle* blocking the channel, the *Revenge* could not pass. They would have to either take one of the secondary channels, or wait until the *Belle* was off the bar.

The *Belle* trembled and creaked, and Melissa could hear the shouts of the men working the grasshoppers.

Jubal was still yelling down the tube, and Martha, looking stunned, and for once silent, was sitting calmly on the deck, as if afraid to move.

Again, the *Belle* shuddered and moaned, her timbers groaning. Again, the *Revenge* loosed an angry whistle behind them. And then, in a movement that spoke volumes for Simon Crouse's impatience and determination to win at all costs, the packet lunged to the right, swerving around the *Belle*'s stern, and headed for the righthand channel.

Jubal looked around in time to see the maneuver. "They'll never make it, the dad-damned fools! That channel's lower than it looks!"

Melissa stared through the window, unable to look away as the *Revenge*, steam billowing from her tall stacks, sparks flying, headed for the channel at full speed.

"The damned idiots! Crouse is hoping that if he hits the channel at full speed, she'll skim over the top, but if he hits a bar or a snag at that speed, they're goners. Just look at that smoke. The boilers are stoked too high. She'll blow herself apart, if'n she don't bottom out first."

Melissa felt both awe and apprehension. She hated Simon Crouse, and all that he stood for, but she did not want him to die this way; besides, there were others on the *Revenge*.

Yet she knew that if he made it through the channel intact, the race was as good as his.

With dry mouth, and sweaty palms, she watched the *Revenge* as it hit the channel. Twenty feet, thirty, forty! The boat was moving fast. Now it was directly opposite the *Belle*. On their decks, she could see the cheering men, hats off and waving, as the *Revenge* sped past not a hundred feet distant.

She sagged with despair. They were going to make it. The *Belle* had lost the race! A soft cry escaped her. She did not even notice when the wheelhouse door opened, and she did not hear Luke until he touched her arm.

Her eyes flooded with tears. "Oh, Luke, they've won! We have lost everything! And Amalie! Poor Amalie!"

As he reached out for her, sympathy and tenderness in his eyes, Melissa caught, past his shoulder, the first glimpse of the fire that preceded the explosion.

Great sheets of flame suddenly enveloped the *Revenge*, until her stacks looked as if they rode high upon a hell ship. At the same instant, the *Revenge* bucked and rose in the air in an awful parody of a high jumper.

The air split with a tremendous clap of thunderous sound, and as Melissa watched in horror, the *Revenge* broke in the middle, like a child's toy. Fire engulfed her, and then clawed for the sky.

Melissa screamed, but the sound was lost in the noise that now overwhelmed them. The *Belle* rocked wildly, and both Luke and Melissa were thrown to the floor. The glass from the pilot house windows flew inward like a deadly, glittering rain, and Melissa felt her arms sting from the glass.

Luke took her by the arms, and helped her to her

feet. Jubal, his face also cut by the flying glass, was desperately clinging to the wheel as the *Belle* rocked and quivered.

Melissa could hear shrill cries of alarm from the lower decks. Luke, after making sure that she was not seriously hurt, shouted to her to stay where she was, and raced out of the wheelhouse.

Dazed, she glanced around. Martha, apparently unhurt, was still sitting on the floor. Tears streamed down her pale cheeks, and her hands were clenched to her breasts. Holding onto the sides of the wheelhouse for support, Melissa went to her, kneeled down, and took the woman into her arms. Martha did not speak, only continued to weep, as the *Belle* slowly stopped rocking and settled down.

"The blast threw us off the bar, damned if it didn't!" Jubal shouted. "We're clear. Is Martha all right?"

"I think so. She's just badly frightened."

Jubal spoke into the tube. "Hold her right there, Amos. We got to look for survivors."

Melissa heard the engines throttle back, followed by sounds of activity on the decks. She helped Martha up, and led her to the glassless windows.

There was nothing left of the *Revenge*, except for a few pieces of debris which were being swept downstream by the current. The stench of burning oil and wood fouled the air, and as she watched, Luke and Beau hoisted a blackened figure out of the water and onto the lower deck.

Later, she was to learn that only ten men were saved. Only ten out of the twenty-five that one survivor told them had been on board the *Revenge*.

404

And, still later, she learned that Crouse had been using great amounts of oil and pitch to make the fires hotter; that he had insisted that they tie down the safety valves, so that they could generate more steam.

A boat was destroyed, and fifteen men were dead, including Crouse himself, because of the villainy of Simon Crouse. Indeed, the Carpetbagger would be mourned by none!

The *Belle* had sustained minor damage from the explosion. In addition to the broken windows, a falling smoke stack had broken one of the paddles on the wheel, and there had been a small fire on the boiler deck, but it had been snuffed out before it could do much harm.

As they steamed slowly upriver, Jubal said, "It was a dad-damned miracle that we got off so easy. If'n that fire on the boiler deck had got out of hand, the *Belle* would've joined the *Revenge* at the bottom of old Miss'ip'l!"

Melissa and Luke stood in the wheelhouse of the *Belle*, observing the colorful spectacle of the St. Louis docks.

Watching the bustle, the comings and goings, Melissa was struck by the difference between the docks here and those in New Orleans, which had appeared to her to be more cosmopolitan. Here, there was a raw, frontier flavor, and from where they stood, Melissa could see Indians in breechclouts, freighters with long blacksnake whips, and cowboys in tall hats and chaps.

"Fascinating, isn't it?" Luke commented.

"Yes, but it smells." She wrinkled her nose.

Luke laughed. "So does New Orleans."

"But it smells of fruit, spice, and," she smiled, "everything nice."

"And this smells of cattle, horses, cured hides, dung, and dead rats, eh?"

He broke off to step closer to the empty window-frame, staring down at the deck below.

Jubal was in town trying to buy glass to replace the windows broken in the explosion, and most of the others had accompanied him.

They had decided not to give any performances in St. Louis, for the city was not on their itinerary since many other showboats made it a regular stop. Their stay here would be a rest stop. They would remain here until the damage to the *Belle* had been repaired, and they were to take on fresh supplies.

Melissa stretched, yawning. She felt pleasantly tired and very contented, totally relaxed for the first time since Great Oaks had gone under the auctioneer's hammer. It was sad that her contentment should come about because of a man's death, yet there was no denying that the explosion of the *Revenge* had rid the world of a man whose absence would be little mourned.

"Melissa?"

She gave a start, and glanced up.

Luke pointed toward the bow of the lower deck. "You seem to be losing a member of your troupe."

Melissa craned forward. It was Beau Vermillian, carpetbag in hand, trudging toward the stage plank, head bowed.

Watching him, Melissa felt a pang of regret.

"Well?" Luke said softly, his voice noncommittal.

"Well what?" She did not look at him.

"It would seem that you are losing your leading man. How did that come about?"

Still not looking at him, Melissa felt heat color her cheeks. "He wanted me to marry him, and I had to refuse. Under the circumstances . . ."

Her cheeks still hot, she raised her head and looked Luke full in the face. Why should she be afraid to face him? He valued honesty, and that was what she was giving him.

"Well, at least now I won't have to fight a duel for you," he said lightly. "Although I would have, you know. Why, Melissa?"

She pretended ignorance. "Why what?"

"Damnit, Melissa, you're being deliberately dense. Why did you turn him down?"

"Because I don't love him. Beau is a fine man, and I am fond of him, but it was not love," she said firmly, knowing as she spoke that the words were true.

His arm went around her waist, and after a moment's pause, he said, "Do you love *me*, Melissa?"

His words created a soft panic within her, and she pulled slightly away. "I don't know. I'm not sure. I . . ." she said in a small voice.

He caught her chin in his hand, and turned her face toward him. "Look at me, Melissa, and answer me honestly. I love you. I love you very much, and I've never said those words to another woman. Do you love me?"

A sobbing laugh escaped her taut throat. "Yes, I love you, Luke Devereaux! I love you!"

He laughed joyously, and drew her close, his mouth near to hers as he spoke. "Then will you marry me?"

Melissa leaned back in his arms, drawing her face away. She shook her head, smiling. "No."

He stared at her in bewilderment. "What are you saying? You just said that you loved me!"

She nodded. "And I do, but as someone once told me, intimacy between a man and a woman does not always lead to marriage. It would seem to me that the same applies to love. I am quite happy the way things are. Why change them? Of course, I don't know if I will always feel this way. Maybe, after our season is finished, if you should ask me again, I might say yes."

His expression was disgruntled. "And what am I supposed to do in the meantime?"

"Well," she gave him a sly look, "we could use you on board the *Belle*. It seems that I no longer have a leading man, and you are acceptable-looking enough to play the part."

"Acceptable, is it?" He laughed. "But me, an actor?"

She pretended indifference. "Suit yourself, but we have been doing well, and shall continue to do so, now that Crouse is gone. It's not a bad life. After all, you've been with us for a while. Is it a bad life?"

"No," he said grudgingly, and then, after a long pause, he blurted out, "All right, damnit! You've got yourself a leading man!"

Melissa smiled, a secretive, contented smile, and a companionable silence ensued, as they stood in one another's arms, looking out the ruined window.

Then Melissa's glance fell on two figures on the deck below, strolling arm in arm—Amalie and Amos.

Melissa said dreamily, "Who would ever have thought, that day last spring at Great Oaks, that this would ever come about? And it wouldn't have, but for something that happened that day. Luke, do you remember my mother's music box, that you bought back for me?"

"I remember." His voice was guarded.

"There is something I have never told you. In that music box I found two thousand dollars. It was that money that started the *Belle* on her way. Without it, the *Belle* would still be sitting on the river bank at Natchez, and Amalie and I—well, I hate to think what might have become of us."

She frowned. "I still don't know who put the money there. At first I thought it was Daddy. He seemed the only logical one. And yet the money was in Yankee dollars, not Confederate . . ."

As Luke cleared his throat, she glanced around at him. "Luke?"

He turned his face away.

In a sudden leap of intuition, she knew. "You! You put that money in the music box! But why?"

He smiled boyishly, his face reddening. "Well, I think I told you once that I'm a man of impulse."

"Impulse? But so much money, and to give it to a virtual stranger . . ."

He took her into his arms, looking deeply into her eyes. "You were never a stranger to me, Melissa. From that first moment, when I saw you on the veranda at Great Oaks, your chin so high and proud, and your eyes so full of sorrow, so beautiful in that worn and patched dress . . . I reckon I knew even then that you were the one woman I could truly love."

Feeling a surge of love and tenderness so intense that it was almost painful, she reached up to pull his head down to hers, pressing her mouth to his fiercely.

After a moment she leaned back to say gravely, "You know, my darling, in a way this makes you half-owner of the *Belle*."

"I don't know," he said solemnly. "I've never been a man to settle for half of anything."

She smiled impishly. "Well, now you may only have half of the showboat, but you have all of me. Will you settle for that?"

He gave a whoop of laughter. "Now that is a bargain I will certainly settle for, now and forever!"

PREVIEW

The Birthright
by Clayton Matthews

This is a readers' preview of the first book in a new trilogy—*The Moraghan Saga*—by Clayton Matthews, who is the husband of Patricia Matthews. Together, the Matthews are a formidable writing team working out of their home in Pasadena, California. Pat is best known for her historical romances, while Clayton's most recent successes have been *The Power Seekers* and *The Harvesters*.

In *The Birthright* we meet the Moraghans. They came to East Texas on the *El Camino Real,* a parched and rugged trail, in August of 1835.

Sean Moraghan and his wife, Nora, had been traveling for weeks, from Tennessee. Just the two of them, and their mule and cart, which held all they owned in the world.

They came to start a new life. And it began quickly enough when Nora gave birth to their first child, Brian, under an oak tree by the side of the trail.

Sean Moraghan, the defrocked priest, his lovely bride, and their love-child, Brian. Together they'd challenge the primitive land and betrayal, greed and murder.

Birthright, a powerful story of a hot-blooded family and the secret that bound them together and tore them apart!

Now on sale wherever paperbacks are sold.

The sun's rays stabbed, like the devil's breath, through the thin blanket stretched over the sides of the two-wheeled cart.

Pain.

The labor pains were only seconds apart now, the contractions squeezing her swollen belly like some torture instrument. The jostling of the cart didn't help, and the pain was a thousand knives digging, gouging, twisting, causing agony unbearable.

But she was determined not to call out to Sean. The poor man had had enough travail and trouble this past year. As another spasm seized her, she bit down hard on her lower lip to keep from crying out, bit so hard that the brassy taste of her own blood filled her mouth.

A final monster contraction squeezed, and consciousness began to slide away from her. She tried desperately to hold on, but the engulfing darkness offered surcease and she finally gave way to it. Just before she slipped under, she was sure that she felt the pain ease, and warm wetness flooded her upper thighs . . .

Sean Moraghan plodded, leaning into the crude harness he'd improvised from the one he'd used on the mule. The two-wheeled cart carrying Nora and all their worldly goods—precious little—resisted stubbornly, almost miring in the dusty ruts of the trail with every step Sean took. Their mule had drowned fording the Sabine River three days before. Thanks be to the Lord, Nora hadn't been taken with the animal.

Trail!

El Camino Real, they called it, stretching the breadth of Texas. What grandiose name for such a primitive road!

Lord God, he was tired, bone-tired, mind-tired. For the first weeks of their journey from Tennessee, the arduous physical labor had left Sean so benumbed with weariness at the end of the day that he wasn't able to think, so tired he could sleep where he dropped. But now he had gone beyond mere weariness, until his mind had become a separate entity from his body. At times he was almost in a state of spiritual ecstasy, and he moved like a man in a dream, his mind free to probe the questions of the universe, of the relationship between man and God, questions for which he had no answers, to which there were no answers.

How many times had Monsignor Riley chided him in that gentle voice? "Questions. Always the questions, Sean. True faith requires no questions. Questions reveal a fatal flaw in us . . ."

A faint cry brought Sean's head up. At first he thought it was the cry of some small animal in distress. It came again, and he finally identified it. Panting in his haste, he grappled with the harness until he could step free of it. Lowering the stays to the ground, he hurried around to the rear of the cart and pushed back the blanket.

He stood frozen in astonishment and awe. Nora's swollen belly was flat, and there between her spread thighs was the source of the thin cry he'd heard—a red, feebly thrashing infant! He saw at a glance that it was a boy.

His son!

A year ago, even six months ago, never in his wildest imaginings would Sean have dreamed that he would ever sire a child. Nora had been three months pregnant before she had informed him.

"Lord God," he whispered in reverence. "By the Virgin Mary!"

Nora stirred, responding with that bawdy chuckle of hers. Her voice so weak as to be barely audible, she said, "I hardly think that applies, my darling. It was not an immaculate conception, if you will recall." Then she raised her head, face pale and beaded with sweat, to stare down the length of her body at him. "Don't just stand there like some great oaf, Sean! You have things to do. Quickly! I can't do everything. Heat some water. The baby has to be washed, and the tad's still attached to me, you dunce. You have to cut the cord."

"Nora, I can't be doing that!"

"Men! If there *was* some way an immaculate conception could be carried out, we women could very well do without men."

Stretching her forearms along the bed of the cart, she levered herself up onto her elbows, then propped her back against the side. Before Sean's horrified gaze, she picked the baby up gently in both hands, bent almost double, and severed the umbilical cord with one bite of strong white teeth.

"God above, woman, what are you after doing?"

"Doing what has to be done." Quickly she tied the cord off, deposited the baby back onto the blanket, and sank back with a sigh. "Now, dear man, will you get on with what I asked you to do?"

The urgency in her voice galvanized Sean into action. He was honest enough with himself to admit that he was glad of an excuse to escape. During the past six months with Nora, Sean, who had known as much about a female as he did about a camel in the African desert, had been constantly dazzled and astounded at the ways of women.

Still Nora, he was positive, was an exceptional woman. Even in his abysmal ignorance, he would have been willing to wager that very few women were capable of doing what she had just done.

Sean rolled the cart off the trail and under the shade of a live oak. Other travelers had scoured the sides of the trail clean of all deadwood, and he had to range back into the trees. The August day was sweltering, the air so thick and humid it was like moving underwater.

The piney woods had a resiny scent. Insects sang a drowsy melody in the heat. The rich red earth had a fecund odor.

Before he had gathered enough wood for a fire, he came out of the edge of the trees onto the brink of a shallow valley. About two miles distant smoke rose straight up into the still air. It was most likely Nacogdoches, the town he had been informed he would eventually come to along this trail.

For just a moment Sean debated with himself—should he hurry Nora and the baby into the town for a doctor, and proper care?

But he knew that it would be too much of a risk, to both Nora and the baby. Many of these towns, he had learned, had no doctors. He would have to tend to her and the child as best he could himself.

The cart was quiet when he returned with an armful of wood. Apprehensive, he stuck his head under the blanket. "Is the baby after being all right?" He swore at himself for the lapse into brogue, something he was apt to do in moments of stress or anger.

"He will be, Sean, when you get on with it." In counterpoint to her tart reply, the baby yowled lustily.

Hurriedly, Sean built a pyramid of dry wood, whittled a few curlicues of kindling, and labored with his flint and piece of steel. Sparks flew, and finally one caught.

Then he constructed a tripod of greenwood from which to suspend a kettle, and went to fetch the water keg. Water had been scarce since they left the Sabine, but there was enough to fill the kettle, with a little to spare. He hung the kettle over the flames, then crossed again to the cart.

"Nora, I spread a blanket on the ground. Can I help you out and onto it?"

"You can, and thank heaven for small favors! I thought you were going to leave me in here in my own piss and stink forever! Not to mention the baby!"

"Nora, I do wish you'd watch your language. That's no way for a lady to be talking."

"Who said I was a lady? Not I. If I had been, I

wouldn't be here now, birthing the bastard son of Sean Moraghan!"

Sean winced. "Sweet, he's not a bastard."

"Perhaps not, strictly speaking. But considering we've only been wed six months, it's not far from the mark. Now can you deny that?"

Sean sighed. In one respect he was relieved. If Nora could talk like this, it meant she was all right, but it also meant that he would be receiving the rasp of her tongue. Not that he minded all that much; her frankness was one of her attractions, and she usually managed to pretend the proper lady when in the company of others. And God knows, he thought, she wasn't a complainer. If she had been, there had been ample to complain about these past few months.

Gingerly, he helped her out of the cart, handed her the baby, and supported her to the blanket under the tree. She sank down with a grateful sigh, leaning back against the trunk of the tree, and took the boy into her arms.

Sean squatted by the fire, waiting for the water to heat. He was a tall, lean man by nature, but the hard work and a scarcity of food had gaunted him even more. His hair was long, almost to his shoulders, so black as to be almost blue. He would have been handsome except for a rather prominent nose. His full-lipped mouth customarily shaped a smile, but of late there had been little to smile about, and the dark eyes, usually gentle, had begun to harden.

He stretched his long hands toward the fire, not to warm them, but to examine them. Unaccustomed to physical labor for most of his thirty years, they had blistered over and over on the trail, and calluses had finally started to form; yet they still pained him considerably.

Sean turned his thoughts to pleasanter subjects—to his son. Closing his eyes, he voiced a silent prayer of thanksgiving. Before it was completed, he began to smile wryly. Did he still believe in God? He wasn't sure, but the long habit of prayer was hard to break.

Faith. That was the knotty nub of it. Was his faith still intact?

Certainly Monsignor Riley hadn't thought so. "Faith above all else, Sean. Faith in Our Father. Without faith, what are you?"

"A man, Monsignor. No more, no less."

"You are not as other men, Sean. When you made the decision to become a priest, you elevated yourself above the ordinary man."

"Yet I am still a man. I thirst like a man, I hunger like a man, I have desires like a man."

"Carnal desire, in my opinion, is one test of our faith. A means by which God has seen fit to judge us worthy in His eyes. You must scourge yourself of all lusts of the flesh, my son. We have all gone through it. You will emerge the better priest for it."

"But I don't know if I wish to be a better priest, or any kind of priest, if it means giving up Nora."

"This woman has been sent by God as the ultimate test of your faith. Triumph over this temptation and you shall belong to God forever!"

"I'm not sure I want to be God's forever . . ."

"The pleasures of the flesh are transitory. The love of God endures into eternity."

"I love Nora. I love her more than life itself. Perhaps I love her more than God."

"Blasphemy! Rank sacrilege! Fall to your knees and pray. . . ."

Nora's tart voice broke into Sean's thoughts. "Sean! Are you going to let the water boil away?"

He glanced at the kettle and saw that it was boiling merrily. "Sorry," he mumbled, and hastily unhooked the kettle scalding his hand in the process. A great oath exploded from him.

"Such language," she said mockingly. "And from a priest yet!"

"Ex, Nora. Defrocked. Excommunicated."

Her face grew still as he came toward her carrying the kettle. "Any regrets, darling?"

"None," he said promptly, and stoutly.

How true was that? He had to wonder.

Then he kneeled beside her and clumsily picked up the baby, fingers feeling big as sausages. His face bloomed in a foolish smile, and he said, "How can I feel any regret, with what you have just presented me?"

"No need to handle him like a porcelain doll, dunce head," she scolded. "He's not going to break."

With a cloth and a rough towel, he washed his son with loving if awkward care. Done, he laid the infant on the blanket and stood up.

"Aren't you going to do the same for me?"

Sean felt his face flushing. Despite all the times he had held Nora naked in his arms, he was still agonizingly embarrassed when he came upon her in daylight without clothing.

"I . . ." He swallowed. "Can you manage by yourself? We have nothing to eat but the remains of the jerky, tough as old leather and about as tasty. You must be starved; I know I am. I'll take my pistol and scout around for a hare for our supper."

"Yes, darling." Her mouth curved in that smile he'd come to think of as special, special just for him. "I wouldn't want you any other way."

"What?" he said in confusion.

"Never mind, just run along with you," she said crossly. "I'll manage very well, thank you."

Sean went to the front of the cart and removed his pistol from the wooden holster hooked to the cart, kept there so it would be handy when he was pulling the vehicle. He checked the priming of the percussion firearm, called a caplock.

He said, "I won't be far away, Nora. There are some rough types along this trail. If you need me, just call out."

She waved a hand at him, without speaking, and Sean stepped among the trees, the pistol at ready. Until he had started on this trek, he had never fired a weapon in his life; but knowing what might confront them on this trip to Texas, he had spent precious money on both a pistol and a musket. To his amazement, Sean discovered that he had a natural aptitude for firearms, and was now a reasonably good shot.

The supreme irony—a disciple of the Prince of Peace handy with weapons!

He moved slowly, carefully, farther into the woods, his gaze darting about in search of a cottontail rabbit, that tasty animal abounding in this area—a ball of fur on its rump remarkably like a flowering cotton ball.

It was Sean's intention to settle in East Texas. In the small trunk in the cart he had a letter from the hand of an empresario, affirming that Sean's application for land near Nacogdoches had been approved.

Back in Tennessee he had heard tales of 12-foot cotton plants in Texas that renewed themselves each season. It was said that the soil in the territory was so rich that "if you plant tenpenny nails in the ground, you will harvest a crop of iron bolts."

Conceding that much of this was probably the extravagant embroidery frontiersmen loved to weave into their tales, it still opened up exciting vistas for a man who was not averse to hard work. Sean knew absolutely nothing about farming, and he had little money with which to purchase needed farm implements; but he would manage, he was sure of it.

A chattering sound and a movement on the branch of a live oak drew his attention. Sean froze, squinting his eyes in an attempt to penetrate the foliage. Then he saw a blur of brown, and spotted a plump squirrel squatting on its haunches on the tree limb, nibbling on an acorn held in its forepaws. The animal was less than ten yards from where Sean stood, and apparently hadn't noticed him.

He had never eaten squirrel, but he had been told that the meat was most tasty, if not as plentiful as that on a rabbit. Avoiding any sudden move, he slowly raised the pistol, cocking it and sighting down the barrel.

Much of the food they had subsisted on during the long journey had come from Sean's hunting of game. Yet he still had to force himself to kill, using his vivid imagination to conjure up images of Nora starving because he was unable to provide food for her belly. Now there was a third mouth to feed. The baby couldn't eat meat yet, of course, but Nora had to eat to provide milk for him.

Sean fired. Smoke puffed up, and the pistol ball whacked into the limb beneath the squirrel, knocking the animal to the ground, momentarily stunning it. The practice of "barking" a squirrel was favored over a direct hit; a pistol ball could rip all the meat from the small animal. Sean loped over to the fallen squirrel, and delivered the killing blow with a rock.

Before picking the animal up, Sean carefully made the pistol ready for firing again. Back in Louisiana Territory, a grizzled fur trapper had watched Sean kill a rabbit, then ram his unprimed pistol into his belt in his haste to pick up his kill.

"Nere do that, hoss. Out here, when a man fire his oney weapon, better reload then and there. Your life may depend on it."

Taking the Barlow knife from his belt, Sean squatted and quickly skinned and gutted his prize before hurrying back to camp with it. He grinned when he saw Nora holding his son to her breast. Involuntarily his glance jumped away from the sight of her bared breast, full, blue-veined. Even though he had not touched her in passion for some weeks because of her condition, Sean was ashamed of the quick hardening at his loins.

With that unfailing knack of hers Nora said, "It won't be long now, Sean, until it'll be all right again. A few weeks."

"I don't fathom your meaning, Nora."

She hooted. "Not much you don't, Sean Moraghan!"

Face burning, Sean went about preparing the squirrel for cooking. Then he stoked up the fire, spitted the squirrel with a long, sharpened stick, and held it over the flames, cooking slowly.

By the time it was nicely brown, dripping grease spitting on the flames, the sun had gone down. Twilight brought, if not a cooling, at least an illusion of it.

When the squirrel was done, Sean dismembered it, arranged the pieces on a board they had been using as a plate, and carried it to his wife. He was relieved to see that the baby had ceased sucking and was asleep in Nora's lap. Her breast was adequately covered, and she had her head back against the tree trunk, eyes closed.

"Supper's prepared, Nora," he said with false cheer.

Nora's eyes fluttered open. She carefully placed the infant on the blanket beside her and sat up straighter. Sean extended the board, and she selected a piece, biting into it.

Chewing, she said, "Ah, it's delicious." Her eyes glinted with mischief. "Did anyone ever tell you, darling, that you'd make some woman a fine husband?"

"Not so fine, I fear," he said glumly. "A boy of ten could kill a squirrel with a stick and cook it. So far, I've managed to get us banished from Tennessee, and we're out here in the wilderness, impoverished, with another mouth to feed, and . . ."

"Hellfire and spit, Sean!" Nora said, eyes flashing. "I'll not listen to you bad-mouthing yourself, nor to your Black Irish glooming about! As my grandpa used to say, you'd complain if hung with a new rope! You've fed us, fathered a fine son, got that allotment of 4,428 acres in that Texas land grant, which is fine cotton land, so you've been telling me . . ."

"I've only been telling you what *I* have been told. But I've also heard some disquieting rumors along the way. I've hesitated to tell you because of your delicate condition . . ." This wrung a snort from Nora. "But you're entitled to know. It's said that some of these empresarios are fraudulent. True, they're empowered by the Mexican government to sell those acres to American families for sixty dollars, but it is rumored that many sell their allotments many times over, and when a man arrives to claim his land, the empresario is gone, and there is no land to claim."

Concern shadowed her eyes. "And you think this empresario is such a man?"

Sean shrugged. "I don't know, sweet. Unfortunately, the world is peopled by the wicked."

"Spoken like a true crusading priest." Amusement brightened her eyes. "Tell me . . . Did it sore try your conscience to have to swear you were a Roman Catholic?"

"I did not lie, Nora. I am still a Roman Catholic."

"Are you now?"

"And besides, it is my understanding that the Mexican authorities do not enforce this rule. It is merely an edict handed down by the central government in Mexico City that an American family taking up land in Texas should swear allegiance to the Church."

"I know, darling, I know." She stretched out a greasy hand. "I'm sorry, Sean. I should be horsewhipped for bedeviling you the way I do. Any other man but my gentle Sean would not tolerate my tongue."

He took her hand absently, his thoughts still occupied with the Church. "There is a problem, however, one that has been in my mind all along. If it becomes known that I was once a priest of the Church, now in disgrace, it could go hard for us . . ."

"And that is my doing!"

"Now stop that, Nora!" He squeezed her hand so hard she winced. "We agreed that we would never mention that again. But we must remember never to breathe a word of it. Since I have taken a new surname for us, there is no reason my past should become known."

"Unless someone from Tennessee who knows us should come here."

He nodded gravely. "There is that chance, but it is such a remote possibility that I think we needn't worry." Privately he was not so confident. If they had migrated to Texas, wouldn't others who knew him do so as well? It was a worry that he would have to live with from this day forward.

He essayed a smile. "We have enough to worry about without adding to it. Do you think you would be safe alone here if I were to ride into Nacogdoches in the morning? It's just up ahead. I don't think you should travel for a day or so, but I want to check on our land as soon as possible."

"I will be fine, darling. Leave your pistol, ball and powder. I'm a fair shot, as you know. If any villain should try to molest me, I'll give him a pistol ball in the . . . What is it they call them here? *Cojones?*" She laughed. "If we're going to live among Mexicans, we have to learn the language."

Sean smiled palely. "It's my understanding that the Mexican population is sparse here in East Texas, out-numbered by Americans ten to one."

"Well, whatever. You go ahead, Sean. I'll be fine. Who would bother a woman with a new baby?"

From Sean's journal, August 18, 1835:

Conferred with the empresario this day. A busy individual, and could spare little time for me. But he assures me that our land is there for the claim-ing. It is the custom, I understand, for the empre-sario to allow a newcomer 30 days to study the countryside, so he therefore may be content with his choice. Then his selected acres are plotted, and he is issued title. But this man, thinking that he might not be present upon our arrival, has already performed this chore for me, and assures me that I will be pleased by his selection.

Since he seems a man of some substance, a Christian man, I put my faith in him.

The land is ours! Although we have yet to set foot on it, I am transported. As is my dear Nora.

The empresario did mention that I was favored by fortune in one respect. The Mexican govern-ment had, for a time, rescinded its liberal immi-gration laws, forbidding any new settlers. But recently, as recently as our departure from Tennes-see, the Mexicans again began welcoming us to their country. Fortunate indeed we are!

The empresario did pass on some disquieting news, the reason, I gather, for his imminent depar-ture. Texas is in turmoil, and trembles on the verge of open rebellion again Mexico! A convention of Texas delegates has been called for Oct. 8, in San Felipe. What action will be taken there, no one seems to know. It would appear that we Americans are too long accustomed to freedom, and averse to the strictures imposed on us by the tyrant, Santa Anna, known hereabouts by the derisive name of Santy Anny.

What effect this will have on us I cannot foresee, but it strikes an ominous, somber note for our new life.

In Nacogdoches, a village of some 800 hardy souls, yet the largest settlement in Texas, I am informed, I met a fellow Tennessean, a man of whom I have heard much. Mr. Sam Houston! A man of many parts. A renowned soldier, a member of the United States Congress, once the governor of Tennessee. He is also a known womanizer, a man of vile temper, and an immoderate drinker. By his many friends, he is known as the Raven; by his enemies, Big Drunk.

I met him by chance on the outskirts of the village. What a splendid figure he cuts! Riding a great white horse, with a Mexican saddle and bridle, elaborately ornamented. Wearing a Mexican outer garment, called a poncho, also elaborately embroidered. Mr. Houston is the most magnificent specimen of physical manhood I have ever seen!

I was told that Sam Houston now makes his home in Nacogdoches. Has a practice of law there.

With such a man as Sam Houston abiding here, the omens for the future can only be good!

Nora agrees wholeheartedly.

Another momentous event this day.

We selected a name for our firstborn. Brian. Brian Patrick Moraghan.

It has a strong, yet melodious ring to it.

May the Lord God bless you for all your days, Brian Patrick Moraghan!